WHEN BLOOD DIVIDES

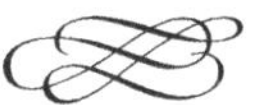

J.B. CROFT

*To all the readers who found a home in books.
I hope you find a new one here.*

PROLOGUE

Emelia screeched into the night and gave a last push. She collapsed onto the cot beneath her as her son was finally delivered into the waiting healer's arms. Tears ran down her cheeks as his wailing cry filled the tent.

Madden rushed in at the sound, the tan cotton of the tent flap catching in the breeze behind him. He brushed past Emelia's outstretched hand, not even sparing her a glance. Her arm dropped helplessly onto the cot, landing with a muted thud that went unacknowledged amid her child's screams.

"My son." Madden seized him out of the healer's arms and cradled the child's small sticky body to his chest, turning his back to her.

Emelia struggled to sit up. "Let me hold him," she whispered hoarsely, her throat sore from all the screaming.

She flinched at the harsh glint in Madden's eyes as his head whipped towards her. She had hoped their son would bring him back to reality; instead, it had done the opposite. He looked more deranged than ever.

"I have a shaman waiting for him. You know the effort I've put into getting one here. If he's an enchanter, he could be the key to everything." He strode out through the tent flap before she could respond.

"Madden." She attempted to yell, but her voice broke on his name. "Bring him back." The tent flap taunted her. It blew in the breeze giving the illusion that someone was about to walk back inside, but she knew he was gone. The remnants of her body's hurt echoed through her, and she slumped onto the cot again in defeat as she was overtaken by dizziness.

The healer rushed to her side. "You must rest."

"No." Emelia panted. "Fix it. Fix me." She gestured at her useless body, which had delivered a life but was now incapable of moving.

"You should really . . ."

"That was an order," she snapped. Her thoughts were only of her son and what Madden could be doing to him.

Reluctantly the healer brought her hands to Emelia's stomach. She sighed in relief as a pleasant warmth flowed through her, lessening her body's soreness until it disappeared completely.

"You need rest," the healer implored.

"Not yet." Emelia pushed her away, finally standing. She swayed on her feet, regaining her balance after lying for so long. Her son had not been quick or easy to deliver.

She wrapped a cloak around her to hide the signs she'd just given birth. If she was lucky, everyone would still be eating dinner, and no one would question her haggard form walking through the campsite.

Emelia left the tent, blinking as her eyes adjusted to the darkness. Torches lit the way to Madden's tent, and she stumbled along the path towards it. There were more people in this camp than Emelia knew, and they were all here for Madden. They called themselves the "Disciples", and they had been the ones to follow Madden into this *Reign of Terror*, as it was now known. In a city where power was everything, she had loved Madden despite his powerlessness. He was barren, a status akin to being an Othersider - someone living on Earth - where magic was sealed away. To be barren was shameful. For Madden, who came from the most powerful family in the land, the Theobesians, it was the greatest shame of all.

Like everyone else in the camp, Emelia had fallen for his visions of equality, foolishly thinking a world could exist where magical power didn't define your status in society. But Madden's plan to achieve it was far more sinister than any social disparity could ever be. By the time she'd realised her mistake she was already pregnant and forsaken by everyone who loved her.

Emelia slipped inside Madden's tent, relieved to have made her way through the campsite unnoticed. His eyes flicked to her, but he didn't object to her presence. He was too focused on the robed woman in front of him, bent over their son. Her fingers were pressed lightly against his temples, and he was sleeping peacefully on a strip of cloth laid on the floor. The shaman was in the process of determining which of his chakras were open. From this, she would be able to tell his manipulation: the type of magical power he possessed. Finally, the shaman took her fingers away although the child remained sleeping.

"What is he?" Emelia whispered, her voice a mixture of anticipation and dread.

"Enchanter." The shaman's glazed eyes found hers and Emelia knew she wouldn't remember being here. Whatever dark magic Madden had done to her would ensure her memories of this time were nothing but a blank spot.

"Are you happy now? Can I hold him?" Emelia moved forward, but Madden held out a muscled arm, blocking her.

"He can serve a greater purpose, Em. He is the final piece."

Emelia's stomach twisted at the reverence in Madden's voice. His obsession with power had never come from a place of purity. Emelia should've known that his motive wasn't to bring equality back to their world but back to himself. His twin sister, Lydia Theobesian, had been born as the highest-ranking power in the alchemist world, an enchanter. In his eyes, Lydia had taken all his power. She had taken all the glory.

And that was the injustice he was determined to right using a type of magic that anyone, even barrens, could perform, known as mortificatio: a forbidden magic which harnessed death to perform acts of evil. Madden used it to kill other enchanters and harvest their power, claiming it as his own. He dismissed the deaths as necessary for the cause. He'd told Emelia that he only targeted enchanters who believed themselves to be better than everyone else, as if that had made it acceptable. But she'd recently heard that a young boy enchanter had been killed because he was said to possess great power; power Madden had wanted. Now, Madden would soon be strong enough to overthrow his sister and claim Namire's throne as his own. Something Emelia feared would lead to their world's demise.

"I won't let you sacrifice our son." It had been a long time since she'd felt Madden was present in this world. The dark magic he'd used had diseased him, changing his soul into this unrecognisable horror.

She lunged forward, trying to get to her son, but Madden knocked her back. She fell to the ground, and her head smacked the dirt. Her eyes swam with tears as she tried to focus on him.

Madden was physically stronger than her, but she was still more powerful. Madden had never cared that she was an enchanter, although it was the reason they'd first met. When they were younger, she had been inseparable from Lydia Theobesian. Lydia was the only other female enchanter her age and that had been as much of a bond as they'd needed to become friends.

During their childhood, Madden had never left Lydia's side. It wasn't until they grew older and understood that there was a difference between them that Madden distanced himself from his sister. But he had always kept Emelia close. She had wanted to support him. She had wanted him to change the world. But not like this.

Emelia had never before used her power against him. But she couldn't stand idly by while he threatened their son's life. She raised her hand, shooting a stunning cast at Madden. Her blurry vision sent the cast astray and instead the small ball of blinding white light hit her son. Madden spun around in shock. She sent another cast at him, blocking out her panic, and this time it was on target. He crumpled to the ground with a heavy thud.

Instantly, she was on her feet and at her son's side. He was only knocked out, but on a baby, she wasn't sure the effect the stunning cast would have. There was a mark on his head where the cast must've struck him, and it had turned strands of his black hair white. Other than that, he seemed unharmed. He was still breathing, and Emelia sent a prayer to the goddess that he would wake soon. She swept a blanket from the bed and wrapped it around her baby, then she ran to the only place that would provide her help in this camp.

Emelia hadn't made many friends after Lydia, but in Catherine Ives, she had found a kinship. Catherine, too, had fallen for a man she'd thought was different. Lucky for her, she was smart enough not to get pregnant with his child.

Emelia burst into her tent, and Catherine looked up, dropping the book she'd been reading.

"Emelia, I thought you were still in labour. What happened?"

"Madden. He's deranged. My son was confirmed as an enchanter, and he wants to use him for the cause," she spat.

Catherine was instantly on her feet. "What are you going to do?"

"I stunned him, but he'll wake soon."

Catherine nodded. "If we can get to the horses, we can be down the mountain and in the city, before he's searched the campground."

"The High Guard will recognise me. You'll have to take him through the gates. I know a different way through for me. Madden and I have used it before."

Catherine worried a hand through her hair. "Madden hasn't heard the news yet, has he?"

"What news?"

"The High Alchemist is about to have a baby."

Emelia felt an old wound deep inside her tear open at the words. "Lydia," she whispered. "How do you know?"

"A spy at the palace. It appears, like you, she's been concealing the pregnancy to protect the child. But I guess she didn't keep it secret enough. Once Madden hears word, he'll go after her."

"I need to warn her." Lydia had been Madden's target for some time now. But he'd known he didn't stand a chance against her until he built his own power. Now Lydia was pregnant, he'd want to eliminate her before a new heir was born.

"Catherine, you have to keep him safe while I'm gone," she said, holding out her son. "I accidentally stunned him when I was trying to subdue Madden, so he should sleep most of the journey to the city, but when he wakes, he'll need someone," she begged. It killed her to leave him, but she could never live with herself if Madden got to Lydia before she did.

"Of course. What have you named him?"

"We never decided." She hadn't wanted to name him alone and Madden had never been around to discuss any options. Emelia wondered if he had always planned to harvest his power and that was why he'd chosen to keep him nameless. It was easier to kill your son when you treated him like a lamb for slaughter.

Catherine nodded. "You can choose a name after."

Emelia looked at her son, suddenly realising the enormity of what she was about to do. "If I don't come back . . ."

"You'll come back." Catherine's voice held an assurance she didn't feel.

"If I don't. Raise him as your own, say you concealed the pregnancy. No one in the city suspects you as a Disciple. I know you'll keep him safe."

"What about Madden? What about anyone who's seen him?"

"With any luck, Madden and the Disciples won't be a problem after tonight. The shaman won't even remember she was here, Madden made sure of that, and the healer will stay quiet. She won't want to risk being tied to the Disciples. You know I've kept my own pregnancy concealed, and bar you no one else would be aware of his existence. And if by chance they are, many of the people in this camp are still undercover, like you, and they'd never blow it by revealing any information."

"Okay," Catherine conceded, allowing Emelia to place her son in her arms. Everything about the act felt wrong. She had carried his weight for nine months and now she had to let him go.

Emelia brushed back the soft hairs from his face and kissed the top of his head. "I'll come back for you," she whispered. She wanted the words to be true, but she knew all the same that she may never kiss her baby again. She allowed herself that one moment to mourn the life she'd envisioned. One small moment in which she wished everything was different.

Then she left to find Lydia.

Lydia Theobesian knew her life wasn't guaranteed. It had been forfeited the day her brother had murdered their parents. But, as she curved a hand around her swollen belly and felt the life pulsing inside, she hoped she could buy her child a chance to live.

Lydia was going for her twilight walk around the palace gardens. She'd started the practice when she'd first fallen pregnant. It soothed her to watch the flowers close over for the night, and the birds finally find a place to rest. Her hand came to her chest in a gesture of comfort, and she rubbed the pendant on her necklace, allowing the feel of smooth metal to calm her.

It was a necklace that had been passed down through generations of Theobesian women and was now the root of so much turmoil. The necklace was known as the Ancient Triad and consisted of three pendants hanging on three separate chains. It had been a gift to her ancestors from the goddess Hecate. The pendants were in the form of two crescent moons connected to a full moon, representing the moon stages of the triple goddess. Mother. Maiden. Crone. They were responsible for creating their world. And they also had the potential to unmake it. Something Lydia was trying desperately to avoid.

She stopped by the lake. The marble balustrade still held warmth from the summer's day, and it seeped into her skin as she leant against it. She looked over the glassy water, remembering the time she, Madden, and Emelia had dragged an old boat from the southern bank and paddled it across the lake. Her mother had found them and demanded they come in, claiming the water wasn't a place for a lady like her.

Her heart ached thinking about her brother and her once best friend. She could never hate them, even after everything that had happened. There was a time when Lydia had hoped for reconciliation. That was before Madden had descended into dark magic. More than anything, she knew he wanted to claim the Ancient Triad as his own. Their power was traditionally passed down the female side of the family. The death of the current owner meant the necklace's allegiance transferred to the next eldest female within the Theobesian bloodline. However, this could be changed if the current owner was killed and there were no remaining female heirs.

Madden had killed their mother out of necessity and their father out of spite. Luckily, their mother had been smart enough to keep the necklaces protected; unlike Lydia, she'd known the lengths her son would go to in order to possess them. Now the necklaces and their power were her responsibility. They also put a target on her back.

When she'd fallen pregnant, it should've been a happy occasion, but all Lydia could think about was what would happen if Madden found out. Using simple enchantment on her body, she'd kept the pregnancy concealed and prayed for a boy. But when it was confirmed a female, her heart had split a little. She knew if Madden got a hint there was another girl in the line; he would stop at nothing to ensure they were both eliminated.

Lydia was preparing for bed when she saw a flicker of light outside. At first, she thought she'd imagined it. But then it happened again. It had been the sign she and Emelia used as teens when they would sneak out in the night. She waited, watching as the light continued flashing. She wasn't naive enough to think it couldn't be a trap. But deep down, she hoped Emelia was finally returning to her. Even though Lydia knew it was reckless, she rushed down the stairs and out the door. A protective hand came around her belly as she crept to the bush the light was coming from.

"Emelia?" she hissed.

The trees rustled, and Emelia stepped out. Her hair was stuck to her flushed face, and she smelt horribly of dried blood and sweat.

"What's happened to you?" Lydia reeled back. The years they'd been apart seemed to melt through her fingers. All she wanted to do was wipe the dirt from her cheek and brush the tangles out of her hair. Lydia had imagined the day she would see Emelia again many times, but she had never quite been able to picture her face. Now, standing in front of her, she could see everything clearly. Every new line on her skin. The dark shadows under her eyes which held a weariness that hadn't been there before. But, despite these changes, she was still her best-friend. She was still the person Lydia knew as well as she knew her own self.

Emelia swatted a hand at her. "Never mind. I came to warn you."

"About what?"

"Madden. He will know soon enough that you're pregnant. Is it a girl?"

Lydia felt like she'd been struck. Emelia couldn't tell she was pregnant by looking at her. To plain eyes, she looked the same as she always had. Which meant that, somehow, the news had gotten out. "How do you know?"

"Someone in your palace isn't loyal to you. Madden will be coming. He has grown stronger. He believes he is ready."

"I can't fight him now, not in this condition."

"Where's your husband, Henrik?"

"I told him to go. We needed to consolidate the werewolves in the north to ensure they didn't side with Madden now that the scope of this war has grown greater. I'm not due for another week."

"It'll still be two against one with me here."

"Emelia." Lydia's voice broke. After all they'd been through, she couldn't believe it had brought them here, back together. "You can't do that."

"I can. I'm sorry, Lydia, I was blinded by love. But, once Madden killed your parents, I knew he had gone too far. I just didn't know how to leave. I was ashamed. But I've left now."

Her voice was resolute, and Lydia knew she wasn't lying. She had always been able to tell when Emelia was lying. It was a skill that had been honed over the years of their friendship and despite their time apart she didn't think it had gone away.

"What do we do then?"

Emelia gave a small smile. "I've got an idea."

They assembled in the throne room. It was the largest room in the palace, and it would be the easiest to repair if a fight broke out, given the only piece of furniture inside was the golden throne on its dais. The throne also provided a perfect hiding place for Emelia. She would take cover when Madden arrived, and once he was distracted by Lydia, hopefully, she would have a clear shot at him.

Lydia had instructed the guards not to interfere if Madden came. They didn't need any more unnecessary deaths. She'd let down the wards that protected the palace from intruders. Now all they had to do was wait.

"Do you have a name picked?" Emelia asked.

Lydia had taken away the glamour she'd cast on her stomach. She rested on the steps that led to the throne, idly stroking her belly.

Lydia smiled. "Bronte."

"Bronte," Emelia repeated. "It's beautiful."

"I thought so."

Emelia sighed heavily. "I always thought I would be around for these important moments. Your marriage, your first child. I always thought my presence here, with you, would be forever. I'm not saying this for pity. I know I chose to leave. But if I could go back, I would've stayed with you."

"You're here now." Lydia reached out a hand squeezing Emelia's, and they shared a smile. Lydia quickly pulled her hand back, holding her stomach as warm water flowed down her leg. She straightened in alarm. "I was meant to have more time."

Emelia looked at her with panicked eyes. "Put the wards back up."

"It's too late," she replied helplessly.

Darkness poured toward them, and with a worried glance Lydia's way, Emelia darted behind the throne. Lydia sent a wave of heat over her body, drying the water as she forced herself to stand. Not a moment later, Madden emerged. He looked exactly as she remembered. Her twin. Except his eyes were darker, swallowed whole by black.

"Hello, sister."

"Madden."

"Thought you would spend your final hours on the throne? I have others coming. You'll be gone by dawn."

Lydia fought the inexplicable urge to laugh. She felt like they were children again, playing a game. When they were younger, they'd spent hours in this room, pretending to be rulers. But now Madden was wholly serious.

"So, is the child a female?"

"You really think I'd tell you?"

"Regardless, once you're dead, it'll be gone too."

His cold tone tore her heart. She had never treated him differently for being barren, but Lydia couldn't deny that, as they'd gotten older, it had been harder to ignore the absence of his power. While she'd gone to school to learn how to harness her magic, Madden had stayed at home. He couldn't leave the palace without sneers following his every move, and despite her parents never showing a hint of favouritism, it was impossible to think they were the same.

It wasn't until she'd reached her last year of schooling that Madden really started to drift away. He'd spent most of his days secluded in the library, hardly coming out unless it was for mealtime. Lydia had snuck in one day to see what was absorbing so much of his time and what she'd found had twisted her stomach with disgust. Books on mortificatio. She'd known it was dark magic, but the horror on the pages was worse than she could have imagined. The texts suggested killing innocent beings in order to perform the most heinous acts of magic she'd ever read about. Harnessing death was a power far more dangerous than anything else.

When she'd confronted Madden, he'd only become defensive, saying she was jealous he'd found something that could make him greater than her. That she'd only ever wanted him to remain her inferior. No matter how hard she'd tried, she couldn't convince him otherwise, and one day he'd simply left. They didn't hear from him until the first murder happened. That was when she'd known it was all over, that she had really lost him.

Madden lashed out with his magic. Lydia could feel its pull. She could feel darkness radiating from it. She quickly flung up a barrier, and the translucent shield wavered as the cast hit it. Lydia flinched at its power. Madden's strength was greater than she'd predicted. She extended her hand, shooting a stunning cast back at him which he easily deflected.

A ripple of pain tore through her stomach, and she gritted her teeth in an attempt to mask it. They parried back and forth, slowly moving around the room until Madden was closer to the throne. Lydia just had to distract him a little longer to allow Emelia to hit him.

Lydia ducked as a deflected cast blasted into the stone wall behind her, raining dust and rock down on the room. She squinted through the debris, hastily blocking Madden's attack. Finally, Lydia managed to position him in front of the throne. She saw Emelia's head peak out from behind it, and she discreetly nodded at her to make a move.

Emelia emerged from the throne, but Madden somehow sensed the movement, whirling around as Emelia cast at him.

"Traitor," Madden roared, deflecting the cast.

He flung out a hand, sending a ball of darkness at Emelia. She gasped as it hit her chest, and she crumpled to the ground. Lydia's scream echoed around the room. A flicker of something close to remorse crossed Madden's face, but when he faced her, it had been replaced by pure hatred.

Lydia saw the first cracks appear in her defence. The power of Madden's casts began slipping through her barrier and waves of dizziness overtook her. A contraction seized her body and pain clawed her stomach. A scream ripped from her throat as she fought to hold her shield in place. In her condition, she wouldn't outlast Madden. She knew the only way to defeat him was if she drew on the Ancient Triad. She rarely used their immense power because it would leave her own abilities sapped for days. A weaker alchemist would be killed if they tried to wield them, but she had been training to harness their power for years. She took a deep breath, relaxing the ever-present resistance to their pull and allowed their power to fill her up. The next cast she sent tore through Madden's barrier, and he was propelled back, landing hard on the floor where he remained unmoving.

Lydia approached him. She knelt next to his immobile body and placed a hand on his chest. She felt his heartbeat faintly against her palm. His life was in her hands. His soul. If she willed it to be, she knew she could end him. But she wouldn't. Unlike her brother, she didn't feel bloodlust. Instead, she found another way to keep him contained.

One of the Ancient Triad's most sought-after powers was their ability to open realms. They were keys, not only into the spirit world but all other worlds. Lydia knew this would be her solution. Using the necklace's power, she opened a rift in the fabric of their world. It was a realm between life and death. She took Madden's soul, the ugly, twisted thing it had become, and cast it into everlasting blackness. Here it would stay, unattached to Madden's body and unable to find rest. He would remain in eternal purgatory.

Lydia could lie to herself and claim morality was the reason she didn't kill Madden. In reality, she knew this fate was a much crueller one. Death would've been too kind a gift for a man who had caused so much ruin.

Lydia ripped down stones from the wall, unable to look at him any longer. She created a tomb around his body, which would remain preserved as long as he was sealed inside.

"Lydia," Emelia's weak voice called to her when the last brick slotted itself in place.

Lydia rushed to her side. While she was still in touch with the Ancient Triad's power, she reached through Emelia, feeling the magic that had stuck her down. It felt like death, corrupt and rotting. She tried to pull it out of her, but it had spread too far. The best she could do was contain the effects. She bound the magic together, entrapping it as far away from Emelia's heart as possible. Lydia didn't know what the long-term consequences would be, but for now, her friend was alive.

Lydia finally released her hold on the Ancient Triad, and her legs gave out from under her. The pain in her stomach was unbearable. Emelia grasped her hand, and Lydia latched onto it. She knew she was squeezing too hard, but she couldn't help it. A scream tore from her throat as another contraction came. Emelia tried to ease her into a more comfortable position.

"Breathe, Lydia. You're almost there, I promise."

She groaned through the pain, over and over again. Her screams filled the throne room. They echoed off the domed ceiling playing the horrible sound back to her in distorted voices.

She gasped in relief when she finally felt her daughter emerge. Emelia was there ready to gather her in the robe she'd stripped off. She brought her to Lydia's chest. Tears streamed down her face as she held her, taking in her scrunched face.

"She's perfect," Lydia whispered. She looked at Emelia whose own eyes were swimming with unshed tears. "Thank you for being here." Her breath caught on the words. The pain in her stomach hadn't eased. There was too much blood around her, and it wasn't stopping.

"Let me get a healer. Where is the healer?" Emelia asked frantically.

"No, Emelia, there isn't time." Lydia's strength had faded. After the magic she'd used, her body was depleted, and birth had taken all her remaining energy. "Madden said others were coming. Once they know he's gone, this will be the end of his reign. But they need to think my child is dead too, and that the necklaces have disappeared. Bronte has inherited the Ancient Triad's power now and I can't put her at risk. They must think there is no hope of anyone ever gaining power again. You have to take her and the necklaces and leave. Go to the Otherside, where she will be safe, where you can hide her. That's all that matters now. Once Bronte is strong enough, she will return, and hopefully, all of this will be over. She will find her way to the truth."

"What about Henrik?"

"He will understand."

"Lydia . . ."

"Emelia, what's keeping you here? This is your way out."

Remorse flickered across Emelia's eyes, but she blinked, and it was gone. "Okay. For you, I'll do it."

Lydia's heart broke completely at the words. They'd wasted so much time and now they would never get it back. "I love you, Em."

"I love you too. Always have, always will." Their voices echoed together, a phrase they'd used many times growing up.

Lydia knew she couldn't hold on much longer. Blood pooled around her, and she felt its sticky warmth spreading. Passing quietly, she sent a final prayer to the goddess that her daughter would forgive her for sending her away.

CHAPTER 1

Bronte Evans woke up sweating to incessant knocking coming from her front door. The blanket she'd pulled over herself the night before had twisted around her leg, and she had a doughy feeling in her mouth that made her tongue gluey. But it wasn't the glueyness that bothered her. It was the heavy heat of the summer morning that had turned her apartment into an oven.

Something hard was jabbing her hip, and she fumbled to pull her phone out of her pocket, clicking it on. Guilt twisted her stomach into a tight knot as she saw the missed call notification from the hospice number appear on her screen. After finishing a double shift at the fish and chip shop across the street, Bronte had crashed on the lounge. She hadn't called her mum even though she knew she should have. She hadn't visited her bedside for two days.

The knocking wouldn't stop, and Bronte cursed, rubbing sleep from her eyes as she stalked to open the door. A tall, dark-skinned man with muscles Bronte wasn't sure would fit through her doorframe loomed before her.

"Bronte Everett?" he asked.

"It's Evans," she corrected while rolling out a crick in her neck. He frowned at her. "My name is Bronte Evans," she repeated. "And you are?"

"Tyrell Baros. We received word from your mother, Emelia Everett, about her illness. She explained everything to us. You're a strange case, I must say."

"Emelia Evans," she muttered. Social worker. Bronte had trusted her mum when she'd said things were figured out. It was the one thought Bronte couldn't bring herself to have . . . what would happen to her after her mother died. The possibility of entering foster care had Bronte calculating the meagre savings in her bank account and how far they would stretch if she slipped away and left this guy none the wiser.

"Children are made orphans every day. I'm not sure what could be so strange about another one entering the system."

Tyrell's brow wrinkled. "System? I don't think you understand why I'm here. I have to speak with your mother before it's too late."

"If you were in that much of a hurry, why not just go to the hospice? If you knew where to find me, I assume you have the address."

"I had to validate your existence."

Bronte thought that sounded unnecessarily formal. She made a sweeping gesture to her body. "Validated." She left him standing in the doorway, walking over to their small kitchen to fill up a glass of water. She chugged it down, washing away the feeling of the night.

"Would you like something?" she asked. Bronte supposed she should invite him in. "We have water." They weren't rolling in money, and without her mum's income, there were no second options.

He shifted awkwardly. "I'm good, thanks. I think it's time we go."

She raised a brow. "We?"

"Aren't you coming to see your mother?"

Bronte considered the bleak prospect of staying in the apartment alone and letting guilt eat away at her. Not a productive use of her time, something she knew from experience. She had the day off work, and if she didn't visit her mum today, Bronte would have to think of an excuse as to why. Lies rolled easily off her tongue: to worried school teachers, counsellors, and even hospice nurses. She'd found people didn't usually question the daughter of a dying woman. Bronte tried not to lie to her mum though.

"Alright." She placed her cup in the sink and collected her keys from the counter where she'd dumped them the night before. "Let's go."

Bronte lagged after Tyrell when they arrived at the hospice, letting the door close slowly behind her to block out the unrelenting roar of inner London traffic and the sour heat of late summer. She smiled mechanically at the woman sitting behind the reception desk. The woman smiled back, but her expression quickly gave way to pity. It was a look Bronte had become accustomed to.

"She's just through here," Bronte told Tyrell, leading him down the hallway.

She quietly entered the familiar chestnut door of room seven. Immediately, her nose filled with the clashing scent of the flowers decorating the bedside table and windowsill. Bronte knew they were gestures of consolation - from her mum's friends and acquaintances - but she had grown to hate the smell of them.

Her mum lay in bed. She was too weak to turn her head, but her eyes tracked Bronte's movements.

"Bronte," she breathed, her faint voice edged with pain.

Bronte wavered, ready to turn back. "Do you need me to get the nurse?" she asked.

Her mum shook her head. The movement was hardly more than a twitch from side to side. "She just left."

"There's someone here to speak with you." Bronte shifted, allowing Tyrell to enter.

"We received your letter," he said by way of greeting.

Bronte's mum perked up at his words, seeming to recognise the visitor instantly. Her eyes flickered to Bronte's. "Could you give us a moment, perhaps get me a cup of tea?"

Bronte nodded despite the questions she wanted to ask about who exactly Tyrell was and why her mother was involved with him. She closed the door behind her and made her way to the small visitor's kitchen.

Bronte filled the kettle with water and switched it on, all the while thinking about what her mum and Tyrell could possibly be discussing. The water boiled, and she tipped it into a cardboard cup, dunking the peppermint tea bag in and out until the liquid turned a reddish-brown colour.

"You got our call then?"

Bronte turned to see a nurse standing in the doorway. She had a familiar face. Bronte had seen her around the Centre but could never remember her name.

The missed call notification flashed in her mind. "No, I was on my way to visit when I saw it. Was it something important?"

The nurse walked into the room, coming to stand beside her. "She doesn't have long now, Bronte. We weren't sure if she would make it through the night."

Bronte's skin prickled as an unpleasant warmth spread to her face. It was an unfamiliar sensation that had her reaching for the kitchen counter. "Oh."

"I suggest you go spend what time you have left with her. She's had her medication, but if you need anything, come and find me."

"Right, I will." Bronte nodded stiffly.

The nurse gave her a pitying look before leaving. Bronte gripped the cup of tea, the heat seeping into her hands. She knew how she looked. The daughter who didn't bother to show up for her sick mum. But she wasn't a bad daughter, and it wasn't that she didn't care: rather, she cared too much. People constantly told her to enjoy the time she had left with her mum, but she couldn't look at her without thinking about how different life would be when she was gone. Bronte figured if she peeled the band-aid back early, it wouldn't hurt so much when she finally ripped it off. The more distance she put between her and her mum during that time, the easier it would be . . . after. She was a coward, but at least she was honest enough to admit that.

Bronte reached her mum's door and raised voices could be heard inside.

"You need to tell her," Tyrell implored.

"I can't, not now."

"It's the right thing to do."

"You're too late for lectures," her mum snapped.

Bronte pushed the door open. "Is everything okay?"

Her mum's icy blue eyes found hers, and her face softened. "Of course. Come in. Tyrell was just leaving."

Tyrell didn't look at all like he wanted to leave, but after an awkward moment of silence, he turned and strode out the door. He shot Bronte a meaningful glance as he passed, which she couldn't decipher. She barely knew the man. She couldn't communicate telepathically with him, but it was clear his conversation with Bronte's mum hadn't gone well. Bronte passed the tea to her mum carefully, and she took a sip, closing her eyes as she let out a tired sigh.

"Sit," her mum told her.

Bronte pulled the only chair in the room over to her mum's side. She sank deep into its plush, too-soft cushioning and chewed on her bottom lip as she scanned her mum's face. Her once creamy white skin - unlike Bronte's golden-brown tone - was tinged with a greyness that made it seem like death had already come and gone. The nurse had been right. She didn't have long left.

"I have something for you," her mum said. She shifted, reaching behind her neck to where, Bronte knew, was the clasp of her necklace. Bronte had never seen her without her necklace. It was attached to her like a fifth limb.

"What are you doing? I can't take that," she protested hastily. The last thing Bronte deserved was that necklace.

Her mum smiled ruefully. "You should've taken it years ago. It was selfish of me to keep it."

"I don't want it, mum," she said firmly.

Her mum had always kept the necklace tucked beneath whatever she was wearing so only the chain was visible. But attached to the necklace was a circular pendant slightly smaller than Bronte's palm. It was engraved with a series of lines that formed a maze-like symbol leading to its centre, where a golden gem lay.

"Bronte, I need you to promise to wear this necklace when I'm gone. Keep it hidden, but always on you. You'll figure out why soon enough."

"Or you could just tell me why."

Her mum's face softened. "It wouldn't make sense now. Just promise you'll wear it."

Bronte frowned and nodded reluctantly, allowing her mum to hand over the necklace. She hated cryptic statements and would've preferred a straight answer, but she didn't want to spend these last moments arguing.

"Put it on," her mum urged.

Bronte fastened the necklace around her neck and tucked the pendant beneath her shirt. The metal was warm as it settled against her sternum. Bronte looked up, expecting a prideful expression on her mum's face, but her eyes had closed. Bronte's heart constricted. "Mum? Mum? What do I do? Mum!"

Her voice sounded desperate and glaringly loud inside the small room. She reached out a hand and gently wrapped it around her mum's. Her fingers were cold, and blue-green veins protruded under the fragile skin. Her mum's pulse was barely perceptible beneath her touch, but each beat was a silent comfort that ebbed some of the tension in Bronte's body. Finally, her mum's eyes opened, and their icy blue colour was alight with a truth that Bronte wasn't ready to accept.

"It's okay. Tyrell's here," her mum murmured. "He'll take you to your godfather."

"Who?"

"Your godfather . . . my brother, Frank."

Her mum smiled. It was an effortlessly happy smile that Bronte couldn't return. She didn't have a godfather or . . . uncle? Her mum didn't have any family. It had always been just the two of them.

Bronte wondered if this was another strange vision. The more her mum's sickness had progressed, the more she'd talked nonsense about people Bronte didn't know and places that didn't exist. She was suffering from an undiagnosed terminal illness. It wasn't cancer, organ failure, or heart disease. But it was death, that much was certain. Her body seemed to be decaying at a rate unrelated to her age.

It was a medical mystery and, unfortunately for them, an incurable one.

She hadn't told the nurse about her mum's strange spells. It could have been a side effect of the medication. Or maybe her mum was going crazy. Maybe from disease. Probably with pain. Bronte's eyes welled with tears, and she blinked rapidly, but they still managed to escape down her cheeks.

Her mum squeezed her hand. "It's going to be okay, Bronte. Don't cry. Not over this. Not over me. I love you. I want to stay with you, but . . . I've done everything I needed to. I've kept my promises. Maybe I kept them a little too long. I was hiding from my past, and it's time for you to find your future."

Bronte fixed her eyes on the ceiling. The artificial glow of the light turned her vision fuzzy, and she wiped away the remaining dampness on her cheeks. She inhaled, held it, and exhaled deeply. "Is this what Tyrell wanted you to tell me? That I have an uncle?"

"That was part of it. Just promise me you'll go with him."

Bronte wanted answers and an explanation, but she could see her mum didn't have the time to give her one. "I promise."

"Good. I love you, Bronte."

"I love you too. Always have, always will." They finished together, both their voices barely above a whisper.

They had spoken those words so many times, but Bronte had never thought they would be the last ones she would hear from her mum. Her mum's eyelids closed. A faint smile rested on her lips, and Bronte felt the band-aid over her pain finally rip open.

"Wait, mum! I, I don't have a godfather! What are you talking about? Mum! Answer me. Open your eyes," Bronte pleaded in a voice that sounded nothing like her own.

Anger spiked through her. Her cheeks were wet. She closed her eyes and swallowed thickly. Bronte had to tell the nurse that she couldn't find her mum's pulse anymore, that the slight lift and drop of her chest had stopped, but she couldn't move. She let out an animalistic yell, and heard a rush of footsteps from the hall. It didn't matter who was coming. They were already too late.

CHAPTER 2

Bronte sat in the waiting room and watched the ceiling fan rotate slowly. Its soft whirring filled the silence, coupled with the sound of the receptionist tapping on her keyboard with acrylic nails. Bronte wasn't smiling at her now. The receptionist glanced at her every few minutes, her expression fixed in a look of sorrowful regret. Bronte wanted to slap her. Instead, she absently picked at a loose bit of skin beside her thumbnail and waited.

Tyrell had been the one to find her with her mum. She'd been sobbing uncontrollably at the time, and he'd had to drag her from the room. Once she'd calmed down enough, he'd left to speak to the nurses. Bronte had finally managed to stop crying now, and her tears had been replaced by numbness.

Tyrell appeared beside her. "I've explained to the nurse where the body must go per your uncle's request."

Bronte stiffened. The thought of her mum's body leaving the hospice lifeless was something she'd never be ready to accept.

"Come on, I'll walk you home." Tyrell offered his hand, and she let him pull her up, mutely following.

It was a short walk to her apartment. A cramped one-story above the street with dripping taps and hot water that only liked to work half the time. She shoved open the foyer door, swollen from the humid summer air. Her puffy eyes stung when she blinked, and it was a relief to get away from the sunlight.

Bronte dragged her feet up the stairs and unlocked their apartment, stooping as she walked inside. The lintel had always been too low for her. Her mum used to joke that they were giants living in a doll's house.

It wasn't the first time Bronte had come home to an empty apartment, but it was the first time she had to accept there was no possibility of seeing her mum here again. No more returning from school to find her bent in an odd yoga position that Bronte would be forced to copy in preparation for the classes her mum used to teach. No more strange aromas from burning incense or candles. Her chest ached from that knowing.

"You can't stay here Bronte. I know this is hard, but I need to take you to your uncle."

She felt a spike of anger toward Tyrell, annoyed that he was pushing this on her when all she wanted to do was collapse into bed. "Where exactly am I being taken, and why are you the one that has to do it? Why didn't my uncle come himself?" If he was indeed a blood relative and her mum's brother, he would surely want to be here. Unless he didn't care. A shiver ran through her at what this man might be like. Perhaps he hated children, and she was about to be delivered into his cruel clutches.

"It's my role as emissary to transport you safely to Hallowless and into your uncle's care. He couldn't come himself because it is not allowed."

Bronte's thoughts of evil child-hating men faded. "Transport me where?"

"Hallowless," Tyrell repeated calmly.

Hallowless. The name struck something inside her. It was a word her mum had repeated on and off during her sickness. She'd assumed it was nonsense. She was sure it was nonsense. There was no place she knew of, in England or anywhere else, called 'Hallowless'.

"And where is that?"

"In a pocket of space between this realm and the spirit world."

He delivered the line with a straight face, but Bronte couldn't take him seriously. "Where is it really?"

"Your mother warned me this might be the case."

"That I wouldn't want to travel with you to a pocket realm?"

"That you would be unwilling to leave because you don't know your history."

"What is there to know? I've lived in England my whole life. Never before has this Hallowless place been mentioned. Well, never before the last month," she amended.

"You were not born in England. Hallowless is your homeland. You're what's known as an alchemist, and your alchemical blood allows you to travel through the barrier that separates Hallowless from Earth."

"Did my uncle put you up to this? Did he create some weird, elaborate story? Because as much as I appreciate the effort to lighten the mood, I do not see the humour in this situation."

"It's not your uncle's doing. It's the truth. If you want to blame someone for your ignorance, blame your mother for not telling you all this years ago."

"Don't speak like that about my mum," she snapped.

Tyrell sighed. "I'm sorry, but she is the reason we're in this situation. If you come with me, your uncle will explain everything."

Bronte was certain she wasn't going anywhere with this man. If her uncle wanted her to come, he could get her himself. She didn't care about the mysterious rules prohibiting it.

"No." She may as well have stomped her foot along with the word. She knew she looked like a bratty little girl throwing a tantrum.

"It is in your best interest to come willingly."

"Are you threatening to kidnap me now?"

"I told you, it is my duty to transport you there one way or another. It was your mother's last wish."

Bronte froze. She thought back to what her mum had made her promise. She had told her to go, but Bronte hadn't known this was what she'd agreed to.

"Prove it. Prove that this place exists."

"I can't. I have to show you. Pack a bag if you wish, but I suggest keeping it light. Most of it won't be useful where we're going."

Bronte debated staying in the apartment alone and waiting for the real social services to show up or following her mum's wish and letting Tyrell take her to her uncle. She grabbed her backpack from beside the door.

"Does this mean you're agreeing to come?" Tyrell's shoulders relaxed as he watched her.

"I'm considering." But she could pack while she considered. "What about all my stuff, my school, my work, my mum's funeral?" Her voice broke slightly on the last question as her throat tightened.

"Frank will have that all under control."

It wasn't exactly an answer she trusted, but she wanted to believe it was true. Bronte hated to admit it, but she wasn't ready to deal with the things she'd listed, so palming them off on someone else would be a relief. She shoved a change of clothes, toiletries, and her phone into her bag.

"You won't need that," Tyrell said as she ripped her phone charger out of the electrical socket.

"Why? Does this pocket realm have no reception?"

"Something like that."

Bronte packed it anyway. She'd promised her mum she would go. If this was what she wanted from her, Bronte had to at least entertain the possibility that it was real.

"Take me to Hallowless."

They'd left the city behind. After driving for a few hours, they arrived at an empty estate where overgrown vines had claimed the rusted gate. It was a Georgian rectory that had fallen into disrepair. The car snaked its way through the untended garden, stopping in front of a worn set of steps leading to a decayed oak door.

"I'm not going in there." Bronte eyed the warped roof of the house in distaste.

"You don't have to. We're going in there." Tyrell pointed to the tree line surrounding the property.

"That's not much better," she muttered. But she slung her backpack on and followed him towards the trees.

They walked through the forest in silence. Soon the sunlight disappeared, and so did the view of the house. The muted sound of running water reached Bronte's ears, and she saw a stream ahead. A strange oblong stone structure had been erected by the water's edge. Bronte could see runes drawn on several of the stones as they approached.

"We call these Arches," explained Tyrell before she could ask.

"That's a very literal name." Though she supposed it would be easy to remember.

They stood together a few meters away from the base of the Arch. A translucent veil filled the space inside, its slight sheen marring the air and blurring the image of the stream behind it.

"How does this take us to Hallowless?" It wasn't exactly a portal inside a cupboard door, but it seemed just as unrealistic.

"These four blank stones," said Tyrell, pointing to the keystone, the stone at the base of the structure - half covered by dirt - and two adjacent stones on either side, "indicate north, south, east and west. The runes drawn on the stones between them give the Arch its magic. It connects to Hallowless like a gateway."

Bronte cursed whatever genius had decided to build the Arch by the water's edge and hoped like crazy she didn't fall face-first into the stream when she went through.

"Ladies first," said Tyrell gesturing for her to go.

"I'm more of a watch-and-learn kind of person."

Tyrell crossed his arms. "I need to make sure you arrive safely. That includes watching you go through the Arch."

Despite his words, Bronte refused to budge. Tyrell's lips pinched the longer he waited. "Whenever you're ready, just walk through the Arch, and the magic will do the rest."

Sighing, she slowly edged in front of the stone structure. It was over a head taller than her, and the strange shimmering did little to hide the fact that she was walking straight into water. She was aware of Tyrell's gaze on her back, waiting for her to move, but she couldn't take the final step.

"It's okay to be nervous, Bronte, but it'll be over before you know it."

It wasn't going through the Arch that she was nervous about. It was what would come after. She didn't know how it would feel to see where her mum grew up. The place that had been hidden from her.

Bronte thought of her mum's necklace, now strung around her neck. She didn't know why she'd been given it or what it meant that she had to keep it hidden, but she had a suspicion that Hallowless might hold the answer. It was curiosity that made her take the final step. She knew she could never live with the feeling of what if.

Steeling herself, Bronte closed her eyes and stepped forward. Where her foot should've hit the water, it touched nothing, and her eyes flew open as she fell into darkness.

There was no time to scream, shout, or gasp. One moment, Bronte was standing; the next, she was plummeting into a world of black. Wind whipped at her hair, and the air turned cold as she continued to fall. Then, just when she thought she would be lost in limbo forever, her body seemed to right itself. Colour burst around her, and her feet hit solid ground. It felt as though she'd been sprinting and come to a sudden stop. She was propelled forwards and ended up on her hands and knees with the breath knocked out of her. Slowly, she got to her feet, brushing the dirt from her palms.

She'd landed in the base of a pit. Arches formed a circle around her. Some had glowing runes and the translucent veil shimmering between them, while others looked like plain stone structures with nothing special about them. Something hit her in the back before she could move, and she was thrown forward again.

"Rule one: don't stand in front of an Arch." Tyrell's breathless voice sounded behind her as he grabbed her arm to steady her.

"Got it, thanks," she gasped, finding her feet. "Where do all these Arches go?"

"To Earth. The active ones mean some people are yet to come back."

"You can travel back and forth whenever?"

"No, these are only used by emissaries, like me, or in special circumstances if you're approved for travel. It can be dangerous for us to be away from Hallowless for extended periods. We are disconnected from our magic when we travel to Earth and, when we return, it's like the effect of plugging one of your electrical devices into a socket and creating a surge. We have to take protective measures like wearing one of these beaded bracelets made of obsidian which we've found helps absorb the shock of our magic when we return. You, however, aren't affected because you've never been in touch with your magic, and it isn't until we connect with our power that we face any risk." He pulled up his sleeve to reveal a bracelet of black stones.

"Sounds intense."

Tyrell shrugged. "Small price to pay. The exit is at the top of the steps. Let's go."

Bronte didn't think she could call the large stone slabs that surrounded the pit steps. They were so big she practically had to climb up them. Two sets of guards stood outside, and Tyrell nodded at them as they passed. They emerged into bright sunlight, and if Bronte didn't know better, she would think she was merely stepping out into the London afternoon they'd left behind. But as she took in the view, it was clear she was far away from everything she knew. Bronte looked out on a sprawling city of colour. Green mountains bordered the city to the right, and a shimmering sea could be seen to her left.

"Welcome to Namire, the alchemist city of Hallowless."

"It's beautiful." She couldn't think of a reason her mum would hide such a place from her.

"Before I take you to your uncle, we need to visit the Shrine. You must be read to determine your powers and that's the only place to have it done."

"What do you mean, 'read'?"

"Every alchemist is usually read at birth by a shaman. They're the ones who will place you into a certain manipulation based on the power you possess. I'll let the shaman explain how this works once we get there. I wouldn't want to mess it up and complicate things." Tyrell led the way down the stone steps and into the street.

Bronte's mind could hardly process what Tyrell had said. She couldn't accept the possibility that she had powers or that her mum had once had them too. She couldn't be anything other than human. She was sure of it.

They followed the path through the streets of Namire. It was unlike any city she'd ever seen. There were no sky-scraping buildings or roads lined with cars, no electricity, or people walking around absorbed with their phones. Instead, the people they passed greeted them happily, and it felt like she'd entered a small town despite its size. Horseless carriages trundled through the streets, and Bronte caught a glimpse of ladies sitting inside, fanning their faces to keep cool in the heat. The strangest thing by far was the fashion. Women wore dresses with voluminous skirts and corsets, while the men were attired in formal coats over vests and long pants. Everything was a step into the past, and Bronte felt herself begin to sweat just looking at them. Her own shorts and a t-shirt garnered many strange looks, although no one openly questioned her about them. She assumed it was due to Tyrell's presence. It helped that he was also dressed in clothes that didn't suit Namire.

"Why is everything so old-fashioned. I assume you've seen phones, computers, and cars if you can travel from here to Earth?"

"We have. We've also seen the way your world has been destroyed by them. But that's not the reason we haven't adopted your technologies. Why would we need cars when we have a way to transport almost anywhere instantaneously? Why do we need electric lights when we have stones that glow in the dark? A lot of your technology was made in the absence of magic to fill the void of things we can already do. But above all these reasons, we have tried using your technologies and found that they fail in the presence of magic. Lights surge and shatter, and phone signals go haywire in the presence of so much energy. It simply doesn't work. Nevertheless, our way of living works, so we've kept it unchanged." Bronte supposed that was as good a reason as any.

Finally, they reach what looked like a wide, dead-end street. On either side were two raised platforms. Lined down the length of these platforms were stone Arches. One of the platforms had the sign 'Arrivals' hanging above it, and the other, 'Departures'. It reminded Bronte of a train station. The major difference was that people kept appearing out of the Arches and striding away as though they hadn't just travelled through space and time.

"These are the Gateways. They'll take you everywhere you need to be in Namire. They're the same as the Arch you just came through, except they don't lead out of Hallowless."

They made their way to the departure platform. Above each Arch was a sign with a number and the name of a destination. Tyrell led them to number eleven, which, according to the sign, would take them to the Shrine.

"After you," Tyrell prompted.

Bronte stepped through the Arch, and she was hit by the same unpleasant feeling of falling through a dark, cold abyss, and then she was stumbling onto solid ground.

She managed to keep herself upright this time, but barely, and she quickly moved away from the Arch. Her heart was pounding as she took in her surroundings. Everything was green, and she wondered how far away from the centre of the city they'd travelled. Nestled among the trees was a white temple. The moss-covered stones she was standing on formed a path to the temple door.

Tyrell appeared behind her, and together they made their way towards it. As she got closer, Bronte spied a tall female figure clothed in white robes standing by the entrance. She found herself regretting not asking what exactly a reading involved. Although, from the sounds of it, it couldn't be anything too sinister.

They ascended the white stone steps and approached the silent woman. She had tan skin and hair that fanned around her head, held back from her face by a golden band. Her brows were arched delicately, highlighting her bright green eyes. She looked like a goddess.

"Bronte Everett," said the woman. Her voice was toneless, and though Bronte knew it wasn't a question, she found herself nodding.

The woman's stillness and unearthly presence unnerved her. "I am shaman Paloma. You may come with me." She turned and walked into the temple. Bronte glanced uncertainly at Tyrell, who gave her an encouraging smile.

"I'll be here when you're done," he assured her.

Bronte forced her legs to move further into the temple. It was beautiful inside. The walls were decorated with mosaic art. She could make out images of the sun, moon, trees, and flowing rivers. Paloma glided across the tiled floor. Her robes fluttered behind her as though an invisible breeze was lifting them off the ground.

The sound of laughter reached Bronte's ears, and two young girls rounded the corner wearing robes of purple. They fell silent immediately when they saw Paloma and passed by her with their heads lowered. They looked no older than twelve, and Bronte wondered who they were.

"They're fledglings," came the answer from Paloma. Bronte eyed her back quizzically, wondering if shamans could read minds. "To an extent."

A shiver ran through her. Bronte tried to wipe any thoughts from her brain, but they kept popping up. "Why are they so young?" she finally asked.

"They are here to learn the ways of the goddess. They are her daughters. Eventually, they will become true shamans. When the children are read at birth and found to be shamans, they are surrendered by their parents and brought up under our care. Although we have great gifts, we must sacrifice a lot for them."

Bronte thought it sounded like a harsh future to be taken away from your parents at birth. "How are you different from a normal alchemist?"

"We are neither full alchemists nor like our witch ancestors. Our abilities mean we are attuned to the energy around us. We can detect what magic an alchemist possesses or what sort of magic has been performed. We can manipulate the elements in small matters, like summoning fire or shifting wind but that is where our limit lies."

They arrived at a room as big as a cathedral. Open arches formed the walls, and a stone slab lay in the middle of the space. Runes lined the base of the stone in jagged lines.

"Please lie down." Paloma motioned with a slender arm toward the block of stone.

Bronte crossed the room and awkwardly manoeuvred herself until prone atop the block. She tensed as the exposed skin of her arms and legs came in contact with the cold surface, unable to shake the feeling that she was about to be sacrificed in some holy ritual.

"The process of being read is simple. First, you will enter a state of unconsciousness that will feel like merely blinking. During that time, I will read your body's energy to figure out what chakras you have open. The seven core chakras determine what type of alchemist you are. Most alchemists have four that are open. The seventh, fifth, and first are the core chakras, and the last chakra is the deciding chakra for your specific magic. If your sacral chakra is open, you are known as a transmuter, capable of altering both physical and mental states. If your solar plexus is open, you're an enchanter. This is often the most desired chakra because it's believed that you possess 'true magic' and, for that reason, enchanters are seen as akin to our witch ancestors. Thirdly, the heart chakra is responsible for healer magic. Finally, the third eye chakra creates clairvoyants, who have the gift of the Sight." Paloma recited the information quickly, and Bronte nodded, too out of her depth to speak. "This won't hurt a bit."

Bronte's tense body unwillingly relaxed as Paloma placed a cool hand against her forehead. Gradually she drifted into the calmness of sleep. Bronte came back to consciousness as subtly as the tide returns to the sea to find Paloma looking down at her with clear emerald eyes.

"Your crown, throat, and root chakras are open, along with your solar plexus, meaning you're an enchanter."

Her toneless voice set Bronte on edge. She couldn't accept she possessed any type of magic, let alone the one most desired by alchemists. "How do you know you're right?" she blurted out, but Bronte immediately regretted asking when Paloma's lips pressed together in a firm line.

"It is not wise to question the goddess. Accept what you are given and give back only what you cannot take. But never refuse. It is time for you to leave," Paloma said bluntly, motioning her to rise.

Bronte pushed off the cold concrete block and followed Paloma back to the entrance. She was reeling from she had been told, but she didn't dare speak again, knowing she wouldn't get a straight answer. Her body flooded with relief when she saw Tyrell waiting for her at the door. Paloma left her there before drifting silently back into the Shrine.

"What did you get?" Tyrell asked once Paloma was out of earshot.

"Enchanter."

His eyes widened. "Blessed by the goddess, I see."

"Who?"

"Hecate, the goddess of magic and witchcraft. Thousands of years ago, she blessed the first human with magic. Have you ever heard of the witches of Thessaly?" Bronte shook her head. "Dating back to the 1st century BC, Hecate blessed Annis Theobesian with the gift of magic."

"And that's how witches came to be? Why are you not all witches, then? What happened?"

"There was once a time when magic belonged solely on Earth. It was slowly passed down through the Theobesian bloodline, gradually spreading around Thessaly. But soon non-magical beings began to notice strange happenings, and witchcraft was blamed. They grew fearful of magic, and the witches went into hiding. But magic continued to prosper and expand to other parts of the world. Hallowless was created from that fear. We needed a place we could live freely. But, as a result, we lost part of our powers. So, when someone is born an enchanter, we say they're blessed by the goddess because they're the closest to our witch ancestors' abilities."

"Is it just random what power you get?"

Tyrell shrugged. "Mostly. It's more common for children to inherit the same manipulation as one of their parents. Your mother was a powerful enchanter, so you would likely be too."

A heaviness settled inside her at the mention of her mum. It was grief that made her want to go to sleep and forget the world existed.

She wished she knew why her mum had run from all of this. Then, another thought broke through her haze of pain.

"If you said I was born here, was my father an alchemist too?" Her mum had always claimed Bronte was the result of a one-night stand, and with no phone number or name to follow up on, she had decided to raise her daughter alone. But it was clear now that wasn't the truth.

Tyrell shifted uncomfortably. "I think that's a question to ask you, godfather. I'll take you there now."

CHAPTER 3

Frank's house was in a part of Namire Tyrell referred to as the lower north. The sun disappeared behind the horizon as they walked along the stone path towards it. Bronte's feet dragged as exhaustion and hunger set in.

Finally, they arrived at a modest two-story house. Bronte relaxed as they reached the wooden door. A comforting glow could be seen through the curtained front windows. The sound of someone playing the piano inside filtered out into the night.

Tyrell knocked loudly, but no one came to answer. He tried again, but the piano must've drowned out the noise.

"Is it unlocked?" she asked.

Tyrell tried the handle, which turned freely and opened into a small foyer. In an adjacent room, the source of the piano playing was found. Bronte could see the back of a boy sitting bent over the keys. His bronze hair hung in front of his eyes which Bronte could only assume were closed given there was no sheet music in front of him, and his neck was bent at an angle that would be uncomfortable if he really was looking at the keys. The music seemed to pour from his fingertips, resonate and full of emotion. She felt guilty interrupting him, but the rest of the house was silent, and there was no sign of her godfather.

"Hello?" she called.

The music came to a halt, and the boy whipped around, pushing his hair back from his face as he did so. She assumed he was around her age or maybe a little older. He had what her mum would've called the 'James Dean look', tousled hair and high cheekbones. His hazel eyes met hers, and she found herself locked in his gaze.

"Who are you?" he asked.

His deep voice carried a transatlantic accent that reminded her of the way actors spoke in old Hollywood movies. It was the same accent she'd been surrounded with all day, but she hadn't placed why it was familiar until now.

"Bronte. Who are you?"

"You're the Disciple's daughter?" His question sounded like an accusation.

"Excuse me?"

"I have to go." His mouth flattened into a hard line, and he brushed past her and Tyrell, leaving through the still-open door.

"Is that voices I hear?" A bespectacled man with shaggy brown hair appeared further down the hallway. "Bronte! How long have you been there? Sorry, it's so loud in the kitchen, and I didn't hear the door over the piano." He walked down the hallway to greet her. Behind him came a short, dark-skinned woman with long wavy hair and a tall boy with tight short curls. "Has Nick gone?" he peered into the room with the piano.

"He just left." Bronte still didn't know what to make of the interaction with the boy or what his relation was to Frank, but she hoped she wouldn't be seeing him again soon.

"I'll take her from here. Thanks, Tyrell."

Bronte was handed over like a piece of cattle and, with a nod of his head, Tyrell left, closing the door behind him. Bronte had to stop herself from following him. After the overwhelming day he'd become an unexpected form of comfort

"As you may have guessed, I'm Frank. This is my wife, Nina, and our son Eli. I'm so glad you made it okay."

Bronte forced a smile. "Nice to meet you."

"Come in. We were just setting out dinner." Frank beckoned her down the hallway. "I'm sorry we're meeting under these circumstances. It's been a strange couple of days. As I'm sure, it's been for you. Forgive me if I'm still in shock, but I was under the impression that Emelia had passed many years ago. To find out she was alive and with a daughter has been a surprise to all of us."

"What do you mean passed years ago?"

"There are many things to catch you up on, but I think food comes first."

Bronte was ushered into a small kitchen brimming with delicious smells. The round wooden table in the middle of the room was covered by a collection of dishes. Steaming vegetables, roast chicken, peas, and gravy in a pot. It was just like the traditional dinners Bronte was familiar with, and this partially quelled the anxiety within her.

"Help yourself," Nina prompted kindly once they'd all taken a seat at the table.

Bronte filled her plate with a bit of everything, her stomach growling at the sight of food after the long day she'd had.

"How is the Otherside?" Eli asked. He was almost the perfect blend of his parents. He had Frank's curls but Nina's almond-shaped eyes, although he was taller than both.

"The Otherside?" Bronte frowned.

"Earth, where you're from."

"She's *from* here. She just happened to grow up there," Nina corrected.

"It's not so different to here. We do have working cell service and Wi-Fi, though." Bronte had quickly discovered that Tyrell had been right, and her phone was about as useful as a brick here.

Eli nodded. "We've studied the Otherside a bit in school, but I've never been particularly fascinated. Of course, if you're an emissary, that's all they care about. I'm too fond of my powers to want to cross the barrier."

"How does that work? The barrier? How did this all come to be? Tyrell told me a bit about Hecate, but why exactly did moving to Hallowless mean there are no longer full witches?"

Frank nodded, absorbing her questions before responding. "It's all a balancing act. Hallowless was created by three women known as the Theobesian sisters. Descendants from the First Witch Annis Theobesian. In the fourteenth century, magical beings, including werewolves, Fae, and many other creatures were hunted relentlessly, and the creation of guns meant they could be killed easily. One of the sisters, Eleni, had clairvoyant powers, and she saw an eternal war between the two kinds. So, the sisters called upon the goddess Hecate for guidance." Frank paused his explanation to take a sip of water. "Hecate gave them what became known as the Ancient Triad. Three necklaces instilled with a small piece of her own power. When joined and wielded correctly, they could open gateways between realms. The sisters used them to open a realm and seal magic away. But for this realm to exist, it had to be created in balance with Earth. It was quickly discovered that the process had caused a shift in the witch's abilities. Not everyone could wield their powers as they used to. The barrier had taken a part of the witch's magic to make up for the magic they were sealing off from Earth. They no longer had access to the full gifts Hecate had blessed them with so many years ago. This is how alchemists came to be and how manipulations were created. Speaking of powers, I know it was planned that you were read today. What was the result?"

"Um, enchanter." There were choked sounds around the table. "What are you all?" Bronte quickly asked in the hope of distracting them.

"Healer," said Nina.

"Same," echoed Eli.

"I'm a transmuter," Frank finished.

Bronte still didn't understand the full capabilities of each manipulation. She hardly understood what being an enchanter meant she was capable of. "Tyrell told me my mum was an enchanter, but when I asked about my father, he said to ask you. My father was from here, wasn't he?"

There was silence around the table, and Bronte searched the three faces, not liking the hesitancy she saw.

Finally, Frank opened his mouth. "Yes. Your father was Madden Theobesian."

"Theobesian, as in related to the Theobesian sisters?"

"A direct descendent. He died around the same time as your birth, if my estimations are correct. It was right before Emelia disappeared."

"What happened?" Eli had begun toying with his food, and she could tell the answer to come wouldn't be good.

Frank cleared his throat. "The Theobesian bloodline has been the most powerful throughout Namire's history. They are our leaders. But Madden was born barren, meaning he had no power. This is a rare occurrence, but it does happen. His twin sister Lydia was born an enchanter and was in line to inherit the throne. It is believed this was the root of his jealousy. Some people in Namire don't think the barrier is for the greater good. They believe that the magic that's trapped is rightfully theirs. If it were to come down, it would mean no more manipulations, as everyone would essentially be a full witch again. However, it would cause the collapse of our realm, and we would be back where we started."

"What does this have to do with my dad?"

"Your dad formed a group known as the Disciples." Bronte frowned at the name, remembering what that boy had called her, the Disciple's daughter. "They sought to bring down the barrier, but the only way to do so was if Madden had control of the Ancient Triad. The necklaces respond to the most powerful member of the Theobesian bloodline. At the time, that person was Madden's mother, but he killed her, causing the power to pass to his sister. He wanted to kill her too and take the necklaces. However, the plan didn't go the way he intended. Lydia was found dead, but Madden was killed too. The Ancient Triad was lost, and the Disciples fell apart without their leader. This all happened the same night you and your mother went missing and were later assumed dead. The truth of that night will likely always be a mystery."

Bronte's face flushed with heat. Her mother wasn't a bad person. She'd never done anything to harm anyone. Bronte refused to believe she was the daughter of murderers. Another sinking suspicion crept to the front of her mind. She thought of the necklace that hung around her neck. It was likely just a coincidence that it had been the one thing her mum had never taken off and the one thing she had given her in parting. She had told her to keep it hidden, and her mum must've known Bronte would end up here, in a place where the necklace could possibly mean something. But she didn't know anything for certain, and until she learned more about her history, she wasn't about to draw attention to it.

"My mother would never do something so cruel."

"I don't believe Emelia knew the full extent of Madden's plans nor his capabilities for evil before it was too late. As a boy, I was friendly with Madden, and he always seemed levelheaded. But whatever was brewing within clearly got the better of him. It's easy to lose yourself in dark magic, it can make you hunger for things you wouldn't usually, and it turned him into a monster."

Bronte didn't want to think of her mum as evil. She couldn't believe it, when she had known her to be a kind and loving woman all her life. But there were so many things pointing towards one truth; Bronte's mum wasn't who she thought she had been. Bronte felt like any control she'd previously had over her life was slipping away.

"Where does that leave me then? How would I fit into this world if my dad was a killer, and my mum was a known deserter? What am I supposed to do here? Everyone my age likely already has a hold on whatever powers they possess. I don't even know where to start with that. Everything I've ever known is on the other side of this place, and I'm not sure this is where I'm meant to be."

Frank's face creased with sympathy. "I know today has been a lot to take in, but I promise it's not as daunting as it seems. We have a school here in Namire, Welkin, the School of Alchemy, which will teach you how to gain control over your power. You will be starting later than your peers, but that doesn't mean you won't be able to learn."

No part of Bronte wished to return to her old school. She had only been attending for a year, during the time when her mum had fallen ill and needed constant care in London. Before then, they'd moved around a lot. Her mum had always claimed it eased her perpetual boredom, but now Bronte wondered if she was trying to remain undiscovered from any alchemists who may have been looking for her. Although if they believed her dead, it could simply have been her own paranoia.

"Do I have a choice here? What about my old life? My schooling? Everything in my apartment. The apartment!" She proclaimed. "You can't just leave it uninhibited, with all of our stuff inside. And my mum." Her voice broke. "I have medical debts to pay and a funeral to organise."

"Bronte, you're sixteen. No one expects you to do those things. I have taken responsibility for selling the apartment and sorting out your things. I see you brought some of your possessions already, but if there's anything else you'd like, let me know, and I can retrieve it. As for Emelia's body, it is being transported here so we can have a traditional funeral for her."

Something eased inside Bronte with the knowledge that her mum was being taken care of. But the thought that her whole existence was being erased stirred an unpleasant feeling. She knew she had no use for the things she'd owned on Earth, but that didn't mean they weren't hers. With all the moving, Bronte had learnt to cut down on possessions early in life, keeping only what was absolutely necessary, but that didn't make parting with them any less challenging. Exhaustion and grief weighed on her, and she found she couldn't take another bite of her food. "I think I'd like to go to bed."

Nina nodded understandingly. "Of course, I'll take you to your room."

Following a series of goodnights, Nina led Bronte up a short flight of stairs to a cramped hallway. At the end of the hallway, she opened a door revealing a room containing a single bed, chest of drawers, and a desk.

"I hadn't expected . . . Well, it's the best we could do on a day's notice. But we can buy you new things, different curtains perhaps?"

Bronte shrugged. "The curtains are fine. It's all fine. Thank you."

"We'll take you into town tomorrow anyway. To get clothes."

Bronte didn't know what was wrong with her clothes, but she was too exhausted to argue. "That sounds good."

"Goodnight then."

"Goodnight."

Bronte sat on the bed after the door clicked shut. She slid her phone out of her bag and curled onto her side. Her phone battery was down to the last quarter of charge. She had no way to call or text, but there was no one she wanted to contact. She opened her gallery and scrolled through the pictures of her and her mum. She tried to ingrain each smiling photo into her brain, knowing that once her charge ran out, she wouldn't be seeing them again. The pressure in her throat eventually built up to the point where she couldn't stop her tears. Bronte turned off her phone, unable to bear the memories any longer, and fell asleep with salt-dried cheeks.

CHAPTER 4

Nick took a deep breath of night air, drawing in the distinct smells of Namire at the height of summer. The city was divided by smell. The south smelt of rotting seaweed and salt; the north of tangy pine and the type of fresh air you associate with crisp mornings. The easiest way to notice an outsider in the south was from their expression. If they had wrinkled noses and scrunched eyes, it was a tell-tale sign that they didn't belong in that part of the city. Nick hardly registered the putrid stench anymore.

The street in front of him was deserted. At this time of night, respectable people were home with their families. Those who weren't so respectable were in bars drinking so much ale they'd forget their own names. Later, the ones who had been prosperous at the gambling tables would stumble home singing nonsense songs, and the losers would walk with their heads down, mumbling to themselves or yelling at shadows. Nick liked to avoid both kinds.

He took a deep breath to calm his ever-present, simmering anger. He hadn't expected to run into the new girl, Bronte Everett. Rationally he knew she wasn't to blame for her parent's actions, but she was the closest he'd gotten to a Disciple walking around in daylight.

He doubted she was aware of her own history. There was no way she could've known her parents were responsible for his brother, Nathaniel's, death. Yet, Nick couldn't let go of his fear that she was returning to finish her parent's job. Something he would never let happen. Nick admitted he hadn't been subtle in hiding his anger, and if he was going to figure out if Bronte was genuinely clueless, or just acting, he would need to mask it better.

The soft glow of sunstones encased inside streetlamps lit his path to The Sparrow. Every so often, one or more of the lamps that should've lit his way had been smashed, and the sunstones were stolen, leaving him to walk through patches of darkness. The stones weren't worth much. They were so plentiful that hardly anyone would pay more than a few copias for one. The way the stones worked reminded him of the solar panels he'd read about from the Otherside. They absorbed sunlight which was reflected out when night fell. He couldn't judge people for stealing them, though. He'd thought about doing the same once or twice himself. Desperate times meant you would do almost anything for a single copia.

Nick registered a particularly foul smell coming from the shadows of an alley, and even his nose wrinkled from the stench. Whatever had died in there was something he didn't want to know about.

Two shadowed figures appeared on the path before him, coming his way. He noted the dark uniform of the High Guard and the flash of silver at their side. Nick scoffed to himself. He'd rarely seen more than the occasional patrol by the city watch in Namire's south. The wealthy northerners made sure of that, keeping their streets well-lit and heavily patrolled, even though the city Council always blamed any trouble on the south. It wasn't slander if it was the truth, though.

Nick passed the guards without making eye contact. Beneath one watchman's cloak, a slip of long blond hair had spilt out. It wasn't rare to see a female High Guard; they were usually the most ruthless. If you ever wanted to bribe a guard, you would have more luck with the men. With enough coin, you could get them thinking about ale or whores, and for a small cut, they turned a blind eye if they caught you with moonwood or some other contraband. Nick had never had any trouble with them, though, and he would like to keep it that way.

He neared the gambling house, and sounds from inside leaked into the quiet night: raucous, drunken noises that would soon envelope him. Girls leant against the wall outside, their bodies expertly curved to display their bare legs and full chests. Moonlight caught the glittering powders that shimmered on their faces. Their makeup had been skilfully applied to hide the shadows under their eyes or blemishes on their skin, flaws that would turn a proud man away.

He wanted to tell them that most of the patrons they ended up spending the night with would be too drunk to notice anything more than the shape of their bodies. But he thought they probably knew that already.

"Why don't you come and play with me tonight, Nicholas?" a woman called. She curled her voice around his name, giving it a sensuous feel that made his skin prickle.

He didn't have to look to know the voice belonged to Goldie. The 'Women of the Wall' never used their real names. They always picked short and meaningless alternatives. In all the years he'd known Goldie, she'd never revealed her identity. He supposed she had a reason for hiding behind the image she'd created for herself. It would be easier to pretend you were someone else in a profession like hers. After all, he didn't think any of the men who slipped her money at the end of the night cared about her name; they just liked how she looked.

Nick kept his face fixed ahead as he walked by. He could see the ocean in the distance, its surface painted silver by the moonlight. He wished he'd arrived early enough to go down to the docks and sit by the sea so he could listen to the waves. In those quiet, stolen moments at dawn or dusk, it was as though he was the only person in existence. It allowed him to forget what the world was like - a dirty, unforgiving place. But it was just a wish, and he shut it away as he walked through the door of The Sparrow.

The only thing in the south that was more overpowering than the smell of rotting seaweed was the stench of stale sweat, and it clung to The Sparrow like moss on the roots of a tree. Summer only made it worse. The long months of unforgiving heat trapped every odour inside the small space. Most of the time, he breathed through his mouth. He was sure his nose hairs would singe off otherwise.

Nick spotted Celia balancing a tray of drinks by the bar. She gave him a stern look, and her eyes flicked to the pianoforte in the corner. Nick wove through the crowd, dodging tables full of men sweating as they drank tankards of ale, played at cards and dice, or waved their arms wildly with voices raised mid-argument. Finally, he made it to the small stage in the corner. It was just big enough to fit the pianoforte and a stool. The stool tilted to the side as he sat. The pianoforte's keys had faded with age to the pale yellow colour of unclean teeth.

It was nothing like the piano he played at Eli's, yet he knew it better than he knew himself: which keys rang off-tune, which ones needed to be pressed down hard to get any sound and even the few keys that made no sound at all, just a muffled thud when played.

He turned away from the crowd and picked up a glass jar he kept hidden behind the black curtain that covered the peeling paint on the walls. Nick placed the jar beside the leg of the pianoforte, hoping to tempt patrons into dropping their loose coins inside. Then he began to play.

When Nick walked home in the morning, his pocket jingled with the weight of the new coin he'd earned. He passed the same alley he had gone by hours earlier and choked as the smell hit his nose. He glanced down the short alley, and he could make out a pile of what looked like old balled-up rags heaped against the back wall. But as he stepped closer, he noticed they had tails. He wasn't unfamiliar with rodents in this part of the city, but he had never seen that many together, especially dead.

He glanced at the apartments above, wondering what kind of infestation had occurred to produce such a massacre. As he continued his walk home, he prayed to the goddess that the smell would soon disappear, at least for the sake of his nose.

CHAPTER 5

Bronte woke to the sounds of clattering dishes and muffled voices below her. It was another day in her new reality, and it felt just as impossible that this world existed as it had yesterday. She quickly dressed and joined Frank and Eli downstairs, where they were already sitting at the table with breakfast laid out between them. A moment later, Nina came bustling into the room. She grabbed a slice of bread and slathered on some jam.

"I'm late," she sighed, taking a bite out of the bread. "I own an apothecary in town, and, right now, it remains closed because I'm all the way over here," she told Bronte between bites. "You all have a nice day, and I'll see you tonight." She kissed Frank on the head. "Fai will be wondering where I am," she muttered as she hurried out the door.

"She does that every morning so get used to it," Eli said with a smile.

"Bronte, I'm afraid I also need to head to work. But you and Eli are free to go into town by yourselves. Have a look at the shops and perhaps buy some clothes more suited to Namire? I don't want you to feel out of place."

Bronte shifted in her seat. "I'm sure that would be great, but I don't have any money. At least not here."

She thought of all the hours she'd worked in the greasy fish and chip shop and how it had all been for nothing, given her money was stuck on the Otherside, as Eli called it.

She'd sent a quick text message to her manager yesterday to let her know she was resigning. Bronte had received a short message back thanking her for her work and wishing her well. In all honesty, it was good riddance to that place and its hot vats of oil and sticky floors.

Frank waved her off. "You're under my care now. Put everything on my account and here, Eli, take this for anything else you need." He handed him a heavy-looking leather pouch. "That should be enough trillings and copias to get you through the day."

Bronte looked at him as though he'd spoken gibberish. "What currency are you talking about?"

"Oh, right, I forgot you don't know." Eli opened the bag and pulled out a bone-coloured coin that looked slightly bigger than a pound. It had a complicated gold symbol etched onto one side with lots of triangles and semi-circles, and little numbers around the outside, which Bronte assumed was some sort of serial code. "This is a trilling and this one," he pulled out a similar-looking coin the size of a penny and coloured lime green, "is a copia, and there are sixty copias to a trilling," he finished, putting the coins back in the bag.

After a quick breakfast, they set off in the direction she and Tyrell had come from yesterday. Outside one of the houses, they passed a man in a big straw hat kneeling as he tended to his beautifully manicured garden. Bountiful flowers in every colour filled the neatly trimmed beds, bordering a lush expanse of grass. From his curved posture and slow movements, Bronte could tell he was on the later side of life. He waved at the two of them as they approached.

"That's Xander, one of the most powerful enchanters in the realm," Eli explained as they waved back. "He mentors Welkin students in their senior year, too." Eli veered off the path towards him, leaving Bronte to follow. "Morning, Xander. I wanted to introduce Namire's newest enchanter, Bronte Everett," Eli announced.

"Welcome," Xander said happily, standing to greet her.

"Thank you." Bronte cast a look at the bent old man. She imagined pulling out weeds was hard on his back. "If you're an enchanter, how come you don't just magic a garden the way you want?"

He smiled knowingly. "I've learnt that magic is a sacred thing. I use it only when necessary. It would be a lot quicker for me to pull out all the weeds using my power, and if I really had to, I could. But I find it enjoyable to be out in the sun doing the work by hand."

"I'm not sure I'd share your philosophy if I could do the same," she replied.

"I was like that at your age, too, using my magic in any way I could. But I was frivolous with it, almost arrogant, and that's not why we have these gifts. I'm sure once you learn, you won't make the same mistake. I look forward to watching you grow. Just as I am proud of my seedlings that sprout into these flowers, I'm sure you'll make your family proud too."

Bronte felt a rush of warmth. The words were more of a comfort to her than he probably realised. She'd needed to hear them if only to soothe her own doubt that she was anything more than a weed in this new world.

A cat suddenly popped out of the bush in front of them, giving a loud meow. Then it trotted across the grass and into the shade of a tree before vanishing. Bronte blinked, thinking it must've run off. She turned to find Xander smiling at her.

"Ghost cats," Xander explained. "They can transport using shadows. That one doesn't belong to me, but he likes to visit from time to time. Go enjoy your day, kids."

"Thanks, Xander," they echoed as they continued their walk.

The road slanted upwards the further they went. As the sun burnt away the cloud cover green mountains emerged in the distance, creating a border around the city. Their peaks disappeared into the sky, and Bronte spied a castle tucked away into the rock on a ridge near the summit of one of the mountains. It was bone white, standing out among the green.

"Who lives there?" she asked, pointing it out to Eli.

"No one. That's Welkin."

Bronte's eyes widened. The last school she'd attended, so briefly, in London had been a small collection of temporary buildings shoved awkwardly onto a narrow block in a busy suburb. Welkin, in comparison, looked like a palace.

Bronte was beginning to think she was dreaming. There was no way this could all be real. She bit the inside of her gum surreptitiously, and it hurt enough to reassure her that she wasn't inside some elaborate illusion.

"Welcome to the Canal, the heart of Namire," Eli announced as they turned the corner of a street.

Bronte found herself immersed in a sea of glimmering gold. The colour winked at her from rooftops and window frames, glowing in the midmorning light. The buildings which weren't paved with gold were every other colour imaginable, turning the strip into a rainbow.

A canal filled with clear water split the road in half with arched bridges made of gold providing access to both sides of the avenue. Quaint-looking shop fronts lined the street, and people darted in and out, carrying paper bags and baskets filled with purchases.

Eli was taking her to a clothing shop first, but Bronte wished they could stop and look at all the shops. She was eager to see what each of them sold, but with the crowd and hurrying to keep up with Eli, she only caught brief glimpses of window-front displays.

From what she could make out, though, these shops were not like those she knew. Some claimed to sell unusual wares like dragon blood or dried widowsweed. One shop was advertising their quality furrows, and when Bronte peeked through the window, it took her a moment to work out what she was looking at. A colourful array of furry creatures met her eyes. They looked like a combination of a squirrel, a possum, and a mouse. However, instead of the usual four legs, furrows had six, an extra pair emerging from their mid-region. They also had furry bat-like wings that were tucked against their bodies.

Bronte instantly wanted to go into the store and hold one. Instead, she read the sign next to their enclosure, which claimed that they had an excellent sense of direction and were the best mode of mail delivery in the city.

When Bronte finished reading, she looked to find Eli, but she couldn't spy his curly head anywhere. She took a deep breath and reminded herself that he couldn't have gone far. She decided to keep walking in the direction they'd been heading and hope that, sooner or later, she would run into him.

Bronte's anxiety grew, however, the longer she walked without seeing him. The back of her neck dampened with sweat, and she tugged at the neckline of her shirt uncomfortably. Looking across the canal, wondering if Eli had somehow ended up on the other side, Bronte stumbled straight into an elderly woman carrying a basket of herbs.

"Oh! I'm so sorry." She reeled backwards, reaching out a hand to steady the woman before her, who was in danger of overbalancing. As she did so, she took note of her short greying hair that curled around her head like a halo.

"Relax, all will be well, girl." The woman repositioned her basket in the crook of her elbow. "Here, chew this. You look like you need it." She passed Bronte a leaf of some black-coloured herb, before going on her way.

Bronte eyed the leaf lying in the palm of her hand. Cautiously, she brought it to her nose and sniffed. It smelt like liquorice and cinnamon. Then, tentatively, she nibbled a small piece off the corner, hoping it wasn't some poisonous plant the woman had given her to enact revenge for her clumsiness.

An icy feeling swept through Bronte's body, and her heartbeat quickened. She was about to spit the remaining leaf out of her mouth when all her anxiety suddenly melted away. An immense calmness followed in its wake. Everything that had troubled her disappeared, and she was struck by the realisation that there was no need for her to panic. If she went on her way, she would find Eli soon enough.

With that comforting thought in her mind, she set off, walking much slower than before, listening to the chatter around her and savouring the smell of mint and strawberry wafting towards her from an iced lolly stand a few meters away.

She'd only been walking again for a few minutes when she spied Eli standing by the entrance of a shop called "Quinn's Apothecary". Bronte absently wondered if that was where the woman had bought the strange black leaf. She noticed another boy standing beside Eli. It only took her a moment to recognise the wavy bronze hair of the boy she'd met yesterday at Eli's house. A tall girl with long strawberry-blond hair was also leaning against the wall of the apothecary, listening to their conversation. Bronte watched as she laughed at something the boy had said, throwing her head back unabashedly as though nothing in the world had ever been so funny. An unwelcome stab of jealousy cut through her haze of calmness. It was an ugly feeling, and it consumed Bronte entirely as she pushed her way through the rest of the crowd and emerged next to Eli.

"There you are. I thought I'd lost you," Eli said, turning to Bronte.

"You didn't make much of an effort to find me." Her voice came out brittle, and she realised she'd entirely lost the calm feeling the leaf had given her only moments earlier.

"I knew you'd turn up eventually," quipped Eli.

The girl laughed again; it was a jarring, unexpected sound. Up close, she looked like she was made from strawberries and cream. Her hair was offset by the paleness of her skin, which was blemish free and shone in the sunlight.

"Bronte, this is Leora Hartfell and Nicolas Henderson," Eli introduced.

"Just Nick," the boy corrected.

"Oh, nice to meet you." Bronte plastered a smile on her face that felt stiff and robotic. She performed the pleasantries for Eli's sake, since he clearly didn't know she'd met Nick last night and hadn't found him pleasant in the slightest.

Leora gave her a bright smile. "Likewise, I'm glad we'll have another girl in our group. You have no idea how frustrating these two can be."

Bronte's smile turned into something real, and she cursed herself for being judgemental. Her mum used to warn her about her unap-proachable personality. She was always the one to wait for the olive branch to be extended to her and not the other way around. Bronte would reply that if she wasn't dragged halfway across the country every year, she might have a chance to make real friends. Her mum never liked it when she said those things. She regretted them now.

"Believe me, I can imagine. Just half a day with Eli has shown me more than enough," she said. Eli gave her a faux wounded look, and she grinned.

"Maybe Eli and I will form our own group, given you're both unhappy having us around," remarked Nick, who seemed to be in a much better mood than when he'd met her yesterday.

"But then, who would be there to make fun of you?" asked Leora.

Nick rolled his eyes at her. "That would be the point. There wouldn't be."

"Ah, boys, they're so sensitive." Leora looked at her as she spoke as if they were sharing an inside joke, and Bronte smirked back.

The shop door opened beside them, and Nina emerged. "What are you four doing lingering out here. Come in so I can give Bronte a tour before you go!"

"This is your shop?" Bronte asked in surprise.

"It's been a part of my family for years. Quinn is my maiden name."

The shop was a quaint space. Shelves lined the walls stacked with jars of herbs and substances Bronte didn't recognise. The pungent smell made Bronte's nose wrinkle, and she held back a sneeze as Nina guided her through the narrow aisles, explaining as she went.

Before she'd finished, a crash came from behind a closed door at the back of the room. As the door flew open, a short boy with shaved black hair emerged.

"Sorry, Mrs Quinn, I tripped on a crate. All the supplies are fine," he said breathlessly.

"Bronte, this is Fai. He's my enchanter apprentice."

"Enchanter? Do you not have to be a healer to work here?"

"It's a more suited manipulation, yes. But Fai has always had an interest in natural healing. You don't need any power to make poultices or a bottle of herbs. Plus, his enchanter abilities are useful in performing day-to-day tasks, like stacking shelves and doing stock take. If he can learn to stop tripping over the crates, that is," she added jokingly. "Anyway, this is my shop. Come in anytime you need. I won't hold you all up any longer, so get going." She shooed them onto the street, the door clanging shut behind them.

"Where were you both heading?" Eli asked.

"I was on my way to Miss Taffeta's, and Nick just happened to have nothing better to do today," said Leora. "Maybe we can meet up later?"

"Oh, we were going there too, to find Bronte some clothes."

"Let me take her shopping! Neither of you know anything about fashion."

Eli glanced at Bronte, waiting for her to respond. "I would love that," she replied, and for once her answer wasn't a lie.

"Great! You and Nick occupy yourselves, and we'll meet at Merlin's Beard later." Leora patted Nick on the shoulder before linking arms with Bronte. Her clothing smelt strongly of orange blossom, making Bronte's nose itch as Leora guided her across the pavement into the growing crowd of shoppers.

CHAPTER 6

"So, I heard you're an enchanter," Leora said as they made their way further up the Canal.

"Yes, but I can't do a thing, so it doesn't really matter."

Leora shrugged. "You'll learn."

Bronte hoped she was right. "What's your manipulation?"

"Transmuter."

"Did you always know you were going to be a transmuter?"

"No one ever really knows. After all, you're a baby when you're read, but most of my family are transmuters, so they weren't surprised."

"What can transmuters do?" Paloma had told her they could manipulate physical and mental states, but she wasn't sure what that meant.

Leora's face brightened at the question. "Transmutation's really fun. You learn how to manipulate all kinds of things. There's the simple stuff, like changing one material into another. There's the classic example of water into wine, or I could shift a stick into a steel pipe. The hard part is changing things that aren't matter, like emotions or thoughts."

"You can change people's emotions?" Bronte asked in disbelief.

"I can't yet. Even those who can find it difficult. But people go to transmuters to make themselves happy, change a memory, or even alter their physical appearance.”

“Is that common?”

“Sort of. It’s a rare transmutation skill, though, and even if you successfully change someone, it’s not permanent, and the length it persists depends on the strength of the transmuter. Getting those alterations done is also really expensive, but if people have the money, they won’t hold back from doing it.”

Leora suddenly veered off the path pulling Bronte with her. The shop they’d arrived in front of had large windowfront displays showcasing the mannequins adorned with finely made dresses. The door was painted to look like it had been wrapped in pink ribbon with a bow tied above the gold metal mailbox in the center. Bronte imagined it was meant to replicate receiving a package from the dressmaker.

“Leora!” cried a lady as they entered.

“Miss Taffeta, I’d like you to meet my newest friend, Bronte.”

Miss Taffeta was a large round-faced woman whose thin brown hair had been swept back into a tight bun. The hairstyle only highlighted the layers of eccentric makeup caking her face. She wore bright red lipstick and purple eyeshadow. Strangely, the look reminded Bronte of the time she’d gotten into her mum’s makeup stash and decorated her doll’s face with everything she could get her hands on. Unfortunately, her mum hadn’t been impressed with the makeover, and her poor doll had spent a long night under the bathroom tap getting it cleaned off.

“I’ve heard talk about you, Bronte. What can I do for you?”

“Talk?”

“People gossip, especially when supposedly dead daughters return very much alive.”

“Oh.” She’d forgotten that people here would know about her past, something she’d only learnt about yesterday. It wasn’t easy to forget that her mother and father had been involved in the once notorious Disciples, as Frank had told her. It was something she still found difficult to accept.

"I wouldn't worry about the talk, though. No one has the guts to say anything to you."

Nick might have, she thought dubiously.

Leora forged ahead, seeming ready to move on from the topic. "Bronte needs everything. She's got nothing but these Otherside clothes." Her mouth twisted in distaste at Bronte's shirt and shorts. "I'm guessing you need a school uniform too?" Leora asked.

"Um, yeah. Frank mentioned something about starting school here." That was another thing she'd ignored but knew she would eventually have to face.

"Really, are you just starting at Welkin? That's exciting!" Miss Taffeta swept across the room past racks of black tunics stitched with gold. On the front of each was the emblem of a burning torch. "I commission uniforms for the High Guard," she said, noticing Bronte's gaze. "As well as tunics for their training and fighting leathers. The school uniform business is only fruitful at a certain time of year." She stopped in front of a clothes rack lined with dark plaid pleated skirts and white blouses.

"Try these." Miss Taffeta pulled a blouse and skirt off the rack and handed them to Bronte, pointing her towards a dressing room.

Slipping behind the curtain, Bronte changed into the clothes she'd been given. Surprisingly, they fitted her perfectly, even though they had no tags or size labelling on them. The blouse was white with navy stitching, and the skirt was navy plaid. Bronte inspected the school crest covering the breast pocket of her shirt. The words μελέτη το παν had been embroidered beneath it. Which she guessed, roughly translated to, "practice is everything". Her mum had encouraged her to take Ancient Greek for three years in high school without ever telling her why. Bronte wouldn't say she was an expert. And she certainly thought she'd be needing a lot of practice when it came to enchanting.

"How does it look?" Miss Taffeta called to her.

"Perfect," she said, smiling at herself in the mirror. Seeing herself in the official school uniform made the idea of going to Welkin real. For the first time the thought of remaining in Hallowless didn't make her stomach twist with nerves.

When she emerged from the changing room, Miss Taffeta was waiting to take the clothes from her, but Leora had disappeared.

"She's just popped outside," Miss Taffeta explained, noticing her straying eyes. "Leora's such a lovely girl. You're lucky to have her as a friend." She smiled, as she hung up the clothes Bronte had tried on.

Bronte glanced out the window, watching Leora as she laughed, at ease with the other girls surrounding her in various coloured dresses. Even among company, she was the one that drew the eye, and Bronte noticed the glances of passer-byers that flickered towards her.

"You're going to want three blouses and two skirts, that's what most of the school kids get, and some socks, a jumper. All that stuff." Miss Taffeta noted down the order. "Where is this being billed and delivered?"

Bronte pulled her eyes away from the window. "Um, Frank Everett." She felt a stab of guilt. She hated having to rely on others financially, but she knew she had no other choice.

"Ah, yes. I already have his details in my book from when Eli bought his school uniform. Now on to the fun stuff!" Miss Taffeta positioned Bronte onto a raised pedestal in the centre of the room and took a measuring tape to her.

"Why do you still wear these outdated clothes anyway?" Bronte asked, nodding towards the dresses the girls outside wore.

"I've seen the likes of the Otherside with your mass-produced outfits and fleeting trends. Here we take pride in each stitch and length of cloth. Higher members of society adopted this fashion style, keeping people like me in business. It's just the way we've always done things."

Leora re-entered the shop with the tinkle of a bell. "Oh, perfect. My favourite part. Choosing the colours and silks. I think a burnt orange would go well with your eyes, or maybe yellow to bring out your complexion."

Swaths of fabric were held up to her and assessed. Leora's predictions had been right. The burnt orange made her olive skin glow and highlighted her auburn eyes. Bronte used to think her eye colour unusual. Bright auburn was not a colour she'd ever seen during her time on Earth. She'd questioned her mum about it when she was younger because her light blue eyes couldn't have been more different from Bronte's, but been told they come from her dad's side. Bronte had quickly learnt that even if it was a mysterious gene from her father, it didn't make them any less strange. Rather than become a scientific anomaly, she would tell anyone who asked that they were brown, and it was simply the light that made them look otherwise. Yet, in Namire, her eye colour didn't seem so peculiar. She'd noticed many strangers passing her outside with eye colours equally unique. Some were amethyst or deep ruby. Even Leora's eyes were a vibrant green, a shade Bronte had never seen before.

"How come there're so many different eye colours here? It's not a common thing on Earth."

"It's a sign of your magic presenting itself to the outside world. Although many people still have common eye colours, we do get a whole variety because of our powers," Leora told her.

"Do you have any preference?" Miss Taffeta asked, holding up a strip of red fabric against the skin of Bronte's arm.

"I give you full artistic license."

Miss Taffeta took every measurement she could, down to the length of Bronte's feet, scribbling furiously in her notepad the whole time. Then, finally, the tape measure was rolled up, and she was allowed to step off the pedestal.

"Excellent, I shall have your school uniform and dresses delivered by week's end."

"Thank you."

"Oh, I almost forgot," Leora said as they turned to leave. "I meant to ask about that blue dress we were discussing. Have you had a chance to finish it?"

"Not yet, darling. Come back for it tomorrow." Miss Taffeta smiled fondly at Leora as she waved them out the door.

"I'm guessing you've never tried the fairy floss in Namire?" Leora asked when they were back on the street.

"It's not made from real fairies, is it?"

Leora rolled her eyes. "No, although I've always suspected it has some sort of Fae dust in it because it tastes so divine."

Leora grinned at her and tugged her by the hand toward a colourful stand by the canal's edge. Bronte found her feet moving willingly after her, squeezing Leora's hand back as they went.

She hadn't realised how much she missed female company. Bronte had spent almost every minute of her life with her mum. And the gap that caused was wide open, waiting to be filled by new friendships.

They were walking towards Merlin's Beard, the café where Leora had told the boys they'd meet. The fairy floss had been eaten, and Bronte was licking her sugary lips when she spied something that caught her attention. It was a two-story shop with the words *'Solomon's and Solomon's. Collecting unique wares since 1718'* written above the door in flaking gold paint. But it wasn't the name that caught her eye. Instead, it was the set of necklaces on display in the glass window. One of them was identical to the necklace her mum had given her. Bronte froze, staring at it to ensure she wasn't seeing things. Leora took a few more steps before realising her new friend had stopped.

"Are you alright?" she asked, turning back to where Bronte stood transfixed.

"Yes, I just . . . can we go in here for a moment? I think I saw something."

Bronte ignored Leora's quizzical look as she peered through the window into the dark shop. She tried the door, and it swung inward slowly. A tinkling bell was set off above her as she walked through. The room was lit by a single lantern, illuminating the shelves stacked with an array of strange objects. Necklaces inlaid with jewels the size of her palm glittered beneath the light. She saw oil lamps, rings, and even a sword propped up against the wall. Everything was coated in a thin layer of dust and her nose tickled as she tried not to sneeze.

But it was the necklaces in the window that most interested her. It was a three-part necklace joined together, with two crescent moons and what Bronte assumed was meant to be a full moon in the centre.

The centre part was engraved with a series of lines forming a circular maze-like symbol that looked the same as the necklace she had tucked beneath her shirt. She was reaching a finger to touch it when a rough voice sounded behind her.

"What are you doing?" it asked in a harsh whisper.

Bronte pulled her hand back and turned to find a short man wearing a suit glaring at her. "I was just, um . . . looking," she stuttered.

"Shhh, you don't want to wake them," he hissed, making her flinch.

"Wake them?" she asked in hushed tones, wondering what an earth he was talking about.

"The spells on my wares. You wouldn't want to trigger one, would you?" he asked, as though the answer were obvious.

"Oh." She looked at Leora standing on the other side of the shop, hoping she would intervene for her. But she hadn't noticed the man or, if she had, she was staying as far away as possible. As the man continued to watch Bronte with beady eyes, she had a grim feeling it was the latter.

"Well, don't just stand there, look, look." He gestured wildly around the shop. Bronte gave the objects a wary glance. She had no intentions of buying anything or setting off one of their supposed spells. "Are you interested in the Ancient Triad?" he prompted with a pointed look at the necklaces. "These are very close replicas, nothing like the cheap versions you'll find sold out there by the canal. Mine are authentic. How much do you know about the Triad and its history?"

"A little." She recalled what Frank had said about the powerful necklaces last night.

The man frowned. "They'll bring you luck," he continued. "They may not have the powers of the true Triad. But those have been lost for years. These are the closest replicas you'll find."

"Do you have any idea where the real ones are?"

"Of course not. No one does. It's not the worst thing that they're lost. After all, we know what would have happened if they'd fallen into the wrong hands."

A chill ran through her. "You mean the Disciples?"

"Who else? With the Triad lost, I can rest easy knowing our world is safe. Although there are still people who search for them. They'd have better luck finding trout in a desert."

"What exactly can they do? How important are they?"

His eyes widened. "Oh, my girl, they are everything. Their power is infinite. However, to access that power, so it's said, you must already possess great power of your own. It is difficult to control such magic, and weaker alchemists would fail in the attempt. But Madden could've done terrible things had he got his hands on them."

"What do you mean?"

"Well, of course, the Disciples wanted them to break down the barrier between our world and Earth. The magic trapped would be released, and Madden would get what he'd always craved; power."

"Is that why people still search for them?"

The man tilted his head in consideration. "There is perhaps another reason."

"What?"

"Another myth circulates for those Disciples committed to finding the Ancient Triad. They believed Madden never really died, that perhaps these necklaces are the key to releasing his body from the afterlife."

Bronte's stomach turned. The man reached out to readjust one of the necklace chains, seeming not to notice the change in energy. "So, are you interested in purchasing these?"

"They're very nice," she said awkwardly. "But I think I'll leave them for today. Thanks for your help."

"My pleasure." He gave her a searching look before walking back into the depths of his shop.

Bronte joined Leora, who was inspecting a coiled-up metal whip that looked as though it had once been a snake.

"I'm ready to go," she whispered, still wary of the mysterious spells the man had warned her about.

"Finally. This place creeps me out." Leora shivered as she led the way outside.

Tucked between a barber's shop and a florist was a bricked building the colour of sunflowers. A sign hung from the door with the words "Merlin's Beard" written on it in sparkly purple paint. Bronte spotted the boys hidden away at a table in the corner as they pushed their way inside. Eli waved at them, and they began weaving their way toward him. Tables and chairs were strewn everywhere, with people sitting in every available space. Waiters and waitresses navigated the chaos, serving food and drinks, which did everything from steam to smoke, and bubble. Bronte even saw a woman sipping a strange liquid that changed colour every few seconds.

"Finally!" Nick said, yelling slightly over the noise. "We're starving!"

They sat, and immediately Nick shoved a menu into her hands. After reading it twice over, Bronte ordered a stack of pancakes. While they waited for their food, Leora launched into a story, and despite trying to understand what she was saying, Bronte quickly became lost. There were just too many names, places, and people she didn't recognise. Her focus waned, and her eyes wandered above her. The ceiling was inlaid with multi-coloured tiles that sparkled like the scales on a dragon's back, and she wondered if dragons existed here. She opened her mouth to ask but quickly shut it, not wanting to interrupt Leora.

Something jostled her shoulder, and she turned to see a waitress carrying a full tray of drinks stumble by her. The girl managed to right herself a step before colliding with a man sitting at the opposite table.

"Lucky I'm wearing this, aye," he said, nodding to the chain around his neck. Bronte saw the shiny gold and recognised it as a part of the Ancient Triad the man at Solomon's and Solomon's had been talking about. "Protect me from harm and all that."

The waitress gave a shaky laugh and continued. Looking around the room, Bronte now saw many chains tucked beneath people's clothes or on full display. Obviously, the Ancient Triad was as revered as the man in the shop had suggested.

"Those bits of metal are about as useless as a twig in a hurricane," the man's friend said.

"You don't believe in them?"

"Yeah, sure, I believe the sisters' had the favour of Hecate. But that was an age ago, and the Ancient Triad is lost now," the man harrumphed. "I heard the Disciples ransacked the Theobesian residence. They probably took them after murdering Lydia. Who knows where they ended up? After all, their leader's dead, ain't he?"

Bronte shrunk in her seat. Their leader had been her father, and she wondered whether they would recognise her if they saw her face. Miss Taffeta said there had been rumours about her, but she doubted they had reached many ears so soon after her arrival. She shifted in her seat, turning her back on them. A waiter appeared at their table, and her pancakes were placed in front of her. Their sweet smell quelled the rottenness of her feelings, and she tried to ignore the man's words as she cut into them.

When Bronte had finished eating, she sunk back into her chair, her eyes drifting closed due to the food and the warmth of the cafe. However, Eli had other plans besides letting her nap.

"Dad will be expecting us home soon," he said with a glance at the darkening sky.

"Nice meeting you." Leora smiled as Bronte got up from her chair.

"Bye, Bronte," Nick added a moment later, seeming to debate whether she was even worthy of his attention. They were the first words he'd directed to her all afternoon, and she found they grated on her. She was on edge after everything she'd heard today, and he was an easy target.

"What, you've finally learnt my name?" She couldn't help the comment slipping out.

Nick looked up, startled by her tone. But he quickly recovered. "Looks like it. It wasn't hard once I really put my mind to it."

"That must've been an effort for you since your little nickname sounded so catchy yesterday."

He gave her a soft smile. "Not at all."

Bronte ground her teeth as she turned away, following Eli out the door.

"What did you mean by that? Did he say something to you?"

Bronte shrugged off his words. "Just last night when I arrived, he made some comment, calling me the Disciple's daughter. But I didn't understand it at the time."

Eli's mouth flattened. "Nick's had a difficult history with the Disciples. His brother was an enchanter who was murdered by them. Nick was only a baby at the time, but he's been intent ever since on ensuring they never return. As have the rest of us. But maybe seeing you and knowing your connection brought his anger to the surface. I'm sure he'll get over it, though."

Bronte's stomach twisted at the horror. She felt heavy with guilt over a past she hadn't known until yesterday. But she didn't blame Nick for his actions. She only wished he'd given her a chance to prove she wasn't like her parents.

CHAPTER 7

Nick shifted uncomfortably beneath his heavy clothing as he walked home from Merlin's Beard. He cursed the people in the north who decided that long pants and jackets were appropriate to wear in the summer. Yet whenever he ventured into that part of the city, he had no desire to advertise his lower-class status to everyone. Which meant he was forced to don his own formal wear and put up with the unbearable heat.

Now that he was returning to the south, he removed his jacket and rolled up his shirt sleeves, loosening the top button to cool himself further. The back of his neck was damp with sweat, making the ends of his hair curl. It would be hell tonight at The Sparrow, all those bodies pressed together in the low-ceilinged room. He kicked at a stray pebble as he walked, sending it skittering into the shadows of an alleyway.

He walked in a daze. His mind still caught up in thoughts of Bronte. He wanted to hate her, but everything from her long wavy brown hair to the crooked way she smiled went against those feelings. But he wouldn't let himself change. He couldn't have those feelings for the daughter of the people responsible for his brother's death.

It wasn't until Nick registered the putrid smell of seaweed baking in the sun that he realised he was almost home. From a distance, he could see that the door to his parent's house was ajar. He couldn't remember the last time it had been shut properly, and he supposed it was a miracle no one had ever robbed them.

It was a modest house, but like a mansion in terms of the south. His family clung to the last of their good name and money, which was enough to keep out the drab. But for how much longer, he wasn't sure. It also helped that people felt sorry for them. They were the family that had lost a son to the Disciples' Reign of Terror. Nick had only been a few months old when his twelve-year-old brother Nathaniel had been murdered by the Disciples. Drained of his enchanter magic, he had been left cold and lifeless for his family to find. The Disciples liked to harvest magic only from enchanters. They believed enchanter magic was the purest, and if their leader was provided with enough of it, he could utilise that power to control the Ancient Triad and break down the barrier. But such a goal couldn't be achieved without murdering others and taking their magic in the process.

Nick still mourned the life he and his brother should've had together. The life that could've been if their family had been whole. He imagined them fishing together or playing dice in the street with other kids. It was a nice fantasy. But, in truth, he'd grown up despising the thought of fishing, and he had always avoided the other kids when they'd asked him to come outside.

"Who's there?" The harsh voice of his mother called from some-where in the house as he walked inside, the door clanging shut behind him.

"It's me. Nick." He walked towards her voice, even though the silence that followed should've turned him away. He found his mother sprawled on a chair behind the desk in the study. It was a decrepit room that had lost its glory many years ago. The shelves were littered with scholarly treasures: a globe hand painted with as fine a map of Hallow-less as had ever been made; an alchemical barometer swirling with misty blues and greens; leatherbound books and journals by the hundreds, long unopened; a portable telescope, its brass now tarnished, hiding the fine workmanship.

His mother had once been a scholar, and Nick wondered if the part of her that longed for knowledge still drove her. Dusty volumes lined the walls of the room, and empty pots of ink cluttered the desk.

"Been progging up north again, have you?" she asked, taking in his clothes.

He shifted in the doorway, his jacket behind him as though he could hide the evidence. His mother straightened in her seat, pouring whiskey into the shot glasses in front of her.

"Have a drink," she said, nudging it towards him. The room stunk of liquor, a smell which could never be erased.

"No, thank you," he replied coolly.

She drank them both without a word, and he suspected that even if he had accepted, she wouldn't have given it to him, never mind that he was also underage.

"Do you want me to get you something to eat?" he asked.

His mother's head was bowed, and her lank hair had fallen across her face. You wouldn't know from looking at her that it had once been the colour of roasted chestnuts and that before the smell of alcohol had overtaken everything, she had smelt like old parchment and ink.

"Not hungry," she said shortly.

He hadn't expected any other answer. "Where's dad?"

She shrugged and took another swig of liquor, this time not even bothering with the charade of pouring it into a glass.

"I'll be back late tonight," he said, hoping she might ask where he was going, what he was doing, or take any interest in him at all.

"Suit yourself," she replied.

Nick knew some kids would love the freedom of his life: kids who longed for the chance to do whatever they wanted, whenever they wanted. But those kids didn't know how lonely it felt when the people who were supposed to love you the most didn't bother to look at you as they said, "suit yourself". It was as if they couldn't care less whether you'd just told them you were going away forever and that this was the last time they would ever see you.

Suit yourself.

He left his mum in the study and walked out of the house, making sure to close the door behind him. He wished he could dredge up some shred of pity or understanding when he saw his mother like that. But he had long ago stopped caring.

Sometimes he wished his mum had never become pregnant with him. Because from the moment he'd been able to comprehend his existence in this world, he'd realised it wasn't a good one. Most kids didn't have to spend their life scraping together enough money to feed and clothe themselves. But when your grief-stricken parents poured all their money away on whatever stimulant they could get their hands on, you had no choice but to fend for yourself.

Nick had almost completed his walk to The Sparrow in peace when he caught sight of a figure that instantly ruined his mood. He saw the black first. Everything his most hated rival wore - from his shoes to his long coat - was black. Always black, even at the height of summer. It made Nick sweat just looking at him, but Isaac Ives' brow was impossibly dry. He was pale, as usual, not even a hint of flushed skin to suggest he felt the heat that pulsed around them. His hair was black, too, making him look like a walking shadow. Black, that is, apart from a single white lock. Everyone knew that a witchlock was the result of a powerful cast being performed on you. Magic like that always left a trace, but Isaac had never admitted what had happened, and Nick sometimes wondered if he even knew.

Isaac held a thick book under his arm as he stalked directly toward him, not taking a single step to avoid a collision. Nick cursed silently. He hadn't thought about him all summer, hadn't seen his pale face for so long that he'd almost forgotten it. He hadn't expected to run into him here, of all places.

"Ives," Nick said when they were face to face, neither willing to give the other a centimeter.

"Henderson." Isaac flicked a glance his way. His blue eyes were so light they looked almost translucent.

"What are you doing slumming down south?" Isaac never hesitated to rub his family's old money status in Nick's face. He lived way north, past the Canal. He would never come down here unless he had a good reason.

"I saw you with a girl today. Do I know her?" he replied, ignoring Nick's question.

"I wouldn't think so."

Nick moved to pass him, but Isaac reached out a gloved hand, catching his arm. "What's her name?"

"Whose name?" he asked, feigning confusion as he yanked himself free of Isaac's grasp.

Isaac's mouth curled into a sneer. "Don't play dumb, Henderson."

"You mean Bronte Everett? I'd thought you'd already know. Wasn't it your father's job to gather information when he was in the Disciples?" Nick had long since suspected Isaac's father had been a Disciple. He'd read every scrap of information he could find on the members and listened to all the stories he could dredge out of people, and he wasn't the only one who believed the rumour that Bastian Ives, the clairvoyant who had once been Chancellor of Namire, was a member. But it had never been proven. Bastain had been found dead in his office one day near the end of the Disciples' reign. The official verdict was suicide. But the private information being leaked to the Disciples from the Council mysteriously halted after his death.

"Speculate all you want, Nick, but you should search for the actual person responsible because if they hadn't been so good at their job, then maybe your brother would still be alive."

Nick's stomach twisted with rage. "Get out of my way."

"Or what? You'll turn me into a frog?" Isaac goaded. "We both know I'm the one who has more power here. Shame you weren't born an enchanter. Though, I have to say, it's a pity your brother was."

Nick lunged, drawing his arm up to strike Isaac's face. Isaac flicked his hand out lazily, and Nick was sent crashing into the wall. His breath left his body in a sharp exhale. His elbow took the brunt of the hit, and a blinding pain shot through him. He groaned, blinking away his blurred vision.

"See you at school." Isaac walked away, not sparing him a second glance.

Nick wanted to get up and fight back, but Isaac was right. When it came to power, he didn't stand a chance because he had been born a transmuter, not an enchanter. His power meant he could change a lot of things, buttons into coins, water into wine, but Isaac's words were a fact he couldn't change.

He roughly wiped away the tears of pain that brimmed in his eyes, cradling his broken arm to his chest as he pushed himself to his feet and continued his walk to The Sparrow. Celia would know what to do.

Nick spotted her immediately, wiping down empty tables with a rag. From the looks of the rag, the tables would be better off without it. The lunch crowd had left, and the room was deserted. Soon it would be full of night revellers, who he hoped would be in the mood to empty their pockets. But it was Sunday, and most people who came in tonight left early in preparation for the week. Fridays were always the best days to make money when the freedom of two days off work loosened everyone's shoulders, and the beer flowed freely, making people more careless with their coins.

"What happened?" Celia asked, a line creasing her forehead as soon as she saw the awkward angle of his arm.

She was a skinny woman, all sharp edges and bone. Years ago, she'd been one of the girls that had hung around outside The Sparrow. Nick remembered the strange green makeup she would smear around her eyes and how she'd plaited her dirty blond hair loosely over her shoulder.

Back then, he'd been a lonely child wandering the darkening streets, desperate for company and food. He would walk past her, and she would wave to him. He had been too timid to wave back. He would only ever go near The Sparrow because sometimes drunks would stumble out, and their change would tumble from their pockets, littering the ground. Nick would hide in the shadows and collect the coins once the patrons were gone. The women that haunted the doorway would berate him for it, but Celia had told them in no uncertain terms to shut up. She'd even gone as far as to give him a coin that had tumbled into her path.

When she'd fallen pregnant, she'd begged the gambling house owner for a job. Nick didn't know what kind of deal they'd struck. It wasn't uncommon for the 'Women of the Wall' to fall pregnant. It was uncommon for the gambling house owner to take pity on them though. Nick had tried asking once. It had been the only time Celia had truly become angry with him. Now it was an unspoken agreement that Nick wouldn't bring up the topic again.

Celia was a healer, but her power had never been strong enough to earn her a better life. Before getting pregnant, she'd been studying at the hospital and only ever taken to the streets to make money to pay for her classes. But the baby had become a priority and now she was stuck here working every spare second as a barmaid to afford a life for her and her daughter. The dark circles beneath her eyes meant Nick would never forget that.

"Isaac happened," he said, slumping on the chair she'd drawn up.

She pressed her lips together as she examined his arm. Although she was only a few years older than him, deep lines creased her forehead as she frowned. "He was here earlier," Celia told him as she gently took his arm. Her hands were thin, the nails chipped from the hours she spent here.

Nick hissed from the pain, but he was quickly distracted by her words. "He was here?"

He'd never seen Isaac here. Celia nodded but didn't speak. Her head was tilted to one side, her eyes closed. She'd wrapped her hands around his arm and was squeezing gently. A warmth that reminded him of spring days flowed through him, and the pain began to ease. Sweat beaded on her forehead. Powerful healers could mend bones in the blink of an eye, but Celia didn't have that sort of power, and she needed all her concentration to fix him. It would leave her drained, and he knew it would take at least a week before her power fully returned. Nick felt a pang of overwhelming guilt. It had been his own stupidity that had caused this, even if Isaac had provoked it. Nick bent his arm after Celia released it, relishing the absence of pain.

"Thank you." The two words sounded horribly inadequate.

She waved him off, sinking into the seat beside him and holding her head.

"I'll get you some water." Nick quickly walked to the bar and grabbed a cup. He pulled on the iron lever that released the water and filled it. Instantly, he was back at Celia's side, bringing the cup to her lips. She gulped it down and afterwards was able to sit straight.

"He came in and sat over there." She tilted her head towards the shadows on the far side of the room. "A man came to the same table. I didn't recognise him. They ordered a round of drinks, then sent me away."

"Strange." Nick glanced at the table in the corner, imagining the scene Celia had painted for him.

Celia snapped to attention as people walked through the door, her weariness masked to keep her job. "I think his name was Rhett. I didn't catch the last name, though."

Nick wasn't familiar with the name, but it was something to go off, at least. He could ask around and see if anyone knew of him.

"Take it easy tonight," Celia whispered to him with a significant look at his arm and then at the pianoforte before walking away to serve the customers.

It was due to her that Nick could even play the pianoforte. One night he'd been hanging around outside the doors of The Sparrow, and she'd poked her head out to ask if he wanted to come inside out of the cold. The owner was out, she'd said, and she had food. Celia had known he would do anything if there was food involved. Back then, he had been too young to go to Welkin, and he'd spent his days scouring the streets for anything edible, constantly on the verge of starvation. So he'd gone into The Sparrow willingly, and she'd given him her meal, claiming she wasn't hungry. Nick knew now that she must've been lying. She'd been eating for two at the time.

He'd seen the dusty pianoforte that day and been fascinated. He'd sat and attempted a tune, and while his fingers had fumbled over the keys, Celia had noticed his interest and encouraged him to continue. Nick had liked the sounds it made, how they'd filled the emptiness and made him forget, even for a moment, about his hunger.

This became a pattern. She would coax him in, give him food, and let him play. Months passed, and gradually his playing improved. He couldn't afford sheet music. Nick hadn't even known what a key or a note was. But he'd made his own melodies. Things that sounded happy to his ears, things that sounded sad. Impressed, Celia had taken him to The Sparrow's owner, claiming she'd heard him play on the streets and that he would be a good acquisition. The owner had been hesitant, but she'd insisted. Eventually, he'd conceded, saying that he required seventy per cent of whatever Nick made during the night. At the time, that had been almost everything, and he was often left with barely two copias to rub together. But, as he improved, the money went up and soon, he wasn't hungry every second of the day.

Tonight, Nick played mindlessly. He let his fingers run across the keys, hardly listening to the sounds they made. He couldn't stop thinking about Isaac. He needed to know why he'd come here and what he'd been doing.

As the night wore on, the crowd grew boisterous, their ever-full tankards responsible for their loss of control. Thankfully for his coin jar, it meant more tips.

Nick watched Celia as he played. She weaved her way through the tables, depositing drinks and taking orders. He didn't miss the sneers some men sent her way, given mainly by the ones who hadn't forgotten her old occupation. Their eyes would linger on her cleavage, and their hands would stray to places they shouldn't as they spoke the word "whore". They believed they had ownership over her body simply because she didn't deny him. She laughed them off, dodging away swiftly. Nick knew she could do nothing more or risk losing her job.

One man, bald and with a beer gut that prevented him from sitting close to the table, reached out a hand as she walked by, earning him grins from his friends. Nick watched him do it, playing the keys harder so the music swelled over the noise in the room. He didn't take his eyes off the man the rest of the night.

When the morning light finally brightened the room, the bald man stumbled towards the exit. Nick sprung to his feet. He dumped his tips into his pocket and tucked the jar behind the curtain before darting off the stage. The man had just reached the door. Nick waved goodbye to Celia, promising to see her soon. On his way out, he threw the owner's cut of the coins he'd made into the small chest left out for him.

The street was empty. He quickly spotted a solitary dark shape stumbling away. Nick weighed his options. There was no way the man could be an enchanter; at least not a powerful one, because powerful enchanters didn't wear the tattered clothes he had on. Nick's best hope was that he was a healer. They weren't much use in a fight until after it was over. It might be a problem if he was a clairvoyant: hopefully the alcohol would mess with his abilities, rendering them useless.

Nick spied an empty bottle of wine by The Sparrow's door. The top had been smashed as though someone had bashed it against the wall. Broken shards lay on the ground, and he picked one up, careful not to slice himself on the serrated edge. He stared at the bottom of it, willing it smooth. The glass softened beneath his hand, and he shaped it until it looked like the hilt of a sword, the top remaining sharp and jagged.

His quarry was still stumbling about, mumbling nonsense to himself. Nick wished, not for the first time, that he could use his powers on himself. It would be helpful if he could change his face to look like someone else. Instead, he prayed to the goddess the man would be too drunk to remember him.

He approached the man, careful to keep his steps light. When he was a step away, Nick hit a pebble, sending it skittering across the path, and the man turned. Nick pounced, slamming him against the wall, holding the blade to his meaty neck. The man instantly stilled, fear clouding his eyes and Nick smiled, letting the blade dig in just enough so that beads of red formed against the knife's edge.

"Don't touch Celia again," he said. His voice was cold, and though the man's breath smelt of alcohol, he seemed to have instantly sobered. The fear of death overriding his intoxication. "Say it. Tell me that you won't touch her or any other woman again."

"I . . . I won't," he spluttered.

"I don't believe you." Nick dug in the blade further, and the man winced.

"I won't. I swear it on the goddess."

"You best hope she looks kindly on men like you when the time comes." Nick dropped the blade, letting it pass over the man's arm as he did so, as though he were being careless. Blood ran from the wound, and the man made a sound of pain, keeling over.

"You should probably get that looked at."

Nick threw the knife at the wall behind him, letting the built-up rage of the past day course through him. The glass shattered, raining to the ground in glittering diamonds. Some were rubies, stained red with blood.

The man flinched, but Nick didn't spare him a glance as he walked away with his back straight. He had to consciously slow his stride, making it seem like he was unbothered and didn't want to run into an alley and vomit. Nick hated blood. But for Celia, he would do it, if it meant even one man would think twice before he touched her again. He turned the corner, longing for the sun to rise completely and warm his chilled body.

CHAPTER 8

Bronte was in the parlour at the front of the house. Frank sat beside her on the threadbare lounge facing the large windows. An ancient-looking fireplace took up most of one wall, and the piano Nick had played the day she'd arrived stood in the corner of the room. Bronte flexed her fingers at the sight of it. She'd once tried to learn how to play on an old keyboard. Her fingers had fumbled over the keys and, as any young child did when things didn't turn out the way they wanted, she'd thrown a tantrum. The keyboard had been stuffed into a closet and sold at the next yard sale. Bronte hadn't missed it.

Her legs were crossed tightly, and she'd unknowingly taken to bouncing one of her feet up and down as they waited. She stilled her leg when Frank sent a worried glance her way.

"It's going to be fine. There's no need to be nervous," he assured her.

"I know," she said, more to convince herself of the fact.

When she and Eli had arrived home yesterday afternoon, Frank had broached the subject of her schooling again. If she was to live here, she needed to learn how to use her powers, and she saw no argument against attending school, especially after seeing what it looked like on their walk to the Canal. However, Bronte would have to meet with a representative from Welkin to discuss her future. The meeting had been promptly scheduled for the following afternoon which was any minute now. There was a knock at the door, and Bronte glanced at Frank to ensure he'd heard it too.

"Ready?" Frank asked, giving her a reassuring smile.

She nodded, unable to form words, and Bronte followed him to the door, quickly straightening her clothes as she walked.

"Jules. Please come in." Frank opened the door and welcomed the tall thin woman inside with a wide smile. But Bronte noticed that the edges of his mouth were pulled back tightly. It was the type of smile she'd mimicked herself these past few days.

"Frank, it's so good to see you!" Jules exclaimed, hugging him tightly and giving him, if possible, an even wider smile than was plastered on his face. Her white teeth gleamed in the chandelier light, and her perky blond ponytail swayed as she turned to face her. "And you must be Bronte. It's a pleasure to meet you." Before Bronte could respond, Jules grasped her shoulders and pulled her into a stiff-armed hug.

"You too," Bronte gasped while her ribs were painfully crushed beneath Jules' embrace. Thankfully, the hug only lasted a few seconds before Bronte was abruptly released.

Not waiting to be invited, Jules strode into the parlour. Bronte's eyes strayed to Frank, and she wasn't surprised to see a frown on his face as he watched Jules. He looked as though he wished to run in the opposite direction. Bronte was inclined to do the same, but she reluctantly trailed after her.

When they were seated - Jules on an armchair, her and Frank on the lounge - Jules pulled out a clipboard and pen from her bag. She straightened and made a gleefully sound as she clicked her pen open.

"I'm going to ask a series of questions now, Bronte. Is that all right?" She had her pen held poised above the paper and didn't wait for a response as she forged ahead. "Tell me, what is your full name?" Jules' voice had gone up a decibel, and Bronte grimaced at its high-pitched sound.

"Bronte Maria Evans," she replied coolly. Her nerves had settled, and a mild annoyance with Jules had taken their place.

"And your mother's name?"

"Em-Emelia Ev-erett," she stuttered, correcting herself before saying the name "Emily Evans" as she would normally.

"Ah yes," said Jules, nodding her head in approval. "But that would make you Bronte Maria Everett, would it not?"

"My mistake," Bronte said, giving Jules an airy smile as though she couldn't believe how silly she'd been.

"And your father's name?"

"Jules, you should already have these details. Bronte's father was Madden Theobesian."

Jules' lips pinched at Frank's interruption. She took a calming breath and tucked a stray piece of hair behind her ear. "Moving on. You're sixteen, correct?"

"Yes."

"Seventeen next year?"

"Yes," Bronte repeated blandly.

"Hmm, obviously, you are late to be starting at Welkin School of Alchemy. However, we really have no choice but to put you in with the other students of your age." She peered at Bronte sternly over her clipboard. "Don't worry, I believe you'll be a fast learner! Especially when your mother was so powerful, you're bound to have inherited some ability."

"Your belief in me is appreciated." Bronte could hardly keep the sarcasm out of her voice.

Jules smiled at her widely. "Just a few more details. Bronte, you will be taking the core subjects with the rest of the fifth years, which include history of alchemy, concoction studies, and rune translations. In addition, I've been notified that you're an enchanter, meaning your manipulation-based studies will be taken with the other enchanters in your year." Jules scanned her clipboard as she spoke, her eyes skimming back and forth across whatever was written there. "Oh, and here's your supplies list." She handed Bronte a sheet of paper from somewhere on her clipboard. "Term starts on the first Monday of September, and you'll be under the excellent guidance of headmistress Maldorf. Any questions?"

Bronte realised with a start that the date was only a week away. "I think you've covered everything," she managed to get out.

"Good, I'll be going then. Don't bother getting up. I'll show myself out." Jules stood briskly and walked to the door. "Goodbye and good luck!" she called as she left.

Bronte glanced down at the sheet in her hand feeling drained in the wake of Jules' departure.

Welkin School of Alchemy 5th year student supply list: Miss Bronte Maria Everett.

Textbooks:

1001 Runes for every Transcription, by Snell Hefford

The Complete Alchemical History (grade 5), by August Hollifinger

The Art of Potions, Elixirs, and Spagyrics, by Robert Peltier

A Guide to Botany, by Lucy Redgrave

The Theory behind Enchanting, by Anthony Beak

Other:

1 Scriber

"What's a scriber?" she asked, looking up at Frank.

"It's like a pen. Shaman charge scribers with a small amount of their energy, like batteries on the Otherside. Any alchemist can use them to perform small tasks, like heating and cooling. All you have to do is draw the correlating symbol onto the object for it to have an effect. You'll learn these things in school, though. I'll have Eli take you to buy one another day, along with all your other school things."

"Tomorrow?" She was eager to return to the Canal. She wanted to taste the fairy floss again and explore the shops. Particularly the one selling the strange animals called furrows.

Frank sighed. "Not tomorrow. I know this is something you probably haven't wanted to think about, but we need to discuss your mother's funeral. Her body has been transported to the Shrine and is being prepared for the service. We will go at dawn tomorrow for the funeral."

Bronte felt as though she'd been plunged into ice. She'd forgotten about death for fleeting moments these past few days, but there would be no way to escape it now. She would have to face what had happened. She still couldn't accept that her mum was really gone. Bronte felt as though she could walk outside now, and her mum would be standing there waiting for her, waiting to take her back home, back to a place that was nothing like this.

"There's something else. Since your mother never told you about Namire, I'm assuming that she never told you who your grandparents are?"

Bronte shook her head. Her mum had told her they'd died in a house fire. When Bronte was younger, she used to ask to see photos of them or visit their graves, but that had only upset her mum, and she'd quickly stopped asking, knowing the answer would always be no.

"Their names are Cora and Mason. They're eager to meet you but have held off visiting because they didn't want to overwhelm you. They'll be at the funeral tomorrow, though. I wanted to tell you now, so it wasn't sprung on you when you arrived."

"Oh, thanks." Bronte fiddled with the corner of the paper Jules had given her. "There's something I've been wanting to ask you." She didn't know how to broach the subject of the necklace her mum had given her. Bronte knew it would sound crazy claiming to have a part of the Ancient Triad, but she wanted reassurance that it was just a replica, like the ones from Solomon's and Solomon's. "Before my mum passed, she gave me a necklace. I didn't know it had any importance until I came here." She pulled the chain from beneath her shirt and showed it to Frank. "Could it be real? Is there any chance that maybe she stole it?"

Frank's eyes widened as he took in the necklace. "May I hold it?"

She undid the clasp and handed it to him. He inspected the metal, holding it close. "If it's not real, this is a very convincing replica."

Bronte's stomach tightened. She didn't want to think about what act of blood-chilling violence had led her mum to possess such a thing.

"What am I meant to do?"

"The necklaces were lost around the same time your mother fled. I'm not aware if she had any contact with Lydia before then, but we know Lydia was the last person to have them in her possession. If your mother managed to get a hold of one, we don't know how or why. But these necklaces have powerful protective properties. Not only are they responsible for great acts of magic, but they can also shield you from any harm that may come your way. Perhaps your mother gave this to you so she knew you'd be safe."

"But it's not mine. It would be wrong to wear it."

"Technically, it is yours. You carry Theobesian blood. These necklaces could've been inherited by you eventually."

Bronte didn't want to acknowledge her father's heritage. She certainly didn't want to wear something that tied her to him. "I still wouldn't feel right keeping it."

Frank nodded understandingly. "I work for the Council. It's only a low-level job in the transmutation restoration department. We assist in restoring any transmutations that have gone wrong. Only a few people will be able to determine if this is the real thing. One of them is the Grand Shaman. However, she is highly reclusive and impossible to get in contact with unless you are someone like the Chancellor. If I can set up a meeting with him, we might be able to resolve this. In the meantime, keep that hidden. If people see it, it may arouse suspicion, given who your parents were. We don't want to draw out people that have been waiting for the Ancient Triad to turn up so they can use it to benefit themselves. Many Disciples were never identified, and many would still carry out your father's wish if they were given the chance. The safest place for that necklace is around your neck. Just don't let anyone see it; if they do, simply tell them it's a replica. They won't know the difference. Don't mention this to Eli or Nick, either. The fewer people that know, the better."

"I can do that." Bronte still didn't want to wear it, but she saw no other choice. If her mother had given this to her, there had to be a reason.

"Here, I'll help you." Frank placed the necklace around her neck and fastened it behind her. The weight of the pendant settled against her sternum as she tucked it beneath her shirt. She hated how much comfort it brought her and how a small part of her wasn't willing to give it up.

Bronte had never given much thought to her mum's funeral. It had seemed like a taboo topic and something she'd never wanted to consider. The one thing she'd always known was that she would be attending alone. But as she'd donned the black mourning robe Frank had laid out for her, she had been grateful that she wouldn't have to face this day by herself.

They'd arrived just before dawn at the Shrine where her mother's body had been prepared for cremation. Two people were waiting for them at the entrance, also wearing black robes.

"Bronte meet Cora and Mason, your grandparents," Frank introduced.

Mason had hair that curled the same way as Frank's, though his had turned grey with age. Cora looked just like her mum, and it was a stab in the heart to see her mother's face reflected before her, though it was lined with wrinkles, and her black shoulder-length hair was streaked with grey.

"I'm sorry we have to meet under these circumstances," Cora said, stepping forward and embracing her.

She smelt sweetly of lavender, like Bronte's mum, who'd often dabbed lavender oil on her wrists, claiming it helped with stress. But now Bronte wondered if it was to remind her of her home and a family she'd never see again. Bronte blinked rapidly as tears welled in her eyes, and she tried to stop the wave of hopelessly tangled emotions from swamping her.

"I'm sorry too," she croaked.

Mason squeezed her shoulder. "We need to go in before the sun rises."

The pinkish glow of dawn was brightening the sky, and a waiting shaman ushered them inside. They were led through the Shrine to an outside terrace overlooking a deep valley full of colourful flowers. In the distance, the ocean glittered in the first light of the morning.

Before them, a stone block was erected resembling the stone Bronte had lain on when she'd been read. A pyre had been built atop the block, the branches intertwined with red flowers. Although Bronte knew the body inside was her mum, it didn't feel real. The tan cloth wrapped around the lifeless shape couldn't be covering the woman she loved. She gathered with the rest of the family, a numb feeling spreading through her.

The shaman stood between them and her mother. She clasped her hands together and began speaking. "We are gathered here today to remember the life of Emelia Everett. We ask that the goddess Hecate looks down on her with mercy, taking the ashes of the yew boughs as sufficient sacrifice to grant her safe passage into the afterlife. We shall say goodbye to the past as the sun rises to bless this new day."

The shaman whispered a series of words Bronte couldn't make out. She flinched at the wave of heat as the pyre was suddenly alight with blue flames. Bronte watched her mother burn while the sun's golden glow lit up the horizon. Silent tears ran down her cheeks, and her throat ached from repressed sobs, as though a giant ball had lodged inside her. Looking back on the past few days, she didn't know how she'd remained so calm. But now, everything was so clear to her. Her mother was gone, and she was stuck in this place without her, left to uncover the truths her mother couldn't face.

The shaman whispered more words, and the fire stopped. She then made a gesture, pushing her hands up, and the remaining ashes ascended high above the stone block, shooting outwards before spreading down into the valley of flowers below them and settling in places Bronte was too far away to see.

Eli wrapped an arm around her shoulders, pulling her close. Bronte leaned into his weight, pressing her cheek into the soft material of his robe as though she could disappear into it.

He tilted his head, and she felt the warmth of his breath against the tears on her cheek as he whispered to her. "The flowers grow from past alchemist's ashes. It's called Rainbow Valley. The red flowers around your mother's body on the pyre will be the colour flower she'll become in the valley. They're amaryllis chosen by Cora because the meaning behind them is pride, strength and determination. All the things she valued most about her daughter. So when you see red flowers growing, you can think of them as her coming back to life."

Eli squeezed her shoulder, and slowly Bronte ran out of tears to cry. "That's a nice thought," she said at last, and she looked up to see a bittersweet smile on Eli's face.

"Death doesn't have to be ugly. We just like to torture ourselves with it because we're the ones left behind."

"But what if I want to follow her?" Bronte whispered. It was so quiet she wasn't sure he'd even heard, but after a moment, his response came.

"Are you really ready to let all this go?"

Bronte looked across the valley and knew what her answer would be. The sun had risen above them and its rays were strong enough to hurt her eyes. She blinked away the dark spots that filled her vision as she shook her head.

"Then look for the amaryllises. There's no need to follow her because she'll be right here."

Bronte sat inside her grandparent's house with her hands clasped in her lap.

"Here we are," came Cora's soothing voice as she floated back into the room carrying a tray of tea and cakes. She passed Eli and Bronte porcelain cups, each filled with a dark liquid that smelt enticingly of peppermint and liquorice.

"I wasn't sure how you take it, Bronte, so I made it the same as Eli's. A dash of milk with one sugar, is that alright?" A line dented Cora's forehead, and Bronte smiled broadly before accepting the cup.

"Yes, that's perfect."

Bronte had never been a massive fan of tea. She found the watery taste of it unappealing. Still, she brought the cup to her mouth and took a long sip. She was surprised when she didn't have to feign her enjoyment of the brew as its rich, comforting flavour filled her mouth. Instead, a calmness swept over her as she set the cup on the table. Cora handed the remaining cups to Frank, Nina, and Mason, before sitting in an armchair.

"Oh, Bronte, I almost forgot," she said, jumping up again. She was sprightly for an older woman, unlike Mason, who seemed to have drifted off to sleep in his chair. "I dug up the old family album. It has captures of your mother in it, and I thought you might want to take a look!" She disappeared into the kitchen

"Captures?" Bronte frowned.

"What you would call photos. They're our own version. We have to develop them in special potions, though. We tried Otherside cameras once, but they didn't work properly. They would always go off randomly as a reaction to our magic, and everything came out black," Frank explained.

"Move over," Cora said playfully when she returned with a leather-bound book.

Bronte couldn't help but laugh as Cora squeezed in to sit between her and Eli. She watched her grandmother open the book to a photo of the family. The Everetts were sitting outside on the steps of the same house they were in now. She picked out Frank immediately, though he must've been no more than eight or nine years of age, his curly hair as unruly as ever. Beside him sat her mum. She wore a ruby-coloured dress, and her long black hair had been drawn back using a matching hairband.

"That's Emelia there," Cora said, pointing fondly.

She chuckled softly, although Bronte could hear the sorrow in her voice. In the picture, a much younger Cora and Mason smiled behind their children. Cora's hair was the same straight black as her daughter's at the time. Bronte's hair was a few shades lighter than black and curlier, like Frank's but not quite. She desperately wanted to see parts of herself reflected in the faces of her family. She'd only ever had her mum to judge by, but Emelia had only been one piece of the puzzle, and while Bronte had never doubted their relation, her looks didn't match her mum's. Maybe the missing pieces would click into place if she saw a photo of her dad.

"It's funny, we all look so happy in that photo, but do you remember the moments before it, Frank?" Cora asked.

Frank rolled his eyes, and Nina grinned at him, squeezing his arm. "I stole Emelia's hairband and ran around the yard with it held above my head so she couldn't reach."

"Dad!" said Eli reprovingly.

"You're an only child Eli. You wouldn't understand that sometimes being mean to your sibling is our way of showing love."

Cora spent the rest of the morning telling stories about young Frank and Emelia. Bronte found herself laughing with everyone as they got more ridiculous. She drank two cups of tea and ate countless cakes until her sadness was nothing more than an ache deep inside her, slowly being buried by these slivers of new happiness.

CHAPTER 9

"We'll go to Bertnam's Cottage to get our books first," said Eli.

They were back at the Canal to buy Bronte's things for school. Her dresses from Miss Taffeta's had arrived the day before, and Nina had helped her put on a powder blue coloured one that morning. Bronte couldn't wait to get home and take it off. She hadn't adjusted to the restricted breathing the tie-up back caused, and she much preferred her shorts and t-shirts, even if they weren't acceptable here.

"You know, most women don't constantly pull at their skirts when they walk," commented Nick. He had joined them for the day, and his constant monitoring of her was getting oppressive.

"Then don't look at me," she snapped.

He just shook his head. His hair fell in front of his eyes, and for a fleeting second, Bronte wanted to reach out and brush it away. She couldn't help imagining how it would feel to run her fingers through its soft length, but when she looked at the face hidden beneath, the feeling evaporated. Nick would likely smack her hand away before she got within a centimeter of his hair anyway.

Eli weaved around a group of people and cut across one of the canal's bridges. It was made of stones, unlike the other golden bridges positioned at intervals along the length of the waterway. In between the stones, Bronte could see slips of paper peeking out.

"Are those letters?" she asked Nick.

He gave a confirming nod. "This is Eros's Crossing. People write to Eros about their troubles in love, then throw money into the water as payment in the hope that he will favour them. Some people even go as far as to drink the water that runs below the bridges. They call it the water of love." He winked at her, and heat flared in her cheeks. She may've disliked him, but she couldn't deny he was attractive.

Bronte looked away, leaning over the edge of the bridge. She saw the shimmer of coins glittering beneath the clear water. "Have you ever written a letter?" she asked absently, hoping her careless tone would mask her interest in his answer.

"Do I look like I need help with love?" He cut a sidelong glance at her, his hazel eyes gleaming with mirth. She liked how his eyes changed colour. Sometimes they looked more green than brown, like right now.

Bronte shrugged and set off after Eli. "No, Leora seems to like you plenty." She didn't know why the words came out of her mouth, but it was too late to take them back.

A disbelieving laugh burst out of Nick. "Leora and I aren't like that."

She hated that his answer brought her relief. "What are you like then?" She kept her gaze on Eli as she spoke. Out of the corner of her eye, she could see Nick looking at her.

"Like brother and sister, and I don't fancy the idea of incest. Why do you care anyway?"

"I was just curious." Thankfully, her voice was steady. They arrived at Bertnam's Cottage a moment later, and she was grateful to be saved from further questioning.

Bronte relaxed as they escaped the overcrowded street and entered the solitary comfort of a room full of paper. The light inside the shop was like the soft glow of dawn sunshine. Books were stacked on every available surface, creating a maze of spines to navigate. Bronte tucked in her elbows, not wanting to accidentally knock anything over. In single file, they made their way to the cashier. He was a thin, gangly man whose tufty head of greying hair almost reached the top of the stacks of books. Bronte supposed his height was a good thing, given the books extended well above her own head. At least if she needed something near the top, he would be able to get it for her.

"Gerard, have you found me anything good lately?" Eli asked.

"Got you a whole stack," he replied cheerfully, lifting a collection of books from beneath the counter.

Eli was quickly absorbed in conversation about the different novels. Bronte's eyes slid to Nick, and he cocked his head to the side, indicating she should follow him down an aisle. Neither Eli nor Gerard glanced up as they walked away.

They emerged from the aisle into a corner of the shop with a sign that read 'Academic Texts' hanging from the ceiling. Books with unusual titles, like *A guide to the Creatures of the Night*, and *Spells from the Other Side of the Moon*, were stacked on the shelves. Bronte spied a particularly interesting-looking volume called *Mind Reading for the Dim-Witted*, which she thought she might've picked up if alone.

"What's first?" Nick asked.

Bronte took out the now creased sheet of paper Jules had given her. "*The Complete Alchemical History Grade 5*," she read.

Nick went to a shelf and pulled out a thick book with silver lettering along the spine and passed it to her. Bronte sagged slightly under its weight. He looked at her expectantly, and she glanced hastily back at her list.

"*Runes for every Transcription*." He handed her a slightly smaller but still very large book with a mottled green leather cover. "Um, then *The Art of Potions, Elixirs, and Spagyrics*, *The Theory behind Enchanting*, and lastly, *A Guide to Botany*," she finished.

Nick stacked the final three books on top of Bronte's pile, which she had to carry with two hands to ensure she didn't drop anything. Nick raised a sceptical eyebrow at her teetering under its weight.

"Before you offer, the answer is no," she said, annoyed by how strained her voice sounded.

He rolled his eyes. "I wasn't about to offer anything. I know well enough that a woman can handle herself."

Bronte refrained from responding. The effort required could be put to better use carrying her books. She slowly navigated the aisle back to where Eli and Gerard were still standing together, deep in conversation. Her elbow bumped the edge of a precariously high pile of books. She had to quickly steady them, almost losing her grip on her own books. Nick sniggered behind her, and she wished the tower had fallen on him just to wipe the smirk off his face.

At the register, Bronte watched Eli count out the trillings and copias needed to pay, and Gerard wrapped each of the books in brown paper. Eli had a considerably large pile to carry, having also purchased the books Gerard had found for him.

Bertnam's Cottage was beside a stationary shop called Inscribed, where they bought parchment and special pens that produced endless ink, and thankfully Bronte found a satchel into which she dumped all her purchases. She also bought a scriber. It looked just like a pen, as Frank had told her. The thin cylindrical object was made from wood with a blunted metal top that Bronte assumed was used to draw with.

Bronte spied a set of fancy quills with large colourful feathers at the register, but Nick assured her that they were horrible for writing with and convinced her to get the pens instead. When all the shopping was complete, Bronte realised just how hungry she'd become, and she was grateful when Eli announced that it was time to go to Merlin's Beard for lunch.

It was late afternoon by the time they made their way back to Eli's. Nick still had a few hours until he needed to be at The Sparrow, so he didn't mind walking home with them, if only because he knew it would annoy Bronte. The flat line of her mouth was enough to tell him he'd gotten on her nerves.

"Did you need something?" She raised an arched brow in question.

"What gave you that idea?" Nick replied.

Bronte looked away, readjusting the strap of her satchel. He'd offered to carry it home from Merlin's Beard, knowing the books weighed a lot, but that had simply earned him another dirty look. Nick knew it was his fault she didn't like him. He'd made a terrible first impression, which he admitted to himself now, had been a mistake. As much as Nick had been hostile to her when she'd first arrived, he could see now she truly didn't know anything about this world, and it seemed cruel of him to blame her for her parent's actions. Nick knew well enough that someone's parents weren't an accurate representation of their nature.

"Can you both stop bickering? I would like a moment of peace," Eli begged.

"We weren't bickering," Bronte mumbled.

They were nearing Eli's home when they spied Xander in his garden, waving at them to come over. "Sorry to bother you, kids, but I was wondering if any of you have seen Chester?"

"Who?" Bronte asked.

"The cat you saw a few days ago. He's been missing since that afternoon."

"Oh, no, sorry."

Xander frowned. "He's never disappeared this long. Vaughn - the owner - is sick with worry."

"We'll keep an eye out, Xander," Eli assured him.

Nick sighed as they walked away. "I hope he isn't lost. Chester and I get along really well."

"He's probably sniffing out fish at the docks or something," said Eli.

"Let's hope. I actually should be heading that way. Thanks for the little detour. I'll see you when I see you."

Eli and Bronte waved him off as he turned to the south. He'd asked around the markets that morning if anyone knew of a man named Rhett. After many negative responses, he'd come across a fishmonger who'd said he'd bought a book from a man by that name a few months prior. When asked what the book was about, the man became cagey, suspicious Nick might be an informant for the High Guard. It had taken a lot of convincing, and Nick had even forked out some copias to buy a fish, before the man revealed that Rhett could be found in the furthest house on Cobblers Street, which was where he was heading now.

Nick knocked on the door and the flaking red paint crunched beneath his knuckles. The sounds of someone approaching could be heard inside. The door was flung open to reveal a stout man with four-day-old stubble shadowing his jaw.

"Can I help you, kid?"

Nick appraised the room behind him. There was nothing to suggest he was in the presence of an illegal book trafficker.

"I hear you sell books."

The man's eyes narrowed. "Depends on who you heard it from."

"Isaac Ives," he lied.

"He a friend of yours?"

Nick could think of a few words to describe his relationship with Isaac, but friends wasn't one of them. "Something like that. He bought a book from you a few days ago and pointed me in this direction."

Rhett hesitated, then moved aside, allowing Nick to enter. "What were you after?"

Nick knew of a few types of books that had been banned, but he had no way of knowing precisely what Isaac had bought. "Do you have a second copy of the book you sold Isaac?"

Rhett's persona had entirely switched now that he knew Nick was here to buy something. "I sell originals only. The best I can do is get you a similar genre," he said brightly.

"Can I see what you have available?"

"Of course, follow me." Rhett led him into a cluttered sitting room where contraband books were stacked on a shelf in plain sight.

"Aren't you worried about the High Guard?"

"I like to go by the honour system. You don't tell, I don't tell. It's worked so far. What you're looking at is mortificatio, texts on death, possession, and mind control. That sort of thing."

Nick only knew a little about mortificatio, more commonly known as dark magic. It was a branch of magic outside of the manipulations, and something rarely discussed, even in an educational sense. The Disciples were renowned for using that magic to steal enchanter power. It was also the way they'd killed his brother. Nick had questioned his parents about the death when he was younger, but it was only once his mother had drunk an entire bottle of spirits that she had finally revealed his brother had been found lifeless in the street near their house. He'd had runes cut into his hands and blood smeared across his naked chest. That was as much as Nick knew of mortificatio.

"How did you get these books?"

"It's an inherited business. My mother - goddess bless her - worked in the Grand Library during the book purges. She's only got a bit of transmuting power, but she was able to use it to alter the books enough so that she could smuggle some out. She's a big believer in freedom of knowledge. She used to lend them to friends, but word slowly spread around here, and I found it more profitable to sell them."

"And the book you sold Isaac, what was that about?"

"Something about wanting to contact the dead."

Nick baulked. He thought a book on that topic deserved a bit more gravitas than the offhanded way Rhett had delivered the news. "And you're not worried these books will fall into the wrong hands, like the Disciples?"

"It's not as if people are jumping to buy the books left and right. Every so often, someone comes around who's interested, for research purposes, of course, and I don't see the harm in that. I have a limit of one book per customer, and there hasn't been any trouble yet."

"The reward is better than the risk for you?"

Rhett's eyes narrowed. "Usually, my customers don't have so many questions about why I'm doing this, and I'm starting to think you aren't interested. So I suggest you leave before I begin asking *you* some questions you might find difficult to answer."

Nick could have the upper hand here, threatening Rhett with the High Guard, but he didn't want Isaac alerted that he knew of the book he'd bought. He had enough information to know Isaac was up to something, and it would be mutually beneficial for both Nick and the book dealer if he left now.

"Thanks for your time," Nick said politely as he was shepherded out the door. It slammed shut behind him, a heavy bolt falling into place.

CHAPTER 10

The final week before school passed uneventfully. Bronte spent the days with Eli and sometimes Nick and Leora, investigating every shop along the Canal and eating lunch at Merlin's Beard. But when she awoke on the morning of her first day at Welkin, she wished she hadn't become so lax. Her bag was only half packed, and her room was a mess.

"Bronte! Are you almost ready?" called Eli from outside her door.

"Almost," she yelled back, flipping up the corner of her blanket on her bed to check for her rune translation textbook. She'd been reading it last night, but in the short time between then and now, she'd managed to lose it. Bronte had looked under the bed and inside her drawers, but it was only after she turned over the last cushions that she'd thrown on the floor before going to sleep last night that she found it.

"Aha!" she said, sighing in relief as she picked it up. She shoved the textbook inside her already bulging bag and gave herself one last look in the vanity mirror. Bronte felt strange seeing herself in Welkin's school uniform. The stiff fabric was still too new to look worn in, and she got flashbacks of her first day at high school. Her mum had proudly snapped photos of her outside the school gates while she'd tried to shield her face from the embarrassment. She didn't think her mum would be proud of her today, attending a school in a place she'd spent her whole life hiding from her. A knock came at her door again, and she pulled her gaze away from herself.

"Coming." Bronte shouldered her heavy bag and opened the door to find Eli waiting on the other side.

He shot a worried glance at his watch. "We're going to have to skip breakfast," he muttered.

They hurried down the stairs to find Nina waiting for them. She was holding a tray stacked with buttered pieces of toast.

"Here, take some," she urged. Bronte took a piece despite nerves having claimed her appetite. "Good luck Bronte. I know you'll do well." Nina gave her a warm smile and some of her nerves dissipated.

"Where's my luck?" asked Eli.

Nina swatted him lightly on the arm. "You don't need any."

"Have a good day," Frank called from the kitchen as they left.

Bronte shared a meaningful look with him. She hadn't forgotten about the necklace she wore or its potential power. It had done nothing to suggest it was magical, though, and Bronte was hoping it really was just a replica. Frank had promised that he was trying to get in contact with the Chancellor but, so far, he'd had no luck. Apparently, working in the transmutation restoration department meant you weren't a high priority on the Chancellor's list.

Bronte was ready to collapse by the time they reached the Gateways. Her bag straps dug uncomfortably into her shoulders, and her hair clung to the back of her neck. She wiped sweat from her brow as she followed Eli to the furthest Arch.

"Eli, Bronte!" called a familiar voice.

Bronte turned to see Nick jogging along the platform. He wasn't carrying a bag, only a single textbook clutched in his hand.

"You're late," observed Bronte.

"I wouldn't act so prim if I was you. We're both here at the same time, aren't we?"

She refrained from answering as she turned to Eli, who was waiting by the Arch, bouncing on the balls of his feet.

"Why are we in such a rush?" She didn't want to be late on her first day, but Eli acted as if it were life or death.

"If you're late, you have to sing the school anthem in front of everyone at the next assembly. It's meant to demonstrate school pride or whatever," said Nick.

"I have a terrible singing voice, and I can't say I'm a massive fan of public humiliation, so I'll see you up there." Eli stepped through the Arch and disappeared.

"Does singing in front of the school sound appealing to you?" Nick asked when Bronte hesitated to follow.

"No, but if I make you late too, it might be worth it." She didn't give him a chance to reply as she stepped forward. She stumbled out of the Arch to discover that she'd travelled all the way to the top of Namire. It looked as though a large glade had been cut straight out of the mountaintop. On the far side of the land, a waterfall spilled over the edge of a cliff, filling up the sparkling lake below. Adjacent to the lake, stood a white castle. From the city, it was nothing but a white smudge on the cliff but, up-close, Bronte could see turrets and spires jutting out from the main building, giving it a misshapen profile that extended towards the sky.

"Goddess above!" cried a voice, and a firm hand grabbed Bronte's arm as she was thrown forward.

She was yanked upright, and she gasped, trying to recover the air she'd lost. Nick was centimeters away from her. His hand still wrapped around her arm. Bronte's breathing turned shallow as she stared into his hazel eyes.

"Have you ever heard of rule one?"

His low voice sent a shiver through her, and she swallowed before responding. "Someone might've mentioned it."

"Would you two hurry up!" yelled Eli. He was already halfway down the stone drive leading to the school's entrance.

Bronte shook her arm out of Nick's grasp and followed. She told herself that her ragged breathing was a result of adrenaline and not the feel of Nick's hands on her skin or his eyes looking into hers while they'd breathed the same air. She needed to concentrate today, and that image of him holding her wouldn't help.

The inside of the school was a giant stone maze. Eli rushed them through the empty corridors. They turned a corner, and Bronte instantly heard excited chatter from beyond a tall stone archway. They entered a room full of students sitting at pew-like rows of seats. Eli slid into one of the empty back rows, and Bronte found herself sandwiched between him and Nick.

"This is the Chamber," Eli informed her. "Any important meetings and assemblies are held here."

The room's ceiling was painted like the sky, the powder blue background was dotted with white clouds outlined in gold. There were figures spread across the mural, shadowy images of a tall and slender woman tending to a garden of flowers; a baby whose eyes were a milky white; a man with a chalice of blue liquid in one hand and deep crimson in the other, and, finally a faceless being with halos of gold around its hands that shone like rays of sunshine. Bronte realised they were meant to be representations of the manipulations and that she was the faceless being: the enchanter.

She turned her gaze away from the ceiling, and her eyes locked with a particularly severe-looking red-headed man standing at the side of the room. A port-wine stain birthmark covered his left eye, and his mouth was set in a hard line as he glared at her.

Bronte sunk low in her seat, unsure why she had drawn his attention. The headmistress hadn't arrived yet, so technically, she wasn't late. Eli and Nick had arrived at the same time, and he wasn't paying them any heed. Finally, he looked away, subjecting another student to his stony gaze. Nick elbowed her side, and she turned, narrowing her eyes. Her breath caught as he leant closer, pressing his body against hers.

Nick nodded his head towards the glaring man. "That's Professor Wrathwell. He teaches history."

"Does he always look like that?"

"Angry?" Nick shrugged. "Mostly, or maybe he knew your parents and didn't like them."

Bronte chewed the inside of her gum. It was possible he knew she was the daughter of two renowned Disciples and was now planning to punish her for it. She risked another glance his way. He was tall, and his raised chin and straight back demanded people's attention. He didn't seem like the type of person who tried to go unnoticed.

A woman with sleek black hair and a harsh angular face strode down the middle of the Chamber's central aisle, causing a hush to fall over the room. The clapping of her heels on the stone floor filled the silence. Bronte straightened in her seat as the woman passed. She guessed it was headmistress Maldorf. No one else in the school could have that effect on students. She reached the podium at the front of the room and peered at them through her tortoiseshell-rimmed glasses.

"Welcome back to what I'm sure will be another fabulous year of learning." She smiled, and it turned the hard angles of her face soft. "And welcome to the new students joining us this year. It is an exciting time to be at the beginning of your schooling lives, and I'm sure you will all excel at your differing manipulations under the guidance of our wonderful professors." Headmistress Maldorf's gaze swept over the room before she continued. "I would like to refresh your memory on some of our school rules. First, there is to be no attempt at alchemical practice on other students outside of the classroom. Secondly, I want to remind you that the boundaries of the school end at its gates, which you are not to cross, and the nearby mountains are also out of bounds. Travelling to and from school is to be done only through the Arch located at the front of the school. You will act in an orderly fashion during this process. I would now like to welcome Professor Kirwan to the podium to make some general announcements," concluded the headmistress.

There was a smattering of applause as a frumpy-looking woman with curly grey hair made her way to the front of the Chamber.

"Welcome, welcome students!" she said, beaming around the room. "This is your gentle reminder that if you want to join any school clubs, you must sign up on the notice board outside the Chamber. The school choir can always use some new voices." She paused, eyeing the students meaningfully. Bronte looked at her feet to avoid catching her gaze. She had no inclination to join the school choir because, much like Eli, she had a terrible singing voice. Finally, as Professor Kirwan continued speaking, she felt it was safe to look up again. Bronte zoned out not long after. There was only so much waffle about general school things, like lunchtimes and class rescheduling, that she could listen to. Even if this was a magic school, it didn't change the fact that assemblies were boring.

Another smattering of applause brought Bronte out of her daydream, and headmistress Maldorf returned to the podium. She held up a finger to silence the chatter that had started up. "Please see your year advisors after the assembly for your timetables. Lunch will be served in the Dome as usual. You have a busy semester ahead, so make sure you start on the right foot today." Her eyes narrowed at the sea of students before she stepped off the podium.

Instantly, the room was abuzz with movement. "Who's our year advisor?" Bronte asked as they filed out of their seat and into the crowded aisle.

"Professor Kirwan," said Eli, pointing to the corner of the room where a small group of students had begun to gather. Professor Kirwan's greying hair was barely visible amid the crowd.

Leora was among the group, and a grin spread across her face as she spotted them. "I was expecting to see you three on stage singing any moment," she said ruefully.

"A gentleman is never late," remarked Nick, earning himself an eyeroll from Leora.

"Leora, your timetable." Professor Kirwan handed her a slip of paper, then she ruffled through her pile and pulled out a similar slip for Eli and Nick. "Ah, Bronte, isn't it?" she asked kindly, turning her attention to her.

"Um, yes," Bronte faltered, surprised she knew her name.

"Here we are," Professor Kirwan handed her a slip of her own. "I'll see you soon," she said with a wink.

Leora tugged her away from the remaining students and into an empty corner of the room where Nick and Eli were now standing.

"What do you have first?" she asked, already peering over Bronte's shoulder at her timetable.

"Um, concoction studies?" Bronte read.

"Same!" Leora flashed her piece of paper at her excitedly. Bronte felt an unexpected wave of relief that she would have a familiar face in her class.

"I'm off to runes," sighed Nick. "And I won't even have you there to cheat off this year." He looked mournfully at Leora.

"What a shame," Leora replied with a deadpan face.

A bell sounded throughout the school, breaking up their conversation, and they set off to class, Nick grumbling as they went.

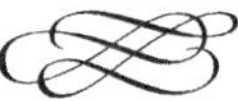

Isaac walked through the door of the rune translation classroom. Nick smiled pleasantly as their eyes met just so he could see Isaac's lip curl. Unfortunately, it had the opposite effect, and Isaac took his smile as an invitation to come over and sit in the seat beside him. He didn't look at Nick's arm. There was no hint of acknowledgement that Isaac had thrown him into a wall the week prior.

"I hear the new girl's an enchanter. I look forward to spending time with her," drawled Isaac as he rested a foot on his opposite knee and invaded all of Nick's personal space. Nick's hand twitched towards Isaac's ankle, and he longed to push it away.

"I doubt she'd bother wasting her time on you." The idea that Bronte would spend a large portion of each day with Isaac made him feel an emotion he didn't want to acknowledge. He convinced himself that if he ignored it for long enough, it would eventually go away.

"I think you'll find some people enjoy my company," Isaac replied blandly.

Nick couldn't help rolling his eyes. "I'm yet to meet one."

Isaac picked off a piece of invisible lint from his pants. "We'll see."

"Actually, I believe I heard someone at The Sparrow was willing to suffer your presence. I think he goes by the name Rhett: a book dealer, I was told." Nick watched Isaac closely, hoping for a sign that he'd been correct.

Isaac's lips thinned. "I was meeting with my mother's old friend," he replied.

His voice was steady, and it piqued Nick's interest. "Lying isn't a good trait."

Isaac turned his icy blue eyes on him, narrowing them slightly. "I would be careful who you call a liar."

Nick smirked. "Then why don't you share the truth?"

"It seems you already know the truth. Your interest in me is flattering, if a little strange. But I'm not ashamed to admit I sought a book to assist me in a certain area of my learning."

"A book on contacting the dead. They're banned for a reason. That kind of magic is harmful. I could report you in an instant."

"I know you think I'm working on some sort of vengeful plot, but the reason is much tamer than you imagine. You know my father's dead. I live alone with my mother, and while that is more than fine, I have always been curious about my past. You'd do the same. Tell me, if you had the chance, you wouldn't try contacting your brother?"

"Not if it meant putting others at risk."

"I couldn't agree more. I am not trying to, nor will I, harm anyone with this information."

"What makes you think I won't report this to the High Guard?"

Isaac scoffed. "Go to them if you wish but remember who you are. I have money and a last name of real significance in this city. You are a boy from the south who has always been jealous of my status and talents and is constantly trying to undermine me. Do you think the High Guard will go after the late Governor's son? Disturb my poor mother's peace? I would love to see that happen, so please feel free to tell them what you think you know, but I have to warn you, you'll only make a fool of yourself if you do." Isaac paused, eyeing Nick quizzically. "But maybe we can work out something mutually beneficial for your silence."

"Like I'd take a bribe from you. I don't want anything you have to offer."

"Not even the opportunity to speak to your brother? Say I do own a book that teaches me how to contact the dead, and say I'm very close to succeeding. You have no interest in seeing if it works?"

Nick hesitated. It was a tempting idea, but Isaac wasn't the type to offer more than he was getting in return. "And all you want from me is to keep quiet? After you just listed the reasons I would need to anyway, without you having to offer anything."

Isaac frowned. "I want you to make sure Bronte likes me."

Nick's suspicion was instantly aroused. "Why?"

"Let's just say I have a vested interest in her, but I know she won't listen to me if you're constantly in her ear telling her how much you hate me."

"What makes you think I have any control over what she thinks?"

"I didn't think you could be so stupid, Henderson, but clearly, you are. Pay attention next time she looks at you. Then maybe you'll see."

Bronte looked at him like he annoyed her and sometimes like she tolerated him. There was nothing special about that. "I thought people 'enjoyed your company' why do you need my help?"

"Think of it as damage control, then. Tell her nice things about me, or at the very least tell her nothing at all and, believe me, I'll know if you do the opposite, and then the deal's off. You can speak to your brother in your dreams."

Nick's stomach twisted. He knew the answer should be no, but a greater part of him longed to see his bother. He longed to ask exactly what to do with the way their family had turned out. If Isaac truly knew a method to contact the dead that didn't put anyone at harm, then what was the risk in at least seeing if it worked? "Fine, I'll keep quiet about you around Bronte, and you let me know when you have things figured out. And don't try to snake your way out of this. I knew when you went to Rhett. I'll know your next plan too."

Isaac only smiled, holding out his hand for Nick to shake. "I have nothing to hide."

Isaac released his hand, leaving Nick's ice cold. He stood up smoothly and moved to another desk. Nick glared at the back of his head.

The lesson started shortly after, and although Nick tried to pay attention, exhaustion weighed on him. He'd hardly slept in the week since he'd assaulted the drunken lecher outside The Sparrow. He'd arrived home and gone straight to the bathroom to wash the night off. The cuff of his white shirt had been flecked with the plump man's blood, and he'd left it discarded at the bottom of his wardrobe, along with a pile of other ruined clothes. Usually, he was more careful, but at least the shirt had been old.

Nick looked down at his hand clasped around his pen. The phantom touch of sticky blood covered it, and he had the urge to wipe it against his pants. But there was nothing there. He was weary, a weariness that couldn't be cured by a good night's sleep. It was as though he existed in this world as a phantom himself. He wondered if it was normal to feel this way.

His parents had barely acknowledged his existence when he'd left this morning. Although, admittedly, he'd left hastily. Nick had arrived home from The Sparrow late and collapsed into bed, thinking he would take a quick nap. The next time he'd opened his eyes, the sunlight had been streaming through his window, and the cawing of seagulls outside had told him that he was extremely late.

"I'm going," Nick had called as he'd rushed towards the door, the closest textbook he'd been able to find clasped in his hand.

"Suit yourself," he'd heard his mum reply.

Nick hadn't seen his dad. The sweet smell of moonwood had hung heavy in the house, and Nick had known that if he'd gone looking for him, he would've appeared to his dad as some strange sort of hallucination and not as his son. But he couldn't bring himself to care. If his parents spent the rest of their lives in that house, littering it with empty bottles and clogging it up with smoke, Nick couldn't bring himself to care one bit. What scared him the most, more than the emptiness, was the fear of that feeling spreading to everything in his life, sapping away any bit of happiness, love, or friendship he'd ever felt until he became a block of ice. The thought sent a shiver through him, and he knew sleep wouldn't come easy that night.

～

Bronte's legs burnt as she climbed the last steps to get to their concoction studies lesson. It was held in the tallest tower of the school. Round tables raised to waist height were scattered around the large circular room. Jars filled with herbs and strange plants submerged in water lined the shelves. There were tall, narrow windows at each compass point, and the door they'd entered through was set between the southern and western windows.

"Right on time," said Eli as another loud bell echoed through the school.

There was a distinct earthy smell to the room, mixed with some essential oil that reminded Bronte of her mum. She was instantly brought back to their shoebox of an apartment, and the pungent oils her mum would dab around to 'clear the energy'. Bronte had never understood where her mum's obsession with natural forms of healing had come from. Along with her dislike of technology, her mum had always veered away from modern advances in medicine. If Bronte ever became sick, her mum would make horrible-tasting herb concoctions to cure her instead of taking her to the doctor. But after seeing all the herb-filled apothecaries in Namire, it was no longer such a mystery.

Eli led the way over to a table by the east window. A cool breeze filtered in, taking away the smell and the memories of her mum it evoked.

"This is the best spot in the room. It gets so hot and steamy once all the cauldrons are heated," Leora said, plonking down on a stool and dumping her bag beside her. She rubbed her shoulder, wincing as she did so. Bronte did the same. Carrying heavy textbooks around, especially up multiple flights of stairs, wasn't enjoyable or easy.

"Welcome back, students!" Professor Kirwan bounded through the door. "I'm sure you are all eager to begin your learning this year." Bronte glanced around the room at the less than enthusiastic faces of the class. "Before we begin, I would like to remind you that your fifth year is a time to hone your skills in preparation for your mentor year. Your other professors and I will be watching each of you closely over the next few months to provide you with the best recommendations for your future, so make sure you try your hardest." A new tension settled over the room as she gave everyone a meaningful look.

"Mentors?" Bronte whispered to Leora and Eli.

"You spend your sixth year with a mentor to help learn more practical real-world uses for our manipulations," Eli explained.

Bronte's stomach tightened with the added pressure to catch up to the rest of her form. She didn't want to end up having to repeat a year because she wasn't ready.

"To get you back in the spirit of things, I thought we would practice making a simple healing elixir to cure a common cold. Turn to page one hundred and three of your textbooks, where you will find the method."

There was a shuffling of movement as people pulled out their textbooks and flipped to the correct page. Unfortunately, the method was written in complicated-looking runes, which Bronte hadn't learnt to read yet. She'd spent the last week pouring over her textbooks. There was only so much information you could cram into the space of seven days though, and now she was cursing herself for not studying harder.

"Excellent. As a refresher, who can tell me why we cannot simply administer the *elixir of life*, otherwise known as the *elixir of immortality*, when someone falls ill?"

A perky-looking girl with brown hair pulled back into a tight bun flung her hand up. "The elixir of immortality was first made by Emmanuel Hunt in the year fourteen eighty-eight AC," she said after Professor Kirwan nodded at her.

"AC?" Bronte whispered to Eli.

"Adapted Calendar," he whispered back. "Hallowless adapted their timekeeping to correlate with the modern-day Earth calendar. Once our Arches allowed us access, we realized there was no time slip between our two realms, and it was easy to sync our calendars."

Scarlett shot Eli a glare while she spoke. "However, upon administering it, he became a shadow of his former self. The elixir cured him of any disease or illness, but it meant he no longer had the impulse to survive. Food lost taste, and yet he wasn't at any risk of starving if he didn't eat because the elixir served as sustenance. He quickly discovered he had lost the ability to feel emotion and instead passed through the world without being able to experience it. He later committed suicide, in fourteen eighty-nine AC, as a result."

"Correct, Scarlett, as usual." Professor Kirwan gave her an approving smile before turning away. Scarlett smirked at the class, a look of superiority on her face. "Remember you are only making one elixir per table; supplies are on your allotted shelves. I have a sick widowsweed here to test your final products on." She placed a black plant with long veil-like leaves that drooped over the edge of the pot on top of her desk. "You may begin."

Noise erupted around the room as everyone began pulling out equipment and collecting ingredients. Bronte watched as Eli took out a large cauldron from underneath their table and placed it on top. She flicked back to the recipe, trying to discern from the method what any of it meant, but the writing on the page just looked like a random combination of lines. Leora returned with the ingredients and began setting them out on the table.

"Do you want to chop up the leech wood?" asked Leora, placing a dish of black stringy bark in front of her. "Just cut it into small even pieces," she explained, holding her thumb and forefinger together to roughly indicated the size.

Bronte took out a knife and wooden cutting board from under the table and began working on the bark, grateful that she could do something. It was a lot harder to cut than she'd expected. It seemed to bend and move under her fingers, and the knife blade kept getting stuck in the wood. She continued to struggle with it and, eventually, she managed to form a small pile of evenly cut pieces. But by the time she'd finished cutting it, all the other ingredients had been prepped.

"Can you fill the cauldron up with water? The tap's just over there." Eli pointed to the deep double sink by the door. "We need it half full."

Bronte picked up the cauldron, which was about the size of a large mixing bowl but considerably heavier, and made her way over to the tap. In front of her stood Scarlett, the girl who'd answered Professor Kirwan's question.

"Oh, hi," said Scarlett, turning around with her full cauldron. "You're the new enchanter, right?"

"Yes," Bronte replied with a smile. "What's your manipulation?" She wasn't cowed by Scarlett's appraising gaze.

"If we're going to use labels, I'm a transmuter." Bronte didn't miss the bitter undertone as she spoke. "I suppose we shouldn't label you just yet. Readings can be wrong. They have been in the past." Scarlett sneered. "And I suppose, given who your parents are, we can't really trust anything about you." She brushed past her; stubby nose raised towards the sky.

Bronte gritted her teeth and turned on the tap to fill the cauldron. She glanced at Scarlett on her way back to the table and saw her whispering something to the girl beside her, her eyes flickering towards Bronte. She avoided their gaze as she placed the heavy cauldron on the middle of the table, careful not to let any of the water slosh out. "What's the next step?"

"First, we put in the stripped olive leaf," said Leora, reading the method. She took a small pile of thin green leaves and sprinkled them into the water. "Eli, do you want to draw the heating rune?"

Eli pulled out his scriber and held it to the side of the cauldron. Bronte watched him closely, because although she'd read about using scribers in her textbook, she hadn't fully understood how they worked.

Carefully, Eli traced a series of lines onto the side of the cauldron. When the rune was complete, it glowed faintly and disappeared. A moment passed when nothing happened, and then the water began to bubble.

"The shamans charge scribers with a small amount of their elemental energy, like batteries on the Otherside. Any alchemist can use them to perform small tasks, like heating and cooling things," he said in response to her questioning look.

Soon the water was simmering away. They added the essence of liquorice, leech wood, the bulb of a firefly, and crushed dandelion root to the water. Eli stirred it anticlockwise three times before letting it distil for five minutes. The water and ingredients blended, turning a deep green colour. After exactly five minutes, Eli drew another rune on the side - this time for cooling - and the water gradually stopped bubbling. As it cooled, the dark green colour of the elixir lightened, giving off a faint smell of mint.

"I think it's finished," said Leora, looking back and forth from the textbook to the liquid in the cauldron.

Bronte had no idea if they'd succeeded in making the elixir properly. Leora had been the one to decipher the instructions because Bronte was still no closer to understanding the gibberish on the pages. She glanced around the room at the other tables. Most of their elixirs were in the process of becoming the green mixture that sat in front of them, so she trusted Leora had gotten it right.

"All right, class, five minutes until testing. Please make sure your elixir is bottled and tables clean before that time," called Professor Kirwan.

They ladled the liquid into a glass bottle and washed out the cauldron. At the end of the five minutes, every table had managed to finish, and they each had a product ready to test. Bronte was happy to see Scarlett's looked almost the same as theirs, only a tiny bit brighter.

"Let's see how you all did. Jake, your elixir first, please." A skinny boy with a blond shock of hair brought his glass vial to Professor Kirwan. She placed a drop into the soil beneath the widowsweed. The plant's leaves lifted slightly, although they still had a distinct droopiness. "Good effort, but I think you may have cut your leech wood a bit too thick," said Professor Kirwan, eyeing the plant critically as she added a drop of dark liquid, which made the leaves droop down again. Bronte cringed inwardly. She hoped her own leech wood had been cut the right way. "Next up, Amy."

Unfortunately, Amy's table's elixir was almost black in colour, and the plant looked even worse after it was administered.

"Better luck next time, girls," said Professor Kirwan ruefully as she handed back the elixir. Amy's table giggled to themselves, and Bronte thought that next time, they probably wouldn't do any better. "Scarlett, your turn."

Pompously Scarlett brought her table's elixir to Professor Kirwan. As much as Bronte wished for Scarlett to fail, the opposite occurred. The plant sprung to life, its leaves lifted all the way up, and the webbing hanging off the ends made it look like a black veil. Bronte suddenly understood why it was called a widowsweed. "Excellent effort from your table Scarlett. This is exactly the effect a correct healing elixir should have." She nodded approvingly, and Scarlett gave her a beaming smile in return. But when she turned around, her face dropped into a smug grin as her eyes met Bronte's. Bronte ignored her, keeping her attention on Professor Kirwan.

"And lastly, Leora."

Bronte chewed her lip as Leora walked up with their elixir. They'd been careful to follow the instructions, but if the elixir didn't work, she didn't want Professor Kirwan to think she'd let the group down or that she wasn't good enough to be here.

Bronte breathed a sigh of relief as the elixir was poured over the widowsweed, and the leaves sprung up. It didn't stand up as high as it had when Scarlett's elixir was administered, but it wasn't the worst in the room. Bronte looked over at Scarlett, and she was pleased to see that her face was pinched with contained anger.

"Excellent effort, class. Before you go, Wednesday morning, I want a one-page paper on why the *elixir of life* doesn't work effectively as a healing elixir."

A collective groan sounded around the room. But Professor Kirwan turned a deaf ear to the complaints, and people soon began filing out the door.

"Bronte, I was wondering if I could have a quick word?" Professor Kirwan called just before she reached the door.

Bronte told Eli and Leora not to bother waiting and made her way back to the front of the room. "Yes?" she asked hesitantly, wondering if Scarlett had said something about her.

"It must be a very difficult time for you, starting at a new school. Your mother was a powerful alchemist, though, and I'm sure you'll follow in her footsteps. If you need any help, don't hesitate to ask me."

"Oh, thanks, I will." She masked the instant pang of hurt at the mention of her mum with a smile.

"Now hurry to your next lesson," Professor Kirwan said, shooing her out the door and into the empty stairwell.

CHAPTER 12

Bronte quickly realised that it had been a mistake not getting anyone to wait for her. She'd descended the staircase to find herself lost. Her timetable said she had history of alchemy in A12, but that meant nothing more to her than the runes in her textbooks did. She tried to remember if Leora had mentioned where the history classrooms were on their way to concoction studies, but everything had been such a blur that she couldn't recall a single detail.

Deciding that she couldn't stand around in the hallway all morning, Bronte set off down the left corridor, hoping she would find the right classroom soon. After five minutes of walking the empty corridors, Bronte couldn't tell if she was making any progress or just going in circles. All the hallways were lined with the same lanterns and plain stone. Some had artwork, but she didn't recognise any of it. Then, right when she was prepared to go into a random classroom and ask for directions, a smooth voice sounded behind her.

"Lost?"

She spun around. Standing before her was one of the most beautiful yet cold-looking people she had ever seen. He was tall, with black hair that had a streak of white at the front. His brows were raised at her, and Bronte realised she hadn't answered his question.

"Um, yes. I'm meant to be in history of alchemy, room A12."

He gave her an amused look, a small smile tugging at his lips. "Fortunately for you, I'm going there now." He began walking down the corridor, and Bronte stood frozen, gazing after him. "Don't just stand there. Come on," he called without turning around.

Snapping out of her stupor, she forced her feet to move. "I'm Bronte," she told him when she was back at his side.

"I know." After a beat of silence, he said reluctantly. "I'm Isaac."

Bronte noticed that he had very light eyes, almost translucent blue in colour. They stood out against the darkness of his hair and the pallor of this skin. It was almost as though she knew his face, but she couldn't remember where from.

"What?" he asked, and she looked away quickly.

"Nothing," she muttered, her cheeks reddening.

They walked up a flight of stairs and along another identical hallway that Bronte didn't recognise. Isaac strode beside her, not saying a word. She risked another glance at him. He had a face that reminded her of art, so intricately carved it looked to be made of marble.

"Here we are," said Isaac, coming to a stop. The wooden door stood imposingly in front of them, and Bronte waited expectantly.

"Don't just stand there. Go in," she urged, mimicking his comment from earlier.

Rolling his eyes at her, he opened the door, and Bronte froze on the threshold as every head in the room turned towards them.

"Making lateness a habit, I see Miss Everett," said the professor sternly.

Bronte instantly recognised Professor Wrathwell's red hair and realised it was the teacher who had glared at her in the Chamber this morning.

"Sorry, Professor, we got held up in concoction studies. It won't happen again," Isaac replied, his voice like silk.

"Mmmm, see that it doesn't." He eyed them severely before turning back to the blackboard.

She saw Eli and Nick sitting behind a desk in the front row. Nick's jaw was clenched as he looked at her, but he turned away so quickly, she wondered if she'd imagined it.

There was only one free desk left at the back of the classroom, and she slid into it. Isaac took a seat beside her. "You weren't in concoction studies," she hissed to him as she pulled out her textbook.

"But you were. A half-truth is better than a lie."

"I'm not sure I believe that," she whispered back. However, Isaac was saved from explaining himself because Professor Wrathwell had launched into his lesson.

"Witch hunts during the fourteenth century were significant to our history, why?" He looked around the room, and his port-wine stain birthmark seemed to twitch in displeasure at the blank expressions on everyone's face. "No one knows? Not one single fact about them. What about you, Miss Everett?"

She hated the way he said her last name. It was a name she was still getting used to hearing, but when he called her that, it was as though he was referring to some inside joke she knew nothing about. "No, sir," she replied edgily, a chill running through her as she met his steely gaze.

"Maybe try to turn up to class on time, and you would."

She nodded mechanically, fury boiling within.

"The witch hunts were significant because they marked the period before Hallowless was created," said Nick. Bronte's eyes shot to him, but he was turned away from her. "Non-magical beings were intimidated by the power of witches, and they believed killing them was the only solution."

Professor Wrathwell gave Nick a slight nod of approval before his face turned hard again. "It looks like someone came prepared. As for the rest of you, kindly turn to section one in your textbooks on witch-hunts and read the passage specifically on the fourteenth century. Then, maybe when I next ask you a question, more of you will be able to answer me."

The class opened their textbooks in unison and settled into an uneasy silence. Bronte quickly learnt the answer to Professor Wrathwell's question. Not only were witch hunts significant because they marked the final period before Hallowless was created, but they also continued well after magic had disappeared from the world. For many centuries, innocent mortals were accused of practising witchcraft, and they were persecuted mercilessly, with punishments that made Bronte's stomach turn.

It took Bronte a considerable time to absorb this information, however, because as she read, she could feel Professor Wrathwell's eyes boring into her. Thankfully, for the remainder of the lesson, he didn't call on her again, and she happily remained silent. She spent her time trying to read as much as possible, hoping that when Professor Wrathwell decided to target her next, she would be more prepared.

Bronte counted the bricks on the wall to keep her mind occupied as she waited for her enchanting lesson to begin. She was ridiculously early to class, but she didn't want a repeat of History. Being on the wrong side of one professor was enough.

The only saving grace from this morning had been rune translations. She'd managed to get through the class without incident, and young Professor Faingold had complimented her on picking up the information so quickly.

The door to the classroom opened, and a tall girl walked in. "Bronte?" she asked, eyeing her curiously.

"Yes, Reyna, isn't it? We had history together." Bronte immediately recognised the long mess of brown curls and dark skin.

"That's me." Her face lit up as she sat in the chair beside Bronte. She had strange eyes. One was brown and the other blue. "Don't worry about Professor Wrathwell. I remember in my first year, I turned up almost half an hour late to History, and he hated me for the rest of the semester. But he forgives eventually."

"Let's hope sooner rather than later." Bronte cringed at the thought of spending the next year being glared at by his beady little eyes.

"Hi, Jake," Reyna said as a lanky, pale figure entered the room. "This is Bronte."

"Yeah, we had concoction studies together. Nice to meet you." Jake smiled timidly as he sat on the other side of Reyna. "I'm surprised Isaac isn't here yet."

Bronte perked up. She hadn't realised Isaac was an enchanter.

"I know. At least now, there will be four of us to practice with, so no one will have to partner up with Professor Latoux anymore." A shiver ran over Jake's body as Reyna spoke, and Bronte wondered how bad Professor Latoux could be.

"I'm not going with Isaac. Just because I'm a guy doesn't mean we're friends." Jake held up his hands in opposition to the idea.

"Not me," said Reyna, with a shake of her head, her puffy hair swaying around her.

"I will," Bronte volunteered. "He seems nice enough." Reyna and Jake raised their eyebrows, but were prevented from explaining as Isaac entered the room.

"I see you've all made it here before me," he said coolly, pulling up a seat next to Bronte. "I heard Professor Latoux's heels down the hallway. She's bound to walk in any second."

On cue, the demanding sound of heels on stone met their ears, and they all straightened in their chairs. Bronte's eyes were glued to the door, and her heart rate increased as the sound of Professor Latoux approaching got louder. Bronte's first thought when she saw her was that she looked like a librarian. Her hair was pulled back into a severe bun, and there were glasses perched on the end of her beak-like nose. She peered at Bronte down the bridge of that nose.

"I was told I would have a new pupil. Bronte Everett?"

"Yes, Professor." Bronte was grateful her voice came out steady.

"I'm Professor Latoux. I will be teaching you how to master your ability to manipulate the energy of enchanting." Bronte felt a tingling spread through her body at the words, nervous energy or something else she didn't know. "As with each of the manipulations, your magical abilities are unique to you. When you were born, you possessed a certain amount of power that remains unchanged regardless of age. I am here to teach you how to access this power to its full capabilities. But first, you need to master the basics. Something your classmates have been practising for a long time. Isaac, summon this pencil." Professor Latoux held out a pencil on her palm. She seemed to have conjured it out of thin air. Without so much as a word uttered or a funny arm movement, the pencil flew across the room into Isaac's outstretched hand. "Good," said Professor Latoux with an approving nod. "Do you think you could do that?" she asked, turning her attention back to Bronte. Her eyes were the colour of a lemon, and her piercing gaze made Bronte's palms sweat.

"Maybe." In all honesty, Bronte didn't think she could make a pencil fly across the room with her mind.

Professor Latoux's eyes narrowed to slits of yellow. "I'm not asking for a maybe response."

"Yes," said Bronte after a momentary pause. "I can do that." Holding Professor Latoux's burning gaze, she waited to be yelled at or sent from the room, but none of those things happened. Instead, Professor Latoux's lips split into a wide smile.

"Then let's begin."

Professor Latoux brought them outside, and the sunshine warmed Bronte after walking through the draughty corridors of the castle. Their small group assembled in the middle of the grounds. In the distance, the faint echo of the waterfall drifted across the space to them, filling the silence.

"The first and most basic rule to enchanting is learning how to cast." Professor Latoux stood before them. She was an intimidating figure against the mountains towering behind her, as though she could bring them crumbling down at any moment if she wished. Bronte wondered if such a feat was possible for enchanters. It would definitely be a far cry from simply summoning a pencil. "Essentially, you are fixing your power on a single goal, whether lighting a fire or summoning an object, as we'll be practising today. How powerful you are as an enchanter is determined by how easily you can do this. You saw Isaac summon the pencil from my hand as though it were nothing, but the further away an object is, the harder it will be for you to summon it. Furthermore, the heavier something is, the harder it can be to summon." Professor Latoux pointed to four smooth white rocks the size of apples placed in a line a few meters in front of them. "You each have a rock laid out for you to summon. If you summon your rock successfully, we'll increase the distance." Bronte stared at Professor Latoux in bewilderment. Surely, she couldn't believe Bronte was capable of summoning a rock by just standing here and staring at it? "Spread out in a line, please and begin."

Thankfully, as soon as Professor Latoux issued that order, she came over to Bronte. "Summoning from a small distance is the most basic exercise for a beginner enchanter. To cast, you first need to visualise the result you want. In this instance, it's the rock landing in your palm. Second, you need to focus the energy inside you on fulfilling that desire. However, it can be difficult for beginners to get in touch with their powers. It's like drawing out a long-buried anchor. You must first find the tether. This is why visualising is so important because it helps attune your body to perform the task. Now stretch out your hand and focus on the rock. Will it to come to you," Professor Latoux urged.

Bronte did as she was told. With her palm outstretched, she stared at the rock in the grass and, feeling slightly stupid, she willed it to come to her. Unsurprisingly, it didn't. Professor Latoux didn't say anything, though. She just left her to practise and went to observe the others.

Bronte couldn't help but notice that they were doing much better than her. Isaac's rock had already made it almost halfway to the lake's edge. It flew back and forth between wherever he placed it and his hand without hesitation. Reyna was summoning her rock just as easily. Jake was struggling the most, although he'd still managed to summon it into his hand, which was more than she could say. Turning back to her own rock, Bronte tried to do what Professor Latoux had asked her.

In her mind, she yelled at her rock to come to her. She asked it nicely. She didn't say anything and just hoped it would jump into her hand, but it stayed firmly put. Bronte thought at one point she felt a tingling in her hand, and she wondered if that meant she was getting closer to summoning, but it could've just been the blood loss from having her arm outstretched for so long.

They spent the whole afternoon outside summoning or, in Bronte's case, standing like a one-armed zombie. By the time Professor Latoux released them for the day, Bronte had a pounding headache and a bruised ego. She hadn't exactly expected wonders today, but she'd hoped at least something would happen. On top of everything else, she'd been assigned a long list of books from the library to read about enchanting, and she expected by the time she graduated she still wouldn't have finished them.

Bronte trudged back to the entrance of the school alone. Isaac, Reyna, and Jake had all returned to the city, but she was meant to meet Eli out the front of the school so they could travel home together, and the final bell was yet to ring.

Bronte lingered at the entrance of the school. She hadn't had the chance to inspect it properly when they'd rushed inside this morning. She climbed the wide flight of stairs to the first level, where three golden statues greeted her. They were women, each twice the size of Bronte, with waist-length hair, heart-shaped faces, and eyes fixed in solemn stares. A small gold plaque at their feet labelled them the Theobesian sisters. They were the infamous founders of the school and partially responsible for the barrier that protected them.

The wall surrounding the statues was covered in framed class portraits or captures, as Cora had called them. As Bronte got closer, she realised they were from past graduating classes. Instantly, her eyes scanned the wall to find her mum's picture. She traced back through the years, a tingling sense of expectation rising through her until she found it.

The capture had been taken on the steps in front of the school. The white stone of the castle stood out starkly against the black gowns of the graduates. She read the names at the bottom, and her heart gave a jolt when she saw her mum's: Emelia Everett, first row on the left. Listed beside her was a name Bronte had become all too familiar with: Lydia Theobesian. Listed in the back row, she also found the name Madden Theobesian and her heartbeat quickened.

Hesitantly, her eyes went to the faces in the picture. She found her mum instantly, but the woman looking back at her was a version of her mum she'd never known. Her mum's whole life before her birth had been a woven series of lies that Bronte had willingly accepted. Yet here she was, clearly framed in the truth, standing in front of a school Bronte hadn't heard of until a few weeks ago. Her hair was cut into a bob that framed her face, and her cheeks were rounded with youth. Beside her, Lydia had equally dark hair, but it was curlier than her mum's and fanned out around her thin face. She found her father in the back row, fourth to the right. His hair had been shaven, making the sharp edges of his face more pronounced. The capture had been taken from too far away for Bronte to notice any details of him she might share.

"What are you looking at?"

Bronte's head snapped to the side and she breathed in relief when she saw it was only Leora. Nick was standing beside her, and she avoided his curious gaze as she replied.

"Nothing. I was just waiting for Eli. Are your parents in one of these?" she asked, diverting the attention away from her. She gestured to the frames, and Leora's gaze shifted.

"Yes." Leora found a frame a few spots beside the one her mum had been in. "That's them." She pointed out a woman who looked like Leora's twin and a man with light fair hair and a chiselled face. It was no wonder Leora had turned out so beautiful.

"High school sweethearts," she said. Bronte didn't miss the resentful undertone, but Leora turned away from the portraits before she could question her. "How was enchanting?" she asked lightly.

"Horrible. I couldn't do a thing." Bronte hated admitting it, especially after what Scarlett had said. She couldn't help wondering if shaman Paloma had read her wrong, and she really wasn't an enchanter. She hadn't felt the slightest bit of power the whole lesson.

"Don't worry about it. It'll get easier," Nick consoled.

Bronte nodded but thought bitterly that that was always the type of encouraging answer people gave you when things were hard. But, more often than not, things just got harder still.

The bell rang, and soon the corridor was flooded with students. They found Eli among the masses and headed towards the Arch. As Bronte left the school behind, she couldn't get the image of Lydia Theobesian out of her head. Had the necklace she wore truly once belonged to her? She felt for the chain's familiar presence, wondering what kind of betrayal had occurred for it to come into her possession.

CHAPTER 13

"Have you read any of the texts I assigned you yesterday?" asked Professor Latoux, who had come over to check on Bronte's progress in summoning.

A prickle of warmth spread through her. "Um, I've skimmed a few of them," she lied. In truth, she'd been so tired after the first day of lessons yesterday she hadn't even made it to the library and instead gone home and fallen straight into bed.

Professor Latoux's mouth tightened. "I'm not expecting any miracles from you. Enchanting is difficult, especially for someone starting so late, but I do expect you to work as hard as possible to catch up."

Guilt slid into her stomach. "Yes, Professor." The words were a promise to herself, and Bronte silently vowed that she would find the books after class.

"Good, and if you ever need an empty space to practice in private, come and find me."

Bronte nodded, turning her concentration back to the rock she was trying to transport into her hand. Out of the corner of her eye, she saw Isaac glance at her, but she kept her head facing forward. It was embarrassing enough having to stand next to him while he outperformed her. She didn't need him listening in on her lies.

"Don't be so tense. Enchanting's all about energy flow and not so much about hand placement. In fact, you could summon without your hand outstretched. Professor Latoux just likes to do that while we're learning, so it's easier," he said in a low voice.

"But I am learning," she whispered through gritted teeth. A sound like a breath being cut short met her ears, and she turned to see a grin on his face, his cold features turning soft. For a moment, she saw her mum in the way his eyes crinkled at the edges and the dimple that only formed in one of his cheeks, just as hers had, but then it was gone. She blinked away the memory, trying to focus on his words.

"Here." He took a step closer, and she tensed, but he looked at her with a question in his eyes, and she didn't flinch away as he reached out a hand and touched her lightly on the shoulder. "Relax."

Bronte resisted the urge to roll her eyes. Relaxing wasn't such an easy thing to do when someone was invading your personal space. Still, she let out a breath and dropped her shoulders away from her ears. His hand drifted down her arm. Immediately, she tensed again, wanting to pull away, but she forced herself to remain calm before his searching gaze. He reached for her hand and turned her palm towards the sky, curving it slightly, like you would if you were to cup water in your hand.

"Now it's like you're beckoning the rock to come to you, not turning it away." He whispered the words in her ear, and her body froze; every muscle tightened at the mere feel of his breath against her skin.

"Oh." The word came out softly, and she swallowed hard.

He stepped away from her, and her eyes glanced down to where his hand had been. She could still feel a tingling on her skin where he'd touched her. She flexed her fingers and tried to regain control, but it took her more than a few seconds to focus again on her rock.

The remainder of the lesson elapsed uneventfully, and by the time they were released for the day, Bronte had been utterly unsuccessful in summoning anything. She returned to the castle in search of the library and hoped one of the books she'd been assigned held the answer to finding her power.

"Quiet down, quiet down." The papery voice of Professor Endacott sounded from the front of the room, and the class fell into a reluctant hush. "Today, we will be working on altering emotions. This is a very complex and fragile part of transmutation, and I will be surprised if any of you will be able to grasp the concept within the space of this single lesson."

On the desk across from Nick's, Scarlett sat with pursed lips: no doubt being told that she couldn't do something had rubbed her the wrong way. The rest of the class whispered excitedly. Manipulating emotion was one of the final skills taught to transmuters. The physical world had to be mastered before you could even think about taking on the mental.

Professor Endacott launched into the theory for the lesson, but Nick was hardly listening. If Leora hadn't personally dragged him here, he might've feigned sickness and retreated to the library for the remainder of the day. There was nothing wrong with him. Things just felt dull. He blamed it on lack of sleep the night before.

"Pair up, please and begin. If you need help, give me a shout," Professor Endacott's voice broke through Nick's thoughts, and he forced himself to focus on the lesson.

Instinctively, his eyes went to Leora. There was no one else he would consider partnering up with.

"Were you even listening?" She accused, her brows raised.

Nick shrugged; the movement was so familiar it was almost a reflex. "I heard enough."

She glared at him, and he met her gaze with a grin. This only made her roll her eyes. Leora was constantly infuriated that he managed to perfect almost every transmuting skill with only the slightest effort. He would tell her it was natural talent but, in truth, reading his textbooks had always been a way to distract himself when he'd felt alone.

"You can go first. I don't want my inevitable success to dampen your enthusiasm," he said.

"One day, your cockiness is going to be the death of you."

"I don't doubt it."

They turned their chairs to face each other, and he held his hand for her to take. It was essential for transmuters to touch whatever they were attempting to alter, and while you couldn't touch emotions, you had to be in contact with the person.

Leora's skin was cold, but not as cold as Isaac's had been when they'd shaken hands on their deal yesterday. Nick knew he'd made the right decision, or at least the decision that most benefited him, so he didn't know why it felt so wrong. It wasn't as if he was selling out Bronte for his own gain. What was the worst that could happen to her if Isaac wanted to be her friend? But no matter how much Nick tried to convince himself that was true, everything sounded like a lie.

Nick could feel Leora's pulse beat steadily where their palms met, and he let out a breath, relaxing into his seat. Leora closed her eyes, concentrating on the transformation. He wasn't sure what emotion she was trying to give him, but he gazed over her shoulder and waited to feel something. Looking down through the window, he could see figures standing in a line on the grounds far below. He spotted Professor Latoux and instantly knew who the others must be. He swept the line again, and his eyes found Bronte. Her untamable brown hair was plaited down her back, and her arm was extended in front of her. He wondered how long she'd been like that, standing unmoving and still, like a mime frozen in place.

He could make out Isaac beside her. He knew it was him from the way he stood, shoulders back and head raised, as though he were above everything else around him. Isaac turned and spoke to Bronte, who tilted her head to look at him. Nick couldn't see the expression on her face, but he could picture what it would be. Her auburn eyes would be wide and curious, and she would smile, her slightly crooked smile that caused a dimple to form at the point of her chin. Isaac moved closer to her, touching her arm as he showed her something. Nick looked away, feeling emptier than he had before.

Leora opened her eyes. "Do you feel happier?" she asked, her voice so hopeful that he hated to disappoint her.

"A little," he said, offering a smile.

"That's a start." He made his smile wider until she seemed pleased. "Now you try."

Nick closed his eyes. In his mind, the image of Bronte and Isaac kept playing over and over. Isaac touching her skin, his words making her smile. Nick gritted his teeth and forced it away.

Nick had been reading theory about altering emotions for years now. As a child, he had thought that if he could learn how to do it, then it would be the solution to his parent's problems, and that he would be the one to finally make them better. But when he'd eventually been skilled enough to attempt that complicated process, he'd found he'd lost his childhood desire. He was never going to be the reason his parents changed, and he didn't care enough anymore to bother forcing them to.

It was complex and uncertain, altering emotions. First, you had to conjure the emotion you needed in yourself, like happiness, and it had to be so strong that it filled you up inside. Then, while you remained in contact with the other person, you sent the emotion through to them as though you were two sides of an electric current. If you wanted the other person to feel the emotion for a prolonged period, like days or weeks, then you needed a well of emotion to draw on, but for right now, he only needed it to last a moment. Nick wished he could give Leora a pleasant emotion, like joy or love. But he couldn't feel them, at least not now, so he reached for the closest thing; anger. The ever-present burning rage that simmered below everything else.

"How do you feel?" he asked, opening his eyes.

"Like I want to punch you in the face." Her spring green eyes had taken on a steely glint, and he released her quickly. She blinked, her pupils going out of focus for a second before she recovered.

"You weren't meant to project your anger back onto me," he grumbled.

"It's not my fault. Your face was the first thing I saw," she said exasperatedly.

"Yeah, well . . ." his words were swallowed by the sound of the bell, and he settled for glaring at her in mock annoyance.

Eli was waiting for them when they reached the front of the school, but Bronte was nowhere in sight.

"Maybe she went home without you," suggested Leora when Eli asked if they knew where she was.

Eli shook his head. "We agreed to go together. Dad doesn't want her walking through the city by herself just yet."

Nick sighed, running a hand through his hair. Suspicion sliced through him as he wondered if Isaac was fulfilling some sort of evil plot against her.

"I'll look for her inside. Maybe she ended up at an after-school club somehow. You check the city, and we'll meet back at Merlin's," he said.

Leora had given Bronte some vague directions about where the library was located the day before, and following her instructions, she found herself in a long empty hallway. On one side of the hallway, the wall was split open by an archway. Bronte made her way to it and peeked inside. The room before her was the size of a cathedral. Shelves of books ran across its length, reaching up to the roof, which was raised high above her.

An elderly man whose back was bent like the hunchback of Notre Dame looked up as she entered the room. He was sitting behind a large L-shaped desk, a thick book lay open in front of him. His finger was paused midway down the page.

"May I help you?" If an old piece of parchment could talk, his voice was how Bronte imagined it would sound.

"Yes, I was looking for these books." The man beckoned for her to come closer, and she handed him the parchment. He scanned it quickly, his brow furrowing behind his glasses.

"Enchanter, are you?" he asked finally.

"Trying to be," she admitted.

"Ah, well, that's all that you can do."

He gave her a watery-eyed look as he picked up a battered walking stick and slowly made his way around the desk. He hobbled down one of the aisles without a word, and Bronte took that as an invitation to follow. He stopped midway down the aisle and lifted his cane up to tap a section of books.

"All the information on enchanting you could ever need is here. Just read the book's title, and it will come to you."

Bronte stared at him. She was waiting for him to say he was joking, but he looked at her expectantly. "Um, *The Method Behind Enchanting,* by Henry Grove," she read in a clear voice. Somewhere near the top of the shelf, a thin book shot out and floated down in front of her.

"Read out the others," the man urged. "They'll follow you wherever you go. Apart from outside the library. You have to borrow them if you want to take them past the archway."

"What sort of magic is this?" Life would be much easier if she could figure out how to replicate it. She could levitate everything instead of carrying it.

"My magic."

"You're an enchanter!"

"A very old one," he said gruffly.

"Have you always worked here?" she asked, intrigued.

"Since the previous librarian retired. I love being among books. They give me a sense of peace I find I cannot achieve around people. Good luck with your reading." The librarian began hobbling away to his desk.

Turning back to her list, Bronte read out the remaining titles. She soon had a collection of books hovering around her like a swarm of bees. She was planning on returning to the front desk to borrow them when a book title caught her eye. *Tracing the Theobesians Through History.* Bronte pulled it from the shelf and flicked it open. On the first few pages were the family trees of the three Theobesian sisters, Maria, Eleni, and Sophia, outlining their descendants through history.

Interestingly, Sophia never married, so her line ended abruptly, but the other two genealogies were long and complex, extending over multiple pages. Bronte studied the most recent names. She recognised Lydia Theobesian, who was a descendant of Maria's and connected to her was her brother Madden. Under both their names was the same date of decease, confirming what Frank had told her.

"Bronte!" A whispered voice broke her concentration, and she looked up to see Nick standing in front of her. His floppy hair was drifting dangerously close to his eyes. "I've been searching the whole school for you," he said in exasperation. "What are you reading anyway?"

He swiped the book out of her hand before she could stop him, and frowned as he read the cover. Bronte lunged to take it back, but he dodged her with a grin.

"I was wondering about my dad," she explained with a glare. But nowhere did the text mention her mum or her own existence. However, Frank had said they weren't married when her mum had fallen pregnant, so that must've been why. "I know it's stupid, but I thought maybe this would prove that he was really my father. I know it's the truth, but it still doesn't explain why my mum fled or why she'd hide this world from me."

"Why do you need an answer? Sometimes it's better not to know," he muttered.

"My father did terrible things, and my mum . . .Well, I wish I knew what happened. You might not care for comfort or closure, but I feel like I need these answers so I can move on."

Nick ran a hand through his hair, which fell back into place immediately and released a breath. "Come on, I want to show you something."

"But the books . . ." They were still floating around her head like a loyal paper swarm.

In a few short seconds, Nick had plucked them out of the air and carried the pile to the front desk. He placed them beside the librarian and muttered something to him before returning to her. "Any other objections?"

"Where are Eli and Leora?" She'd been released early from her enchanting lesson today, but if Nick was here, that meant the school day was over. She hadn't even heard the bell. It was as though time had warped while she'd been inside the library.

"At Merlin's. We thought maybe you'd gone back to the city already. Now can we please go?"

Resigned, Bronte motioned for him to go wherever he was taking her. They arrived at the far side of the library, stopping in front of a section of books dedicated to cooking. "Thinking of becoming a chef?" she asked blandly. Eli and Leora were probably wondering if they'd been abducted by now.

"I hardly think anyone would want to eat the food I cook." Before she could agree, Nick reached out and pulled on a book titled *"How to Appropriately use Frog Spawn in Cooking"*. Except the book didn't leave the shelf, it tilted forwards, and the whole section of shelving swung open to reveal a gloomy passageway.

Bronte eyed the dank space sceptically. "Only someone with a death wish would be stupid enough to go down there alone."

"But you're not alone."

"Exactly. I'm with a guy, which would be even more stupid."

"If I wanted to murder you, I would've done it days ago."

"Comforting. You go first, then." Nick looked at her like she was being ridiculous, but she'd had too many lectures from her mum in the past to simply traipse willing into some dark passage with a young man she barely knew. "Get moving," she urged.

Nick muttered something that sounded a lot like a curse as he walked by, and Bronte debated whether to shut the door behind him and lock him inside. She settled for glaring at his back as she followed him. The shelf door closed behind her, and there was a beat of darkness before the lamps on the wall flamed to life.

The passage led to a dead end, but Nick pulled on a candelabra, and a section of the wall descended into the floor, revealing an exposed balcony, really just a small semicircle of space jutting out from the side of the castle. A stone balustrade was all that prevented them from plummeting to their death. Bronte edged backwards until she was pressed against the stone wall. She needed its solidness as a reminder that she was safe.

Nick had already walked onto the platform, but when he noticed she wasn't with him, he turned back. He frowned, his face scrunching in a way Bronte may well have found funny if she wasn't standing near the edge of a two-hundred-meter drop.

"You've gone white."

No kidding. Bronte swallowed and took a deep breath. "I don't like heights," she said, her voice strained.

She didn't know where she'd gotten her fear from. It was one of those things that she forgot existed until she was standing on the edge of something, and she couldn't bring herself to look down. Bronte silently cursed him for bringing her here.

She waited for the witty comeback or sarcastic joke, but Nick's face turned serious. He came towards her and held out a hand. "You're not going to fall."

She batted his hand away. "I'm fine. I just need a minute." Shaking his head, a small grin on his face, Nick backed away from her and waited. "Stop staring at me like a wild animal. I'm not about to run away."

"No need to bite my head off about it."

There wasn't a look withering enough to give him, but Bronte tried her best. She slowly eased her back away from the wall and stepped towards the balcony. "I swear if you come close to me, you're dead. Actually, if you could just stand over there, that would be great." She pointed to the corner of the balcony. It wasn't a very large space, so the corner was only a few steps away, but she needed him in her sights, but also far enough away that she didn't fear him suddenly throwing her over.

Nick held up his hands and retreated to where she'd pointed. Satisfied, she took another step, then another. Bronte forced herself to keep moving even though her mind screamed at her that she was doing something stupid. When she was in the open, she stretched her arms out as far as they would go until she touched the stone balustrade, then she wrapped her hands around it, her knuckles turning white as she did so.

From the corner of her eye, she could see Nick had pressed his lips together in an effort to hold back a laugh. Bronte would slap the grin off his face if her legs could move another step. But, instead, she shuffled forward, closing the remaining space between her and the edge. The primal part inside Bronte was urging her to retreat, or at least close her eyes and imagine she was somewhere at ground level, but as she turned her gaze outwards, that part of her quietened.

The sun had sunk low, and the last rays painted the sky in electric pink. The balcony was so high that stray clouds drifted below her, but when they shifted just the right way, she could see Namire. The city was coming alight in preparation for nightfall, and it glowed at her like a whole clump of fallen stars had landed together. It was an unreal feeling, looking down on the world from so high up and so far away. It was as though she was spying, like an angel who peeked through the clouds when God had forbidden her to look. A cold wind blew across the castle walls, yet Bronte didn't wrap her arms around herself. She stood in the breeze, clutching the stone balustrade and reminded herself that she wouldn't fall.

"Can I move yet?"

Nick's voice broke through her thoughts, and she was forced to acknowledge his existence. For a moment, she'd felt like the only person alive. "Yes. But keep your distance," she warned. He took up a place an arm's length away from her.

"There's the Canal." Nick pointed out.

Bronte looked at the tiny strip of blue with small figures moving around it. The whole of Namire was in front of them at a bird's eye view. She could see from the ocean to the left all the way to the mountains on the right. Bronte even located the Shrine. It was a white blob amongst the trees, and the valley behind it was a blur of colour from all the flowers of the dead. She hoped her mother's had grown. Then they, too, would get to look out on this beautiful world.

"What's out that way?" she asked. Beyond the city line was a blanket of green that extended until it met the horizon.

Nick followed her gaze. "Everything else. The Whispering Wood, the Merrylands where the Fae live, and Velkrian, the homeland of the werewolves."

She remembered Frank mentioning the other beings that lived in

Hallowless. She didn't know why she hadn't asked about them earlier. "Have you ever seen them, the Fae or the werewolves?"

"No. When Hallowless was first created, the world wasn't split into regions. But a few years later, a treaty was signed after a disagreement over land, which gave each of the major species their own territory. Think of Hallowless as like a triangle. We each occupy one end, and the Whispering Wood is where all types of creature's roam.

"And no one ever mixes together?"

She found it hard to believe that they all stayed in their neat little territories, but Nick shook his head. "The boundary is heavily secured by protective wards as well as the High Guard. Since I've been alive, I don't recall there ever being a breach."

The wind had blown his hair back from his face, and for once, it wasn't at risk of covering his eyes. They fell silent, and Bronte watched him as he watched the darkening sky. Somehow, he'd drawn closer to her during the conversation, but she didn't step away. She took in his sharp jaw and straight nose. If she reached out and traced those hard lines, she imagined they would mould beneath her fingers like clay, because Nick was one of those people that you looked at and wondered if they were real or if they had been handcrafted by the gods and could just as easily be unmade.

He opened his mouth and spoke, and before the wind could snatch his words away, she caught them. "You'll find your answers. And even though they might not be what you want, you won't have to discover them alone. I'll be here."

Bronte didn't have any words to express what that sentence meant to her, so she edged her fingers closer to his until their pinkies were touching. He moved his hand and covered hers with it. Nick's fingers were warm and firm as they intertwined with her own. Everything felt heightened; her thundering pulse and beating heart, her shortened breath, and her shaking limbs. As she peeked over the edge of the balustrade and took in the sheer drop below, Bronte realised that she had never really been fearful of heights, only of falling.

CHAPTER 14

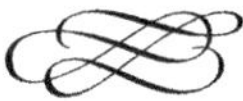

Nick was at The Sparrow again. Night had barely fallen, yet the room was crowded. The gambling tables were already full of patrons believing that tonight would be their night, and that the goddess would bless them alone with luck, as if the people around them weren't all praying for the same thing.

Nick enjoyed watching the hope in someone's face rise every time they had a small win. But what he liked even more was the slow, crushing realisation that followed, as their luck begun to ebb away, until finally it hit them that they had just blown all their money on a stupid game. But no matter how disheartened they were by the night's end, they would always return the following day with their hope renewed, offering their prayers to the goddess once again.

Nick watched this cycle occur from behind the safety of his pianoforte, constantly wondering if tonight would be the night that finally broke them; that would finally make them quit. But when an addict craved something, it didn't matter the harm it caused, the fix was always better, and that intense moment of exhilaration when they won kept them coming back, night after night.

Nick's eyes found Celia in the crowd, delivering drinks to a table in the corner. Her face was open and smiling now, but she'd been frowning when Nick had arrived. He'd been late again. After returning to Namire with Bronte, they'd gone to Merlin's Beard, where they'd met an extremely worried Eli and Leora. It hadn't taken long to assure them that Bronte was fine, and soon they were all eating food and drinking beneath Merlin's Beard's glittering ceiling. They'd been having such a good time that Nick hadn't noticed the darkening sky. He'd rushed out, followed by the fleeting look of gratitude on Bronte's face as she'd watched him go.

Nick didn't know why he'd shown Bronte the secret passage. It had been an accident when he'd found it back in his first year. Isaac had gotten on his nerves, and he'd scoured the library shelves to find a way to get revenge. His eyes had caught sight of an old decaying book about frog spawn; he'd pulled it out, and suddenly the wall had swung open to reveal a hidden chamber. He remembered the feeling of standing on the edge of the balcony for the first time. It had been so easy to convince himself that nothing was real. That the houses below him were toy models, and the people were figurines, and nothing that happened down there could ever touch him because he was now so far above it all.

Nick had kept the spot a secret for years, venturing there alone when he needed time to think. It had been his, but he didn't regret showing Bronte. Something in her eyes had told him that she needed it.

He smiled, thinking back to her shaking limbs as she'd reached out for the balustrade and the glare she'd shot his way when he'd spoken, as if it was a crime that he'd broken her peace. But there was only so long Nick could remain silent around her. The words just seemed to tumble out without him realising.

The door to The Sparrow opened, and his fingers faltered on the keys as Nick saw who walked in. He would know that dark hair with its single icy white lock anywhere, but he'd never expected to find him here at this time of night. Nick's eyes met Isaac's across the room, and he returned his cold stare. Isaac slunk inside and sat at an empty table directly in Nick's line of vision. Jealousy flared inside him as he thought of Isaac touching Bronte's arm earlier that day. Nick stopped playing mid-song and walked towards him, having no idea what he was doing until he stood before Isaac's table.

"Back so soon?" he asked.

Isaac's mouth tightened. "Why'd you stop?" He gave a lazy tilt of his head towards the pianoforte.

Nick shrugged. "You can only play for so long before all the songs start to sound the same."

Celia appeared beside Nick as though she had transported across the room in the blink of an eye. "What can I get for you?" she asked Isaac sweetly, but Nick noticed the glimmer of distaste behind her eyes.

"I'm not fussed. Any ale will do."

"You're not of legal age," she pointed out, a smile still on her face.

Isaac shrugged. "But these drinks pay your wages, don't they? You know your boss is more worried about getting money in his hands than bending a rule or two." He tossed a full moneybag onto the table, its contents clinking heavily. "Who's going to question me in a place like this anyway?" He raised a brow at her, and Celia's smile turned steely.

"Your order won't be long," she said, her lips set in a thin line of disproval. Her eyes met Nick's for a fraction of a second, long enough for him to see the question behind them. Nick wanted it answered as much as she did. Why was Isaac here?

"I bet you've got enough alcohol stored at your manor, so why bother coming here?"

"Change of scenery. Are you going to sit or just hover?"

"Sitting would make people assume I'm willingly enduring your company, and that's not the kind of image I want for myself. I don't mind standing."

"Suit yourself. I know someone who is willing to spend time with me, though. Bronte seems to be warming up nicely."

Nick ignored the comment. "Did you come all the way here to tell me that, or do you actually have some news about your little project?"

"Turns out contacting the dead isn't as easy as you'd think. But yes, I did come to hold up my end of the deal. I figured coming to you would be less suspicious than anyone seeing us talking at school."

"Fine, so what's the update."

"That is the update, I made an unsuccessful attempt last night, and we won't be able to try again until the next moon cycle is complete. The book says that for beginners it's best to attempt a connection during a new moon when the gates between realms are weakest, and that won't be for another month."

"Your drink, sir." Celia reappeared, placing a full tankard in front of Isaac.

Isaac nodded his thanks, and Celia left. "To the goddess." Isaac raised his tankard at Nick before downing the whole thing. "How are your parents doing? You might end up needing to contact them from beyond the grave if they keep up their *habits*." Isaac paused before the last word, and Nick knew exactly what he was insinuating, but he didn't question how Isaac knew about the drinking.

There was gossip in the south, and it wouldn't be difficult for Isaac to find out a thing like that if he asked around. So instead of reacting, Nick let Isaac's words hang in the space between them until they meant nothing.

"I see you've learnt control. Good for you." Isaac stood. "See you around."

Nick's fingers itched to throw the tankard at the back of Isaac's head, but he remained entirely still until the door closed behind him. One day Isaac would find himself in the wrong place at the wrong time, and he would be there too.

Nick walked home that morning, reeling from his interaction with Isaac. He knew he would be a fool to ever trust him but, for some reason, he'd expected a certain level of respect now they'd entered upon an agreement together. But Isaac wasn't that kind of person.

Nick neared the Arch by his house when an unpleasant smell - even for the south - hit his nose. He quickly located the victim. The gulls were picking at a carcass dumped on the corner of an alley. Nick got closer, and his stomach tightened as he recognised the patterning on the fur. It was Chester, the cat Xander had been looking for over a week ago now. There was nothing to indicate the cause of death, apart perhaps for the birds now picking at it. Luckily, they hadn't done much damage yet, and he waved them off despite their angry caws at being denied a meal.

Nick couldn't leave the cat to be bird feed, so he took off his shirt and wrapped it around the body. He carried it home, leaving it on the porch as he quickly dressed into his school clothes. By the time he took the cat to Xander's, it would be quicker to stay at Eli's until they left for school.

The sky was lightening when he reached Xander's, but it was still the early hours of the morning. Thankfully, a glow came from inside the house, so Nick knocked on the door.

Xander emerged, looking bleary-eyed. "Nicholas?"

"I found Chester."

Xander's eyes fell to the bundle in his arms, and his face dropped as he comprehended what he saw.

"Chester," he sighed. "Where did you find him?"

"By the Arch in the south."

"I didn't think he liked the south," Xander murmured. "I guess he was getting on in years. The goddess will look after him now. I'll take him. I need to go break the news to Vaughn. He'll be devastated."

"I understand. So sorry for your loss." Consolation was all Nick could offer him.

Eli's house was a short walk up the street. Unsurprisingly, all the lights were still off. Eli slept like the dead, and Nick would have more chance of waking Chester than him. But he didn't want to wake Frank or Nina either, so he collected a small pile of pebbles from the path and made his way to where he knew he would find Bronte's window. Nick threw pebble after pebble, waiting patiently for the curtain to open. He just hoped Bronte wasn't like Eli.

By the time he reached his second handful of pebbles, Nick was considering other options. Then finally, the curtain was drawn open.

Bronte's head popped out the window. "Nick, what are you doing?" she hissed.

"I've come to profess my undying love for you," he whisper-shouted.

"Then you're out of luck because anyone who truly loved me would know not to wake me before the sun's risen."

Nick's mouth twisted at the anger in her voice. Yet he didn't feel the slightest bit bad about waking her, if only for the entirely selfish reason that he was happy to see her. "Can you open the door, please?"

Her mouth flattened. He knew she was debating closing the window and leaving him out here, but he shook the remaining pebbles to remind her that he would keep trying until he was let in.

"Fine. But profess your undying love during the day next time." She slammed the window shut and drew the curtain.

He couldn't stop smiling as he walked to the front door, which opened for him within seconds.

"Why do you look like that?" Bronte gestured at him vaguely as she let him in.

"Like what?"

"So happy. It's unnatural this early. What are you doing here anyway?"

"Oh." The smile was quickly wiped off his face when he remembered the reason. "I found Chester the cat. Dead. He was about to become bird feed, so I delivered the body to Xander. It was easier just to come here than go back to the south and leave again for school."

Bronte's mouth opened in horror. "What happened to him?"

Nick shrugged. "Old age."

Bronte frowned. "Poor cat."

They stood in silence for a moment, and Bronte shifted on her feet.

"I thought you wanted to get back to sleep. Nice pyjamas, by the way. What is that thing?" A picture of a brown bear in a red hat and a blue coat was smiling at him.

"It's Paddington Bear." She folded her arms across her stomach defensively. "It's a popular bear on the Otherside. Anyway, I'm up now. Why don't I make us some tea?"

"I could drink some."

He followed Bronte into the kitchen, and his smile returned as he watched her prepare the tea. He forgot all about his run-in with Isaac earlier, or about Chester, the unfortunate cat, because at that moment, Nick felt there were more important things to think about. Like why he was falling for a girl he shouldn't have allowed himself to ever like.

CHAPTER 15

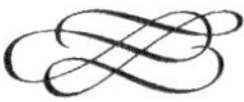

Despite her best wishes, Bronte's attempts at summoning that day were once again fruitless, and she'd finally caved, asking Professor Latoux if there was a space where she could practice alone. Bronte hadn't thought she could stand another second outside, staring at her stupid rock as it remained firmly on the ground.

Professor Latoux had led her to an empty classroom in a deserted alcove of the school. Old chairs were stacked against the back wall, and a few tables were scattered around the open floorspace, but Bronte supposed it was the best she could ask for. She'd told Eli she would meet him at Merlin's Beard in an hour, but as the time began to tick past, she had begun to lose hope that she would make any progress before she had to leave.

Dust tickled her nose and, not for the first time since she'd arrived, she sneezed, her eyes watering from the force of it. She turned her gaze back to her pencil once she'd recovered. Bronte had chosen a brand new one in honour of the occasion and sharpened it to a point. But it still lay unmoving on the floor in the middle of the room. She'd failed spectacularly at achieving anything remotely like summoning in the last half hour. No matter how long she stared at the damned thing, it wouldn't move.

A light tread in the hallway broke Bronte's concentration. She wasn't expecting anyone to find her, tucked away in this insignificant and forgotten room, far away from the main part of the school. Perhaps Professor Latoux was returning to check on her. She sighed and waited glumly for the door to open, not looking forward to having to report her failure.

"Bronte." Isaac hesitated on the threshold as though unsure whether he should enter the room.

"Isaac. I thought you'd already gone home."

He finally entered the room but remained close to the door. "I had to go to the library," he explained. "Any luck?" he asked, with a meaningful glance at the pencil. "Professor Latoux suggested I should check on you and see whether you needed any help, given I'm the most advanced in the class."

Bronte shook her head. "It won't budge."

Isaac effortlessly made the pencil fly into his hand without so much as a twitch of his fingers.

Bronte shot him a mock glare. "There's no need to show off. I know you're capable of summoning anything."

"And so are you. Learning your first skill as an enchanter is hard. It's like trying to connect wires in the dark. But once you do, once you get that first spark, everything else will come easily."

"Or maybe I'll be stumbling around forever, accidentally shocking myself every now and then."

Isaac's stare was enough to tell her that he didn't appreciate her attempt at a joke. He sent the pencil back to the floor with a swift flick of his hand. "Your power runs through your whole body - every vein, every bone - and in every beat of your heart. You just have to call it. Close your eyes."

She raised her brows, suspicion instantly creeping through her. "Why?"

He sighed, running a hand through his black hair. The gesture instantly made her think of Nick, and for a moment, guilt gripped her stomach, although she had no real reason to feel that way. She and Nick were no more than friends, as were her and Isaac. But Bronte couldn't help thinking back to this morning. Despite her original annoyance at being woken up she'd enjoyed his company as they'd drunk their tea. They hadn't spoken much but his presence had been enough. Bronte had found herself needing company more than ever these days. If only to distract herself from the cloud of thoughts that came when she was alone. Reluctantly, she shoved aside the image of Nick sipping dark liquid from a porcelain teacup and instead forced herself to focus on Isaac.

His light blue eyes were fixed on her. "You'll just have to trust me."

At this point, Bronte didn't have anything to lose by complying, so she shut her eyes. She heard Isaac walk toward her, and she tensed.

"Take a deep breath," he whispered close to her ear. The warmth of his breath tickled her skin. Blocking him out, she breathed in, letting the air fill her lungs before she exhaled slowly.

"Can you feel it?" Isaac asked, his voice further away now.

Bronte let her body relax, listening to the quiet sound of her lungs as she inhaled and exhaled. She was reminded of the afternoons when she joined her mum in yoga, constantly told to turn within. As a child she had never been good at complying. She had always been too focused on what was happening around her: the sounds of someone breathing too loudly on the mat beside hers; the traffic rushing past outside; the soft hum of the air conditioner that she never seemed able to ignore. But, as Bronte had gotten older, on the rare occasions when she'd sat in on a class with her mum, she'd found she no longer had those issues. She could've lain for hours, unmoving. Her outside problems hadn't touched her in those moments. Her mum's illness. The looming prospect of orphanhood. It had all seemed irrelevant.

Bronte tuned out all her worry and focused on herself. In the space between one breath and the next, she felt the faint, almost imperceptible, hum of energy within her. Just as the deepest rivers run silent, she'd never noticed its sound before. Bronte called to it until it pulsed urgently within, a solid beat that seemed to say, I'm here, I've always been here, you just didn't know. Envisioning the pencil on the ground, she held her palm up like Isaac had shown her. Come, she asked, come to me. And Bronte knew as sure as a mother knows her own child that it would. The light weight of the pencil landed in her hand, but she jerked away as a stabbing pain shot through her. She opened her eyes to see that the top of the pencil had impaled itself at the base of her palm. Without thinking she pulled it out and winced as blood welled in the wound.

"Control is what you need to work on now." Isaac observed.

The blood was starting to run, and she reached into her pocket with her good hand, knowing she had a tissue somewhere. Finding it, she pulled it out but, in her haste, dropped it on the floor. She quickly bent to pick it up but, as she did, the necklace's pendant fell out from beneath her shirt. Bronte hastily tucked it back, holding the tissue to her palm as she did so.

"Where'd you get that?" Isaac asked, looking at the spot where her necklace had just been.

Bronte silently cursed as she stood. She'd hoped he hadn't noticed. "Oh, it was my mum's. It's nothing, just a replica," she assured him.

"Why would your mum leave you a replica of the Ancient Triad? Those necklaces are sold all through Namire, but they're pretty worthless. Did it mean something special?"

Frank still hadn't made any headway in his attempt to get her a meeting with the Grand Shaman, but she didn't trust Isaac enough to reveal her suspicions about its true meaning.

"She just liked the way it looks. Were your parent's enchanters?" Bronte asked to change the subject. Although she'd seen Isaac every day this week, she realised she didn't know a lot about him.

Isaac hesitated, but eventually, he answered. "My mother's an enchanter, but my father was a clairvoyant. He died when I was a baby, though." He was looking out the window, the side of his jaw a hard line that drew her eyes.

Her stomach lurched. "I'm so sorry. I didn't know."

Isaac's face remained blank as he spoke. "It's hard to mourn someone you never knew."

"But . . . your mum must've been happy when she found out you were an enchanter."

He gave a half-shrug. "She had her reservations."

"Why? Isn't having true magic seen as a gift or a blessing?"

"Because of the Disciples. She didn't want me to grow up in fear. She was always over-protective of me."

Renewed guilt washed over her. "I'm sorry. I know it must've been difficult. Growing up after what my father did."

Isaac shook his head. "Nobody blames you."

"I think a few people definitely do. I'll always be a reminder of something bad, something horrific. Thankfully, the Disciples are gone now."

"Nothing's ever really gone," Isaac said, his voice barely above a whisper. "Regardless, I'm sorry about your mother's death. She was a powerful enchanter in her day. I'm sure you'll be a great enchanter too."

The look on his face was sincere, and she felt warmth spread through her. Bronte reached out and squeezed his hand. It was cold, and she pulled back slightly in surprise but kept ahold of it. "I'll have you to thank for getting me started. I think I would've gone insane tomorrow staring at my rock, not knowing how to summon it."

Isaac smiled and pulled back his hand. "Bronte, given who your parents are, do you really think that necklace is just a replica?"

Bronte froze at the question. "What do you mean?"

"You can trust me. I have connections on the Council. My father was the late Chancellor. I think it's worth getting someone to look at it because I think that could be the real thing."

"I . . . I have doubts. Frank said the only way to know for certain is to have the Grand Shaman assess it, but she's been harder to get into contact with than expected."

Isaac nodded. "Leave it to me. I'll make sure you find out."

"Thank you."

"I'd better go. But you should keep practising."

"Oh, right, see you."

He'd already begun walking away, but Bronte couldn't pull her gaze from his stiff figure as Isaac strode out the door. She wanted to call out to him, to tell him again how thankful she was that he had helped her, but the words died on her lips.

She still didn't understand why he had the reputation he did. She'd listened to some of the comments Reyna and Jake made when he wasn't there and seen how people looked at him when he walked by, as though he was someone to be feared or hated. Bronte hoped Isaac didn't notice these things, but something in the way his eyes had flickered when he had pulled his hand away from hers, told her that he was used to being avoided.

"We were wondering when you were going to turn up," said Nick when she arrived at their table in Merlin's Beard. "I was thinking I would have to come find you again."

"Did your extra training help?" Eli swallowed his last forkful of food, watching her expectantly.

Bronte could still feel the pulse of her power beneath her skin, and she found it comforting to know that if she wanted to, she could summon the muffin on Nick's plate into her hand. And just to prove it to herself, she did. Everyone's mouths fell open as it flew to her, and she took a bite, sitting down in the spare chair beside Eli.

"You can summon!" Leora stared at her in surprise.

"You stole my muffin," said Nick indignantly.

Eli gave her an impressed nod. "But how did you do that? I thought it would take a beginner a lot longer."

She shrugged. "I'm a fast learner."

In a split second, Bronte decided to keep the truth of Isaac's help to herself. She also didn't want to share the memories of her time with her mum. Bronte would give anything for one more afternoon with her, laying on their yoga mats with incense burning around them. She suspected that yoga hadn't just been a hobby her mum had forced her into. She must've known that one day Bronte would return here and that all the years of yoga would help her navigate her magic.

"We should get going. Dad will be expecting us for dinner soon." Eli glanced at the darkening sky.

"My mum's probably already wondering where I am," Leora sighed.

They left Merlin's Beard hastily, Leora walking in the other direction towards the upper north and the rest of them towards the border of the city.

"Are you coming to dinner?" Eli asked Nick.

"I've got a bit of time. I'm sure Frank and Nina miss me."

Bronte couldn't help rolling her eyes at his self-importance, but a small part of her was happy he was staying.

They arrived home to the smell of stew cooking on the stove. Nina poked her head out from the kitchen as they shut the door. "I was about to send a search party out for you!"

"Sorry, I had to stay late to practice my enchanting." Bronte grimaced.

"Ooo, how did it go?"

"Good, I managed to summon a pencil which is better than nothing."

"Congratulations! Double dessert for you tonight." Nina grinned.

Bronte's stomach grumbled in response. She hadn't realised how hungry she was. It felt like she hadn't eaten all day, but Professor Latoux had warned that she may feel tired or hungrier than usual as a response to using her magic.

"Boys, come help set the table. Bronte gets the night off."

"Thanks, Nina. Where's Frank?" She peered into the kitchen.

"Upstairs in the study."

Bronte wasn't sure the term 'study' was accurate for the tiny room Frank had crammed a desk into. Bronte knocked tentatively on the door and waited for him to call her in.

"Bronte! I wasn't expecting you."

She edged inside. "I just wanted to ask if you've heard anything from the Grand Shaman?"

Frank sighed, his deep chocolate-coloured eyes softening. "I'm sorry, there's still nothing."

Bronte chewed her lip. "Today at school, the necklace slipped out, and Isaac noticed it. I think he made the same connection we have and suspects it may be real. He said he'd help me contact the Grand Shaman."

Frank's brow creased. "Isaac Ives? I suppose he would have better connections than me, given his father was the Chancellor once. Be careful placing too much trust in him, though. I'm sure he's only trying to help, but there was speculation after his death that Isaac's father was a member of the Disciples. I've never put much stock in this talk because it was never proven, and I don't want you to have any prejudice against Isaac because of it. But be wary about his motives."

Bronte nodded, but she didn't doubt Isaac's motives. She believed he'd been honest in his offer to help her. She felt she understood him more deeply now.

"Frank, Bronte, dinner's ready," Nina called up the stairs.

Frank looked at her seriously. "Remember, always keep it hidden."

CHAPTER 16

"Thank the goddess, it's almost Friday," groaned Reyna as they waited out the front of the school for Professor Latoux. "I couldn't take many more days of mindless summoning."

"It's like she forgets that we already learnt this stuff back in first year," complained Jake.

Bronte remained silent. For the first time this week, she was looking forward to their lesson, but it was impossible to ignore the fact that, despite her success yesterday, she was still years behind the others.

"Jake, if anyone needs the extra practice, it's you," drawled Isaac. He was sitting on the front steps. His face was turned away from them towards the sun. His eyes flicked to Bronte's. "And when he says we learnt it back in first year, he means we learnt how to summon a grain of rice from our desks into our hands because that's all the range a young enchanter can manage."

Jake rolled his eyes at the comment, but Bronte couldn't help the small smile of appreciation that came across her face. A moment later, Professor Latoux strutted down the steps of the school. Her gaze swept over them, but she didn't pause to speak as she stalked towards their usual practising area, leaving them to follow.

"Begin." Was all she said when they'd gathered around her.

Nerves settled in Bronte's stomach as she focused on her rock. She could sense Professor Latoux's piercing gaze on her, but she ignored it as she held out her palm. She let her blood crackle with power before she called to it. For a split second, Bronte thought it wouldn't work, that yesterday had merely been a fluke, but she breathed a sigh of relief as the tiny rock dropped into her hand. It was cool and smooth, and solid.

"I see your time alone yesterday helped. This is a very promising sign of your power to come, given your late start. Now increase the distance," Professor Latoux instructed.

Bronte looked at her and saw the slightest hint of approval behind her hard eyes, but that was as much praise as she would get. Professor Latoux drifted away to check on Jake, who was struggling with his own rock.

As she increased the distance between her and her rock, a slight pressure began to weigh on Bronte's head, like the beginnings of a headache. It only worsened when Professor Latoux paused their lesson and enlarged each of their rocks to the size of a boulder.

"Think of your magic as like a muscle. The more it gets used, the stronger and more capable you'll be. Draw your rock to you and place it at your feet," Professor Latoux directed, eyeing the four of them intensely.

Bronte's eyes bored into her rock, and she called to her magic to lift it from the ground. She clenched her jaw with effort, and it rose shakily from the grass. It was as though a great weight was pulling her into the earth, but she fought the urge to release her hold on her magic as she drew the rock towards her. Cool sweat prickled at her neckline, wetting the base of her hair. Bronte tried to hold her focus, but black spots darkened her vision, and her legs gave out from under her. She collapsed on the ground, her rock thudding down with her. Bronte blinked away her dizziness, a headache already pounding at the base of her skull.

Isaac stood over her, blocking out the sun. "Are you okay?"

Reyna and Jake had also stopped to watch her, their faces lined with concern.

"Isaac, move over, everyone, back to your summoning." Professor Latoux came to her side. "How are you feeling?" she asked, looking her up and down with a sharp eye. "Headache? Burning in your muscles?"

Bronte nodded, feeling both of those things.

"You have to be careful, Bronte. All magic has a price, and you need to know your limits, physical and alchemical, or you might burn yourself out. You've done very well today, but perhaps I shouldn't have pushed you so far. When you get home, make sure you rest and take it easy over the weekend. Once you're feeling better, I expect you to practice your summoning of small objects daily and slowly progress from there to build your endurance."

The sound of music woke Bronte from her sleep. She'd been ordered into bed rest by Nina when she'd arrived home, and she didn't remember anything after her head touched the pillow. Her curtains were still open, and it was dark outside, although she guessed she'd only slept for an hour or so if there was still noise from downstairs. Her stomach grumbled angrily, reminding her it needed food after the magic she'd performed. Despite her nap, her muscles still ached, and it was an effort to get out of bed. Thankfully, her headache had gone.

Bronte slowly descended the stairs to find Nick playing the piano. He was facing away from her, but she recognised him immediately. He'd only played the piano once - on the day she first arrived - and she'd begun to assume it was simply for decorative purposes. Bronte thought about retreating upstairs, but from the way his head was bent over the keys, like a fallen angel begging to be let back into heaven, she imagined his eyes were closed. He wouldn't know if she stayed and listened. Just for a moment.

She watched him play, leaning her head against the doorway.

Bronte didn't know what song he was playing. There was no sheet music in front of him, yet his hands moved up and down the piano effortlessly, as though they were being guided by an outside force. It became a song of loss to her, and she was surprised to feel her throat close with the ache of unshed tears the longer she listened.

Bronte wouldn't let herself cry now, not when her mum's death had been weeks ago. Her hand subconsciously found the pendant of her necklace, and she rubbed the metal. Her feelings towards her mum were a mess of overlapping lines, wrung with confusion, sorrow, and longing, but they all pointed to one thing: love. And no matter how much she tried to ignore it, she thought she would always miss her. Even when that feeling wasn't at the forefront of her mind, it would still be a constant ache inside her. Blinking furiously, Bronte stared at the glowing lamp in the corner of the room and waited for the song to be over. Then, as the last notes faded into silence, she took a deep calming breath.

"That was beautiful," she said softly, the words leaving her mouth before she could stop them.

Nick turned around sharply. "Goddess above! Bronte, I didn't know you were there."

"Sorry," she cringed. "I heard the music from upstairs."

"Are you feeling better?"

She shrugged. "A bit."

"You have to be careful. Burnouts are serious."

"I know." She edged further into the room, perching on the arm of the lounge. "What are you doing here, and where is everyone else?"

"Frank had to stay late at work, and there was some sort of stock emergency at the shop Nina needed Eli's help with. Apparently, Fai didn't show up to work, so I said I'd stay in case you woke up. Didn't want you to feel deserted."

"Oh. Well, thanks." She knew Nick could be thoughtful when he wanted to be, but it still took her by surprise.

Nick's eyes narrowed to her throat. "Since when have you had that?"

Bronte realised she was still holding the pendant and quickly tucked it beneath her shirt. "Oh, my mum left it for me."

"It's not real, is it?"

"No! No, it's just a replica."

Thankfully he accepted her answer. "So, that one afternoon alone really made your magic suddenly improve?"

Bronte didn't miss his sceptical tone, but she chose to ignore it. "Isaac helped me a bit," she admitted.

Nick remained silent, and she risked a sidelong glance at his face. His jaw was clenched, the only sign that the words had had any effect on him.

"Why do you hate him so much?" she asked eventually. She hadn't missed the glares he shot Isaac's way across the Dome while they ate lunch. Or the way his lips pressed together if she ever brought him up in conversation.

"I can't tell you," he blurted out after a pause.

Bronte laughed at his grave face. "What do you mean you can't tell me?"

Nick shrugged. "I just mean it would go against my promise that I would respect your friendship with him."

"You never made that sort of promise to me," Bronte pointed out. "Tell me, I'm curious."

He sighed, muttering a curse beneath his breath. "He's from a wealthy family. I'm not."

Bronte hadn't known the financial situation Nick was in, she'd never thought about it before, and now she felt naive for never considering it. "Leora's from a wealthy family. You like her."

"She's not Isaac," he argued. Bronte gave him a questioning look. "We just don't get along. There's no major event or thing that happened between us. It's just a fact, okay?"

"Okay."

Nick sighed again, running a hand through his hair. "You know, the first time I realised there was something . . . different about how I'd grown up was the first time I went to the north. I'd entered a world of people in flashy coats and colourful dresses. There, the world sparkled, when all it had ever done before was show me its shadows. I saw another boy, dressed in pants that didn't cut off above his ankles and shoes that weren't scuffed, and he looked at me like a piece of dirt on his steam-pressed jacket. That look was all I needed to know that I didn't belong, no matter how much I wanted to. I don't trust shiny things. I never will because behind it all is the same grime I know. But at least I grew up around people that aren't afraid to show it."

Bronte felt like a cold bucket of water had been dumped over her. Ice spread through her body as Nick's confession sunk in. It was the most honest he'd ever been with her. It had been stupid of her to assume his past when she'd only ever known him in the present. "Where is it that you belong then? If it's not where you want to be, what place is it?"

Nick didn't hesitate before he answered. "It's a place that I've made. It's with Leora and Eli . . . and now you."

"Not with your family?"

He shifted, the only sign that they were entering uncomfortable territory. "My parents aren't like Frank and Nina, and from what I can gather, they're not like how your mum was either. So, no, not with my family."

Bronte heard the ache of longing behind his words. She had recognised it in her own voice too many times. The need to belong to something, to someone. "I'm sorry for assuming things were different. For never asking you."

Nick shrugged. "I likely wouldn't have told you anyway. But you know now."

"Do you think things could've been different? If your brother was still around."

"But he's not."

"I know, but . . ."

"I've made peace with it, Bronte, and I suggest the sooner you make peace with your own reality, the better. There's no use wishing for things that are gone."

"Wishing is sometimes the only thing that keeps you going," she countered. "It's not bad to remember the past, to want for a time like it again."

"It is if it makes you forget to live. If it drowns out reality. I would know. Wishing is what ruined my parents. They longed so much for the son they'd lost they forgot the one they still have. I'm not saying you should forget your mother, but don't let yourself be forgotten in the process."

"But what if I don't know who I am here? I have so many questions that sometimes I feel like I'm going crazy pretending to understand everything when it's all still a blur. Even the pavement I walk on feels like it could disappear in an instant. I don't know why my mum ran away from everything or what really happened the night my father died. I keep looking for her when I know she's never coming back to answer me, and I don't know how to stop it. I need these answers. I need to know that she was good, that one of the people who made me was good. Because if they're not, then what am I?"

"Bronte, I don't think you need me to answer that question, and you don't need the answer to any of those questions to know that who you are has nothing to do with your parents or your past because, if it did, then we would all be screwed." Nick met her eyes across the remaining space and the fierceness of his gaze tugged at something deep inside her. At that moment, she wished she was a clairvoyant so she could read his mind. The troubling feeling of wondering what he was thinking made her want to turn away. Instead, she watched as he walked over to her and tucked a loose strand of her hair behind her ear. "You're good, Bronte, and that's what matters."

Her heart was pounding against her chest as she looked up at him. His hazel eyes were swallowed by black, and if she could dive into their depths, she would. There was something intoxicating about being the subject of his gaze.

Bronte reached out a hand to cup his cheek and brushed a finger along the bone. He closed his eyes, leaning his forehead against hers. She breathed a sigh of relief, feeling at peace for the first time in a long while. But the fleeting moment ended when the front door was flung open, and Nick and Bronte sprang apart. She whipped around to see Eli and Nina walk in.

"Bronte, you're awake! Are you hungry? I've left stew in the kitchen." Nina instantly fluttered over to her side.

It was only then that Bronte remembered her hunger and the original reason she had come downstairs in the first place. "Starved."

Nick remembered that day so clearly in his mind. The day he'd found out that the world wasn't out to help him but to drag him further down. It had been a harsh realisation, but he was better off because of it. His curiosity had driven him away from the mud and grime of the southern streets into a place he'd always known existed but had never dared to explore. The north was the fabled land of the good and the pure, where he'd heard a river of diamonds flowed, and the sea's smell was nothing more than a whisper in the breeze.

Nick would never forget how the world had sparkled that day. Everything had seemed so new and shiny. Rosy-cheeked women had been carrying baskets of groceries, and men had strutted around with their heads high, and shoulders thrown back. These people had walked with such confidence when all he'd ever known was the walk of the defeated. Nick had wanted to be a part of it so badly because, even at eight years old, he'd been sick of the scrapping and sparring that had been his life since his brother died and his parents had fallen apart.

That had been the day he'd first seen Isaac, and the enemy lines had been drawn. The small dark-haired boy Isaac had been then had seemed like a golden ticket allowing him access into the world before him, but it had been snatched out of his hands before he'd been able to grasp it. Nick had imagined them as friends, but the boy's mouth had twisted in disgust at the first sight of him. He'd pulled at his mother's dress and pointed at Nick. She had looked at him with pity clearly written across her face before leading her son away into the crowd. But even as all the other faces had blurred at the edges, Isaac's cruel sneer had remained.

It had been the face Nick had seen as he'd run through the wide streets, trying to find a safe place where no one looked at him strangely, where no one spared him a glance at all. Nick had realised then that although he'd grown up thinking the opposite, sometimes to go unnoticed was a blessing.

He'd found a corner in a small, quiet park and spent some time trying to throw pebbles into an empty bottle he'd scrounged from a bin. He'd just thrown a particularly bad shot when a girl with strawberry-blond hair hanging in curls around her pale face had stopped beside him.

"You're not very good at that," she'd said.

He'd scowled and thrown another pebble, ignoring her completely. It had been clear from her silky, pale-blue dress that she belonged in the north. The southside women he knew never wore coloured clothing because it was too expensive. Instead, they wore drab, plain grey or brown wool dresses and sensible shoes that wouldn't be ruined by the dirt.

The girl had been carrying a small wicker basket. She'd pulled a muffin - still warm - from it and held it out to him. "Mama asked me to collect these from Pearl's Patisserie, but she won't notice if one's missing. And even if she does, she'll just think I ate it. So, you can have it if you want."

Nick had been all skin and bones then, and he'd taken it greedily, his grimy fingers leaving marks on the casing. The girl hadn't said a word, she'd just sat down next to him.

"You'll get your dress dirty," he'd pointed out.

She'd shrugged at him and rolled her big green eyes as though nothing could have bothered her less. "I have others. I'm Leora, by the way. What's your name?"

They'd spent the rest of the afternoon there, flicking pebbles and eating most of the muffins, until the sun had set, and she'd had to go home. But she'd been the one to peel back the façade of the north. Leora had shown him that it was no different from the world he'd known. They just had a better way of hiding it, behind their pretty clothes and stained-glass shop windows.

Night had truly fallen by the time Nick left Eli's home. He'd wanted to stay, but he knew that if he left then, there would still be time for him to make it to The Sparrow for the evening crowd. There was a cold chill in the air with the approach of winter, and the only people Nick passed on his walk to the south were hurrying home to get back to warmth.

The breeze ruffling his hair made the leaves skid across his path, and he stepped on a stray one, crushing it beneath his foot. He couldn't shake his annoyance that Isaac was helping Bronte. His own prejudice and hatred against him had convinced Nick that his adversary would always be hated by everyone. But he'd overlooked the fact that even monsters could appear as saviours if it suited them.

Nick thought back to his lessons in the transmutation of emotions. If he wanted to, he could make Bronte hate Isaac as he did. Just by reaching out and taking her hand, he could make her despise him. But he could never live with the guilt.

As if conjured by his own thoughts, he looked up to see a flash of white hair coming toward him.

"Why are you out so late? And what's your sudden obsession with the south?" Nick asked accusingly.

"We're both out at the same time." Isaac stopped before him, a sneer curving his lips.

"But for me, it's normal. You, however, should've already been tucked into bed by mummy with a nice mug of warm milk beside you."

"Is that the kind of fantasy you wish for? The love of a mother?"

Nick glared at him. "How's your little project going?

"As a matter of fact, I was just collecting some supplies."

Isaac's hands were empty, though. "What would they be?"

"Our deal is that I let you speak to your brother, not that I tell you how it's done."

"Fine. I'm sure you'll be happy to know I've been holding up my end of the deal."

Isaac smiled. "And I'm sure it's been hard for you. Bronte seems to have taken a liking to me. You've probably noticed she's learnt a new trick. Summoning is one of my strengths, so I shared a few words of wisdom with her yesterday to help her along."

"What exactly do you want from her? What exactly is your motive for all this?"

Isaac frowned. "I don't mind if you make me your villain, but that doesn't make me everyone's. I only want a friend."

Nick almost laughed. "Somehow, I don't believe that."

"I don't see why not." He grinned wickedly at him, and Nick's hands curled into fists. He hurriedly jammed them into his pockets.

Isaac gave him a knowing look. "Let's not have a repeat of last time. I really can't be bothered to make a scene."

"Why don't you give it a try," Nick spat. He spied a rare High Guard patrol lingering further up the street. If Isaac would bite, maybe it would be worth it.

Isaac's gaze followed his. "You're not worth the trouble," he scoffed and walked away.

Nick watched him leave, taking deep breaths to calm himself. He slowly unfolded his hands. It was a losing battle. It had been from the day they'd first seen each other. The order had been set, and he had no chance of being the usurper.

CHAPTER 17

Bronte grabbed four fig leaves, carefully placing each one individually into the simmering cauldron. She eyed them critically, watching as they dissolved into the liquid, turning her potion a light pink colour.

The nerves she'd felt this morning gradually ebbed the further through the method she progressed. She'd spent almost the entire weekend cramming information about how to properly brew a muddlewart potion in preparation for today's test.

If made correctly, the potion altered the features of your face until you were entirely unrecognisable, but it only lasted a certain period of time, depending on how much of the muddlewart herb you used.

Scarlett had sneered at her when Professor Kirwan had announced the test last week, and as Bronte had scribbled down notes from *The Art of Potions, Elixirs, and Spagyrics* over the weekend, it was that sneer that had kept her motivated.

Bronte glanced over to where Scarlett was standing, only one table in front of hers. Her pointed chin was bent over her cauldron, and the steam made the strands of her brown hair curl.

"Bronte," Leora whispered sharply, elbowing her subtly and indicating her potion.

The last fig leaf had dissolved, and she hurriedly grabbed her ladle to sir the liquid twelve times in a clockwise direction. She threw Leora a grateful look, berating herself for getting distracted.

"Fifteen minutes to go, everyone. You should be preparing your potions to bottle soon," announced Professor Kirwan. "Remember to label your vials with your names because I will be storing them until the next lesson so they can get the full eight hours of maturation time."

The extra maturation time just meant Bronte's torture would be prolonged. She would have to wait a total of twenty-four hours before she knew whether her potion had worked, and that was a whole extra day of Scarlett sneering at her.

After she completed the last stir, the liquid in her cauldron turned a deep violet. Bronte drew a cooling rune on the side of the cauldron and let it sit as she prepared her vial for bottling.

They weren't allowed to stopper the potion because it had to be exposed to air to mature properly. Her classmates around her were carefully bringing their final products to the front of the room, where Professor Kirwan had test tube holders ready.

"Listen up, everyone. Your time is almost over. Could the remaining students bring your potions forward, please," called Professor Kirwan.

Bronte looked around the room and saw that most of her classmates had finished. Eli had already brought his potion up, and Leora was ladling hers into a vial. Thankfully, Leora's looked around the same colour as Bronte's. Many of the potions up the front weren't as deeply coloured as hers. But the instructions had said that the potion should look a deep violet by the end. She spied Scarlett's potion, which looked almost identical to hers. It seemed Scarlett noticed the similarities, too, because as Bronte began ladling her potion into the vial, she felt Scarlett's stony glare on her.

Ignoring it, she weaved her way around Eli and walked towards the front of the room. She was so focused on not spilling the potion that she didn't see Scarlett move her foot out from her table. Bronte tripped, splattering poor Ben Higgins in the face.

"Sorry," said Scarlett, smiling sweetly at her as Ben's face erupted in red boils. Bronte's heart dropped as she looked at the empty vial, and she had a strong urge to throw it at Scarlett, but Professor Kirwan appeared beside them before she could act on it.

"Bronte, what happened?" she asked, glancing between her, Scarlett, and Ben.

Scarlett's eyes were innocent and wide. There was no way Professor Kirwan would believe Bronte if she said Scarlett had been the one to trip her. Plus, no one else had been paying enough attention to notice Scarlett intentionally sticking her foot out.

"Nothing, I tripped," she finally mumbled, her cheeks reddening with embarrassment.

"It would be best if you watched where you were going next time, don't you think." Professor Kirwan gave her a rueful look, and Bronte nodded her agreement. "Do you have any potion left in your cauldron?"

"Yes," she said, the realisation dawning on her like a bright sunrise. She turned towards the table but found Leora cringing at her.

"Sorry, I already dumped it while cleaning my cauldron."

Bronte turned back to find Professor Kirwan shaking her head.

"I'm sorry, Bronte, but if you can't produce any work, I can't grade you for anything."

"But . . . but I did do the work. You saw me making the potion. Can't you give me some marks?" she spluttered.

"Unfortunately, no. But don't worry, there will be many more chances over the semester to show your knowledge." She looked at her pitifully, and awkwardly patted her shoulder before turning to Ben. "Oh, Ben," she tsked, inspecting his red face. "Caught in the firing line. You better head off to see the nurse."

Ben brushed past Bronte's shoulder, his face turned down as he left the room. She should've apologised, but she was still frozen in shock. Her throat started to swell, a sure sign that tears were on the way. She blinked furiously, unwilling to let her frustration and embarrassment show.

"Never mind, Bronte. Just don't be so clumsy next time," said Scarlett.

Even though Professor Kirwan had moved away, Scarlett still had a fake smile plastered on her face, as though she was offering Bronte friendly commiseration. Bronte didn't even bother replying. She just numbly returned to her table with the now empty vial clutched in her hand.

"I'm really sorry," said Leora, looking almost close to tears herself. "I never thought that would happen."

Taking a deep breath, Bronte plastered on a smile of her own. "It's fine. I didn't think Scarlett would trip me either."

"She's a sneak. I once saw her put the wrong ingredient in Sophie Pierson's potion just because she didn't want it to beat her own." Eli shook his head in disgust.

"And you never said anything?" asked Bronte.

"No, and for the same reason, you didn't. What teacher wouldn't believe perfect Scarlett?"

As she packed up her things, Bronte knew what Eli said was the truth. There was no way Professor Kirwan would've believed her, but it still stung to know that even though she had been so close to success, she had failed and had nothing to show for herself to disprove that fact.

Bronte stood in front of her mum's old school capture and longed for the time when the smiling woman in it had been by her side. She hadn't let herself dwell on the past, but it was hard to forget that she was walking the same halls her mum had walked, sitting in the same classrooms, and eating at the same tables. Bronte felt like a ghost trapped in a life long gone, making her want things she could never have again. Footsteps sounded down the corridor, and she turned to see Isaac walking toward her.

"Heading to class? I heard what happened with Scarlett."

Bronte had endured her smug face all through rune translation studies, but she was happy to see Ben return boil free from the nurse at lunch.

"Water under the bridge," she said with a shrug. Bronte wouldn't hold a grudge over something so petty.

"I know it must be hard for you with your past, and I'm sorry she acted that way."

"It's not your responsibility to apologise for her."

"I know, but I also know it can be frustrating having to live with people's preconceived opinions of you."

"You're the late Chancellor's son. I can't imagine that's a damning opinion people have of you." Despite knowing the rumors surrounding his death, Bronte had found the vast majority of people still idolised the late Chancellor.

Isaac chuckled. "You're right. All the same, though, I'm still sorry you had to go through that."

"There are worse things."

"I have some news that might improve your mood, though. I invited the Chancellor over for tea, and I mentioned your situation. He told me that the next time the Grand Shaman will be available is during the Lost Night festival. She always attends to bless the ceremony. There will be a short time after when we can approach her, and she can assess the necklace."

"The Lost Night festival?"

"It's kind of like our New Year. The Lost Night is a celebration held on the 31st of October every year. It's the date Hallowless was created."

"That's Halloween."

"The dates overlap. The Theobesian sisters chose that date because it's when the barriers between realms are weakest. All magical beings were to travel to Thrace, where the spell would take place, and the portal between realms would open. If you didn't make it in time, you were sealed off from the magical world and left on Earth. So it's also a time of remembrance for those that didn't make it."

"But don't you have Arches that lead to Earth?"

"They weren't created for over a century. By the time people could return, any hope of contact with those left behind had disappeared."

Halloween was still over a month away, but she supposed it was the best chance she'd get.

"What do you think?" Isaac raised a brow.

"About what?"

Isaac grinned. "I'm asking you to the festival. Will you come with me? I'll be able to get us an introduction to the Grand Shaman once we're there."

"Oh, yes, thank you." The fleeting image of Nick's face crossed her mind, and she hoped he would understand why she'd chosen Isaac. But given she couldn't tell him about her necklace, she felt sure he wouldn't take it well. They were friends, she reminded herself, and nothing more.

They arrived at their enchanting classroom just as the bell rang, but everyone else was already there.

"Hurry up." Professor Latoux shooed them into their seats. "Today, we will be studying blocking. An important skill in an enchanter's self-defence repertoire. Of course, it would be ideal if you never need to use this type of cast, but it doesn't hurt to be prepared. Blocking involves projecting one's magic into a shield that can protect you from both physical and magical attacks. Usually, less powerful shields will manifest as a dark blue sheen in front of you, but as you grow stronger with this skill, the shield should become translucent. Remember that one of the most important steps in any casting is to visualise the desired result. So please take a moment to feel your magic and imagine it forming an impenetrable barrier before you."

Bronte had grown used to the steady hum of magic within her. Since she'd recovered from her minor burnout, she'd spent the past week and a half practising her summoning daily until it had become second nature.

The day prior they had spent the lesson attempting to light a circle of candles. Bronte had thought this task would be well out of her capabilities. But since she'd learnt her first skill as an enchanter the well of power within her had opened up and she'd found accessing it was becoming easier every day.

Bronte had followed Professor Latoux's instructions and focused on the wick of a single candle imagining it growing orange with flames. She'd cast her magic towards it and before her eyes the wick had ignited. She'd followed this process for the other candles until a ring of flames had been flickering before her.

"Your progress has been extremely impressive," Professor Latoux had praised her. "I wouldn't have expected this type of development from just anyone, but we have to take into account your parents. It's clear you've inherited your mother's natural skill. She was an incredible enchanter in her day."

Beside Bronte, Isaac's last candles had flared together, and Professor Latoux had turned sharply. "Control, Isaac," she'd reprimanded.

Quickly the flames had died down, and although his face had been a mask of calm, Bronte could've sworn she'd seen anger in his eyes when Professor Latoux had complimented her.

Now, Bronte focused on Professor Latoux's words as she imagined drawing on her magic to create a barrier.

"Good. I want each of you to partner up and come collect some marshmallows I brought for the lesson."

Bronte and Isaac looked at each other, confirming their partnership without a word. They joined Jake and Reyna at the front of the classroom, where Professor Latoux had placed a bag full of marshmallows. Bronte took a small handful of pellet-sized white marshmallows.

With a sweep of her hand, Professor Latoux sent the tables to the back wall, and the chairs followed, stacking themselves neatly in front.

"In your pairs, choose a side of the classroom. Each of you will take turns throwing marshmallows at the other, whose job is to shield themselves. Later this week, we will practice a cast that is the opposite of summoning, which will send the marshmallow at your target using your power. For today, I want all of your focus to be on casting your barriers."

Isaac and Bronte went to the right side, closest to the windows.

"I'll throw first," said Bronte.

She lightly tossed the marshmallow at him, and a solid blue wall formed in front of him, forcing the marshmallow to the ground. Beside her, Jake had managed the beginnings of a shield. A faint blue sheen appeared in front of him, and the marshmallow Reyna had thrown at him bounced hesitantly off it. The shield immediately collapsed, and Jake let out a shaky breath.

"Good attempts," Professor Latoux praised.

"Ready?" Isaac asked, holding the marshmallow.

Bronte nodded, focusing on her power until it hummed in her ears. He threw the marshmallow, and in front of her, the faint makings of a barrier formed, but it wasn't strong enough, and the marshmallow passed through, hitting her on the cheek.

"You know the point of this is that you don't get hit in the face?" Isaac smirked opposite her.

"Thanks, I had no idea," she replied sarcastically.

The one saving grace was that Bronte could now summon the marshmallow that had fallen at her feet into her hands. She wiped the remnants of white power from her face.

She threw the marshmallow at Isaac harder this time, but it bounced off his barrier before it could hit him.

"How are you picking this up so quickly?" Even Jake had managed a strong blue barrier on his second attempt, and Reyna's was equally good.

"We've had a lot more practice than you. Keep trying."

The next three consecutive throws hit her on various parts of her body.

"This is impossible," Bronte groaned. Her success from yesterday was starting to feel a little less impressive.

"It's not impossible," Professor Latoux said, overhearing her. "You're capable. Your power is, and always has been, a part of you. It is an extension of yourselves, and you need to harness that power in order to wield it as you want. Focus on what you're doing and draw your power out."

When Isaac sent the marshmallow at her the next time, Bronte did what Professor Latoux said. She urged the magic out of her, and a flicker of dark blue appeared before her. The marshmallow didn't bounce off strongly as it had from Isaac's shield, but it didn't hit her in the face. Instead, it dropped to the ground. It wasn't the best, but it was a start.

Bronte felt the necklace pulse at her as though in approval, and she smiled with success. Since she'd been able to summon, she'd noticed the presence of the necklace more. It was like a second heartbeat thrumming along with her magic.

By the time the lesson ended, Bronte had successfully produced several weak shields, although none had had the translucent appearance of a fully formed shield.

"You're improving well," observed Professor Latoux as she gathered her bag.

Isaac had ducked out quickly, claiming he had somewhere in town he needed to be. Reyna and Jake had followed, leaving Bronte alone.

"I have Isaac to thank for that. If you hadn't sent him to find me the other week, I might never have learnt how to summon or connect with my magic."

Professor Latoux's brow wrinkled. "I didn't send him."

"Oh . . . regardless, it was helpful." Bronte thought for sure he had said Professor Latoux had sent him. Although Isaac had also said he'd needed to go to the library, so perhaps she'd misunderstood.

"I'm glad. Isaac is a powerful enchanter. He will be a good influence on you. But he's also very protective of his power."

"What do you mean?"

"He likes to be the best. At the moment, he won't be threatened by you, but at the rate of your development, I can already tell you could be great someday too. Just be wary of him when that time comes."

Bronte left the classroom feeling like she'd walked in on a conversation she wasn't supposed to hear. She couldn't imagine Isaac being jealous of her. If he was so worried about being the most powerful, he wouldn't have helped her find her own power. Bronte didn't know what Professor Latoux had observed to make her think that way, but she chose to trust that Isaac was her friend and not someone who would ever hurt her for something she couldn't change.

CHAPTER 18

"Nick, in here!" Isaac hissed, intercepting him as he walked to the door of Isaac's house.

To call it a house was an understatement because it was nothing short of a mansion. A great block of stone that stood imposingly at the top of Cresthaven Street. It was the wealthiest part of the city, and only a short way down the street lived Leora.

Isaac was standing in front of a barn by the side of the house. Nick followed him inside, and he pulled the door closed. A sunstone lantern emitted a yellowish glow from its position on one of the barn stalls. By the back of the barn a horse stood in the shadow, idly chewing hay.

Nick knew barns were usually a place for animals, but he'd never heard Isaac mention horses in all the years he'd known him, so he felt it was appropriate to ask the following question. "Why do you have a horse?"

"You, of all people, should have some understanding of how mortificatio works."

"Death magic," he replied bitterly.

It was the reason he was here. The night of the new moon had arrived, and Isaac had unwillingly told him that if he wanted to contact his brother, he should come to his house at nightfall. The moral side of

Nick knew he should stay far away from this, but a greater part of him was curious to see if it would actually work. If it did, he would have the chance to talk to his brother tonight, and Nick couldn't let go of that hope. But now that he was here, he regretted ever giving in to that desire.

"Exactly."

"Where did you get this horse?"

"He's my mother's. Lyonn. He's a beauty, isn't he. Or at least he was"

"You're killing your mother's horse?"

"Don't look at me that way. He's reached the end of his life. Better his death serves a purpose."

"What else have you killed?" Nick felt sick at the thought, but he found himself rooted to the spot, unable to leave the barn.

"Just some rodents. A cat. Nothing anyone will miss."

"You killed Chester?"

"Who?"

"The cat. I found it in the south."

Isaac frowned. "I thought it was a stray. But, regardless, I needed something more than rodents or cats. Their deaths aren't powerful enough. Hence, the horse."

"That cat had an owner, and you just killed it." Anger spiked through him.

Isaac couldn't look less bothered. "Death is a part of this process. You shouldn't be here if you can't handle it."

They stood in silence for a moment, and Nick debated what to do, but eventually, he gave in to curiosity. "Fine, how does this work?"

Isaac smirked. "There are a number of ways you can use mortificatio. As I'm sure you're aware, the Disciples used a ritualistic form to kill and harvest magic from their victims. We will be employing a less gruesome method. According to the text, to gain access to the spirit world, we need to draw a series of runes for sacrifice and summoning around the horse using our own blood. Once complete, we will read a line from the text to activate the runes. In theory, you should be given a pathway into the spirit world through the death of the offering, where you can call forth the spirit you seek."

"That sounds unpleasant."

"Well, it's called mortificatio for a reason. It's not fairy magic," Isaac drawled. "I've drawn a line in the sand around Lyonn where our runes must go." Isaac slipped a knife out of the coat he was wearing and passed it to Nick. "Slice your palm and use your finger to draw the runes." Isaac produced a second knife and cut his hand without hesitation. "Don't be a baby. It hardly hurts."

Nick gritted his teeth and sliced his hand. It stung, and red welled out of the cut.

"Good, now copy the runes."

Isaac placed the book on the ground between them, and Nick knelt beside the horse. He drew the runes around half the circle, and Isaac completed the other half.

"Now hold your palm to the runes. When the darkness overtakes you, say the name of the person you wish to speak with. Understand?"

"Yes."

"Good. Repeat after me. Bring forth the Gates. I call upon the spirits to open their realm to me."

Nick did as he was told. When the final word left his mouth, the circle began to glow. The blood runes shone, and a shadow emerged from them. They were enveloped in darkness, and Nick felt like he was suffocating. He wouldn't put it past Isaac to have concocted this whole thing to kill him.

"Nathanial Henderson," Nick yelled into the shadows, remembering Isaac's instructions.

He couldn't hear Isaac or the horse. There was nothing but darkness. Then from the black, a figure emerged. They were blurred at first, but as they grew closer, Nick saw his brother's face. It was the same face of the twelve-year-old boy he had been before he'd died.

"Nate." Nick hadn't expected the gut-wrenching feeling in his stomach when he realised his older brother would forever be younger than him.

"Nick, what are you doing here?"

"I wanted to see you." He couldn't take his eyes off his brother's face. He'd always thought of himself as the kid brother. Nate was the leader, the all-knower, the guide. But Nick was the older one now, and he was beginning to think this had been a bad idea.

"You shouldn't have."

"I needed to know you were okay."

His brother frowned. "Nick, death is not somewhere you need to follow me. But I am okay. How are mother and father?"

"They . . . They miss you." He was suddenly unable to tell Nate what had happened to their family. If he didn't know already, Nick wanted to keep it that way. He wanted his afterlife to be peaceful.

The image of his bother flickered out of focus, but then he reappeared. "I know the type of magic used to do these things. It's the same type of magic they used to kill me. Don't contact me again. The realm of the dead isn't a place for you, or any of the living." Nate's voice was harsh, and Nick's face burnt with shame.

Nate was blurring again, and Nick found himself back in the barn in the space of a blink. Lyonn had fallen to the ground before him, and his body lay lifeless. Opposite him, Isaac's eyes were closed, but his pupils were flickering beneath the lids.

Nick couldn't be there any longer. His mouth tasted like death, and the things Nate had said echoed in his ears. He had killed a living animal simply to satisfy his own curiosity.

Nick left the barn on shaky legs. The walk back to his house passed in a blur. He bypassed The Sparrow. There was nothing that could make him play the piano tonight. When he got home, he went straight to his room and fell onto his bed, praying to the goddess for forgiveness and the oblivion of sleep.

CHAPTER 19

Bronte stared down at the grass-green fur ball at her feet and wondered if she was still asleep. The creature's small bat-like wings were a translucent grey. It tucked them tightly to its back and stood on its hind feet. It stared up at her with wide, curious green eyes. When she'd heard a knock on the door, this hadn't been what she'd expected.

Bronte recognised the creature as a furrow, exactly like the ones from the shop in town, but she'd never seen one here before. She thrust her heavy school bag higher on her shoulder and glanced up the stairs. Eli hadn't come out of his room; Frank was nowhere to be seen, and she knew Nina had already left for the apothecary.

Bronte turned back to the creature, which was gazing at her expectantly. It wore a tiny leather harness, and a rolled-up scroll was neatly secured lengthwise between its wings. She bent down to pat the creature, and it nuzzled its soft head into her open palm. The harness's chest band had the word 'Wilbur' stitched in red thread.

"Hi, Wilbur," she crooned, and the little green creature sat down on its rear end, its toothy mouth splitting in a wide grin.

Bronte slid the scroll out of the harness, and it unrolled easily in her hands. Printed on the front in huge block letters was the ominous headline *'Another animal missing. Hold your horses!'*. The masthead read *"The Scriber"* - Namire's paper.

She scanned the next paragraph, which stated that for the fourth time this month, a horse had gone missing from its stable only to be found a day or two later dumped near an Arch. *'The High Guard are searching for either a beast or person who may be responsible for these attacks. Until they're found, the Guard advise warding your animals with protective casts to prevent further deaths'*.

A shiver ran through her. The missing animals had begun at the start of October, but they hadn't been reported as suspicious until the week before. Wilbur made a keening sound at her feet, bringing her out of her thoughts.

"Wilbur!" Eli's voice sounded behind her, and she turned to see him walking down the stairs towards the door. "He usually flies to my window. I wondered what had happened."

Wilbur flapped off the ground a little when he saw Eli, his tongue lolling happily out of his mouth like an excited dog.

"Here you go." Eli pulled a handful of hazelnuts from his pocket, and Wilbur held out one set of his green paws, taking them greedily. He immediately shoved the entire pile into his mouth.

"Haven't I taught you to eat in moderation," Eli warned, and the little furrow gazed at him with his big, green guilty eyes. He gulped down his mouthful of hazelnuts in a single swallow, flapped into the air and through the still open door, heading back to wherever he'd come from.

"Oh, here." She passed Eli the paper as she watched Wilbur disappear.

Eli frowned as he read the passage. "It's lucky we don't have horses, but I hope they catch whatever this thing is soon." Eli glanced at his watch, something Bronte noticed he did more out of habit than actually to check the time. "We should go. The Arches wait for nobody."

"Today, we will be practising control and accuracy," announced Professor Latoux.

Bronte shared a look of disgust with Isaac. She had been hoping for something easy. It had been nearly two months since she'd started at Welkin, and Bronte was steadily gaining control over her power. She could now summon almost any object effortlessly, and her blocking was always a strong blue shield. She had even managed a translucent barrier a few times.

But control and accuracy were things that required a lot of mental concentration. Just the thought of it exhausted her. Professor Latoux launched into an explanation of what they were expected to do, which only made Bronte grow wearier. To practise their control, they would use a simple levitation cast, similar to summoning.

Professor Latoux had set up four dart boards on the opposite end of the room, and they were each given a dart to shoot at them. The hard part was that they had to use their minds and their magic, not their arms, to direct them. Bronte thought it sounded easy enough, but she'd learnt fast that nothing to do with enchanting was easy.

"Don't give me those looks. Up you get, here are your darts." Professor Latoux passed them each a dart and sent them to the back of the room.

"Best of three?" whispered Isaac as they prepared to shoot.

Bronte considered the proposition. Her skill in enchanting had only grown over the past weeks, and she was no longer so far behind Isaac's capabilities.

"You're on," she whispered back with a grin. Today she was ready to prove that she was truly a powerful enchanter.

Jake had already sent his dart whizzing towards the board, but it veered off course and landed in the singles zone.

"Concentrate, Jake!" reprimanded Professor Latoux, who had taken up a post safely behind them.

Blocking the others out, Bronte focused on her dart, bringing it to eye level. When it was quivering in front of her, she shot out with her magic. It felt as though she was sending the dart through a tunnel. A slight loss in eye contact with the target and her dart would go careening off course. She exhaled sharply as she found her target. It wasn't a direct bullseye. The dart had landed on the smaller outer ring. Still, it wasn't bad.

Isaac shot next. He raised his dart into the air and straightened his shoulders, then he released his magic. Annoyingly the dart found its target, right in the centre of the board.

"Are you sure you can keep up?" he asked mockingly.

Bronte ignored him and summoned her dart back to her hand. On her other side, Reyna made a sound of alarm, and the window by her dartboard shattered, glass falling to the ground in a glittering cascade. A bitter gust of air rushed into the room, sending a shiver through Bronte.

"I'm sorry," cringed Reyna. She anxiously twisted a piece of hair through her fingers as she took in the damage.

"Everyone, hold your darts," called Professor Latoux.

She made a sweeping gesture with her hand, and the fallen glass was gathered into the air. A moment later, it had fitted itself back into the cracked window, and it was as though the damage had never occurred. Professor Latoux then handed Reyna another dart. "Next time, remember we're aiming for the board, and don't lose your hold on your power."

"I understand," mumbled Reyna.

"You go first this time," said Bronte when Isaac had his dart back in his hand.

"Fine." He looked as though he was barely concentrating as he sent his dart across the room. To her disappointment, it sunk into the bullseye.

"Perfect, Isaac," said Professor Latoux approvingly.

"Hear that - I'm perfect," he goaded.

She rolled her eyes at him. "Perfectly annoying." She wasn't about to let him beat her. Bronte shot out her power with a sharp exhale, directing her dart safely into the bullseye. Isaac let out a frustrated sigh, and she glowed inside.

When they both had their darts back in their hands, Isaac motioned for her to go again. "After you."

"It's only fair if we both go at the same time," she pointed out, an innocent smile on her face.

Isaac shrugged. "I'll beat you either way, so it doesn't bother me."

She didn't care to reply. They turned their attention to the dart boards. Bronte could see the small red circle pulsing at her, and the power within her was rising, ready to be used. She took a deep breath, steadying herself, and as Isaac's dart began to move, she let her power go.

Not taking her eyes off her dart, she flicked the tiniest ripple of magic into Isaac's path, and Bronte watched triumphantly as his dart strayed off course, landing on the outside ring as hers hit home.

"Cheater," he said indignantly, a frown gathering on his face.

"You never said we couldn't play dirty. I guess that means I'm the winner." She took a small bow, but the look Professor Latoux shot her way when she lifted her head sent her eyes back to her dartboard.

"You're not the winner. It's a tie." Isaac corrected her, his voice cold.

She shrugged, giving him a friendly smirk. "Same difference."

Isaac took a breath and quickly arranged his features into a mask of calm. "I'll remember that for next time."

Bronte grinned back at him; happy they had no hard feelings over her slight cheating. Ringing filled the castle, signalling the end of the day.

"Remember to keep practising," Professor Latoux reminded them as they packed away their things.

"Have you got your dress ready for the festival?" Isaac asked Bronte as they left the classroom.

It was the week before the Lost Night, and Bronte's anticipation was growing each day. But she was yet to find something to wear. She'd thought she'd just wear one of the dresses she owned, but Leora insisted that Bronte needed to go shopping with her to find something new.

"Not yet, but I have plans to get something." The festival fell on a Monday, so she had plenty of time.

"Great, so are you still planning on speaking with the Grand Shaman?"

"Of course."

They reached the front of the school and joined the rest of the students. She spotted Eli's curly hair above the rest. He was waiting just outside the entrance of the school. Leora and Nick lingered beside him. Immediately her eyes went to Nick, and she saw him tense as he looked at Isaac. Isaac slipped away before she could say goodbye. The day Nick and Isaac got along would be the day Hell froze over. Bronte's eyes flickered to Eli's, and she noticed he too was looking after Isaac with a strange expression on his face.

"Don't tell me you have some problem with him as well," she groaned.

"What? Oh, no." He blinked as if coming out of a dream. "We better get home."

The sun set early now that it was approaching winter, and the castle was already in the shade as they returned to the city. Frank and Nina would be expecting them soon, and with the ominous threat of an attacker loose in the city, there was no time for them to linger.

CHAPTER 20

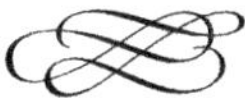

It had been a month since Nick had summoned his brother, and he was still troubled by it. It didn't help that Isaac seemed to have increased the amount of mortificatio he was performing. When Nick had first heard of the missing animals, he'd hoped it really was a beast: that some wild animal had crossed the city gates from the Whispering Wood. But deep down, he'd known the truth of it. Nick's suspicions had been confirmed when Isaac had approached him in their runes lesson that day.

"I'll be performing another summoning tonight if you're interested."

"I already told you I'm not." Nick had been firm in his stance that he didn't want to be involved anymore.

"What exactly did your brother say to you to make you run for the hills?"

"It's not right, killing for your own gain."

Isaac sniffed. "Don't act like a saint now."

"I'm not interested."

"Suit yourself."

"How much longer are you going to be doing this? You're drawing attention. I thought you could only summon on a new moon anyway."

"You can summon at any time. The magic is just more potent on a new moon."

"Just leave me out of it."

But Nick hadn't been able to stay out of it. He'd tried all day. He'd focused on his studies. He'd gone to The Sparrow, but he'd left early, and instead of walking home, Nick found himself at Isaac's place.

The house was dark, but he could make out the telltale glow of light from the barn. Nick wasn't sure what stage of the process Isaac would be at, but he had to know that he hadn't progressed to using anything other than animals. If he needed to report Isaac to the High Guard and consequently condemn himself, then so be it.

The barn door had a large enough gap that Nick could see inside. Once again, a horse stood in the middle of the barn. Isaac was just completing the ring of runes and the final drops of blood settled into place before he put his palm onto the circle.

"Bring forth the Gates. I call upon the spirits to open their realm to me." There was a cloud of shadows, then the shout of Isaac's voice. "Madden Theobesian."

Nick froze, thinking he'd heard wrong. Isaac had told Nick he was contacting his father. The horse began to struggle, whinnying loudly as Isaac's dark magic took effect. Nick burst through the barn door. He couldn't let another animal die, especially when he had the ability to save it. He scuffed the rune line with his foot until it was indistinguishable.

The darkness in the barn began to lift, and the horse calmed down. Isaac's eyes fluttered open, and when their translucent blue colour set on Nick, he saw nothing but anger simmering behind them.

"What the hell have you done?" Isaac shouted.

"Saved you from murdering another innocent animal. Who does this horse belong to anyway?"

Isaac wiped dirt from his palms as he stood. "None of your business. You said you no longer wanted to be a part of this, so why are you trespassing in my barn?"

"Perhaps I changed my mind."

"I highly doubt that. What's your plan now? Play vigilante and save the animals?"

"Why are you contacting Bronte's dad? Is that why you wanted her to like you? So you could rope her into whatever you're concocting."

"You heard that part?" Isaac drawled.

"Arrived just in time."

"Given you cut our little chat short, there's really nothing to tell you."

"I'm not naive enough to think you won't do this again."

"Warn Bronte then. You're just as much an accomplice to the crime as I am. I'm sure she'd love to hear about your involvement. I'm sure that's the reason you also haven't gone to the High Guard earlier, because you know you'd be condemning yourself too. If you feel so self-righteous, then fine, I will spare the horse. You won't find reports of it turning up dead anywhere. But go home now, Nick. I don't want this to turn into something worse than it has to be."

Nick debated his options. But he didn't feel like getting into a fight with Isaac when they both knew what the outcome would be.

"Always a pleasure." Nick nodded his head at Isaac before retreating from the barn. Whatever reason Isaac had for contacting Madden, it couldn't be good, and he knew he had to warn Bronte regardless.

"I'm not saying we don't believe you, but it does sound a little farfetched. Why would Isaac be doing that?" Leora questioned.

"I'm telling you, he's the one behind the animal killings. He's using their deaths to perform mortificatio," Nick insisted.

After what he'd seen last night, he hadn't been able to keep the information to himself, and as soon as they'd gathered in the Dome for lunch, he'd told them everything.

"What's that?" Bronte asked.

"Dark magic. It was what the Disciples used during their reign, but it's banned now. All the texts on it were removed from the library, and we really shouldn't even be talking about it," said Eli, giving a worried look around the Dome. "Which is another point. How would Isaac even learn to do this?"

Nick shifted uncomfortably. "He found a way."

"What way?" Eli pressed.

"There's a guy who sells books illegally in the south. That's how I found out about all this."

Leora raised a brow. "How long have you known?"

"About two months."

"Two months! Nick, why didn't you tell us!" Leora exclaimed.

"I wasn't certain. Now I am. Can we refocus here, please? Why would he be contacting Madden? Do you think he is trying to get the Disciples back together?"

"I highly doubt that." Bronte looked at him sceptically.

"What makes you so sure? You have to agree it's suspicious. Bronte, you can't go to the Lost Night with him. It's not safe," Nick urged.

"I'm not doing that. Isaac has been nothing but helpful to me since I arrived. I understand you have a prejudice against him and, if what you say is true, then it's definitely worrying, but if I suddenly flip, I think he'll find it suspicious."

Nick ran a frustrated hand through his hair. "Say you've changed your mind. Say you're going with me."

"No!"

"Why do you want to go with him so badly?" He hadn't questioned her when she'd announced her intention to go with Isaac, despite everything inside him protesting against the idea. He'd tried all this time to suppress his jealousy, but he wanted answers now.

Bronte chewed on her bottom lip. "There's something I haven't been truthful about either," she admitted. "When my mum passed, she gave me a necklace. I didn't know until I came here, but that necklace was extremely similar to the Ancient Triad. I agreed to go with Isaac to the festival because he told me he'd get me an audience with the Grand Shaman so that we can figure out if it's real. That way, it can be returned to the High Alchemist."

Nick's body went cold. "There is no way you can let him close to that necklace. If he's in contact with Madden, this would only be part of his plan. Once the necklace is confirmed real, he'll be after it. He needs those necklaces for something."

Bronte shook her head. "He's had too many chances to take it before. He wouldn't do something like that."

"You're willing to take the risk?" Nick asked.

"Just give him a fake. I already own one. It's easy." Leora shrugged. She didn't look troubled by any of this.

"I suppose, but the whole point was so that I could find out if it was real," Bronte said.

Leora sighed, looking at everyone else at the table like they were stupid. "The Grand Shaman will be there all night. Get her to look at the fake while Isaac's around, then slip away and show her the real one when he's gone. Problem solved."

Despite Nick's reservations, he could accept the compromise. He wasn't going to let Isaac out of his sight the entire night, though.

CHAPTER 21

"Leora, Bronte. Welcome!" The overly excited voice of Miss Taffeta greeted them as they walked into the shop.

It was the day of the Lost Night festival, and they'd met at Merlin's Beard for lunch before Leora had taken Bronte to Miss Taffeta's.

Today Miss Taffeta had bright orange eyeshadow on, paired with a deep blue lipstick and Bronte couldn't look at her without being reminded of a clownfish with a cold.

"Come on, we don't have all afternoon." Miss Taffeta flipped the little sign on the door handle to read 'closed' and herded them behind the counter. She punched a series of numbers into the cash register, then opened and closed the till. A moment passed, and a door appeared in the solid brick wall in front of them.

"Up you go," Miss Taffeta said to Leora, who was closest.

Leora opened the door to reveal a short staircase, and Bronte followed behind her as they ascended it. When she reached the top, she found herself in a large room bursting with fabrics of every colour. Lengths of material were thrown over every chair or clothes rack available, and sparkly sequins, buttons, and pieces of ribbon littered the floor. A small sewing machine was tucked into the corner of the room, and Bronte assumed it was responsible for producing the line of gowns that hung from the curtain rail above the window.

"The uniform business is my bread and butter, and fabulous frocks are the cream. I like to fill my spare time with things I love," Miss Taffeta said with a wink.

"We'll definitely find something for you here." Leora had gone over to the dresses, running a hand along their skirts. She took down an emerald-coloured dress and held it up, squinting at Bronte from across the room. "Hmmm, maybe."

"I've got a few I think would look perfect on her," Miss Taffeta said as she joined Leora by the window. "Bronte, go to the dressing room and try these on."

She waved a hand towards the corner of the room before turning back to the dresses. Bronte followed her gesture and saw that curtains, which she assumed had previously hung over the window, had been strung up to create a makeshift changing room. Bronte walked over to it, and Miss Taffeta shoved the first dress into her arms before pulling the curtains closed. Bronte could barely hold it. The gown was a mass of red velvet that weighed her down. Luckily, there was a hook on the wall, and she hung it up while she changed.

Bronte manoeuvred herself carefully into the dress and managed to hoist it up. The strapless cut tapered down to a thin waist, which constricted her breathing. By the time she'd tied the thick ribbons that hung from her shoulders and zipped up the back, Leora, and Miss Taffeta were urging her to come out and show them.

There was no mirror in the changing room, but she'd spied one outside and, resigned to the fact Leora and Miss Taffeta were waiting right behind the curtain, Bronte pulled it back. The look on both their faces was enough to tell her that this dress wasn't the one. And Bronte didn't need any more confirmation after she glimpsed herself in the mirror looking as if she'd been stuffed into a giant cherry.

"Try this one next," said Leora, hanging a light blue silk dress on the hook in her changing room.

This new dress was a lot easier to put on, given she just had to slip into it, but it was far too long for her and pooled at her feet. Dress after dress was passed to her, but none of them seemed perfect. The colour was wrong, or the cut didn't fit her figure. She wondered if Eli and Nick's suit shopping was going any better. Bronte still wasn't looking forward to playing peacemaker all night, but she'd already asked Nick to try and be nice to Isaac, and he had grudgingly agreed.

"This is it. I'm certain this is the one," Leora said, flourishing a bright, crimson-coloured gown that had been concealed behind a length of fabric.

The bodice had been stitched with a pattern of delicate flowers, and the chiffon skirts flowed to the floor. Bronte appraised the dress, swallowing down her words of argument. For the first time that afternoon, Leora might have spoken the truth.

Bronte slipped into the dress. The lace up back was threaded with moss-coloured silk, and she released a sharp breath as Leora gave a particularly hard yank on the ends, pulling them tightly before securing them in a small bow. Then, Leora tied the long lengths of chiffon fabric into large bows at her shoulder. The loose ties hung down the back of the dress, stopping just below the waist. Even though Bronte hadn't seen her reflection yet, the look on Leora's face told her enough.

Bronte exited the makeshift change room and walked over to the mirror. She met her eyes in its reflection and allowed herself to really look. It had been a long time since she'd cared about her appearance. The red colouring made her face look flushed, and her tan skin glowed in the dim lamp light. She still wore the necklace her mum had left her. It rested on her upper chest, exposed by the dress's low neckline. But she didn't feel she had to hide it now Leora knew the truth, and she doubted Miss Taffeta would think it was anything other than a replica.

Bronte brushed the dark folds of her hair back from her face, so it fell down her back in one long curtain. It had become a habit to let her hair shadow her face, obscuring it from prying eyes, but she didn't mind people seeing this version of herself. In fact, she didn't care who looked. It was a powerful thing to recognise yourself as a weapon, and for the first time, she understood why Leora took so much care with her appearance. It was important to look the part.

"It's perfect," she said, a real smile appearing on her lips as she spoke.

~

While they'd been inside Miss Taffeta's, the sun had begun to drift below the skyline. Shadows now crept along the road as they walked through the upper north side of the city. Here the small apartments that overlooked the Canal gradually gave way to larger, more stately houses.

Bronte lived in the opposite direction - in a modest neighbourhood - but this was where the wealthy members of Namire lived. This was the north that Nick referred to. Bronte wasn't surprised that one of these houses was Leora's.

It was quiet in this part of the city. They'd left behind the merriment. The Canal had been strung with glowing lights, and food vendors had begun setting out their wares in preparation for the coming festival. It was tradition for people to dress in their fanciest clothes and dance the night away beneath the stars.

Unfortunately, Frank had been stuck down with a virus. Nina had already supplied him with ample herbs to help him recover, but on her orders, they'd been sent from the house for the night so he could have peace and quiet. Instead, they were all meeting at Leora's house before the five of them would go to the festival.

"Home sweet home." Leora stopped beside a little wooden gate.

The house beyond was anything but little. It was a towering edifice of brick that loomed at them in the growing darkness. Leora stood frozen in place, her hand raised towards the gate.

"Are we going in?" Bronte prodded.

Leora had been pestering her to walk faster the whole journey from Miss Taffeta's, yet now it was her feet that seemed glued to the ground. Leora swallowed - the only sign that anything bothered her - then she threw her shoulders back and strutted purposefully through the gate. The front door opened before they reached it, and a beautiful woman with curling strawberry-blond hair identical to Leora's greeted them.

"Bronte! It's so lovely to meet you!" said the woman, beckoning them inside.

"It's nice to meet you too, Mrs Hartfell." She didn't need to guess who the woman was. She was the spitting image of Leora, just older.

"Please, call me Rose. Would you two like anything to eat? A snack, perhaps? We have some lovely cheese that would go well with bread."

"No thanks, mother, we're fine."

"Leora, don't answer for your guest. It's rude," she snapped.

Bronte flinched at the sudden fire in Rose's voice, but Leora seemed undeterred by the change in tone. She stared with intensity back at mother, her lips pressed into a hard line.

Rose's nostrils flared slightly as she locked eyes with her daughter, but when she turned back to Bronte her green eyes were again filled with a welcoming shine.

"Would you like anything, dear?" she asked again.

"No, I'm fine, thanks, Mrs Hartfe- . . . I mean, Rose," Bronte stammered.

"Just give me a shout if you do." Rose walked into the parlour, with a final look of displeasure in Leora's direction.

Leora didn't say another word until she'd led Bronte to her bedroom and shut the door behind them. The room was twice the size of Bronte's own and filled with expensive-looking objects. A golden jewellery box shone on her bedside table, overflowing with glittering necklaces and rings inlaid with different coloured stones. A small carved wooden clock beneath a dome ticked quietly on her dresser, and a silver music box winked under the glowing chandelier. Bronte saw the strange sunstones that were used in most light fixtures in Namire enclosed in glass around the chandelier.

"Just lay the dress on my bed," said Leora before disappearing into her walk-in wardrobe.

Bronte watched her go. Her mouth was half open, but her words died before she could get them out. She wondered if her mother treated Leora like that all the time. It was clear her friend didn't want to discuss the subject, though, so making a mental note to ask Nick or Eli about it later, she turned her attention to her dress.

Miss Taffeta had packaged it for her carefully, but she'd urged Bronte to get home quickly, so it didn't crease. She unfolded the fine fabric layers of chiffon and laid them across Leora's bed. They only had a short time to prepare for the ball before Nick, Eli, and Isaac would be arriving. Bronte's stomach twisted with renewed anxiety at the thought of them all altogether. Leora returned from the closet carrying a large unadorned black box, and she set it down on her vanity.

"Come sit," she beckoned Bronte over to the stool.

Bronte slid into it, watching the box as though a wild furrow might jump out of it. Leora flipped the latch and opened the lid. It expanded into a series of small shelves, each carrying an array of jars and pots. It wasn't the sort of makeup Bronte was used to back in London, with the packaged plastic containers and company labels printed on everything. She'd never considered what sort of beauty products were found in Namire, but it seemed Leora had them all.

"Crushed berries," Leora said. She held a small pot of red powder up to Bronte's face and squinted. "This will make you look a little more alive."

Bronte hid a smile as Leora dipped a finger into the pot and carefully applied it to her cheeks. Her face soon had a rosy tint, which did indeed make her look 'more alive', as Leora had put it. Next, Leora lined her eyes with kohl and stained her lips a deep red. Finally, she opened a small compartment to reveal sparkling powders of every colour. Selecting one, she told Bronte to close her eyes. Leora's finger delicately brushed across the surface of her eyelids and, when she opened them again, they glowed golden.

Even though she'd merely accentuated the features already there, Bronte was surprised at how different it made her look. She appeared older. Hopefully, it would make the Grand Shaman take her seriously.

"I love it." Ridiculously Bronte found her eyes tearing up, and she blinked furiously.

"Don't start crying. You'll ruin my hard work." Leora laughed, but she gave Bronte's shoulder a squeeze, her own eyes suspiciously shiny and bright.

"I'm not crying. You're crying," said Bronte, laughing at how thick her voice sounded.

She caught Leora's eye in the mirror, and soon they were both in fits of laughter. She had to grab onto the table to keep herself from falling off the small stool, and she accidentally upset a pot of glitter, but they were both too happy to care.

"Stop, stop," Bronte pleaded, attempting to regain her composure. "Otherwise, my eyes really are going to water."

Leora took a breath, steeling herself. "You're right. No more." She held up her hands, her face serious. "Now, what are we doing with your hair?"

"Whatever you want." Bronte knew how much Leora valued the freedom to style things the way she wished.

Leora braided the front of her hair and used pins to secure the braids into a small bun. The rest of her hair hung loose down to her waist.

While Leora was doing her own makeup, Bronte walked around her room, inspecting all the interesting objects. There were glittering stones inscribed with runes, some of which Bronte could read now that she'd had a few months of rune translation study. There was a purple stone with a wisdom rune drawn on it and a golden stone with a rune for happiness. A photo, which Bronte now knew to call a capture, caught her eye.

"Who's that?" She pointed to the small girl smiling beside Leora. They looked almost identical, apart from the slight age difference.

Leora's eyes flicked to the photo in the mirror's reflection. "My sister."

Bronte couldn't hide the surprise in her voice. "I didn't know you had a sister. Is she going with us tonight?"

"No, she's sick," Leora replied bluntly.

"Oh . . . that's too bad."

"It is."

"She's not at Welkin, is she?" Bronte had never seen her there, and she assumed if Leora had a sister at the school, she would've at least seen them together sometimes.

Leora sighed, putting down the stick of kohl she'd been using to line her eyes. She turned to Bronte and her face became serious. "What I'm about to tell you is a secret, Nick's the only other person who knows about my sister, and that's only because I used to carry around a capture of her with me, and it slipped out of my pocket once in front of him. So you can't tell anyone. Otherwise, my mum will kill me."

"I promise, I won't say a word." Bronte couldn't think of anything that would be as bad as Leora was making it out to be, but the deadly seriousness of her voice sent a shiver through her.

"Calliope's barren," she said, her voice barely above a whisper.

"She's what?" Bronte asked, thinking she'd heard her wrong.

"She has no power. Only three of her chakras are open, her crown, root, and throat. But Callie has no real abilities, like you or me."

"Oh . . . and that's bad?" She vaguely remembered Frank mentioning that her father had been barren. That his powerlessness had been the reason behind all the terrible things he'd done.

"It is to my parents. My family's . . . powerful, and for them to have a daughter with no ability at all is shameful. They've hidden her away to save their reputation. It was a scandal when they first found out, but everyone seemed to forget and move on to the next thing quickly, and now it's just a hindrance in my parents' eyes. To be barren is a bad thing in this world. They are thought of as scum."

"That's terrible." Bronte's stomach twisted.

"When I leave Welkin, I'll get her away from here. I've been planning, saving up."

There was steel in her voice, and Bronte didn't doubt that that day would come.

"Tell me if there's anything I can do to help."

Leora gave her a tight-lipped smile, but tears shone in her eyes. She took a deep breath and turned back to the mirror, continuing to draw kohl on her eyelids.

Bronte felt as though she'd fallen into a world that had far greater problems than she'd left behind.

"We'd better get changed. The boys will be here any minute," said Leora after a time.

Her eyes were dry now, and she smiled. She glanced at the darkness outside before disappearing into the wardrobe. Bronte slipped into her dress, once again admiring the beautiful material.

Leora came out of the wardrobe wearing a gown that reminded Bronte of autumn. The rust-coloured skirts were detailed with glittering orange sequins, and she seemed to glow in the dim room.

"You look amazing," breathed Bronte, stunned that anyone could be so gorgeous.

Leora waved her off as she helped tie up the back of Bronte's dress.

She scanned Bronte critically. "You're not still wearing those dirty sneakers, are you?"

Leora wrinkled her nose as Bronte stuck out a scuffed shoe from beneath the many skirts of her dress. When Leora wrinkled her nose, it was a sure sign that a lecture would follow, and Bronte braced herself.

"I didn't bring any other shoes, plus the dress covers my feet," she pointed out before Leora could get a word in. She ruffled the long skirts to highlight this fact, but unfortunately, Leora didn't look pleased.

"It's the principle of the thing. You wouldn't get up in the morning, make yourself all pretty and then go out in your pyjamas, would you?"

Bronte thought that didn't sound too bad at all, and from the disgusted look Leora threw her, she assumed she'd noticed. Leora went back into the closet and returned with a pair of white heels.

"Here, you can borrow these." She thrust them into Bronte's hands before she could decline the offer.

The heels had been patterned with golden flowers that matched the detail in the dress's bodice.

"These flowers aren't made using real gold, are they?" Bronte asked, slightly horrified at the idea of wearing something so expensive.

"What if they are? Hurry up and get those dirty shoes off your feet." Leora ordered.

Giving in, Bronte plonked down on the bed with a hiss of chiffon and pulled up the skirts to find her feet. It was an effort to unlace them over the puffy material, but she eventually got them off. Leora's heels were slightly too big for her, but she tightened the straps and, when she stood up, her feet barely moved.

"Now you look perfect." Leora beamed at her. "But we can't forget the final touch." She dug around in her jewellery box before she found what she was looking for. She pulled out a necklace identical to the one around Bronte's neck. "Here."

Bronte took it, replacing her own. Immediately, she missed its comforting presence around her throat. It was as though she had lost a part of herself. The new necklace was cold and felt lighter than the one her mother had given her. There was no beat or connection when it settled against her skin.

"Where am I meant to keep this, if I want the Grand Shaman to look at it?" she asked, holding up her own necklace.

"In your pocket! My favourite thing about Miss Taffeta's dresses is the pockets."

Sure enough, Bronte felt the side of her dress, and there was a small slit where she could keep the necklace without anyone noticing.

A loud knocking sounded downstairs, and Bronte met Leora's eyes in the mirror. The boys had arrived.

CHAPTER 22

"Henderson."

"Ives."

Nick's voice was laced with the same underlying contempt as Isaac's, and he wasn't sure how long he'd be able to keep up this mock civility. He was burning with rage, while Isaac's gaze held a savage gleam of satisfaction. It killed Nick to think that Isaac had the upper hand tonight, and he'd been the one stupid enough to give it to him.

"Glad that's over," grumbled Eli, leading the way toward Leora's front door.

Nick pulled his gaze away from Isaac and followed. In all the time he'd known Leora, Nick had never been inside her house. He had walked by it before, had even gone as far as the front porch, but the residence beyond was a mystery. Leora hadn't invited him over either, claiming her tyrannical mother would never allow it, and maybe Nick should've pressed her on the point, but he never did. He was well-versed in keeping family matters to himself.

Nick reached out a hand and grasped the ornate golden knocker, feeling like he was performing a taboo act. He banged the knocker three times; each one reverberated through the house. Then there was silence, filled only by the sound of their breathing.

A moment later, Leora's muffled voice reached his ears. She was calling to someone, a shushing noise followed, and Nick hid a grin when he recognised the owner of that voice as Bronte. Footsteps tapped across the floor, a latch clicked, and finally, the door was flung open. Leora stood behind it. He distantly heard her greet them, but his eyes instantly fell on Bronte.

She shadowed Leora's side, but there was nothing subtle about the way she looked tonight. The red gown she wore made it seem as though she was glowing. Bronte always looked beautiful, but tonight Nick had a feeling he would be one of many to notice it. A small, selfish part of him wished he could blind all those other eyes. When you found something precious, you didn't want to share it.

But she wasn't his.

She wasn't his.

Something inside Nick caved in at the realisation. He was just like everyone else: an admirer, an onlooker. His arm wouldn't be the one she took as she entered the festival, his hands wouldn't guide her through the steps of the dances, and her eyes wouldn't look at him in joy as music floated around them. He'd made a stupid deal, and now he was paying for it.

For a breath or two, he stood frozen, gripped by the deep-seated ache to have someone, to be someone's. Nick watched on hopelessly as Isaac stepped in front of him, took Bronte's hand and brought it to his mouth. He brushed a kiss across her skin. A blush rose in her cheeks, and she smiled. The whole scene was wrong. Everything was wrong because it should've been him by her side. Yet, he was standing in the background, like a ghost at his own funeral.

"Should we . . ." Bronte began, but her voice faded as though she wasn't sure where the sentence was going.

The sound of heels broke the silence, and they all turned as Leora's mum wobbled towards them, a glass of wine clasped unsteadily in her hand. A red tint flushed her pale cheeks, and Nick noticed that her lipstick had become smeared, an imprint of the deep crimson shade colouring the rim of her glass.

"Where's dad?" Leora asked, gazing at her anxiously.

"He's meeting us at the ball. He got caught at work," Rose replied loosely, taking a long draught of wine.

Nick glanced at Leora and saw disgust flicker across her face. It was so close to what his own face had looked like mere hours ago when he'd said goodbye to his parents. He hadn't been surprised that they'd decided to start celebrating the holiday early.

Rose let out a small hiccup as she swallowed the rest of her drink. "Oops, excuse me," she said, giving them a guilty smile that revealed lipstick-stained front teeth.

Nick felt the familiar need to turn away from the scene unfolding before him, but his gaze remained fixed on Rose, as though his brain knew she was a disaster waiting to happen.

Rose's attention locked on Bronte and Isaac, and she brushed Leora roughly aside as she came to stand by them. "Now, you two make a handsome couple." She reached out a bony hand and gave Bronte's arm a squeeze.

Nick didn't miss the flicker of pain that crossed Bronte's face, and his eyes narrowed at the firm clasp Rose had on her.

"Why can't you find yourself a classy boyfriend like this?" Rose suddenly asked, turning her bloodshot eyes on her daughter. When Leora didn't reply, her eyes narrowed. "You will find a boyfriend. Won't you?"

Leora's face had turned stony, but she plastered on a smile. "Of course. I just haven't found the right one. Not everyone's as lucky in finding love as you and father."

Rose's lips pinched, and she released her hold on Bronte, stepping close to Leora. "Soon, all the good ones will be taken. I had an excellent northside prospect lined up for you as a date, and you cancelled him for your charity case here." Nick didn't miss the cutting look she sent his way before she went on. "I don't want you spending a lifetime alone. Your looks will only last so long and, take it from me, no one's going to want you once they're gone." Rose tucked a loose strand of hair behind Leora's ear, and it became a battle of wills to decide who would break first. Seeming to come back to herself, Rose stepped away, smiling falsely at them. "You kids should get going. The festival will already be underway." She shooed them out the door and gave them a cheery wave before shutting it in their faces.

The cool night air shocked Nick after being inside the warmth of the house. Leora didn't seem to notice the cold. She stalked straight down the porch steps towards the little gate. Nick was still trying to comprehend the scene they'd left behind. The woman on the other side of the door fitted the image Leora had painted in his mind, yet it was a shock to see it for himself. Rose was unhinged and chaotic, and Nick truly believed now that she was capable of locking her own daughter up just to save face.

"Come on," said Eli, breaking them out of their stupors.

"You go ahead," Bronte told Isaac, bending down to adjust the strap of her heel.

"You sure?" he asked, but she waved him off, and he walked away with Eli.

Nick went to follow but hesitated. Bronte stood up before he could decide whether to go or stay. Her eyes locked on his and his mouth went dry.

"You look . . ." he began, but she'd already taken a hurried step forward as though she was fleeing him.

The heel of her shoe caught in the folds of her dress as she moved, and Nick reached out a hand instinctively, catching Bronte's arm to keep her from falling. A nervous breath of laughter escaped her lips as he helped her right herself.

"Thanks." Her voice was barely more than a whisper.

Bronte's arm was cool beneath his touch, and while Nick was cold in his suit, he imagined she must be freezing. As if sensing his thoughts, her eyes strayed to his hand, and he released his grip immediately, revealing a red mark.

"I'm sorry. I didn't mean to-"

"It wasn't you," she said, cutting him off. "Rose has a firm grip."

As if acting on its own accord, his hand reached out, and his fingertips brushed the bruise beginning to form on her forearm. Bronte shivered, and he pulled his hand back, curling it into a fist at his side.

"You look. . . " she began.

"Are you guys coming?" Leora's voice called from the shadows.

Bronte cleared her throat. "Yes," she replied.

Unsaid words hung in the air between them, but the moment had passed and, even if Nick wanted to, he couldn't get a single syllable out of his mouth. Bronte walked down the steps, careful to pick up her dress this time. He trailed an arm's distance behind, just in case.

They joined the others in front of the gate, and Bronte drifted away from him to Isaac's side. Nick took up a place beside Leora, grateful that the shadows hid what was plainly written on his face.

Bronte squinted in the darkness as the sound of wheels rolling over the uneven stone cobblestones reached her ears, and she gradually made out the shape of a carriage approaching. She'd assumed they'd be walking to the festival, but Leora had claimed the distance was far too great to go in heels. Bronte was inclined to agree, having already embarrassed herself in front of Nick. The less walking, the better.

No horses were drawing the carriage, and there was no driver, but it rolled smoothly to a stop in front of them. The shiny black door swung open without any of them moving towards it. The seats inside were lined with deep crimson felt, and delicate curtains covered the small window set into the door. Bronte found it unusual seeing an inanimate object act as though it had a brain and had sensed their presence.

"Perks of being a member of Namire's elite," Eli murmured to her, noticing her confusion. "Only the wealthiest families can afford carriages that are spelled this way."

The five of them piled in without a word. Bronte lifted her dress away from her feet as she climbed up the steps, stooping awkwardly to get to her seat. Somehow, she ended up opposite Nick, his knee casually bumped against hers as they were finding their place, and Bronte crossed her legs tightly, trying to take up as little space as possible. Her heart was still beating from the encounter they'd had moments ago. She swallowed, reminding herself that she couldn't spend the whole night watching Nick. Her eyes didn't want to listen to her thoughts, though. Unbidden, they kept straying in his direction. It had taken all her willpower when Leora had first opened the door not to stare directly at him. Bronte had allowed herself the smallest of glances before fixing her gaze on Isaac, but what she'd seen had been enough to make her catch her breath.

The suit Nick wore was navy blue and tailored to fit him perfectly. It was a suit well above the quality she now knew he could afford. He'd slicked his hair back with some sort of pomade, which made the sharpness of his jaw even more pronounced. She'd had to force her hands together in front of her to keep from reaching out to trace that hard line. The shadows of the dim carriage caused the bronze strands in his hair to glow. A small part of Bronte missed its usual messiness. She forced her eyes away from him. There was no use spending her night looking at something she could never have.

Because he wasn't hers. The thought bothered her more than she cared to admit.

When they'd all stopped shifting about, the carriage door swung shut. Leora cleared her throat and said aloud to no one in particular.

"The Canal."

The carriage must've been listening because it rolled forwards, towards where Leora had directed it. Thankfully, the inside of the carriage was warm compared to the cool night outside. The heat made Bronte think of Christmas time, of winter days, and curling up in front of a fireplace. It was only two months until Christmas, and she wondered how different it would be this year. It would be her first without her mum. The familiar ache of sadness Bronte usually kept at bay rose unbidden inside her. She didn't think the feeling would ever leave. She didn't think she wanted it to either. Even if it hurt to remember her, at least it was a sign her mother would never be forgotten.

Nick bumped her leg, drawing her out of her thoughts. Bronte ignored him, unsure she could hide her feelings if she looked into his eyes. She kept her gaze fixed out the little carriage window. He didn't try to get her attention again, and the remainder of the carriage ride passed by in silence.

CHAPTER 23

The Canal was alive with activity by the time their carriage arrived. Glowing lanterns of every colour had been strung across the street, and everyone was dressed in elaborate gowns and suits. With the stars glittering above, it was a beautiful sight.

The street was too busy for the carriage to get through, so Leora ordered it to stop. The door sprung open, letting in a gust of cool air. Leora climbed out first, and the others followed. When they were on the street, the carriage door closed, and it rolled off to meet its next fare.

The five of them moved towards the Canal's walkway. Leora led the way, and Isaac offered Bronte his arm. She took it, grateful for the support. When she'd first walked on her heels down Leora's stairs, she'd felt like a fawn on new legs, testing the boundaries of what she could do. Bronte didn't need another incident like her stumble with Nick, and she made sure to keep her skirts from getting caught under her feet. When they passed from the street into the Canal, Bronte was again wrapped in warmth, like the carriage.

"How is it so hot?" she asked.

"Just for tonight, the length of the Canal up to the Town Hall is enchanted to remain warm, but anywhere outside that zone will be the normal temperature," Isaac told her.

Eli and Nick walked behind them, and she could feel Nick's gaze on her back, burning a hole through her. She straightened her shoulders and tightened her grip on Isaac's arm. Flowers lined the iron railing of the bridges, perfuming the air with their sweet smell. Bronte took a breath, and suddenly she was back in her mum's hospice room. She remembered so vividly how every available space had been covered in vases of flowers, delivered to her by acquaintances and friends. Now, everything around her was too bright and too loud. Her vision began to blur. Her breath hitched, and she could feel her chest rising and falling desperately beneath her constricting bodice. Bronte cursed herself for letting Leora lace up the back so tightly. Her grip tightened on Isaac's arm as she drew to a stop.

"Are you alright?" he asked, looking at her sharply.

She stared ahead at the lights of the Canal and reminded herself where she was and what she was doing. But nothing could calm her breathing, and her face was beginning to flush. Bronte didn't think she could take another step. A second warmer hand brushed her free arm gently, and she turned to find Nick beside her. He didn't say anything, just looked at her. Like déjà vu, she saw herself reflected in his eyes, just as she had the first time they'd met. He saw her, and she knew that this was real. She was real. Nick's touch grounded her, and, slowly, she allowed herself to relax.

Bronte couldn't remember the last time she'd thought about the scent of blossoms in her mother's hospice room. Something about the intensity of the flowers nearby had made it impossible to ignore the memory. She didn't hate flowers. Especially not after seeing Rainbow Valley. But she hadn't smelt those flowers. They had been a pretty sight. Not a reminder of her pain.

"I'm okay . . . I just . . . Let's go," she said and pulled her eyes away from Nick.

His hand left her arm, and the absence of his warmth sent a shiver through her. She slid a glance up at Isaac, who'd started walking again. His arm had gone rigid beneath her hand.

When they reached the end of the Canal, they joined the crowd that had gathered in front of the Town Hall. A wooden dance floor had been erected in the square, and a buffet table stood behind it, lined with dishes of food. A band was set to the side, filling the night with music.

Leora stood beside her, watching the dancers with displeasure. When she noticed Bronte's gaze, her face smoothed into a smile.

"The food's the best part," Leora told her. "All the vendors and restaurants on the Canal donate dishes to feed the city for a night."

Bronte grinned. "I can't wait to try it."

"Should we dance then?" asked Isaac, holding out his hand.

Bronte stared at his hand. "What about Eli?" she blurted, hoping to get out of it.

"Don't worry about me. I just spotted Remy. She's a healer too." He waved at a short girl standing on the far side of the dancefloor. He walked away, and reluctantly Bronte took Isaac's proffered hand.

"Shall we," said Nick, offering Leora his own hand with a sly grin.

Bronte watched as Leora rolled her eyes before snatching his hand and dragging him onto the dancefloor, where they were immediately lost in the swell of bodies. Bronte was surprised at the wave of jealousy she felt. They were only friends, she reminded herself. She turned to Isaac, hoping he couldn't tell what she was feeling.

"There is a high chance your toes are about to be squashed," she remarked, trying to retain some self-respect before making a fool out of herself.

"I've never been fond of my toes anyway," said Isaac, leading her into the crowd.

Bronte had never done any sort of formal dancing before, and she didn't think the school dances her mum had forced her to attend as a kid counted. All they'd done at those was bob awkwardly to the beat of pop music. But this was ballroom dancing, and it appeared everyone here knew how to do it.

She placed her hand on Isaac's shoulder, knowing that much from watching movies, and he rested his hand lightly on her waist. Bronte could feel its coolness through the thin material of her dress, and she sucked in a shaky breath. He clasped her right hand in his left, and begun to navigate her slowly around the dancefloor.

"See, it's not so bad, is it?" he asked with a grin.

"There are worse things in life," she reluctantly admitted.

With Isaac leading, all she had to do was follow and try not to bump into anyone else. When she felt confident enough that she wasn't about to trip, she shifted her gaze away from the silk cravat at Isaac's throat. Suddenly, the music changed from a slow, easy rhythm to an upbeat tune, and all the couples on the floor moved to form a circle. Isaac tugged on her hand, pulling her into line.

"What's happening?" she hissed over the music.

"Just try to follow along."

She didn't like the wicked grin that had come over Isaac's face. There was a pause in the music, and everyone seemed to take a breath in expectation, straightening their backs and sucking in their stomachs. Then the band took to their instruments, filling the night with a clamour of sound. The couples around them moved in time, the women expertly swished their hips, and the men guided them as they turned across the floor.

Bronte tried to keep up, but her limbs lacked the grace and poise of those around her. Isaac wasn't helping much. He'd taken to laughing at her flailing attempts to follow along. There was a pause in the music again, and Bronte hastily detached herself from Isaac, planning to leave the dance floor but, instead, an unfamiliar man pulled her into his arms, and the music started again. Her eyes shot to Isaac's for help, but another woman had already joined him, twirling him away across the floor.

The man she was dancing with had a kindly face, reminding her of Frank, and she relaxed slightly. She made it through the dance, and when the next pause in the music came, she was in the middle of the floor, which wasn't ideal, but she thanked the man and turned her head down, heading for the safety of the refreshment table.

Bronte had almost made it successfully off the floor when someone tugged her arm, pulling her towards them. She opened her mouth, about to make an excuse, when she saw Nick's face above hers.

"May I have this dance?" he asked.

He was so close to her that she could smell the peppermint on his breath. She didn't reply for a moment, lost in how his body felt pushed up against hers.

"I have time for one more," she conceded.

A quicksilver grin passed over his face and his hand, which had been burning a hole through her shoulder, slid down to grip her waist. He began moving them around the room. The music had taken on a slower rhythm, and Bronte allowed herself to be guided by him. Unwillingly, her eyes flicked to the curve of Nick's lips. In heels, she was only a few centimetres shorter than him. All she needed to do was lean forwards and tilt her head. But surely, he wouldn't return the kiss. She was certain he didn't think of her like that. His eyes found hers and the heat in them told her otherwise. Bronte had to remind herself to breathe before she drowned looking at him.

"You look beautiful." His deep voice reverberated through her. "I've wanted to tell you that since the moment I saw you tonight, well, since the moment I first saw you really, I was just too blind by prejudice to admit it," he amended. "I don't think I ever apologised for the way I acted that day."

"You don't have to. I understand."

"No. I'm sorry. You never deserved that, least of all after what you had just been through."

She squeezed his hand. "I forgive you."

Nick bowed his head, so it rested lightly against hers. The world around them melted away as she gently swayed in his arms.

"Nick?"

"Yes?" He lifted his head, raising his brow in question, and she opened her mouth, but the words she'd been about to utter stuck in her throat. The moment stretched, and she glanced around, trying to think of something to say so she didn't look like an idiot.

"I'm hungry." They had just neared the buffet, and it was the first thought that had popped into her head.

His face fell slightly. "Should we stop then?"

"Yes."

She detached herself from him hurriedly, and though the air was warm, she suddenly felt as if she were out in the cold. Forcing her body to move, Bronte walked to the buffet, cursing herself that she had ruined the dance with him. But Nick didn't seem bothered. He trailed behind her, his hands slipped into his pants pockets casually.

She surveyed the food in front of her. There were platters of fancy meats, crackers piled high with caviar, and long trays of cured fish, all of which she wasn't too keen on trying. She wasn't even hungry. Her nerves had shut down any thoughts of food. Finally, she took a strawberry from next to the dipping chocolate and bit into it. Her eyes slid to Nick's, and she found that he was already watching her. Suddenly her mouth went dry. She mechanically forced herself to chew her food. It was one of the most flavourful strawberries she'd ever tasted. Bronte could've eaten a whole bowl of them and all the chocolate if her stomach wasn't adamant about making her feel sick at the thought of more food.

"We should find Eli," she said. She had no interest in going back to the dance floor.

"Are you sure you don't want anything else?" His eyes were gleaming, and Bronte levelled him with a flat stare.

"I'm full."

He gave her a sceptical look. "Shame. I've seen you when you're hungry, and you never have just one strawberry and call it a day."

She shrugged. "I miscalculated."

She wasn't about to admit the little slip-up she'd experienced on the dance floor. Bronte spotted Eli next to an ice sculpture of what she assumed was a unicorn - given it had just a single, long icy horn - chatting to an older woman that she didn't recognise. She walked over to him without checking to see if Nick followed.

"This is Audrey. She's a friend of Cora's," said Eli, introducing her.

"Nice to meet you," said Bronte, smiling politely at the woman.

She had short greying hair that was streaked in parts with black, and her face was lined with wrinkles that reminded her of the spine of a book which had been opened too many times.

"So, you're the newest enchanter," Audrey said, her voice deep and gravelly. Bronte had to lean forwards to hear her over the music. "Sorry about your mother. She was such a sweet child."

"Oh, thank you." Bronte let the comment wash over her. She'd had months now to accept the death, but every time she was reminded of it, the dull ache inside her thrummed to life.

"Audrey's a healer. She created a potion which can nullify any sort of pain, emotional or physical," explained Eli.

Bronte regarded her with new interest.

Audrey sniffed. "It's good to feel pain. Makes us stronger. Sometimes I regret ever making that potion."

"There's definitely a lot of people who don't share that feeling," Nick muttered, seeming to appear that moment at Bronte's shoulder.

"Do you ever use the potion?" asked Bronte. She imagined it must be of benefit for someone her age.

"Like I said, sometimes it's good to feel pain."

From the distant look in her eyes, Bronte wondered what sort she was referring to. Before she could ask, Audrey trailed off to the buffet table without a goodbye.

Bronte glanced at Nick and Eli, who both had the same expression on their faces she imagined must be on her own. Clearly, they were all thinking the same thing; Audrey seemed slightly unhinged.

Isaac and Leora joined them, coming from the dance floor. Isaac took up a place beside her, and Nick notably shifted away, muttering something to Leora that earned him a reproving look.

"Who's that?" Bronte asked, bridging the tension.

The music had ended abruptly, and silence had fallen in the square as a man appeared at the podium overlooking the dancefloor. He was of medium height, and his plain face surveyed the crowd.

"The Chancellor," Isaac replied.

"It is my pleasure to welcome you all to this wonderful celebration. May you all dance, drink, and revel to the night's end." A cheer went up around them at the words, and the Chancellor's face split into a grin. "And now, I'm delighted to welcome the woman who will bless this celebration."

There was a collective inhalation of breath as a woman appeared by his side. She towered over him. Her dark brown skin had been wrapped in robes of glittering white, and her long hair fell in intricate braids behind her, held in place by a diadem of sliver. In the centre of the diadem lay a white moonstone, which seemed to shine on its own as if a star had been captured inside it. Bronte knew without having to ask that the woman was the Grand Shaman.

"Thank you all for coming." Bronte shivered as the Grand Shaman's voice resounded in the night air. It was as though it had been layered with multiple other voices, both male and female, creating a richly ethereal tone. Although Bronte was on the opposite side of the floor, it sounded like the Grand Shaman was standing beside her, whispering directly into her ear. "Tonight, we celebrate new beginnings brought to us by our ancestors. We thank them, and the goddess Hecate for the sacrifice they made to create this haven. Centuries ago, the magical kind was facing relentless persecution. Our very existence was threatened because non-magical beings feared us. The blood-stained history of that conflict meant losses for both sides. It was Eleni Theobesian who, through her clairvoyance, saw what was ahead for everyone involved. To ensure a future for the magical kind, therefore, the Theobesian sisters contacted the goddess Hecate. A solution was found in which the goddess gifted the sisters three necklaces, infused with a portion of her own power. This allowed them to open a pocket realm and so create a new home for all of us. Not everyone made it to this realm, though. We know there were some who chose to stay behind and some who didn't make it to the portal in time. Let us honour the lives of those before us and protect the lives of those to come. Do not forget that Hecate guided us down this path, and we thank her for allowing us to retain our gifts in this new world. It is our duty to remember our history, so we will never make the same mistake of believing a just harmony can be found on Earth. To the Lost Night!"

All around them, people cheered and clapped. Next, a man appeared in front of the podium. His tall, muscular frame demanded attention, and the crowd's noise instantly stopped.

"That's the High Alchemist," Leora whispered.

Bronte regarded him with new interest.

"I'm sure you're all sick of speeches by now and itching to celebrate on this beautiful night. But I must steal your time and, I hope, your attention for a little longer. However, if your eyes begin to wander, I do not blame you. Our beautiful city's history has not been the easiest. On this night, it is also important to remember the good that has prevailed after the dark years the Disciples brought. They took not just the lives of my wife and daughter but many other valued members of our beloved city. If you could all take a moment to remember those souls tonight, it would be a great comfort to me and to all the other families who lost someone." He paused, allowing a solemn silence to fill the air. "Here with me tonight are representatives from the Fae and wolf lands to symbolise our unity, not just on the Lost Night but through all the nights to come." Beside him stood a tall boy with dark hair and rugged looks. On the High Alchemist's other side was a spritely woman. She had a thin, angular face with delicately arched ears that disappeared into her amber-coloured hair. "That is all the time I will take from you. I wish you nothing but happiness tonight." Another round of clapping and cheering followed as the High Alchemist left the podium, and music once again filled the night.

"I'm going to eat," Leora announced abruptly, cutting through the crowd to the buffet.

Bronte's eyes followed her. She wavered, debating whether the boys could be civil without her there as a buffer. But after deciding that it wasn't her responsibility to mother them, she followed Leora.

"Have you seen your dad yet?" Bronte asked, catching Leora as she piled an excessive amount of caviar onto some bread.

"Nope." She slipped the bread into her mouth, eyes rolling back slightly with pleasure.

Bronte made a face at her. "How can you eat that?"

Leora shrugged as she covered another piece of bread. "Because I have good taste."

It was then that Bronte noticed her slightly dilated pupils, the sweet scent of her breath, and the clumsy way her hand brought the caviar to her mouth. Leora was never clumsy.

"Have you been drinking?" she asked, wincing at the accusation in her voice.

Leora batted a hand at her, rolling her eyes dismissively. "I had a sip of someone's unattended glass. I'm fine."

Bronte opened her mouth, unsure whether a lecture or words of condolence would emerge, but Isaac interrupted before she could decide.

"Bronte! If you want to speak to the Grand Shaman, now's the chance," he insisted.

"Go," Leora said, already busy with her next piece of bread and caviar. "I'll likely still be here when you return."

Bronte nodded. She didn't miss the meaningful look Leora gave her as she turned to Isaac. She hoped their plan worked.

Isaac led her to the steps of the Town Hall. "I'm going to introduce you to the Chancellor first, and he'll bring us to the Grand Shaman."

A couple of High Guards stood at the base of the steps, but Isaac merely looked at them as he passed, and they offered no resistance. Either they knew who he was, or they weren't very good guards.

"Chancellor! Happy Lost Night!" Isaac gleefully patted him on the back.

The Chancellor turned, a wide grin on his face that Bronte thought may've had something to do with the flute of sparkling liquid in his hand. "Isaac! I hope you're well. Is this the girl you were telling me about?"

"Yes, do you think we could have that audience with the Grand Shaman?"

"Of course. Follow me. She's in a particularly good mood tonight, meaning that she's actually speaking instead of staring into space." He shivered. "Always slightly disturbing. Makes me wonder if she knows how I'm going to die, but is too kind to tell me." He shared a covert look with them as they reached the Grand Shaman's side. "Grand Shaman, I have something you may be interested in."

The Grand Shaman turned from her spot at the small banquet table set up for the night's honoured guests. Her eyes looked clouded, as though shrouded by an opaque mist. Bronte flinched slightly, but then the woman blinked, revealing the clear blue eyes beneath.

"Yes?"

"This girl here believes she possesses one pendant from the Ancient Triad." It was clear from his tone that the Chancellor was only indulging her for Isaac's sake, and Bronte's cheeks reddened.

"Leave us." The Grand Shaman told the Chancellor.

He looked affronted but did as he was told. The Grand Shaman's eyes fell on Bronte's throat, where the necklace was.

"That necklace is not the real thing," she said once the Chancellor was out of earshot.

"You can tell just by looking at it?" Isaac pressed.

"Yes, energy doesn't lie. Although . . ." Her eyes dropped to where the real necklace was stashed in Bronte's pocket. "What did you say your name was again?"

"Bronte Everett."

"Hmm, interesting."

"Why?"

"I believe you'll soon find out. Won't she?" The Grand Shaman addressed her question to Isaac, who stiffened.

"I beg your pardon?"

"I suggest you go enjoy the party." She dismissed them, turning her back.

Isaac was speechless, but Bronte tugged his arm, drawing him down the stairs and into the crowd.

"Where is it?" he demanded. There was a feral gleam in his eyes that revealed a side of Isaac Bronte had never seen before.

"Where is what?" she asked, feigning cluelessness.

"The necklace. You have to have the real one."

"Isaac, calm down," she urged.

He blinked and seemed to come back to himself. "Right, sorry."

"I think I need a drink." The Grand Shaman had all but confirmed that the necklace in her pocket was the real thing. Bronte didn't know what to do with it now. She just knew she needed to get away from Isaac. He moved to follow her, and she held out an arm. "Alone."

Thankfully, Isaac respected her wishes, and she was able to escape into the throng of people. It was clear Isaac knew she was hiding something. Nick had told the truth, and Isaac could no longer be trusted. The sound of laughter. The chink of a glass. The band music. All of it was too loud, and Bronte needed to get out. She barely registered the grunt of disapproval as she brushed too close to a dancing couple, nor did she notice the large vase of flowers she almost toppled in her haste. All she could think about was her need to get away from the crowd.

Bronte made it almost the full length of the Canal before she felt herself begin to calm. It was quieter away from the Town Hall. The Canal had emptied to a few stragglers. It was darker down this way, too, with only some twinkling lights strung up along shop fronts and woven through the bridge's handrails along with the flowers.

Bronte began to cross one of the bridges and then stopped in the middle. She took deep breaths, choking on the flowery scent but forcing it down regardless, as though filling her lungs to their maximum capacity would solve all her issues. In a way, it did. Her racing heart began to calm, and her body relaxed. She picked a flower and absently fiddled with the petals. The smell didn't bother her at that moment. She was too focused on Isaac to think about anything else.

Bronte couldn't believe Isaac was bad. She'd wanted so desperately for him to be good. It was easier to deny what she knew when she had only shadows for company. She went to the edge of the bridge and leaned her forearms against it. The cold metal pressed into her skin. She dropped the flower, watching as it floated down into the canal and began drifting away. The water before her was moving idly, calmer than she could ever be, and she envied it. For a moment, Bronte imagined jumping into it and sinking below it's cool shallows.

She longed for the mute silence that she couldn't find above the surface. She longed for an escape that didn't involve running away from a situation but falling below it, far away into the peaceful darkness. Perhaps it would be a place where she could finally give in and surrender.

Bronte felt as though the water was already coursing through her, diminishing any flame she had managed to coax to life these past months. She would miss the warmth, but she was tired of burning her fingers on flickering embers and scrapping through ash until her nails were stained black, trying to find some semblance of light. Sometimes you burned until there was nothing left, and then it was time to learn to live with the cold.

CHAPTER 24

Nick stood beneath the glowing lights of the dancefloor and wished he was anywhere else. He'd had to steal his father's best suit to wear tonight, since he didn't have the money to buy a new one. Luckily, he'd been able to transmute the outdated buttons to look smart, and he'd altered the drab greyish brow colour of the fabric to navy blue. Next to Isaac and Eli, you could hardly notice the difference, as long as you didn't look too closely. But the way Isaac's mouth had tugged up at the corner when he'd first seen him suggested he hadn't missed the attempted fix-up job.

Celia had been impressed, though. Nick had dropped by The Sparrow on his way to Leora's. Cheap decorations had been put up for the Lost Night celebrations, and the inside looked almost presentable for once. Nick was glad he wasn't working tonight, though. He'd played at The Sparrow during the holiday before, and he didn't feel like getting drenched in beer again. When the clock struck twelve, anyone with a drink would toss the contents into the air in celebration. He didn't know how that tradition had started, but whoever was responsible for it was someone he wasn't very pleased with.

Leora returned to his side, holding a piece of bread topped with caviar. "Has Bronte finished speaking with the Grand Shaman yet?" she asked with a frown.

Nick glanced at the balcony of the Town Hall, but he couldn't see her. "She was just up there." He spotted Isaac standing among the crowd without her, and he made his way over to him, Leora in tow. "Isaac, where's Bronte?"

Isaac cut him a glare. "She went to get a drink."

Nick frowned. He couldn't see her anywhere near the refreshments table. He wondered what the Grand Shaman had said but, if Bronte had disappeared, he couldn't imagine it was anything good. He knew that if he was going to find her, it would be someplace away from all these people.

Bronte heard something move beside her, and she whirled around. A shadow loomed at the start of the bridge. She recognised Nick's face and instantly relaxed.

"I just needed some space," she told him as he reached her side.

"What did she say?"

Bronte didn't have to ask to know who he meant. "That it was a fake, but we already knew that." She allowed herself to meet his eyes, and her breath caught. He was so close to her. In the darkness, the shadows cut his face into angles, and again she found her hands wanting to reach out and trace his cheekbones and his lips. But now wasn't the time or place. "I think you're right about Isaac."

"What changed your mind?" His voice was barely above a whisper.

"Just something the Grand Shaman said. She looked at my pocket, where the real necklace is, and then addressed Isaac, saying I'll soon find out about something. Ominous, I know," she said with a laugh.

"So, the Grand Shaman knows you have the real necklace but didn't do anything about it?"

"That's what it seemed like to me. And then Isaac got really intense, insisting I must have the real necklace."

"You didn't tell him, did you?"

"Of course not! I told him to calm down, and then I got away from him as soon as I could. I'm just hoping there's some other explanation for why he was acting like that."

Nick didn't say anything, and Bronte knew he disagreed with her.

"Come with me," he said after they'd stood in silence for a moment. "I want to show you something."

Bronte felt a warm hand take hers, and she allowed herself to be pulled away from the bridge.

They made it to Nina's apothecary, and Nick led her down the small alley beside the shop. At the back was a door where Nina took in supplies.

"We're breaking into Nina's shop?" Bronte asked dryly.

"No. See this ladder. Nina uses it in the shop if she has to reach the top shelves. It also happens to be the perfect height to reach the gutter." He pointed out the section of guttering he was talking about.

Maybe it was the adrenaline in her or her need to simply get away from everything, but Bronte didn't argue when Nick scaled the ladder and hoisted himself onto the roof.

"Come up," he urged her.

She took off her heels and climbed the rungs. He held out his hand, and Bronte allowed him to pull her up. The roof was slated, but the angle wasn't steep enough to pose any risk. It allowed them to sit comfortably so they could take in the view of the Canal. Bronte could see the Town Hall lit up in the distance and the faint swell of the music reached her ears.

She flinched as a loud bang overwhelmed the music, looking skyward as the star-strewn sky was decorated with what appeared to be a rainbow of glowing gems. A faint whistling sound reached her ears, and she watched as a ball of white light climbed from the direction of the Town Hall into the sky, exploding in a kaleidoscope of colour. It was like a firework, but instead of the embers dying out, they hung there, suspended in the night air.

Nick looked down at the wonder on her face and smiled. "The legend is that those white balls of light are fallen stars being released back into the sky. The beams of colour that emerge from them are the wishes people made upon the star as it was falling. Every Lost Night, at midnight exactly, hundreds are let off until it looks as if gems have been scattered across the sky. The stars have returned to where they belong, and the wishes go with them so the universe can see them and call them into reality. People call them dreamcatchers."

"That's a pretty story," she whispered, leaning back as she watched them.

One after another, the dreamcatchers soared into the sky, releasing the supposed wishes into the night. Bronte could've watched them forever. As time passed, the sky really did look like it had been scattered with gems. Millions of colourful glowing flecks stood out against the blackness, mixed with real stars, though it was hard to discern one from the other. She wished the sky could look like this every night, covered in hopeful dreams cast upon falling things.

"Have you ever made a wish?" she asked Nick. Her voice sounded strange to her ears after sitting in silence for so long.

"I used to when I was younger, when I thought there was something out there listening."

"And now?"

"Now, I don't think there's anything out there at all." There was a coldness in his voice that she hadn't heard before, and when she looked at him, his mouth was set in a hard line.

"You know, when my mum was sick, I would sit by the window and look at the stars. I liked to think she was one of them, watching me from above. Now I like to think she's still up there and that the thousands of glittering diamonds that wink at me from the darkness are all people who were once loved but had to leave. When they fall from the sky, it's because they have no one left to watch over." During those nights, she'd felt so hopelessly alone, but at the same time, the stars had brought her comfort.

Nick was looking at her intensely, his eyes were dark, and she lent forwards. He flinched, and she froze, heat rising through her.

"If you don't want to . . ."

"I do," he cut in. "You have to know that I do." He reached out, cupping her face with his hands, and tilting it up, so she was forced to meet his eyes. They were almost entirely swallowed by black, desire clearly written in them.

Her breath stilled. "Then why don't you?"

"Because you came here with *him*. You chose him." His last words were only a whispered breath, and Bronte had to lean closer to catch them.

She couldn't believe he was holding that against her. "I didn't have a choice."

"We all have choices, Bronte. And as much as I want to . . ." His lips were centimeters away from hers now. She could practically feel them move against her skin as he spoke. "I won't. Not tonight, at least."

She frowned. "So, you're punishing me?"

His lips brushed against her jaw, and he kissed her there softly, then dipped lower, below her ear. His breath was warm against her neck as he trailed a line of kisses down to her collarbone. "I've had to watch you all night with him. You don't know anything about punishment."

She groaned as he softly nuzzled her skin. "Then put us both out of our misery," she gasped. She didn't often beg but, for this, she would do so gladly. "Nick."

A grin tugged at his lips, and he brought his eyes back to hers. "Bronte, I . . ."

There was a crash beneath them, and her eyes widened in alarm. "That was from inside the shop."

"You don't think someone's broken in?" Nick asked.

"We'd better check."

Nick was already hurrying toward the ladder.

Bronte grabbed her heels and followed, cursing Leora for making her take off her sneakers.

"Nina keeps a spare key beneath a loose brick four rows from the bottom," Nick told her when they'd reached the ground. He sought out the brick and dislodged it. Sure enough, a key was lying in the space behind. "We'll go in the back door, so they don't see us in the window."

Bronte nodded. There had been no other sounds from inside, and she hoped the noise had just been caused by stock falling over and not a burglar.

Nick unlocked the door, easing it open. He peeked inside, but they couldn't see anything in the dark. They were in the back stock room, and a second door led to the main shop.

Nick picked up a broomstick. "Stay behind me."

Bronte fought a laugh at how ridiculous he looked holding the broom for protection, but she kept her mouth shut so she didn't give them away.

Nick opened the door to the dark interior of the shop. Nobody was in front of them, and they crept out together. Suddenly, there was a blinding flash, and Nick dropped to the ground.

"Nick!" There was a second flash, but instinctively Bronte flung up a barrier absorbing the cast. She turned to the corner where the attack had come from, and a shadow loomed. Her heart dropped. "Isaac."

A moment passed when neither of them moved. Bronte knew she should run, but she couldn't leave Nick on the ground. He was still breathing, which was a comfort, and Bronte hoped Isaac had merely hit him with a stunning cast. During their lessons on creating barriers, Professor Latoux mentioned that stunning was a form of cast that they may need to protect themselves against. If hit by a stunning cast, it would leave you unconscious for a period of time, depending on the strength of the person casting. It could be as short as a few minutes or extend to hours.

"What are you doing?" Bronte knew it was a stupid question. It was very clear what Isaac was doing. But she still couldn't process the betrayal.

"Just hand me the necklace. I know you have it. Or is it at your house? Should I go see what Frank and Nina are up to?"

A flush of anger warmed her face. "No! No. I have it, but I'd never give it to you. Why are you doing this? The Disciples are the reason your father is dead. How could you want to be like them?"

Isaac raised a disdainful eyebrow. "You still haven't figured out who I am, have you? It is my best-kept secret. I thought Nick may've worked it out, though. What did he tell you about me? I assume he's the one responsible for your sudden change of mind."

"He told me that he saw you contacting Madden. What other reason would you have for talking to my father other than wanting the Ancient Triad? What kind of deal have you made with him?"

Isaac let out a cold laugh. "Madden isn't your father. He's my father. Your father is still very much alive. In fact, you saw him tonight. I'm surprised he didn't recognise his little girl, although I think the Grand Shaman caught on."

Bronte's body had begun to tingle, and the warmth had spread to her cheeks. "What are you talking about? Your father was the Chancellor."

"My adoptive father was, although I never knew him, so he wasn't really anyone to me. My real father was Madden Theobesian, and my mother was Emelia Everett."

"That can't be true," Bronte protested abruptly. Isaac had to be weaving a story to distract her.

"I've contacted Madden multiple times now to learn the full story. We were both entangled in a complicated past. But I think you have a right to know the truth. Your father is the current High Alchemist, and your mother was Lydia Theobesian."

Bronte's stomach twisted. "You're lying," she insisted in a faint voice. Emelia was her mum. She always had been. She couldn't have lied to her for all those years.

"I'm not. My adoptive mother, Cathrine, felt too guilty to keep this information a secret and I've known since the age of five that my true parents died long ago. Catherine couldn't tell me exactly what happened that night, though, and I'd always accepted the rumours surrounding their deaths. It wasn't until you returned that I realised the facts didn't add up."

"So you've known all this time and didn't say a thing? You let everyone believe I was the daughter of Madden and Emelia while their actual son has been pantomiming as some tragic fatherless kid?" Bronte spat.

"I've merely been playing the cards I was dealt. I didn't control my parents' actions that night, nor yours. What good would it do if everyone in Namire knew the truth about my heritage? Being the Chancellor's son gave me safety and, up until this point, I haven't had any reason to change that."

"But now you do?"

"The name Ives no longer serves me."

"This makes no sense. Why would your own mother leave you here? She wasn't friends with Lydia anymore. She had no reason to take me away."

"I've since learnt through my contact with Madden that she was protecting you from certain death. Because the Ancient Triad is passed down through the Theobesian bloodline Lydia knew that once Madden heard of your birth, he would hunt you down as well. She kept the pregnancy concealed, but right before you were born the secret got out. Emelia deserted Madden to warn Lydia that he was coming, and they constructed a plan to stop him. Madden was led into a trap and sealed away in a tomb for eternity. What happened after is guesswork, but it is believed Lydia died in childbirth and Emelia fled through the barrier with you. To keep you *protected*," he spat the word, "from any Disciples who might try to avenge their leader. Clearly none succeeded but once I find the Ancient Triad, I can free him. I can undo all my mother's mistakes. Because she didn't just desert Madden, she deserted me. Did you know that we were born mere hours apart? Then she abandoned me here, and instead chose to go with you."

"How would that even work? Didn't people know Emelia was pregnant?"

"Emelia concealed her pregnancy too. It's possible to cast an illusion on the body so no one would know. She and Lydia were both women in prominent positions, and because of that they would be made targets. But after I was born, I was left with Cathrine, a trusted friend of my mother and liaison with the Disciples on behalf of her husband. Conveniently, her status as wife of the Chancellor, meant it wasn't surprising when she revealed she'd been pregnant. So, I've lived with that lie my whole life. Knowing that a time would come when the truth would serve me."

"So, you're doing all of this to remake the Disciples?"

Isaac scoffed. "I couldn't care less about the Disciples. I'll bring my father back. His wife may've betrayed him, but his son won't."

"Why did you wait so long? Why not kill me the moment I returned to Namire? Why did you even bother being nice to me? Why pretend to be my friend? Was all of that just a joke?" Bronte let the tumble of questions fall from her mouth. It was all she could do to keep herself distracted from what Isaac had just told her.

"It was really Nick who motivated me to be your friend," Isaac said.

Bronte's mind focused on Nick's name. "What?"

Isaac shrugged. "You have simply been a pawn from the moment you arrived here. Nick's convinced I'm a bad person. But I think you'll agree, at least, that I can be pleasant when I want to be. We made a deal. If he kept quiet about his opinion of me, then I would help him contact his brother. Of course, the deal served my purpose, which was the reason I proposed it. I wanted you to feel what I felt: used. Used by the people who were supposed to care about you, used for your power. I also needed to see if you possessed any part of the Ancient Triad and I knew if I wasn't close to you I wouldn't get the chance."

Nick had told them he'd only seen Isaac contacting Madden, not that he was a part of it. Bronte's stomach clenched. "I don't think you're a bad person," she said. Even after everything he'd told her, she couldn't make herself believe it. He had laughed with her, helped her, comforted her, and she didn't think it had all been just for show. "You're a person who's been wronged, but that doesn't have to take away all the good in you."

"Don't try to force morality on me now. You'll only make a fool of yourself." Isaac's laugh was cruel and cold, brushing against her like the freezing winter rains. "Wanting power is not a crime."

"But your means to get it is."

"I'm a realist."

"I suppose that's what all the other tyrants told themselves," she mumbled.

Isaac's eyes took on a sharp gleam. "Give me the necklace."

Bronte took a steadying breath, readying herself. "No."

Isaac raised a hand, and a ball of darkness was sent towards her. Instinctively, her training kicked in, and she flung up a blocking cast. She flinched despite herself, even as her barrier absorbed the attack. Bronte's eyes darted wildly around for an escape, but the Canal was deserted, and all she could do was hope that someone would come this way.

She faced Isaac and drew on her power. Bronte only had a moment to prepare herself before another shadow was hurled at her. Bronte didn't know this kind of magic. She didn't know how to fight it either. The best she could do was block and hope. The casts kept coming, and she continued to deflect them, but her power flickered, and a faint sheet of darkness slipped through her barrier, sending a wave of dizziness over her.

Bronte shook it off, throwing up a new barrier. A pounding headache had begun in her temples and sweat dripped down her neck. The heavy curls of her hair stuck to her skin, and they felt like a weight pulling her down, but she didn't stop. Her breath came in ragged pants as she continued to block, but it was only a matter of time before she would be hit.

Bronte heaved in air, her breath coming out in ragged bursts as she tried to remain strong. She'd never had to use her power so rapidly and in such an uncontrolled situation. Performing so many blocking casts at once had sent the magic inside her wild. It felt like an ocean during a storm waging and waring within, and she was on a boat trying to keep herself from drowning. The waves could easily become too much. They could easily tip her over if she didn't ride them the right way. If she went overboard, that would be it. Bronte begged the sea to be calm and to help her, but it was no use.

Another shadow came in a dark blur, hitting her hastily cast barrier. Her arms were seizing up as she held it, but it was holding, at least for the moment. Isaac wasn't relenting, though. The casts began seeping through the cracks of her barriers, hitting her one after the other. They were dizzying blows which sent her mind spinning and magic wavering. A haywire cast hit the shop windows, shattering the glass, which rained to the floor.

Finally, darkness punched through her barrier, hitting her square in the chest, and she didn't have time to react as she fell to the ground, a wave of nausea overtaking her. Then, through her blurry vision, she saw Isaac approaching. She tried to move, but her limbs were heavy, and she struggled helplessly as he crouched down before her.

His pale hand reached out and clasped her necklace. He yanked her up by the chain, and she choked as the metal bit into her throat.

"Where is the real necklace." He breathed the words, his eyes transfixed on the metal circle at the end of the chain.

Bronte struggled desperately to keep her weight off the ground, but she was at his mercy. It was then that she noticed the flash of silver in the moonlight as he produced a blade from his coat pocket.

"In the dress pocket," Bronte begged. "Please just take it."

Isaac stuck his hand into her pocket and drew out the necklace. "The line must end with you."

He brought the blade to her neck, just above the chain and pressed it against her skin. She felt the sticky warmth of blood running down her neck as it bit into her. Bronte found herself praying then, even though she didn't really believe anyone was listening. She prayed to Hecate that everything would stop and that she would be okay or that, at the very least, wherever she ended up, she would no longer be in pain.

Bronte didn't know whether she was delusional or if her prayers had worked. But a moment later, she thought she could hear voices behind her. Isaac paused too, and that was how she knew it was real.

She summoned her remaining strength and shoved out against him. The chain of her necklace snapped, and they were separated, both falling onto the ground. The approaching voices were thundering in her ears now. She turned to Isaac, but he had disappeared, taking the necklace with him. All that was left was a cloud of inky darkness.

It was then that Bronte took note of the pain in her body. Her bones ached, and the cut on her throat was bleeding. A wave of dizziness overtook her, and she let her body go, falling back against the solid floor beneath her. She looked to the side, and stars shone high above her out the window, mingled with the glowing lights of the dream catchers, and she wished more than anything that she could disappear.

Nick stirred beside her, and his head appeared above hers as he rushed to her side. Clearly, he'd recovered from whatever cast Isaac had hit him with. His hair hung over her, and she reached out a hand, brushing it away from his eyes. He took her hand in his and held it against his mouth.

"Bronte," he whispered. His breath was warm against her skin. "I thought . . ." he started between breaths, but he didn't finish his sentence, and he pressed a kiss against her hand. She closed her eyes and focused on the warmth of his skin against hers. He didn't speak, only held her as she rested.

"Nick! Nick! Open the door."

She forced her eyes open. Through the glass Bronte could make out the blurry shapes of Leora and Eli, and behind them a crowd of people streaming past. A few gave curious glances into the shop but no one else stopped to offer help.

Nick promptly got to his feet, unlocking the door and opening it.

"What happened? We noticed the broken glass, but we never thought we'd find you both inside." Eli's face was scrunched with worry.

"Isaac happened. We need a healer," Nick urged.

"Isaac did this?" Leora's wide eyes trailed over Bronte, snagging when they reached the blood at her throat.

Eli knelt by her side. "I can do it."

Nick ran a hand through his hair, peering at Eli in concern. "Are you sure?"

"Don't insult me, Nick." Eli moved his hands over Bronte's body with surprising gentleness. A deep warmth flowed through her, calming her, but when Eli reached the cut on her throat her muscles tensed. "Shh, it's alright." Eli's smooth fingers lay against her skin, and the pain receded.

"Thank you," said Bronte though her words were barely audible to the point where she wasn't sure she had spoken at all.

The physical signs of Bronte's pain may've been healed, but exhaustion weighed heavy on her bones.

"Leora, you need to find the High Alchemist . . ."

Bronte tried to remain conscious to hear the rest of what Nick was saying but sleep eventually pulled her under.

CHAPTER 25

The house was dark when Leora crept inside. She wasn't surprised that her mother had never made it to the festival. Rose drank herself to sleep most nights and then blacked out in the parlour. She hadn't expected to see her father either. He was probably at another woman's house.

Leora had pulled off her heels as soon as the carriage dropped her off outside, and she was now standing barefoot on the cold floor. Blisters had formed on the outside of her little toes from where the skin had rubbed against the narrow interior of her shoes. She knew walking tomorrow was going to hurt. Creeping soundlessly across the foyer, she had almost reached the base of the stairs when she heard her mother's voice calling from the shadows.

"Leora, Leo, is that you, honey?"

Leora winced. She hated it when her mother used that nickname. It was what her younger sister had called her when she'd been too young to pronounce her full name correctly, but it wasn't for her mum to use.

"Yes, mum," she called back, resigned to the fact that she couldn't creep away unnoticed.

"Come here, darling. Talk to me."

Her mother's voice was saccharine, but Leora wasn't stupid enough to think they would share a friendly mother-daughter conversation. They never had friendly conversations. It was always veiled threats, snide comments, and petty remarks. Still, Leora turned from the foyer and walked into the dark parlour. She lit the oil lamp before joining her mother on the lounge. She smelt sweetly of wine, the empty bottle on the table evidence of how her night had gone.

"So, tell me, darling, did you have fun?" her mother asked.

Leora thought of the bubbling alcohol she'd downed and the heaviness it hadn't been able to lift. She thought of what had happened to Bronte, what they'd learnt.

"Yes," she lied.

"Did you see your father there?" her mother pressed.

"No." Leora immediately regretted her answer.

She should've been smarter than this. Her mother's eyes turned hard as she straightened beside her, and Leora felt herself unwillingly shrink in response.

"I didn't think he would be. I don't know why I'm surprised," her mother snapped. Just like that, the façade had slipped. She reached out a hand and grabbed Leora's wrist, inspecting the bronze bracelet she wore. Her grip was tight, but Leora knew not to pull away.

"Pretty," she said absently, releasing her. "Did you at least meet any prospective husbands?"

"Unfortunately, there seemed to be a complete lack of those. I did, however, meet quite a few prospective wives." She couldn't help the words from tumbling out of her mouth. She knew her mother would never take them seriously, but she had grown tired of hiding the truth.

"Don't use that tone to joke with me."

As quick as a whip, her mother lashed out, smacking her hard across the face with the back of her hand. The cold metal of the numerous rings she wore bruised her cheek. Leora released an involutory gasp, tears springing to her eyes, but she didn't lift a hand to defend herself. She didn't move. Her body was numb to the pain. She dropped her eyes away from her mother, who had broken down sobbing beside her. Leora's own fingers lay bare in her lap. She never wore rings. They were cursed pieces of jewellery in her mind.

"I'm sorry. I'm so sorry, Leo . . . I . . . I didn't . . . didn't mean to," sobbed her mum.

The words came out in disjointed gasps. Maybe she should feel pity, but cool hatred flowed through her instead as she listened to her mum cry.

"It's fine," Leora said in a flat voice.

She knew her mum wasn't listening anyway. She had long ago stopped accepting the role of the villain, but Leora knew it was better to act as though she was one, to stop fighting and simply give her mother the forgiveness she didn't deserve. She was just a shadow, a ghost, a pawn in her mother's game. She didn't know exactly what game they were playing or when it started. Probably it had begun around the time her parents found out her sister was barren. That was when her dad had turned to other women, ashamed that he had bred something seen as so useless to the alchemist world, and her mother had turned to wine.

Her mother dried her eyes and cupped Leora's face in her hands. She turned it towards her, so she was forced to look directly into her bloodshot, grass-green eyes. Leora could see herself in their reflection. She looked like a marble figure gazing lifelessly back. She hated that she shared her mother's eyes, her mother's hair, and her mother's face. She hated that she was a living depiction of the very thing she was trying to escape. Her mother's hands turned to ice as they held her, and Leora felt true numbness spread over her.

"There, now it's like it never happened." She released her face, patting her tenderly on the shoulder. "Now go."

Leora left. She climbed the stairs to her room and shut the door, turning the lock even though her mother had a key to every room in the house. She went to the mirror to inspect her face, and just as she'd thought, there was nothing there. Her mother truly believed that if she continued to heal Leora every time she hit her, if she erased all the evidence, it never really happened. Sometimes Leora managed to convince herself that was the truth as well.

She turned away from the mirror in disgust, sliding her hand into the pocket of her dress. It was a small cut that she'd instructed Miss

Taffeta to make on all her gowns. A lady needed pockets; otherwise, how would she hide things. She took out a small white box. It was a party favour given out each year at the festival. It was usually a cheaply made piece of jewellery or a pretty stone. But it wasn't hers to unwrap.

Leora went into her closet. It was a monstrous thing filled with all sorts of beautiful clothes and shoes. The dress she'd worn tonight had been greatly overpriced, and she'd likely never wear it again, but she'd built an image for herself as someone who only settled for the best. It was an identity that suffocated her sometimes, especially when she viewed herself as deserving of the worst.

"Calliope?" she whispered. She knelt on the floor at the back of her cupboard, where a hole had been cut into the wall. It was only big enough for a mouse to fit through or a small object like the one she held. "Callie?" she said again, hoping her sister hadn't already fallen asleep.

"Leo!"

Leora breathed in relief as the excited voice reached her ears. "I brought you something." She pushed the box through the hole, and Callie snatched it up eagerly. She could hear her unwrapping it and then a small gasp. "What is it?" Leora asked.

"A ring! look."

Leora pressed her eye to the hole and peeped through. She saw a thin finger adorned with a silver band that had a small auburn gemstone in the middle. The colour reminded her of Bronte's eyes, and her stomach tightened in a lurch of worry. Bronte had been covered in blood when they'd reached her, and though Leora knew she was safe now, she couldn't shake the crippling panic that had seized her when they'd arrived at Nina's shop.

Leora didn't want to think about the attack now, though, or what it could possibly mean for the future. Things were a lot more complicated than they'd originally thought.

"It looks beautiful," she replied in a tense voice.

Even though her sister wasn't her mum, she still hated the sight of the ring on her finger. Leora was always struck by how fragile her sister looked. Her wrist was so thin, and her hand was deathly pale. She didn't know how she stayed sane, stuck in this house for so long. Her mother locked Callie's door at night. During the day, she let her out but always kept her in sight as though she was some pet.

"Tell me about your night, please?" Callie asked.

The question was in earnest, unlike her mother's. A lump formed in Leora's throat as she thought about her sister being stuck here while she had been dancing and eating outside, but she swallowed it down.

They had a no-crying policy and a pact that one day they would both escape and move into a small apartment on the Canal, where they would open a shop selling used things that they would make beautiful again.

Leora whispered to Callie through the hole, telling her about the carriage they'd taken there, the caviar she'd eaten, and the dream-catchers that had been let off into the sky. How the night had sparkled with all the colours of the rainbow, just as it had when they were younger.

"I wish I could've been there," whispered Callie, her voice soft and full of longing.

Leora's heart ached. "You will be soon, I promise."

They sat in silence for a while, enjoying each other's company. Although it was late and she was tired, she would never leave Callie alone. Soon, her sister's breathing turned heavy.

"Good night," she whispered to the sleeping child.

Leora pressed her fingers to the wall as though she could reach through and give her a hug. Eventually, she pulled herself to her feet with a groan and threw off her dress, letting it crumple to the ground like a deflated souffle.

She was changing into her night clothes when she heard the front door lock click downstairs. She didn't have to look to know who it was. The heavy sound of boots on the floor reached her ears, and she tensed. Leora would know that tread anywhere. It was her father. She could already sense the argument brewing, and though she knew she shouldn't, she crept over to her door. She edged it open so she could hear better.

"Who were you out with tonight?" asked her mother in the same saccharine tone she'd used with Leora.

"No one. I got stuck at work," replied the deep voice of her father. He was a member of the Council, and it was expected he would attend the festival. But perhaps, just this once, he was telling the truth.

"Don't lie to me, Ethan."

"I'm not. Did you hear the news?"

"What news?" Her mother loved gossip, and Leora imagined her sitting up eagerly on the lounge.

"The High Alchemist's daughter has returned."

Her mother scoffed. "Are these the lengths you'll go to, just to get me to believe you weren't out cheating on me? Feeding me rumours that the long-lost heir is alive?"

"It's the truth . . ." her father protested.

"That can't be true," her mother immediately cut in. "Leora would've mentioned it."

Her father murmured a reply, but Leora couldn't catch his words.

"You're lying," spat her mother, the disgust clear in her voice.

Her father's footsteps approached the stairs. Silently, Leora closed her door and slipped into bed. This was one of the rare times her father was telling the truth, but he didn't know the full story. Two heirs had been revealed tonight, on opposite sides of the divide between good and evil. Nick had been right to be suspicions of Isaac, and she didn't know what that would mean for their future.

Nick scrubbed his hands in the cold water. Gradually the dried blood washed off his skin, turning the contents of the bowl a murky brown. He used a bit of cloth to wipe off the more stubborn marks. The linen had become a sodden red mess by the time he was finished, and he dumped it atop his dresser beside the water bowl. The blood was gone, but the image of it across Bronte's neck hadn't left his mind. Nick shuddered to think what Isaac might've done if the crowd of people hadn't arrived.

After all the dreamcatchers had been let off, many people had decided to return home for the night. He was just thankful Eli and Leora had been among them. Nick had heard the end of Isaac's little speech. The stunning cast Isaac had hit him with meant he'd been unable to move or speak at the time, but he'd regained consciousness and had been able to open his eyes. It had killed him having to watch Isaac hurt Bronte. Nick curled his hands into fists as he collapsed onto the bed with a loud groan.

He knew Bronte was safe now yet that didn't calm his anxiety. Nick hated having to leave her but there was no arguing with the High Alchemist. Luckily, Leora had returned shortly after Nick had sent her away, the High Alchemist and Grand Shaman in tow. Apparently, the Grand Shaman was already aware of Bronte's true heritage so that saved Nick from having to explain what he'd overheard for a second time. Eli and Leora had been hard enough to convince. Unfortunately, the three of them had been sent from the scene before he could get any more information.

Sighing, Nick ran a hand through his hair. The night had become a mess. He needed a distraction. He needed to feel like he was doing something. Nick changed out of his rumpled suit and pulled on a pair of pants and a loose white shirt. He also ditched his dress shoes for his old boots. They were scuffed around the edges, but he liked them better.

"Nick, where are you going?" His mother's voice called from her office when he returned downstairs.

He flinched at the sound. She'd been blacked out when he'd come home, but she seemed coherent now, as though she were sober for once. "Out," he called back. He waited for her to tell him to stay. Or at least to warn him to be careful. But she did neither or those things.

"Suit yourself."

He heard her slump back on her chair, and he left through the door. It was nearing daybreak, and the brightening sky revealed the events of the night before. Shattered glass littered the road, and there was more than one comatose straggler slumped against the walls of apartment buildings, too drunk to go any further.

Nick dodged them all as he made his way to The Sparrow. The last of the revellers were still there despite the early hour. He immediately spotted Celia. She was gathering empty glasses from tables, and he made his way towards her. As Nick got closer, he noticed the dark shadows under her eyes, and he hesitated, but before he could turn away, she looked up and spotted him.

"Nick!" she said when she saw him. "I've already heard the rumours that the High Alchemist was seen with your friend Bronte. Is it true? Is she really the heir? Are you okay? You look haggard." She immediately set down the tray of drinks and came to inspect him. It was the tone he sometimes wished his own mother would use. The tone of someone who cared about you.

"I'm fine." He tried to move away, but she pulled him closer. She ran her eyes over every visible part of him until she was satisfied that he really was unharmed.

"Sit," she ordered, not giving him an option as she shoved him down onto a wooden stool. It was sticky with spilt beer, but he didn't protest. "Tell me."

Nick explained the attack as vaguely as possible, not wanting to worry her more than necessary. He still couldn't believe what Isaac had done. Nick had known he was planning something, but he'd never thought that would include killing Bronte.

"That's why I came here. I wanted to know if you've seen anything suspicious tonight. Or if Isaac had come back to meet with anyone?"

"You know a lot of shady people come here, but, no, I don't think he'd be stupid enough to do that tonight."

Sighing, Nick nodded. He hadn't expected it to be that easy.

"Nick, the High Alchemist is the one who will get to the bottom of this, not you," Celia pleaded, her eyes wide with fear.

"I know." But he wasn't certain the High Alchemist would get to the bottom of it. "I have to go," he said, looking up at Celia, who had resumed cleaning the mess left behind from the night.

"Be careful." She held out a hand and squeezed his. And just because she hadn't simply told him 'suit yourself', he looked her in the eyes and promised he would be.

CHAPTER 26

Bronte opened her eyes to a bright room. It reminded her of Leora's bedroom. She was lying in a four-poster bed that could comfortably fit three people. Creamy white drapes patterned with golden leaves were drawn back from the windows, letting in buttery morning sunlight.

"You're awake."

The surprised voice came from her side, and she turned her head to see the High Alchemist staring at her. He had the same auburn eyes as hers. Her father. Bronte pressed herself against the headboard in shock and drew the sheet up to cover her as though it was a protective shield.

"Please, relax," he urged. "I'm not going to hurt you."

Relax, what an insane thing to suggest, she thought. "Where am I?" She remembered her fight with Isaac and losing the necklace. Her hand went to her throat, and she felt nothing but smooth skin. There was no chain to wrap her fingers around. There wasn't any blood or a cut either. Eli's healing had clearly worked.

"Inside my palace. As I'm sure you know, I am the High Alchemist. My full name is Henrik Theobesian . . . and I am your father. I took your mother's last name, given she was the one in power."

Bronte noticed his hesitation and thought back reluctantly to what Isaac had told her. She needed the truth now, but it was already staring her in the face. She had the same tawny skin as he did, the same straight nose and thick brows. He was the missing piece of the genetic puzzle she had been trying to figure out for years, but she didn't know if she liked the picture she saw. Bronte was the daughter of the High Alchemist, the enchanter the Disciples had wanted dead. The person Isaac wanted dead.

"How long have you known I was in Namire, and that I'm your daughter?"

He pulled his hand away from her bed. "Not until the Grand Shaman brought it to my attention last night. I was under the impression, as all of us were, that you were Madden's child," he said finally.

It felt like a blow to the stomach, worse than the cast Isaac had hit her with.

"You were lost to me for a long time, from the night your mother died." His face went deathly pale after speaking the words. "I thought you had been killed as well. It was only a rumour that you had been saved. I clung to that rumour, though. I searched for you everywhere, but you were on the other side all this time, and I had no idea."

"Where were you that night?"

"I had left for Velkrain to try and ensure the support of the werewolves. Madden was rallying forces to build a bigger army, and we couldn't have the wolves taking his side. It is my greatest regret that I left you and your mother here."

"What happened to Isaac?" Bronte couldn't get the manic look in his eyes out of her mind. They were so cold and so cunning.

"Isaac's gone. He shadow-walked before we arrived. It's a form of realm manipulation very few can achieve, aligned with the dark magic he's been responsible for these past months. We haven't found him yet."

Bronte nodded. She didn't think he would be easy to find.

"You're safe now, though," The High Alchemist said, awkwardly patting the edge of her comforter.

Bronte was sick of hearing that phrase. She had come to realise that no one could give her safety or the comfort that came with it. She had to find it for herself and accept that reality was cruel.

"Isaac has the necklace. One of them at least," she said dully.

"He can't do anything with it. At least not until he's found the others, and then . . ." He cut himself off.

Bronte's body felt heavy as she realised why. Because Isaac needed to kill her first.

"How much do you know about the Ancient Triad?" her father asked instead.

"Isaac's planning on using it to free Madden. Is that true, is he really not dead?"

"Your mother couldn't bring herself to kill him, and so his soul was suspended in a purgatory between the spirit realm and reality. The Ancient Triad can be used as a key to release his soul from that jail and reconnect it with his body, which is entombed in the crypt beneath this castle. I'm not sure how Isaac knew that, though."

A chill went through Bronte. "Isaac is the real son of Emelia Everett and Madden Theobesian. He's been contacting Madden using mortificatio," she explained.

"He had us all fooled then."

"He did." And she had been the one who had been tricked the most. She had been so convinced of his goodness. She supposed Nick must be feeling fairly pleased with himself now. But she didn't want to think about Nick. "What day is it? Should I be at school?" she asked suddenly.

A faint smile came across the High Alchemist's face, and Bronte knew, after everything, how ridiculous her question sounded.

"It's only been a day since the Lost Night. You slept all morning. But I don't want you returning to Welkin. It's too dangerous. You will stay here. The palace is warded, and guards are posted at all entrances to keep you protected."

Bronte wasn't about to be cloistered up like a damsel, relying on the words and actions of others. She thought about Frank, Eli, and Nina. They were no doubt worried about her and wondering when she'd be coming home. But Bronte guessed she had finally found her true home, even if everything about it was unfamiliar. "I have to go back to school," she protested. "There's no way Isaac would risk attacking me there, and I still have over half a year to go."

Her father's mouth flattened. "We can get you tutors."

"No, I want to go. Get me a personal guard if you have to, but I'm not staying holed up here."

"We'll discuss this later. At the very least, you will wait until next week to return."

"Fine," she conceded. "What about my friends? When can I see them?"

"You may write to them to inform them that you're safe, but these are uncertain times. We do not know who can be trusted. Therefore, it is best for you to remain here until we have a plan of attack."

A plan of attack against an enemy who could be anywhere. She ground her jaw in frustration, but before she could argue against her new quarantine inside the palace, a loud ringing interrupted her thoughts. A few moments later, a guard appeared at the door. Bronte eyed the woman who was watching her sternly. Her hair was pulled back into severe braids, and her dark eyes were fierce.

"A Nicholas Henderson is here. He's making trouble at the gates and claims he needs to speak with . . . your daughter," she said coolly.

"Send him away . . ." Began the High Alchemist.

"No," Bronte interjected. He looked at her in surprise, hesitation written on his face. "Please, he's harmless."

She remembered what Isaac had told her about their deal. She hadn't been able to accept it last night, but it had finally sunk in. Nick had used her, and whether he regretted it now or not, it still hurt.

"Fine," her father agreed.

Bronte jumped from the bed, before he could go back on his word. She was in a slip, but a dressing gown lay on a chair beside her. She put it on, tying it tightly around her.

"Let Sloane take you down. She's the captain of the guard and someone you'll see around the palace a lot," he told her.

Bronte followed the woman out the door. Leaving her father behind.

The palace was a maze of corridors. Finally, after descending a large flight of stairs they reached the front doors, which were a golden, ornately carved monstrosity.

"I'll take it from here," Bronte told Sloane.

The woman gave a pert nod before walking away. Bronte stared at the doors. Her hands frozen by her side. She could picture Nick behind them, but she didn't know what she would say when she saw him. Taking a deep breath, she reached out an arm and opened them. She had to use all her strength to pull them back.

"Nick?"

He was sitting on the steps outside.

"Bronte!" He jumped up, relief evident in his voice as he made his way to her. He reached out a hand, but she shifted away.

"Why did you come here?" Her icy voice stopped him in his tracks.

"Isn't it obvious. I wanted to see that you were okay." He was watching her hesitantly now.

"I'm fine." She gestured to her body, which showed no physical signs of hurt.

He nodded, his stupid hair falling across his eyes. "I'm glad." When she remained silent, he cast around for something else to say. "So, you're the High Alchemist's daughter." He gestured to the palace behind them, gleaming in the sun.

"It seems so."

"And Isaac is evil."

Though he said it more matter-of-factly, Bronte couldn't help biting back. "Yes, I'm sure you must be pleased. You were right." A fire burned within her; a fire she was certain had died the day before.

"I'm not . . . I never wanted this to happen." He stumbled over the words.

"Then why did you use me as a pawn for your little deal?" she spat.

Nick ran a hand through his hair in desperation. "Let me explain. Please."

His voice broke, but it only hardened her resolve. She didn't want to hear what he had to say. "You don't need to explain. I know why you did it. What's the risk of using me to get what you wanted when we were hardly even friends? But then we were friends, more than friends. Yet you never said anything to me even then." She hated the desperate way her voice sounded as she tried to fight back the involuntary burn of tears. She wasn't about to cry, especially not over something as trivial as this.

"Because I started to believe he'd changed, and that the deal was stupid, harmless."

Nick's hazel eyes were swimming with remorse. They were eyes that she had fallen in love with, and her chest ached as she stared into them, knowing she would never be able to see him without thinking of the hurt he'd caused.

"I thought the same about you. That you were harmless, good for me even. It seems I was wrong. You knew how badly I needed . . ." She cut herself off, her throat burning. Bronte didn't want to admit the stability he had given her, or how much she had come to rely on him, which was why this hurt so badly.

"You don't understand. I had to."

"We all have choices, Nick," she said flatly, echoing the words he'd said to her on the Lost Night. He opened his mouth, about to protest, but she shook her head. "You need to leave." She couldn't speak any longer, or she was sure she would start to cry.

"I'm sorry."

It was two words too late. "So am I," she said bluntly.

She turned away from him and retreated inside the palace. The heavy door closed behind her with finality. Bronte shut her eyes and bit her lip hard, using the pain to distract herself from the emotions inside her.

She felt like part of her was slipping away. The part of her that believed the world was good and that broken things could be fixed if they got the right amount of love and care. Bronte was starting to realise that broken things stayed broken, and their jagged edges tore at everything they touched. It took her a moment to shove away the hurt and let something cool and icy settle in its place. When she opened her eyes again, she was confident she wasn't about to fall apart.

The foyer was empty, and gold gleamed at her from every surface. It was inlaid in the design of the wallpaper and the lining of the marble floor. She didn't know how the High Alchemist, how her *father*, could stand to live in a place that was so shiny.

Bronte laughed. It was a bitter sound echoing around her. She thought back to the tiny apartments she and her mum - or the person she'd thought was her mum - had lived in all their lives. This was a completely different lifestyle and one she didn't think she would get used to quickly.

Bronte walked up the stairs to her room, distracting herself by thinking of the letters she needed to send to Leora, Eli, Frank, and Nina, who would no doubt be wondering how she was.

She took one turn after another, and soon she found herself in an unknown part of the palace. Bronte wasn't surprised that she'd become lost. After all, she hadn't been paying much attention when Sloane had led her to the front door. She'd now found herself in a dim hallway. Dust covered the floor, and spider webs hung from the ceiling. The flickering candlelight cast long shadows as she walked further down the hall, and the gold around her no longer seemed cheery and bright, but dark and sinister.

She knew she should turn back, but curiosity made her continue. Finally, she reached an oil painting of a man and woman. She immediately recognised the High Alchemist, and the woman beside him must be Lydia. These were her parents: her mother and father. They were strangers to her. No more familiar than the people she passed on the street.

Leaving the picture, she continued down the hallway. Coming to a partly open door, she listened carefully, checking that no one was in the room before pushing it fully open. The door swung back with a loud creak. The room looked like it hadn't been entered in years. The furniture was blanketed in dust, and the windows were covered in patches of mould. She wrinkled her nose at the musty smell.

On the wall was a mural depicting a glade and a shimmering waterfall. From the roof hung a mobile of glittering crystals. All the furniture was colourful, yet it had faded with age, and a small cot was placed by the window. The realisation slowly dawned on her that the room was a nursery, and it was waiting for a child that would never come. It was her own nursery. Bronte didn't know what to feel. But right now, she felt like an imposter, a girl who had fallen into another life: an alternate dream.

She left the room and its haunted feel and hurried back down the hallway, still unsure where she was going. But all the gold was giving her a headache, and she knew she needed to get out. She took the hallway she did recognise, and it led her back to the foyer.

"Lost?"

She'd heard that same question before, and her heart clenched as she turned. But it wasn't Isaac she saw. It was a different boy. Or man would be more accurate. He had golden skin and golden hair, fitting in perfectly with the palace's decor. He was dressed in a guard's uniform, and he smiled as though he knew something she didn't.

"I'm Peirce. I've been assigned to you as your personal bodyguard."

So, her father had taken that suggestion literally, then. "Perfect."

"I thought so."

Bronte wasn't in the mood to joke. "Could you take me back to my room?"

He arched a brow. "You don't want a tour?"

"Not when I'm wearing a dressing gown, thanks."

He nodded. "Follow me then."

Bronte couldn't believe that she had gone from being nobody to having guards escort her around a palace in the space of a day. Nothing felt certain to her anymore, but she knew one thing for sure, that the girl who had come into this world searching for answers was no longer the same girl who had now found them.

CHAPTER 27

Bronte was convinced she was burning from the inside out. Despite it being mid-winter, with snow covering the ground around her, she was sweating beneath her tunic.

"Again," Sloane ordered.

Bronte focused her gaze on the captain of the guard. She'd gotten all too familiar with her over the past weeks. Bronte had insisted she learn combat. Never again did she want to feel weak and defenseless as she had when facing Isaac, and that meant she couldn't rely solely on her magic. Sloane's barking voice and stiff demeanour had even slipped into Bronte's dreams at night: a voice that wouldn't be silenced, demanding things of her. She'd wake up feeling achy and sore and overall disgruntled that she could no longer view sleep as a respite.

They were in one of the palace's smaller courtyards, shielded from the cool breeze blowing off the water surrounding the estate and its grounds. The palace was located at the base of the mountains, and the waterfall from Welkin tumbled down the side of the mountain, feeding into the river that ran around the palace and on to the Canal. Bronte had asked why she'd never seen the palace from Welkin, but the wards meant it was undetectable to the naked eye and so, from the school, the area looked like nothing more than forestland.

Bronte wiped the sweat from her brow and adjusted her stance. She tightened her grip around the wooden sword and braced herself for Sloane's attack. Effortlessly, Sloane raised her sword and advanced on her. She swung the blade in a high arc, and Bronte blocked it using the technique she'd been shown. The blow was hard enough to make her arms quake. Sloane didn't wait for her to recover. She brought her sword back and, with a sweeping movement, slashed at Bronte's right side. Bronte just managed to block it in time, letting out a grunt as the wood clashed. They parried back and forth, as Bronte defended herself from Sloane's assault. Her arms were growing heavy, though, and she could feel her reflexes slowing. They had been practising for almost an hour, and it was beginning to show.

Sloane aimed a direct blow at Bronte's midriff, and then darted back. But just as Bronte decided she would aim another blow to her side, Sloane brought the sword down in a flash and swept it towards Bronte's feet. She was too slow to jump, and she lost her balance, landing hard on the unyielding flagstones, her sword clattering as she lost her grip, breaking her fall with her hands. She turned around to find Sloane's sword pointed at her heart.

"And now you're dead."

Bronte heard a laugh and whipped her head to the right to see Peirce in the shadows from the parapet, stifling a grin.

Sloane gazed down at her. "I suggest you head to your chambers and prepare for the ceremony. Your father will be expecting you shortly."

Bronte grunted her agreement, still catching her breath. Today was Solstice Eve, the first day of the Winter Solstice Festival, meaning she was finally allowed to leave the palace for something other than school.

She would attend the blessing ceremony in town along with her father. Bronte had quickly learnt that Christmas wasn't traditionally celebrated in Namire. Instead, they participated in a twelve-day festival which involved providing offerings to the goddess Hecate to ensure the coming year was full of light rather than darkness. Gifts were exchanged tomorrow as a show of gratitude to loved ones, and tonight there would be a ball held at the palace. The first one since the fateful day she had disappeared sixteen years ago.

Bronte had always loved Christmas. She remembered when students at school would talk of their large family gatherings or the copious presents they'd received, but Bronte had liked that it had always been just her and Emelia. They had traditions that she wouldn't have wanted to share with anyone else. Every Christmas, they would buy each other the ugliest sweaters they could find at the dollar store and wear them over their pyjamas. Then they would spend the remainder of the day making an outrageously large Christmas dinner that they never ended up finishing. To top everything off, they would sit in front of the television and watch a rerun of *The Grinch* while they dug into a strawberry jam tart piled high with whipped cream. Bronte guessed that today she would have to start making new traditions. But the idea didn't seem as daunting as it once had. New wasn't always a bad thing.

"Peirce come and take the swords to the armoury," Sloane ordered.

That wiped the grin off his face. Sloane was already marching away, hardly offering Bronte a second glace. Even though she was the High Alchemist's daughter - a status she'd quickly discovered was akin to being a princess - she'd told Sloane to treat her like any other guard she trained, and Sloane had been only too happy to oblige. She was in charge when they were outside, and Bronte was nothing more than a willing student.

Peirce took the sword Sloane offered him as she passed, and then walked towards Bronte. He held out a hand. Grudgingly she took it.

"You're getting better," he said as he pulled her up.

"I don't need pity." She wasn't expecting to become an expert with a sword, but some basic skills were better than nothing. Her father had reluctantly agreed to let her train, just as he'd agreed to let her return to school. It had taken a week of begging and a promise that she would allow Peirce to accompany her. Bronte wasn't allowed to travel through the public Gateways, though. Instead, she used their personal Arch located on the palace grounds, which took her straight to Welkin and returned her home in the afternoon. No going to Merlin's Beard after school, seeing Frank and Nina, or visiting Cora and Mason. Nearly two months had passed since the Lost Night, and Bronte was kept firmly within the perimeter of what her father considered safe.

"That wasn't pity. It was an observation. If I'm forced to stand out here, watching you attempt to fight is more entertaining than watching the clouds pass, if only marginally."

"Standing is your job," she pointed out. "No one's forcing you. If you don't like it, you can quit."

"The situation's hardly that drastic."

"I'm glad. Now, if you'll excuse me, I have to get ready." She gave Peirce a mindless smile she knew would grate on his nerves as she brushed past him.

He shifted to the side with a cough. "After you, *princess*."

Bronte ground her teeth as she walked up the short staircase to the courtyard door, slamming it behind her. She could've sworn she heard a deep chuckle from the other side, and she stormed off in the direction of her room, muttering unpleasant libels about Peirce as she went.

Bronte had been stripped, scrubbed, and plucked within an inch of her life. She was now positioned in front of her mirror while Rowan brushed out the lengths of her hair.

Rowan was her handmaid. She had cornsilk hair, and freckles covered her face like grains of sand. Bronte was still adjusting to life with someone at her beck and call. She'd tried to argue against having a handmaid or a guard stationed outside her room. But her father had been adamant. She liked Rowan, though, and didn't mind the company.

Bronte had learned a lot about living in the palace in the past month and a half: that dinner was served in the dining room at six o'clock sharp every night; that she was never truly alone anymore, there was always someone watching, waiting to escort her from one room to the next; that her father still didn't know where Isaac was, even though it had been nearly two months since he'd attacked her. There had been no more dead animals and no more rumours of dark magic they could use to trace him.

Bronte felt the familiar dip in her stomach and chill on her skin when she thought of Isaac. But that feeling had fueled her training for the past month. Every day she'd risen with him on her mind, knowing he was somewhere out there waiting for her. Despite her father's constant assurance that she didn't need to worry about anything, Bronte knew this was a fight she couldn't avoid forever.

"Time to dress," Rowan instructed, setting the comb down on the table.

She'd braided the top half of Bronte's hair and left the rest to flow down her back. Bronte stood and tucked her robe closer to her body as she made her way to her wardrobe. It was a carnivorous space almost twice the size of Leora's room, decked out with clothes and shoes. They had appeared shortly after Bronte's arrival.

She'd worn nothing more than training gear, her school uniform, and simple dresses for the past weeks, not even touching the glittering gowns that took up almost an entire section of the wall.

"I think this would be an appropriate selection for today." Rowan pulled out a pale-yellow floor-length dress with lace gloves.

Rowan had more knowledge about what was considered suitable for a religious ceremony than her, so Bronte accepted the dress without question. When she'd changed, she slipped on thick-soled boots, lace gloves, and a cream coat to stay warm.

Rowan stepped back, assessing her. "Perfect," she said with a smile.

A loud knocking came from her door and Bronte groaned knowing who was on the other side. She stalked out of her change room and flung the door open.

Peirce looked her up and down, but his face revealed nothing about what he saw. "The High Alchemist is ready for you."

"Patience is a virtue," Bronte mumbled as she followed Peirce down the hall.

A carriage waited for her in front of the palace, and she climbed inside. Her father was sitting stoically on the velvet bench, and he hardly spared her a glance as she found her seat. Peirce closed the door behind her, and then they were rolling towards the palace gates.

"I need you to stay close to me today. We can't risk anything happening."

Bronte sighed. "I doubt Isaac would be stupid enough to try something with you around."

Her father tilted his head in consideration. "Even so . . ."

The carriage brought them to the Town Hall, and they exited directly in front of the building. A pair of High Guard were stationed at the base of both staircases. A crowd had gathered in front of the platform as it had on the Lost Night, but Bronte couldn't make out any faces she recognised.

She knew Leora and Eli were in the crowd somewhere: they'd told her that week at school that they'd be there, but it was clear her father wouldn't let her slip away to find them. Nick would likely be with them, too. Bronte's heart twisted when she thought about Nick. She'd successfully avoided him at school, and with Peirce trailing her everywhere, he hadn't made any effort to talk to her. She'd also conveniently seen that he was left off the guest list for the ball held at the palace that night. Though a small traitorous part of her wished she hadn't been so rash in exiling him from her life.

Bronte had peeked at the invitations sent out at the start of December, and his name hadn't been included. She knew that, if she'd asked, her father would've invited him, but she hadn't said a word. Leora and Eli hadn't brought it up with her either. They would both be attending, given Leora was from a notable family and the Everetts had taken Bronte in.

Since the Lost Night things had been different with Leora and Eli. Bronte kept to herself at school, and although she still spoke to them, she didn't sit in the Dome at lunch and tended to spend most of her spare time at the library away from the prying eyes of other students.

Since her new status as the High Alchemist's daughter had been revealed, she'd become a spectacle to many.

Her father brought her up the stairs where two seats that could only be described as thrones had been placed. Bronte took the slightly smaller one. Peirce stood by her side, having travelled in a separate carriage behind theirs, and Sloane stood by her father. From their vantage point, she could see down the length of the Canal, which was packed with people. It was the first time Bronte had really felt the notoriety of her position. Her stomach clenched with nerves, despite having to do nothing but sit and watch the ceremony. A large fire pit containing a thick log had been built by the platform's stone balustrades.

The doors of the Town Hall opened behind them, and the Grand Shaman walked to the front of the platform. A hush spread through the crowd.

"Welcome all. Today we celebrate the return of light. This is a time for reflection and a reminder that we cannot have light without darkness. Hecate, the triple goddess, will exit her Crone phase and enter her Mother aspect. Now is the time for rebirth and renewal, and it's important to remember that no matter how dark the night becomes, the light will always return! We ask the goddess to please accept our offerings and bless us with a season of prosperity. As a symbol of our gratitude towards the goddess, this yew log will remain lit until midnight of the twelfth day."

The log burst into flames, and the crowd erupted in applause. People came forward, ascending one side of the steps in an orderly line and, as they passed the log, they dropped packages into the fire. They then bowed to the flames and exited down the other side.

"What are they doing?" she whispered to Peirce.

"Providing offerings for Hecate. Usually, eggs, cheese, bread, or meat. This can take a while, so get comfortable."

Peirce was right. Bronte sat for hours watching as people continued to drop offerings into the fire, and yet the line didn't seem to get any shorter. It wasn't until the sun set that her father stood up, motioning her to follow. She felt like she'd aged fifty years as she eased out of the throne on stiff legs. Although she couldn't complain, given Peirce had been standing all that time.

The carriage ride home passed quickly, and although Bronte was ready to fall into bed when she reached her room, she instead found Rowan standing there, ready to prepare her for the ball. The theme was 'Light and Night'. It was apparently chosen to pay homage to Hecate as ruler over both domains.

When the news of Bronte's return had spread through the city, her father had insisted on throwing the traditional Winter Solstice Festival event. Bronte had learnt that it was customary for the ball to be held on the eve of the exact day of the winter solstice, but her father had refused to host it since the apparent death of Bronte and her mother. However, tonight he wished to officially acknowledge her return as the rightful heir.

"The High Alchemist instructed me that you should wear this one." Rowan pulled out a gown from the line of dresses in her closet. It was blindingly white and impossible to miss. The sleeves were made from clear beads and dipped just below her shoulder, while the skirts had a line of lace detailed with swirls that reminded Bronte of snow flurries.

Bronte's mouth pinched in at her father's order. He hadn't said a thing about what she needed to wear. But she knew he wanted to send a message. White was purity and power. Reluctantly, she slipped into the dress, allowing Rowan to help her tie up the back.

"Ah, final touches."

Rowan held up a finger for Bronte to wait, and then she procured a box, flipping the lid open. Inside was a glittering crown rimmed with what Bronte could only assume were diamonds.

"I'm not wearing that." She already felt like a fraud, and she didn't want to shout to the world using shiny jewels that she wasn't one.

"The High Alchemist insisted." Rowan's worried hand touched the side of the box, holding it closer to Bronte.

Bronte pushed it gently back, closing the lid. "Not tonight."

Rowan pursed her lips but didn't say anything more. Bronte knew if they were true friends, she might've argued, but it wasn't her job to speak her mind. And for the first time, Bronte was thankful for that.

Bronte opened her bedroom door, and Peirce turned, ready to escort her to the ballroom. His eyes widened when he saw her.

"It's a bit much, I know," she said, wrapping her arms around her stomach.

He gently took her hands, placing them back at her side. "It's not."

Heat bloomed in her cheeks, and Bronte quickly turned away. Seeking an escape, she hurriedly started down the hallway, leaving him to follow.

Her father was waiting for her at the base of the stairs. He wore robes of gold, and a crown glittered atop his head.

"Bronte."

"Henrik."

She was still unable to say the word father aloud, although, she was slowly growing to think of him that way. She could see he cared for her. He asked her how her day was each night at dinner, and he always made sure she had everything she needed. But the title still felt wrong coming from her lips.

"I see you bypassed the crown."

"I don't deserve it."

"It's important to look the part. You are my daughter. You are a ruler."

I am nothing. "There will be another time for me to announce my rule."

He frowned, the deep grooves in his forehead telling the story of a history of worry. "None as important as this."

"It's too late now."

He let out a resigned sigh. "You're just as stubborn as your mother."

Bronte's blood turned cold, and she didn't reply. Her father offered her his arm, and she took it, walking with him into the teeming ballroom. A hush fell as they entered, and Bronte felt every set of eyes turn towards them.

"Thank you all for coming to celebrate the Winter Solstice ball and to officially acknowledge the return of my daughter. As I'm sure you've heard, the goddess has blessed me in more ways than I could hope for. It is not very often in life that our prayers are answered. Although I prayed every night for her safe return, I had begun to think it would never happen. However, tonight I am honoured to present Bronte Theobesian to you all, firstborn daughter of Lydia Theobesian and future leader of Namire."

A wave of spontaneous applause filled the ballroom. Bronte managed a weak smile in return. Soon guests flooded the space before them, greeting the High Alchemist and his daughter. Bronte couldn't keep up with the names and faces, but she kept a smile on her lips as she shook hands with everyone.

Her smile turned into something real when she saw that Frank and Nina had made it out for the occasion. Nina wore a dark grey gown, and Frank looked smart in his formal suit with his hair combed for once.

"Bronte, happy Winter Solstice!" Nina embraced her with wide arms. When she released her, Frank hugged her in turn, squeezing her gently.

"We've missed you back home. It feels like forever since we've seen you. Did Eli make sure you received everything of yours from the house?"

"Yes, he brought it to me at school." Eli had delivered everything she'd left at Frank and Nina's house, which she hadn't returned to since the Lost Night.

"Good. I know we haven't had much of a chance to talk, apart from the letters, but I wanted to make sure you know that despite everything, we all still consider you family. I'm sure you're safer here, but if you ever need anything, let us know. Cora and Mason also send their regards. They said they were too old for balls, but they hope you have a good night." Frank squeezed her shoulder.

Bronte blinked tears out of her eyes. "Thank you for your kindness."

"Always." Nina gave her a final hug before allowing the next guests a chance to greet her.

When the line of guests finally began to dwindle, she was able to properly look around the room. Bronte's eyes darted across the blur of faces searching for someone familiar, searching for her friends. Bronte knew they would be here tonight, and her skin tingled with excitement.

She saw Eli first. His head of curling hair stood out above the others, and beside him was Leora. She wore a light blue gown whose skirts seemed to float around her as she moved. They turned to her at the same time she looked at them, and Bronte felt herself truly relax for the first time that night. If she could run in her heels, she would've, but she knew her father would disapprove, so she excused herself and settled for a hurried walk towards them. She hugged Eli first, then Leora.

"Merry Christmas!" she exclaimed.

"It's *Winter Solstice*, not Christmas," Leora insisted.

Bronte groaned. She had been subjected to one of Leora's long lectures the day before about how Christmas in Namire wasn't a thing, because alchemists didn't follow the Christian religion. But Bronte thought Winter Solstice and Christmas were virtually interchangeable. People still celebrated together as a family, and Leora had mentioned how tomorrow morning, it was traditional to exchange gifts with loved ones to show gratitude. The only difference was they celebrated a few days earlier.

"Tomato, *tomato*," she said with a shrug. "How is . . ."

"Nick?" Leora prompted.

Bronte nodded.

Eli shrugged. "The same as always."

Bronte hated that she missed him when she knew she shouldn't. She hated that she needed these little slivers of assurance from her friends.

"I need a drink," she announced. Her throat felt suddenly parched. "I'll be back in a moment."

She made her way through the crowd toward a tower of glasses. It was impossible to be inconspicuous tonight. Every movement caused her dress to glitter in the light, and everyone's eyes were constantly on her.

She selected a flute of bubbling liquid and took a sip. The alcohol rushed through her, warming her stomach and settling her nerves.

Bronte knew she shouldn't be drinking but her father was occupied, and no one else was going to question her actions.

"Good to see you've managed to stay upright for the time being."

She turned sharply, only then noticing that Peirce was standing beside her. She'd been so preoccupied with thoughts of Nick she'd forgotten it was his job to tail her everywhere.

"And good to see you still can't keep your mouth shut."

"These are the first words I've spoken since we arrived," he protested.

"You have excellent timing, then."

"I've been told. I do strive to keep a lady satisfied."

Bronte rolled her eyes. "Maybe choose a different lady next time."

"And leave you deprived of my company? I think not."

Despite wanting to keep a straight face, Bronte couldn't help a grin from forming. She took another sip of her drink, letting the bubbles fizz in her mouth before she swallowed.

"I'll survive without it."

"Don't make promises you can't keep."

Bronte tipped the glass back, downing the remaining liquid. She held it out to Peirce, and he reluctantly took it from her. She plastered on a wide smile. "I can assure you, I'm not."

She turned away from him, planning on walking back towards Eli and Leora, but her step faltered when she saw who was standing before her.

CHAPTER 28

Nick had known he wouldn't be able to stay away tonight, even if he should. But he hadn't had a real conversation with Bronte in weeks, and he wasn't going to bypass his chance to make things right.

Nick had assumed she would oversee the list of guests coming to the ball. He also assumed he would be barred from the entrance, so he'd need another way in. The answer had come to him one night at The Sparrow. Music. The High Alchemist had to hire musicians to play. Nick just needed to find the pianist and keep them from being able to attend.

He'd tracked down the man who was meant to play and slipped a herb into his tea. Nothing fatal, but it would cause a sickness that would last for at least twenty-four hours. More than enough time. The desperate band had no other options, and then he had appeared, and they'd reluctantly agreed to let him fill in.

Nick had sat on his piano stool waiting for Bronte to see him but silently praying she wouldn't. When she'd arrived at the ball in her white dress, he'd thought he'd forgotten how to breathe. She was dazzling and it seemed he wasn't the only one to notice. The blonde guard that trailed her everywhere couldn't take his eyes off Bronte tonight, and Nick assumed it wasn't only because of his duties to protect her. Seeing him look at her like that spiked a jealousy in Nick that he hadn't felt since he'd seen her dancing with Isaac on the Lost Night.

Nick hated the way she smiled at him and how she was constantly turning around to talk to him or share some private joke. He hated that a wedge had been driven between them, and now he felt like he didn't know how to talk to her.

Finally, when Nick couldn't stand watching them together any longer, he told the band in between songs that he desperately needed the bathroom, and he disappeared into the crowd before they could stop him.

"Happy Winter Solstice," he said when Bronte was finally in front of him.

She had a frown on her face, and it wasn't the greeting he'd hoped for.

"Thank you," she whispered, gritting her teeth as though to thank him for anything personally pained her. He hated that he'd caused that. "I don't remember inviting you."

The words hurt, but he smiled anyway. "I figured my invitation got lost."

"What are you doing here, Nick?"

"Talk to me, please. Let me explain."

"You used me and put my life in danger. I understand why you did it. I just wish you hadn't."

"I regret . . ."

"Regret doesn't get you forgiveness."

"Then what does? Tell me what does?"

She chewed her bottom lip. "I don't know."

Nick would've said anything, done anything if it meant he could earn back her trust. But from the look on her face, he could tell she still needed time.

"Have there been any new leads on Isaac?"

Bronte's eyes shuttered. "No, and if there were, I'm sure Leora or Eli would've told you."

Her tone wasn't bitter; rather it was filled with resignation. Nick noticed Leora and Eli watching them. Their eyes were wary, as though they were worried to approach and interrupt something, but he wouldn't have minded them coming to break the awkwardness.

"I think the band is missing you." She nodded her head towards the corner of the room, and Nick turned to see the bassist glaring at him.

"Right. Talk later?"

She didn't respond, just gave a noncommittal nod. He walked back through the crowd to the piano.

"Some bathroom break," the bassist hissed.

Nick didn't miss a beat. He just joined in the song they were playing.

Bronte had decided she didn't like balls that much, and if this one wasn't in her honour, she would already have left. Her feet hurt, and her back ached from dancing in heels, but every man under the sun seemed to want to dance with her.

Her current partner was a short man with a mop of messy hair who'd introduced himself as some important member of the Council that Bronte had already forgotten. He wasn't the best dancer, but neither was she, so they manoeuvred awkwardly around the room until the song's final notes rang out. She refused to look at the band as it finished, knowing Nick was watching. Bronte hated that she had been happy to see him. She hated even more how she had blocked him out. But she knew deep down that as much as she wanted things to return to the way they were, she wasn't ready for them to. Because when she looked at Nick, she saw Isaac's cold eyes, and she didn't feel love but pain.

Bronte quickly excused herself from her dance partner and hurried off the floor before she could be swept up again. She found herself back at the drinks table. At least if she had something in her hands, it was an excuse not to dance. She spied Leora and Eli dancing together and she gave them a little wave as she took a sip of the bubbling liquid.

"Having fun?"

Bronte flinched at the voice. "Goddess above! Peirce, stop sneaking up on me."

"It's my job, and usually, you're expecting it."

Bronte sighed. "I've had other things on my mind."

"Care to elaborate."

"No, I'm going to take a walk," she announced.

"I have to accompany you then."

"That won't be necessary."

"As much as you might think the opposite, I do take my job seriously." His grey eyes gleamed with humour that she didn't feel in the mood to reciprocate.

"Me walking out with you will only draw attention to my absence."

"You didn't notice me, and I was standing beside you. I'm invisible in this uniform."

Bronte sniffed. "Still, I'd rather be alone."

"That isn't an option for someone like you."

Bronte was beginning to realise that. She glanced across the room to where her father was standing, talking with a man she didn't know. She was wasting time arguing with Peirce, and her opportunity to leave was slipping away.

"Fine, but don't draw attention to yourself."

He glared at her and motioned for her to go. Discretely she moved around the side of the ballroom and ducked out the opening. They made it through the palace doors, and as the cold winter air enveloped her, she felt like she could finally breathe. Bronte walked around the side of the palace to a secluded balcony that overlooked the garden. The grass was covered by recent snowfall, and everything before her was a blanket of white. The stars were out, and she sighed in relief as the loud noises from inside the ball faded into the quiet night.

"Better?" Peirce asked.

"Much." But she no longer had the warmth of the ballroom to keep her comfortable. She wrapped her arms around herself to stop from shivering. "Why did you become a guard?" she asked, partially to distract herself from the cold but mostly because she'd taken a liking to Peirce and realised she knew little about him despite all the time they were forced to spend together.

"For my sixth birthday, my dad got me a wooden sword and told me to start practicing, because I wouldn't get far without it. He was the previous captain of the guard, but he retired early to look after me. My mother wasn't . . . around. I left school early because he talked Sloane into mentoring me. He's had his sights set on me replacing her since I was born."

Bronte thought that sounded bleak, but Peirce didn't look upset by it. "Did you want to become one?"

He shrugged. "It got me here, looking after one of the most valuable things in the city."

A blush crept across Bronte's cheeks at his intense gaze. "I thought you found watching over me boring."

"No, I said you're the least boring thing about this job."

Bronte stared into Peirce's grey eyes and saw the honesty behind his words. But she found her thoughts caught up on another boy who was playing the piano only a wall away from her. "What's your manipulation?" she asked instead.

"Clairvoyant."

"So, you can predict the future. Do you know what I'm thinking?" she asked, startled.

Peirce laughed. "No. On the scale of powerful to not, I'm closer to being barren."

"Oh." Bronte thought of Leora's sister, and a shiver ran through her. "What can you do then?"

"It's sometimes helpful in a fight. That's why I'm so good with swords. I get flashes of my opponent's next move. It doesn't always work, though."

"I could use that based on today's performance."

"You'll get better."

Bronte shifted on her heels. "Let's hope."

"Why are you so bent on learning to fight anyway? I've seen you use your power. Is that not all the protection you need?"

As well as training with Sloane, Bronte had talked her father into giving her extra enchanting lessons on top of her schoolwork. She spent most afternoons with him practising. She still sometimes felt the shadow of that moment when her power had almost overwhelmed her, and she never wanted to experience that again. "Doesn't hurt to be prepared."

"You're shivering violently," Peirce observed. "I think now would be a good time to return to the ball."

CHAPTER 29

Bronte didn't return to the ball. She hoped Eli and Leora would understand, but she couldn't spend another second there with Nick's gaze on her and strangers constantly asking for a dance. Back in the solitude of her room, she stripped out of her white gown and hung it carefully in the closet, changing into a more comfortable nightdress.

By her bed, a pile of presents had been assembled. Bronte hadn't seen any of the guests carrying them, and if she'd known they were bringing gifts, she would've told her father it wasn't necessary. She didn't need anything, especially from people she didn't know.

Bronte looked aimlessly at the pile. She didn't have the energy to unwrap them tonight. Perhaps, she should call Peirce in, and he could do it for her. She grinned at the thought. She could imagine the look of outrage on his face if she tasked him with such a menial job.

Bronte was preparing for bed when a glimmer of something familiar caught her eye amid the packages. She recognised the amulet of the Ancient Triad, and her heart leapt as she picked up the necklace, but she instantly knew it was wrong. It was a fake.

A piece of paper had been wrapped around the chain that read,

'Happy Winter Solstice, cousin. I hope you didn't think I'd forgotten about you.' Bronte felt the burn of hatred settle in her as she stared at the slanted cursive of Isaac's handwriting. It was the first she'd heard of him since the Lost Night and her skin prickled with anticipation. She knew the day would come when she would see Isaac again and, when that happened, she was determined to get her necklace back. Its absence felt to her like a missing limb. Bronte still reached for the chain despite knowing it hadn't been around her neck for months. There was a knock at the door, and she jumped, hastily stuffing the necklace back into the pile.

"Come in," she called. Bronte turned, expecting to see her father ready to berate her for leaving the party. Instead, Nick was standing in the doorway.

"What are you doing here? Where's Peirce?"

"Attending to a distraction I made. Did you know Mrs Callibary is an awfully loud and disruptive drunk?"

"I wasn't aware of that, and I'm sure Peirce will soon find it to be untrue and quickly wonder why he was lied to."

"It is true, at least partly. All good lies are based on truth." Nick winked, and Bronte felt a spike of heat go through her.

"It doesn't matter whether a lie is good or not. It's still a lie, and you still have to face the consequences for it," she snapped, but her heart wasn't really in it. It had been so much easier hating him from a distance, but now he was in front of her. She couldn't ignore his presence or simply pretend he didn't exist.

"I have something for you," he said softly.

"I don't need more presents," she gestured at the heaping pile beside her bed. Bronte didn't want to take anything from Nick. Having it around would be a constant reminder of him.

"It's not a present, but it is something I should've given you a long time ago." He held out an envelope.

"A letter?"

"An apology. Open it."

Reluctantly her hands went to the seal, and she slipped out the piece of paper. She unfolded it to reveal a blank page. "I see you've put a lot of thought into this."

Nick gave her a wry grin, but it quickly turned into a look of sadness. "I've thought about sending a letter to you every day for the past two months, but I knew you either wouldn't read it or you would, and I was worried the words on the page would mean nothing to you without me here to show you that I meant them. And I only realised once I tried to write a letter that I couldn't get the words out anyway."

"You seem to be doing just fine now," she muttered.

"I've had a lot of time to think. Almost every day I had to stop myself from coming to talk to you. It was driving me mad. I finally understood why Eros's Crossing was stuffed full of letters. I used to think people were fools for writing to a god, but even the tiniest bit of hope that he could fix everything is enough. I've visited the bridge so many times, but I could never bring myself to leave a letter because it wasn't Eros I needed to beg for forgiveness, it was you. I know how it feels when the people you care about too much are the ones who don't seem to care about you at all. I never wanted to make you feel like that. I was blinded by my hatred for Isaac. You have to know . . . you have to know that it scares me how much I care about you, but losing you is a fear far greater, and I'll never be the one to cause you that pain again." He had come closer to her now, only a centimeter away. Nick looked down at her with anguished eyes. "Please, Bronte, forgive me," he whispered, bowing his head.

She felt his pain and knew his reasoning, and she didn't have it in her anymore to hold a grudge. The ice had thawed, and the sting of his betrayal felt like a distant prick. Bronte found her fingers winding their way into his hair, and she gently tilted his head up, so he was looking at her.

"I do." She brought her lips to his, and they both released a sigh.

"I've missed you." He spoke against her skin as he kissed his way across her cheek to the dip of her jaw. His mouth was hot against her, and her breath hitched.

"I know," she managed to get out.

"But you haven't missed me?" He paused, raising his eyes back to hers.

"I've been trying to forget you," she answered honestly, and his eyes dimmed. "But I spent so much time thinking about you that all I did was miss you."

His grip tightened around her waist and the thin material of her night dress bunched against her thighs. He kissed her slowly as though he was trying to imprint the memory of her lips into his brain forever. But she didn't want slow. She wanted him. She felt a wave of wanting so intense that she didn't care that a room full of guests danced not far below her or that, at any moment, Peirce could return knocking on her door and asking if she'd seen anything suspicious. For now, this moment was all she cared about, and after trying not to care for so long, it felt good to finally give in.

Something hard inside Nick's breast pocket pushed into her. "What's that?"

He pulled away, grinning. "Sorry, I actually did get you a present." He reached into his jacket and removed a small rectangular box wrapped in brown paper and secured in red thread.

"Nick, you shouldn't have! What if I hadn't forgiven you?"

"I knew you would."

"Presumptuous." She took the parcel, and his shoulders relaxed. He ran a hand through his hair, but it fell back into his eyes immediately. Bronte watched him, thinking that he needed a haircut more than ever.

"You're staring," he commented.

"Hard not to when you look like a wolverine."

He narrowed his eyes. "A what?"

She suppressed a grin. "Nothing."

Bronte turned her attention to the box. It was heavy, and she pulled at the red string, then ripped off the brown paper. Inside was a small retractable telescope made from brass. It was beautiful and not what she'd expected. She pulled on the smaller end, extending it to its full size, which was about the length of her forearm. Bronte noticed a line of writing inscribed in cursive around the last cylinder. *'For when you feel alone'*, it read. Her throat closed up. She couldn't believe Nick had remembered what she'd told him on the Lost Night. That when she had been at her worst, she would look at the stars and think that her Emelia was watching over her. And no matter what the truth had revealed since then, she would still always love the woman who raised her.

"Nick, this is . . ." *Too much.*

He'd gotten her the perfect gift, and she didn't have anything to give in return. Bronte reached out a hand and intertwined it with his, hoping it would convey the words she couldn't say. She could hardly breathe when he was this close. It felt like everything inside her was attuned to him.

"It's nothing," he replied, though his voice sounded hoarse.

There was a knock at her door, and she sprung away from him.

"Bronte, are you in there?"

It was her father. She turned panicked eyes on Nick. "Get in the closet," she hissed. She shoved him towards the doors. "Yes, just a minute," she called back.

She hid the telescope in the stack of presents, then she straightened her nightgown and pulled on a robe. Quickly Bronte combed her fingers through her hair. She opened the door stifling a yawn behind her hand in an attempt to hide the heat that still bloomed in her cheeks.

"What are you doing up here?" her father asked.

She knew what kind of response her honest answer would get, so she chose to lie instead. "Sorry, I got tired. I'm sure people will hardly notice I'm gone."

"Yes, I'm sure no one's realised that the guest of honour has run away to hide."

"I'm not hiding."

"Your mother didn't like these parties either."

Bronte shifted on her feet. The same awkwardness that arose whenever her mother was mentioned filled her. She didn't know the appropriate response, so she let the silence stretch.

"I noticed Peirce was gone when I came up here. I will remedy that immediately. Get some rest." He paused awkwardly as though wondering whether to hug her. Eventually, he turned around and left the room.

Bronte sagged in relief. "Nick." She hissed towards the closet.

There was no response, and she hurried over, opening the door. Nick was standing across the room examining the glittering crown that had been in the box.

"Leave the crown. You need to go now before Peirce returns."

With a sigh, he placed the crown back and stalked toward her. "Fine, I'll leave, but come into town tomorrow. We can all go to Merlin's like we used to."

Bronte chewed her lip. Her father would never let her out. "I'll see what I can do."

He looked at her intensely, and for a moment, she forgot her panic and the need to rush him away. He pulled her close and kissed her. She fell into him, losing herself in his lips.

With a groan, she pulled herself away. "No time. Go." She brushed past him and opened the door. Thankfully, Peirce hadn't yet returned. "Go," she urged.

"I've missed you," he whispered to her as he slipped past. She watched his figure stride down the hall and out of sight before she clicked the door gently shut behind her.

"I've missed you too," she said to the empty room.

Bronte wished she could remember this warm feeling inside her forever, the glow that made her feel invincible. But she wasn't invincible, and as she turned to the pile of presents by her bed, she was reminded of the fake necklace Isaac had sent her, and she felt the constricting weight of hatred and fear settle over her. She was far from free. These walls and this night reminded her of that. The sacrifices Lydia and Emelia had made hadn't allowed her to escape her fate. They had merely prolonged the inevitable.

She shifted the presents away from her bedside. She would open them tomorrow but, right now, she wanted to sleep. As she moved them, a small package with her grandparents' names caught her eye. Renewed sadness spread through her. She couldn't call them her grandparents anymore. They had no relation to her. Still, she opened the package and inside was a delicate gold ring engraved with a pattern of leaves. She slipped it on her finger and found that it fit perfectly.

Bronte knew it was silly to value material things, but the ring felt like more than that. It felt like they were repeating what Frank had told her tonight, that despite everything, they still wanted her in their life, and she still wanted them in hers. She'd learnt that who you called family had little to do with blood and everything to do with the way you were loved.

CHAPTER 30

Alex Strognov didn't enjoy his life. Unfortunately, he'd been born a shameful excuse of an enchanter. He could vividly remember the look of disappointment on his parent's faces when he'd barely been able to do more than summon a leaf from the ground. He may as well have been barren, given the infinitesimal amount of power he possessed. That's why he'd turned to alcohol.

Alex walked along the streets towards The Sparrow and thought about what he would drink. He liked The Sparrow. The barmaid was easy on the eyes, and a boy sometimes played the pianoforte at night. The sound of music floating above the roll of dice and exchange of coins gave him a little joy.

He was taking a shortcut through a back street when a shadow appeared further down the path. It was hard to tell who it was because there were no sunstones to light his way. It was also a new moon tonight, and the usual silvery glow Alex relied on was non-existent. As he got closer to the figure, he heard a hissing sound as though the person was speaking in another language. It was a strange, harsh noise that sent a shiver through him. Then everything turned black. Alex froze. He was stricken by the thought that he'd suddenly gone blind. But then the darkness shifted. It forced its way inside him. Down his throat, through his nose. He gasped for breath. A horrible wet sound escaped his mouth. Over and over again, he tried to breathe, but he couldn't. Alex tried to reach for his non-existent power, reach for anything, but he felt empty. He crumpled to the ground. His lips parted as he waited for a breath that would never come.

As Nick walked back to the south after the ball, he thought about Winter Solstice and how much he disliked it. He enjoyed the lead-up to it, though. The whole city seemed a tiny bit brighter, and everyone was a little bit nicer. He liked the lights they strung up around shop fronts and through the Canal. And how, despite the cold weather, you felt a warmth inside you looking at the decorations and knowing that soon everyone would gather around fireplaces exchanging gifts and eating meals with their family. But that was where his fondness for the holiday stopped. Because as much as he could fantasise about having a big happy family, he knew that would never be a reality.

There was one Winter Solstice morning that stood out to him, though. It was the year before he'd started school and, on this particular morning, his mum had woken up and decided to act like his caretaker for once. She'd built up the fire, so his room had been warm when he'd opened his eyes, despite the snow that drifted by his window, and a big breakfast of scones, cream, and even jam sat in the middle of the table when he'd come downstairs.

"Happy Solstice, Nick!" His mum had said gleefully when he'd sat at the table.

"Happy Solstice," he'd replied hesitantly, unsure where the sudden cheerfulness had come from.

His dad had come down the stairs behind him. His hair had been combed, and his beard had been shaved for once. Nick hadn't recognised this family sitting before him sharing food as though it were normal. He felt for sure that he was in a dream or living some alternate reality. He'd half expected his brother to walk through the door next.

"We have something for you!"

His dad had passed him a thin book tied with a red ribbon. Inside were pages of music.

"How did you . . ."

"I heard through the grapevine that you play a bit now."

Nick had smiled. "It's great, thanks."

The rest of the meal had passed happily. Nick had eaten five scones piled with cream, and the prospect of getting to learn new music had filled him up even more. He'd helped his mum clean up and then raced to his room. He'd thought he should buy them a present too because, for once, he wanted to impress them. He'd wanted their approval. Not something big, but Nick had been playing at The Sparrow long enough that he'd saved up a small fortune. He could buy a nice candle, or an ornament, or perhaps a bookend. But when Nick had lifted his mattress up, he'd found his money pouch wasn't beneath it. He'd searched his entire room, thinking he'd somehow misplaced it, even though he knew he hadn't. But then everything suddenly made sense: his parent's cheerful mood, the food on the table for once. All unknowingly paid for by him.

Nick hadn't received a gift from them since. He hadn't tried to buy them one either. He'd never confronted his parents about it because he supposed that one perfect morning was gift enough. Even if he'd known he was paying for it at the time, he still didn't think he would've changed a thing.

Nick always bought gifts for Eli and Leora, though. He enjoyed picking out things he knew they would love. He liked his title as a great gift giver. Nick didn't know when he'd decided to buy something for Bronte. He hadn't known for a long time what that thing would even be. He'd just started putting away a little extra money each day for her. It wasn't until she told him the story about the stars that Nick knew what he wanted to get her. It had put a bit of a dent into his savings. But Nick was able to bargain for a good price, and the look on her face was more than worth it.

Snow had begun to fall, and Nick hugged his coat closer to his body, longing for the warmth of his bed. He was cutting down a side alley when he came upon a body lying with limbs spread on the ground. At first, he assumed it was just someone too intoxicated to make it home. But then he saw the blood staining the white flakes. The man's shirt had been ripped open, and it looked like an intricate pattern of runes had been carved into his chest. For a moment, Nick couldn't separate the image before him from that of his brother as he pictured him in death, lying in his own blood with the same pattern carved into his flesh. He felt bile rise in his throat. Beneath the overpowering stench of rotting seaweed, the lingering traces of magic remained in the scent of burnt sugar. The man had fallen on his back. His mouth open in shock, his face a mask of fear. Nick vaguely thought he recognised him from The Sparrow, but he didn't know if he'd been there tonight.

"What's going on here?"

Nick flinched and looked up into the face of two High Guards. He didn't know how they'd found him. Perhaps they'd been following him since he'd walked through from the north. It was the early hours of the morning, and he supposed he could've looked suspicious hunched into his coat alone.

"I don't know. I just found him," he sputtered.

One of the guards narrowed her eyes, and he knew he would instantly be suspected as the culprit, but thankfully she didn't directly accuse him. Her nose wrinkled as she got closer, and Nick knew she smelt it too - death and burnt sugar. She crouched beside the body, testing for a pulse and inspecting the man's airways. Her mouth flattened into a grim line, confirming what Nick already suspected. She shared a look with her partner before turning to Nick.

"When did you find him?"

"Only moments ago."

She sniffed the air again, away from the body and her brow creased. "We need a shaman," she muttered. She eyed him quizzically. "There was no one in the alley when you arrived?"

"Not a soul," he replied confidently.

The woman gave a small nod. "Go straight home, and don't speak to anyone about what you saw here."

"But I . . ." he began to protest. His curiosity had gotten the better of him, and he wanted answers as much as she did. Although, he had a pretty good idea who was responsible for this. He was sure Isaac had finally made a move.

"That's not a request," she snapped.

Silently cursing, Nick left the alley and walked back to his house. It was dark when he entered, and there was no sign of his parents. The fireplace was unlit, and Nick's room felt like an ice box.

He hurriedly changed for bed, burying himself under his blankets. When he finally stopped shivering, he drifted into a restless sleep, but images of the mutilated body he'd found remained trapped in his head. The next morning, Nick awoke wondering if he had dreamed the whole thing. He passed the alley on his way into town that morning, and a blanket of white covered any evidence from the night before, but Nick could still smell it. Burnt sugar and death. That was how he knew it was real.

CHAPTER 31

Bronte entered the large dining area for breakfast to see her father already waiting, seated at the head of the long table.

Worry seeped into her as she took a seat adjacent to him, meeting his vacant eyes. "Is everything okay?"

Her father sighed heavily, running a hand over his face. "There was a suspected murder last night in the south."

Bronte froze. "What? Who was it?"

"An enchanter by the name of Alex Strognov. The murder was near identical to the ones performed during the height of the Disciples reign. His chest had been carved with runes that can only suggest some form of mortificatio was used."

"Do you think Isaac did it?" she whispered.

The High Alchemist frowned. "We have to wait for the Grand Shaman's assessment to be sure but, from the description I received, it looks like Isaac's work. I believe he's finally come out of hiding. I wasn't going to tell you because I don't want to worry you, but I felt you should know."

"You're right. I *should* know. This what we've been waiting for. What I've been training for."

"Bronte, how many times must I tell you, your training is a precaution, nothing more."

Bronte stabbed a cube of melon with her fork in frustration. "And how many times must *I* tell *you* that my training isn't a precaution it's an inevitability. Isaac wants me dead, and I hardly think your worries for my safety are going to get in the way of his plans."

"Let's not get into this today. I don't want our first Winter Solstice together to be ruined."

Bronte shook her head. "That hardly matters." She could only think of Isaac now. She didn't care that today was meant to be a day of celebration. She couldn't relax knowing that Isaac was still out there, potentially growing more powerful by the day.

"It matters to me. I'm sorry I didn't get you anything. I wasn't sure what was appropriate. Is there anything you'd like?"

Bronte thought for a moment. "A lesson. I know you're busy, and technically I'm on school break and should really be studying for my exams, but if Isaac has made a move, it's more important than ever that I hone my skills." She leveled her father with a stare, waiting for him to argue.

He looked back at her wearily. "Go put on your tunic and meet me in the courtyard."

Bronte rushed from the table back upstairs before he could change his mind.

The stiff fabric of the tunic Bronte wore stuck to her back. She pulled on the collar itching her neck.

"Stop fidgeting," her father chided, and she released her hold on the tunic with an annoyed sigh. "You insisted on training today, so don't give me that look."

Bronte pressed her mouth into a line, knowing she couldn't argue.

"Hands up and prepare yourself."

Bronte focused her gaze on her father and did as he said. He sent a flash of light at her, and she blocked it effortlessly. It was second nature now. She sent a dizzying cast back at her father. They parried back and forth until sweat dripped from her. But the drag of her magic didn't pull her under anymore. Bronte was learning to control it, to use it in bits, so it didn't overwhelm her. But her father wasn't weak. He didn't relent.

Sloane entered the courtyard, pausing to watch them. Cast after cast came at her. Eventually, one slipped through, knocking her back, and her shield waivered.

"Go for a run and then come back," her father ordered, turning his attention to Sloane before she could argue.

Peirce moved from the corner of the courtyard where he was standing guard. "Let's go," he groaned.

"I don't need you to come."

"I have to come for your protection. Remember it's my job?"

Bronte set off jogging, following the path that led around the palace and back to the courtyard.

"Why couldn't you just stay inside the palace today and sow pillows or play music or read? Anything that doesn't involve me having to stand in the cold," Peirce complained.

"When Isaac is hunting me down, I'm sure I can gift him a lovely hand stitched pillow, and he'll decide not to kill me."

"I'm glad we're in agreement."

Bronte refrained from talking and instead focused on her breathing. When they rounded the front of the castle, she spotted a green blob flying toward her. She drew to a stop, forcing Peirce to as well.

"Wilbur?" The furrow landed in front of her, and she confirmed that it was really him from the name on his pouch. "What are you doing here, huh?" She reached down and retrieved the note. She recognised Nick's messy scrawl immediately. It was a request for her to meet for lunch at Merlin's Beard.

Bronte hadn't forgotten his request last night, but she had been waiting for the right moment to ask her father. She wondered if Nick had heard about the murder, but she didn't know how, given it had only just happened, and she was sure her father was keeping it quiet.

"What's it say?" Peirce peered over her shoulder.

"You and I might be going on a little trip."

"Like the High Alchemist will let you."

Peirce was right. The second she asked her father if she could go into town, the answer was an immediate "no".

"I will not let you put yourself at risk like that!" he finished, filling the courtyard with his stern voice.

"I haven't left these walls apart from school in two months. Let me go into town just this once, and I won't ask again. I'll even allow Peirce to come along to . . . protect me," she gagged on the word. "Isaac won't attack in the light of day. He won't even know I'm there. It's Winter Solstice. Just let me have this one thing."

She could tell her father was thinking it over by the fact that he remained silent long enough for her to finish talking.

His eyes flickered to Peirce. "You'll make sure she gets back in one piece? Guard her with your life? Sacrifice yourself if you have to?"

Bronte rolled her eyes. They were going to town, not entering battle.

He nodded solemnly. "Of course, sir."

"You may go for one hour and, when you get back, you'll have a lesson with Sloane."

Bronte hid her smile. "Thank you."

Bronte was finally in the midst of the Canal, taking in all its winter glory. Wreaths were strung up along the bridges, and twinkling lights glowed down the length of the street, making Bronte feel like she'd stepped onto the set of a Hallmark movie.

She thought most people would be inside trying to hide from the cold, but it seemed the opposite. The carriage they'd taken here had rolled past countless families on what she could only assume were pre-feast walks. No doubt, back at home, their kitchens were filling up with the smell of roast lunches. She hadn't liked the stares the carriage emblem had drawn on the way, though. Children had pointed it out excitedly to their parents, and even though Bronte was hidden behind the dark windows, she had never felt more exposed.

"To think we could be in front of a nice warm fire at this very moment," whined Peirce, trudging along the snowy path beside her.

"If you're not happy with your role as my protector, I'm sure I can find many willing volunteers to replace you."

"And doom yourself to a droning carriage ride with one of the other guards? You're lucky I saved you from that fate."

"No, you're lucky I saved you from your fate of standing outside the palace in the cold, watching the trees for any mysterious activity. Would you rather that?"

"I would rather be sitting in a nice hot tub until my teeth stopped chattering and my skin turned red. At this moment, I can't even remember what it was ever like to feel warm."

"Stop being dramatic."

"Is that an order?"

Bronte raised a brow at him. "Yes." She felt the need to remind him again that he could be replaced but refrained. She wished it wasn't necessary to have escorts, but she'd known this was the only way her father was going to let her out of the palace, and it wasn't worth the fight to get her way. "We're here now anyway. No need to complain about the cold. We'll soon be inside a warm room."

They had arrived outside Merlin's Beard's butter-coloured front. It was the only place along the Canal that Bronte could see was still open today. In the window, a sign was hung up inviting customers in for Winter Solstice lunch.

"Thank the goddess for that." Peirce opened the door for her and ushered her inside.

Bronte spotted their group at the usual table in the corner. Eli and Leora smiled at her as she came over, but she didn't miss Nick's narrowed eyes as he looked at Peirce. She took the spare seat next to Nick, and Peirce stood behind her.

She turned, pulling over a chair from the empty table beside them. "Sit. You aren't standing behind me like a sentry."

He made a face but didn't argue.

"You finally got let out," Leora said cheerfully.

"Not without a watchdog." Bronte elbowed Peirce.

"What happened to you last night? We barely got a chance to talk," Eli scolded.

Bronte cringed. "Sorry, I . . ." She could feel Nick's foot beneath the table gently nudge her, and she was reminded of exactly what she'd been doing while she'd been absent from the party. "I got tired," she finished.

"And Nick was noticeably missing at the same time?" Leora arched a brow.

"Our paths may have coincided momentarily," Nick conceded.

"And now we're all sitting here about to enjoy a lovely lunch, and you're magically forgiven, I see." Eli raised a brow.

"I don't make the rules," Nick said defensively.

Bronte crossed her arms. "It's not too late to change my mind." There was a stifled cough from Peirce, which sounded a lot like a laugh.

A waiter arrived carrying their food. A steaming plate of pancakes was placed in front of Bronte. "We ordered for you, assuming pancakes are still your usual?" Nick grinned at her, and her heart warmed.

"Thank you. Peirce, did you want any?"

"I'm here to guard, not sit and eat food," he grumbled.

"Don't be stupid. Eat." Bronte shoved the plate towards him.

Nick rolled his eyes, and she kicked him under the table. "What did you do that for?"

"Do what?" she asked sweetly. There were muffled sniggers from Leora and Eli, but Nick just shook his head and cut into his food, ignoring them.

"As much as I'm happy to see you, Bronte, I called this little gathering to discuss what I saw last night. Nobody in the city knows yet, but there was a murder. I filled Leora and Eli in before you arrived, I assume you already know?" he asked her.

"Are you sure you should be talking about these things?" questioned Peirce.

Nick immediately stiffened. "Why shouldn't we? It involves

Bronte, doesn't it? Isaac is dangerous, and he's clearly tired of waiting. What I saw last night was exactly the same as the way I was told my brother died. Isaac is harvesting enchanter magic. Who knows how strong he could grow? And if he gets his hands on the other necklaces, he's even more of a threat."

"Yes, but the High Alchemist is the one who will take care of this, not the detective squad you four have formed."

Bronte's cheeks burned. "My father has no idea where Isaac is. We've got just as much chance of finding him as he has."

Peirce ran a frustrated hand through his hair. "Don't be ridiculous, Bronte."

"I think you're overstepping your place, *Peirce*." An uncomfortable silence settled over the table. Bronte had always had a relaxed relationship with Peirce. But she hated the way he'd spoken to her like she was a child when she knew he was hardly a year older than her.

There was a shout from outside, and the five of them turned towards the windows. Darkness had enveloped the streets. It was a darkness Bronte recognised from the Lost Night. It was Isaac's darkness. Peirce was instantly on his feet, pulling her up by her arm. "We need to go."

He was already pushing her towards the kitchens. Bronte resisted, watching the window. "He has the necklace."

"He also wants to kill you," Nick pointed out, joining Peirce in pulling her away. She struggled against them, trying to get to the door. She thought of the note Isaac had sent her last night, and rage filled her. Bronte needed this shot at him. The months of waiting for him to finally appear had ended, and she couldn't just run away.

"Don't be stupid, Bronte. He probably isn't even carrying the necklace. We need to go," Eli urged.

As she looked back, she saw the shadow of Isaac emerge. But she wouldn't put everyone at risk. She knew if Isaac came after her, he wouldn't hesitate to take down her friends as well. She finally gave in, allowing herself to be pulled away. The group rushed through the kitchen, the confused look of the cooks following them out into the back street.

"This way." Peirce pulled her away from the corner leading her up towards the Gateways.

They sprinted, their footsteps echoing behind them. When they reached the top of the street, Bronte risked a look back and saw that the darkness had spread, coming quickly for them. But the High Guard were on alert and assembling in Isaac's path.

Peirce dragged her along until they made it to the Gateways.

"Divert Isaac, go somewhere safe," Peirce yelled to the others as he shoved her through the Arch that took them to the top of the north and the next second, they were on a frosty road far away from the Canal.

Bronte ran through the trees, following the long road that would take her to the palace. She heaved in breaths of air, her lungs burning from the cold. She was slow in the long skirts of her dress and thick boots, but she didn't stop. Peirce urged her on and then, blessedly, the gates were in sight.

The guards standing alert rushed to help them. Bronte collapsed past the border, panting out clouds of air from her mouth. One of the guards hurried off, and she knew he was going to get her father. She would never be allowed out again. She was going to be kept behind the palace walls forever.

Bronte cursed. She shouldn't have run. She should've faced Isaac. That had been her chance, and she had allowed fear to get in the way. She rolled over to find Peirce looking down at her. He was breathing evenly and didn't seem on the brink of death as she was.

"You should have let me face him," she gasped.

"If I thought you were ready, I would have."

They were harsh words, and their argument from before echoed in her mind. He reached out a hand, and she reluctantly took it, allowing him to pull her up. Her father was striding down the path, and she quickly dusted snow and dirt off her dress.

"What happened?" He demanded.

"It seemed Isaac didn't want to go by my logic after all," Bronte said breathlessly.

"What does that mean?"

"He just appeared in the street, great clouds of darkness enveloping the space around him. How could he have known I was there?"

Deep lines marred her father's brow. "It's possible he put a trace on you somehow. To track you if you leave the palace wards. Are you wearing anything different?" Her father appraised her.

She thought of the necklace Isaac had given her. Surely, that had been the thing he'd put a cast on. But he must've known she would never wear it. "The ring! I was given a ring last night. I thought it was from Cora and Mason, but I suppose he could've sent a fake gift from them."

"Give it to me. I'll have it analysed by the Grand Shaman."

Reluctantly she slid the ring off her finger and handed it to him.

"Go inside and take a bath. I don't want to hear another argument about your freedoms when you can see I'm only trying to protect you now."

Bronte gazed up at the tall palace walls. Her home and prison. But there would be other days to push for her freedom, other days when she hadn't just run for her life.

"Thank you." She told Peirce, but he only nodded at her, and she was surprised to feel a twinge of hurt as she walked away. Bronte hadn't realised that somewhere in the last two months, their relationship had slipped between professional and personal, and she wasn't sure that was a good thing.

CHAPTER 32

"Come in, come in," beckoned Professor Kirwan as they arrived at concoction studies that morning.

The air was pleasantly warm inside the room, and Bronte was grateful for the school's heating. She'd learnt that enchanters could magic cauldrons of water to boil indefinitely for a steep fee. At Welkin, the steam was piped through the castle for radiant heating, staving off the cold turn that had swept through Namire now that it was winter.

Bronte, Leora, and Eli sat at their usual table and pulled out their notebooks to prepare for the day's theory lesson.

"Quiet down," called Professor Kirwan, her voice rising about the chatter. "Today, we're going to talk about the antidotes to poisons." She scrawled the word on the chalkboard. "In light of recent events, I feel it's important that you're all prepared in case such a scenario arises."

A palpable tension had swept through the city since the murder in the south, and the news of Isaac's recent appearance had spread like wildfire. The paper had eventually gotten hold of the story twisting it to make it seem like the Disciples had returned, and people had begun fearing the worst.

Bronte frowned at the board. On top of everything else, she also didn't like the prospect of being potentially poisoned. But she supposed it couldn't hurt to be prepared.

"There is a range of potential biologically active plants that can have detrimental effects on both your powers as an alchemist and your overall health. What are some poisons to be aware of?"

Scarlett's hand shot up. "The rare jaquesbloom is a purple flower whose nectar, when distilled correctly, can nullify an alchemist's abilities completely. One drop is enough to have an effect, and more than two flowers' worth can be fatal. It can also cause nausea, vomiting, hallucinations, and a rise in temperature while it's in your system."

"Correct," Professor Kirwan approved. "The Fae and werewolves also have a range of plants and substances that can prove deadly. A full list of poisons can be found on page sixty-five of your textbooks, and I'd like you each to choose one poison and write me three hundred words describing its origin, effects, and possible antidotes. The most common antidote to be found is nollyleaf." She held up the delicate stem of a flower with a small white bud on the end that looked like a snowflake. "It's plentiful and can be found growing in most gardens around Namire. All you need to do is chew the flower and, within half an hour, the effects of the poison should wear off completely. It works to stop the spread of the poison through the body and even draw its effects out of the patient before it becomes fatal. I've collected some for each of you." She held up a wicker basket full of nollyleaf and passed it to the student closest to her. The girl took a sprig before handing it on. "It stays useable no matter how long you keep it, so I recommend putting some in your pocket wherever you go, just in case."

When the basket came around, Bronte slipped some into her jacket pocket. She hoped she would never have to use it but knowing she had it there was comforting.

"I always knew there was something wrong with Isaac," Reyna claimed. "The way he would just strut around the school. You could tell there was something dark inside."

"I never thought he was capable of murder. We're probably on his hit list if he's after enchanters." Jake shivered.

"Bronte, please tell us the High Alchemist knows where he is," begged Reyna.

Bronte glanced up from her textbook. She was tired of these conversations. Students who had never talked to her before continually came up to her in the hallways asking if she knew where Isaac was or whether her father thought the Disciples had returned. She'd wanted to come back to school so she could have normalcy. But it had never been the same since the Lost Night, and it was only growing worse now Isaac had started stirring up trouble.

"The High Alchemist has things under control," she told them, barely containing her irritation.

"I'm glad to see you all made it safely through the holidays," came Professor Latoux's sharp voice as she clipped into the room, silencing their conversation. "I'm sure you've all read The Scriber by now and have heard of the theories surrounding the attack, but it is still believed to be an isolated event, nothing to worry about."

She didn't mention that the perpetrator had once sat in this very room with them.

"Yes, Reyna?"

Reyna lowered her hand. "Um, what sort of cast was the magic used in the attack? If we learn it, then maybe we will know how to combat it next time."

"There won't be a next time," Professor Latoux said briskly.

"Just for educational purposes, then."

Professor Latoux pursed her lips, but she took in their eager faces and, gradually, a look of resignation came across her. "It's not a branch of enchanting we teach, and its practice had been banned in Namire since its creation, but the magic that we believe Isaac used is what we call *mortificatio*. It can involve the summoning of demons, mind control, bodily possession, or in this case, absorbing another's power.

The unique thing about mortificatio is that you don't necessarily need enchanting power to perform such magic. The energy used arises directly from acts of evil." Professor Latoux didn't look like she wanted to elaborate, but Reyna raised her hand again.

"Such as?" she prompted.

"Death," Professor Latoux replied solemnly. "It doesn't necessarily have to be a human death, although that will create the most powerful magic. Animals and animal blood can also be used. Centuries ago, some witches excelled at such magic. They used their power for evil, but it was considered a crime against the goddess. We were given our powers as a gift, which is why we use them for good."

"Do you really think this was a one-off attack Professor, or do you think the rumours might be true? That the Disciples have really returned?" questioned Jake.

Professor Latoux's face was as hard as marble as she looked at them. "I think jumping to conclusions is never right and that we have strayed off track from today's lesson. While I have previously had you practice summoning fire to light the wick of a candle, today we will be learning how to summon and control fire using only your hands. We'll be going outside for the lesson. I'm hoping the cold will motivate you, and the snow will help us avoid any problems if one of you loses control."

They all groaned as they put on their warm winter coats and followed Professor Latoux outside.

Bronte grinned at Peirce as they walked through the hall. "Time for one of your favorite activities. Standing guard in the snow," she said sarcastically.

Peirce spent most of her lessons seated at the back of the classroom, but on days when they were required to do something practical, he was forced to stand watch.

"I'm sure it'll be entertaining," he replied blandly.

When they were gathered on the snowy lawn Professor Latoux began speaking. "One of Hecate's many gifts was the ability to control the elements. This included being able to summon fire. That same ability lies within you. As with our other lessons, I want you to hold out your hand and visualise fire in your palm."

The three of them did as they were told.

"Is this going to burn us?" Jake asked, his voice wavering.

"No, the wielder will not feel anything but a mild heat when the flames are in your hands. Now make those flames real."

Bronte drew on her power, envisioning it emerging from her palm in the form of fire. Miraculously, the flames she'd imagined burst to life, dancing in her hand.

"Good, Bronte." Professor Latoux praised. "Now, see if you can make it bigger or smaller."

Bronte focused on her flames, willing them to grow. Slowly the flames rose until they were well above her head. She quickly drew back with her power, and they died down again. Bronte cut off her power, and the flames disappeared. She let out a breath, relaxing her tense body and a wide smile spread across her face at her success.

Beside her, a weak flame flickered in Jake's palm, and Reyna was tending to her own raging fire.

"Oh!" Reyna exclaimed when fire leapt from her palm into the snow. It was instantly extinguished, and Reyna quickly controlled the remaining flames.

"That is what happens when we don't have control over our magic. It's important to concentrate, or it can grow wild," Professor Latoux observed.

For the remainder of the lesson, Bronte summoned flames into her hand. She learnt to transfer the fire between her palms, so the flames leapt back and forth. Her face was flushed when the final bell rang, but she was brimming with excitement at the thought of showing her father what she could do.

Her lessons quickly picked up again after the winter break, and although Bronte wanted to focus on finding Isaac, the more pressing issue was passing her impending mid-year exams.

"I'm never going to learn this," sighed Leora, holding her head in her hands.

They were sitting in the library, notepaper and textbooks spread around them in a halo. Bronte's eyes were burning from reading for so long, but Scarlett was sitting at the table opposite theirs, and her presence motivated Bronte to continue. She could clearly envision the smug look on Scarlett's face if she failed her exams.

"You'll be fine. Stop stressing," Nick said airily. He was rolling up balls of paper and flicking them across the table at them. Bronte swatted one away, glaring at him. Leora looked up from her page of notes, smiling sweetly, yet her eyes were burning.

"Nick, if you're just going to sit here and annoy us instead of working, why don't you go find somewhere else to be?"

"Because then I couldn't do this, could I?" He flicked another paper ball at Leora, and it bounced off her forehead.

Her cheeks flamed. "Nick! I swear to . . ."

He held up his hands in defeat, cutting her off. "All right, calm down. I'm going. I was just trying to lighten the mood," he muttered as he climbed out of his chair. He winked at Bronte. "Don't melt your brains." He lingered behind her, his hand brushing against the soft skin of her arm as he passed, leaving behind a trail of goosebumps.

"Stop being disgusting and leave." Leora turned around in her chair and hit him lightly on the arm.

"Jeez, would you relax? Where's Eli, anyway? Wasn't he coming?"

"No idea. Why don't you go find him? Seems like a more worthwhile use of your time," jabbed Leora. Bronte had to bite her lip to keep herself from laughing as Nick skulked away.

"I don't think your father will be happy to hear about this relationship if it's distracting you from your studies," Peirce said dryly. He was absently flicking through a book beside her, but Bronte was sure he hadn't read a word of it.

"It's not a relationship, and my studies are going just fine despite it, thanks." She threw a paper ball at Peirce, and he hit it away.

There had been no further mention of their argument inside

Merlin's Beard, and Bronte was grateful things had gone back to normal between them.

"Whatever you say. We should be getting back to the palace, though, if you still want to have a lesson with Sloane."

Leora groaned. "Don't leave me here alone."

"At least you'll have no distractions once I'm gone."

"True," she grumbled.

Bronte collected her things, and they left the library.

"What's going on between you and Nick?"

Bronte looked up sharply. "Pardon?"

"I know he snuck into your room on the Winter Solstice, and you clearly can't keep your eyes off each other."

Although he wasn't far from the truth, Bronte wasn't going to admit anything. She hadn't been alone with Nick since, and nothing further had happened. "There's nothing going on, Peirce. With you trailing me around everywhere, I hardly get a second to myself."

"Who's the one being dramatic now?"

"I've learnt from the best."

They had reached a door on the far side of the castle, close to the classroom where Bronte had first learnt to summon. Peirce took out a key and unlocked it, allowing Bronte in and locking it behind them. Inside was an Arch built specifically for Bronte's use to take her straight to the palace, which was extremely convenient. She stepped through it without another word to Peirce. She hoped he wouldn't bring up the topic again, because she wasn't sure she even knew the answer.

Bronte's lesson that afternoon with Sloane was brutal. She had just finished a hundred crunches, and now Sloane was ordering a one-minute plank every time she got past Bronte's defences as they sparred.

Bronte wiped sweat from her brow as she got back to her feet, adjusting her grip on her sword. She had progressed to a steel sword now, though the edges were blunt, so no harm would come to them.

Her calluses rubbed against the hilt as she adjusted her grip. What followed was nothing short of torture. She managed to hold Sloane off for a time but, eventually, she broke through, hitting Bronte on her left arm. Immediately, Bronte was on the cold ground, her legs and arms shaking as she held the plank. Then it was straight back into sparring, then another one-minute plank, sparring, one-minute plank, on and on until she had a stitch in her side and physically couldn't lift her sword anymore.

"That's enough," Sloane finally relented.

Bronte collapsed on the ground allowing the cold to seep into her as she looked up at the stars. Her breath came out in white puffs above her. Despite the pain of training, Bronte had begun to look forward to her daily routine with Sloane. It was a release she hadn't known she needed, and it was paying off. She had definition in her body that she'd never had before, and her stamina was growing. She felt powerful. And Bronte liked that it was a strength that had nothing to do with her magic.

CHAPTER 33

The morning of Bronte's first exam arrived on a freezing January day, and she trudged up the stairs to their concoction studies classroom, dreading the torture that lay within. The usual large round tables had been replaced with single desks, and a cauldron sat atop each of them. Bronte chose a spot near the back of the room and tried to calm the nervous energy racing through her.

Professor Kirwan had them all brew a mindfulness potion, and though her mind had felt extremely full upon entering the exam, everything she'd learnt seemed to drain away as she tried to remember the ingredients and method required.

Bronte ended up with a final product that she thought looked about right, but she didn't have long to rejoice because she had to go straight to Professor Wrathwell's classroom to sit his gruelling history paper.

She scribbled down everything she could remember about the original witches of Thrace and the treaties between the three main kinds in Namire: the Fae, wolves, and alchemists. By the end, Bronte's hand was aching, and her brain felt like mush.

She was certain she'd mislabelled the treaty that allowed the free creatures to roam the Whispering Wood, and after the exam, her heart sunk in her chest when she checked her notes and saw that it wasn't called the *'Free Peoples Treaty'* as she'd thought, but the *'Treaty of Self-Governing Beings'*. Although it seemed pretty much the same thing to her, she knew Professor Wrathwell would relish marking her incorrect for that mistake.

Thankfully, rune translations went fairly well. She couldn't remember the symbol for vinegar and ended up drawing a bunch of overlapping squiggles. Still, Bronte thought she answered most of the other questions correctly.

The next morning, she walked into her theory enchanting exam with clammy hands and a heart beating far too quickly. But as she progressed through the paper, her anxiety slowly drained away. All her reading had paid off, and she found she could answer almost every question thoroughly. For their individual practical test, Bronte had been placed in the last time slot. She sat outside the classroom as she waited. The classroom door opened, and Jake walked out looking slightly green. Bronte's nerves spiked as Professor Latoux called her inside.

She was sweating profusely, and she wiped her palms on her skirt as she walked toward the door. The room had been enlarged to the size of a basketball court, and a series of objects were lying about. Professor Latoux stood in the middle of the room, holding a clipboard to her chest. She gazed at Bronte sternly.

"Today, you will be performing a number of individual tasks so I can assess how well you've progressed so far. Please begin by summoning the rock from the opposite end of the room."

The slightest wave of relief passed over Bronte. Summoning had become something she could do in her sleep, and she easily drew the rock across the room towards them, setting it down gently at her feet.

Professor Latoux scribbled something on her clipboard and then ushered Bronte to a desk covered in candles. The task was to light them individually and then extinguish each one separately. This took a little more concentration, as she needed to channel her power on each individual wick. She accidentally lit two at the same time, but she hoped it wouldn't impact her mark too much.

Next, she was faced with the dart board, and Bronte had to make each dart she'd been given hit a specific ring. Her thoughts flickered back to their first lesson using darts, and Isaac's face flashed across her mind, but she forced the image away.

Bronte had prepared for this task, and she swiftly sent each dart towards their targets with precision. Finally, a self-throwing machine shot a spongy ball at her, and she flung up her barrier to protect herself. All the while, Professor Latoux was scribbling things down on her clipboard.

By the end of the test, Bronte was feeling strained and wobbly on her feet, and she longed to be outside relaxing in the sun, which was taunting her by streaming through the windows.

"Good, Bronte. That will be all." Professor Latoux dismissed her.

Bronte walked out of the room feeling lighter than she had in weeks, and she couldn't help the smile that grew on her face as she made her way to the Dome to meet her friends.

As stressful as their exams had been, it had given Bronte a distraction. Now, all her thoughts returned to Isaac and her missing necklace. She had made it through another week of school and, still, there was no more news of Isaac's whereabouts.

When Bronte returned home with Peirce that afternoon she immediately changed into a tunic, meeting her father in the courtyard for training. She forced herself to concentrate as he explained the training drill he'd set up for her. It reminded her of capture the flag. Bronte started on one side of the courtyard, and between her and the other wall was a series of protective barriers she could use as protection to reach the goal, which was a golden banner. Her father stood imposingly before her.

"Ready?" he asked.

Bronte nodded, drawing on the magic inside her. He shot a cast at her, and she blocked it, darting to the nearest barrier. A blast of light hit it just as she ducked behind, shaking the wood. She flung a cast at him. It was a concentration of a small amount of her magic which would cause him to be propelled backwards if it hit him. Unsurprisingly, because he was the High Alchemist, he easily deflected the shot.

Bronte used the small distraction to dart to the next barrier. Here she quickly made snowballs, and she shot them at him using her magic.

"Bronte, you'll have to try harder than that," her father laughed, deflecting the last one.

He drew the snow around him and formed it into one giant snowball, throwing the whole lot at her in one movement. Luckily, she was able to block it in time, and the snow scattered everywhere as it hit her shield.

Bronte sprinted to the next barrier as the snow settled, and she felt a whoosh of power as a blast hit where her feet had just been. She was nearing the flag. She just had to make it to the last barrier, and then she was in the clear.

Bronte heaved in freezing air, wind whipped around her, and the snow flurries were getting thicker, making it hard for her to see. She squinted, making out the next barrier, it was further away than the previous ones, but Bronte would have to risk it.

She shot out into the snow and immediately flung up a barrier. It was getting harder to control her magic, but she stayed focused on her goal. The golden banner.

Centimeters from safety, a cast slipped by her defence, and she was knocked face-first into the snow. She lay there for a moment, absorbing her failure. Her father was by her side when she lifted her head, ready to offer a hand. She took it, allowing him to pull her up.

"That was a good effort," he consoled.

The golden banner waved behind him as though it were taunting her. She wiped her face. The snow was becoming unbearable, and the adrenaline rush had left her body, allowing the cold to seep through again.

"I'm going to take a bath," she informed him, trudging toward the castle. She walked to the side door to see Peirce sniggering at her.

"What?" she snapped.

"Nothing, I just enjoyed that little performance, particularly the end."

She gave a faux smile. "I'm sure you did."

The next week passed tantalizingly slowly. In the fifth form, you had to go for an interview with your manipulation advisor, and it was there that you received your exam results.

Bronte was used to getting marks back in a group, where you could easily blend in if you did badly, but this one-on-one method meant there was no escape. She walked to Professor Latoux's office, dreading what was about to happen. Bronte reminded herself that her exam results couldn't be that bad, but even as she had the thought, half of her was convinced that she'd failed everything. She knocked on the office door, and Professor Latoux's clear voice called to her from within.

"Come in."

Professor Latoux's office was dark but not in a way that evoked the thought of a dungeon or prison cell. It had a stern feel about it, and the Professor was sitting behind a large cherrywood desk, holding a cream-coloured letter in her hands.

A wooden carving of an owl sat beside her, and its beady eyes seemed to watch Bronte as she approached the empty chair opposite the desk. Although the carving wasn't real, as the dim light flickered over its face, Bronte could've sworn it blinked at her. She looked away from it, sliding into the chair.

Silently, Professor Latoux handed her the envelope, and Bronte broke the wax seal with shaking hands. She pulled out the slip of paper inside. Her movements were mechanical, as though someone else was controlling her.

Bronte read over her results once, then twice, then a third time to make sure she was seeing everything correctly. She had managed to pass everything even, to her surprise, history, which she knew wouldn't please Professor Wrathwell. The wave of relief that swept over her was so great she thought she might dissolve into a puddle on the floor.

"Surprised?" Professor Latoux asked, her brows raised.

"A little," she admitted truthfully. She was still holding the paper, staring at it as though she was expecting the numbers on the page to change before her eyes.

"I commend you on your diligence so far. Those marks are no more than you deserve. It is clearer to me now why you have had an accelerated development compared to other enchanters. Your power is far greater than you probably know, and being the daughter of two powerful enchanters means you have inherited a great deal of their skill." Bronte nodded, not sure what other response she should give. "I'm sure the remainder of the schooling year will bring equal success. That will be all."

Bronte walked to the door in a daze. It was only when she reached it that Professor Latoux spoke again.

"And Bronte."

She turned. The usually harsh lines of Professor Latoux's face had softened. "Yes?"

"You have the potential to be far greater than Isaac. Don't ever forget that."

CHAPTER 34

Nick had hardly seen Bronte in weeks. Apart from the short lunch break in school, there was little time they could spend together. He knew she was busy and had a target on her back now, but he wished they could go back to how things were when she was just Bronte Everett and not a Theobesian. Realistically, he knew that wasn't possible, and he hated himself for thinking it.

"Nick stop being morose and eat your food," Leora said, breaking him out of his thoughts. His soup no longer appealed to him, and the chatter inside Merlin's Beard, which he usually found comforting, was too loud and invasive.

Eli looked up from his own food at the darkening sky. "We should be getting home anyway, with Isaac on the loose and everything. My parents are frantic. They've hardly recovered from the Lost Night. I think knowing Bronte is in the safest place she could be is solace to them, though."

"I suppose it is getting dark. I wouldn't want to keep mother waiting, although I could just tell her I was on a date with a potential suitor, and that would satisfy her." Leora grinned.

Nick pushed his soup away. "I'm not having any more. Let's go."

He had never been one to waste food, but he couldn't bring himself to finish it.

His parents were in worse shape than ever. The fear of the Disciple's return had spiked their substance abuse. He wasn't sure either of them had had a single coherent thought that wasn't addled by alcohol or drugs in weeks.

Nick's walk back to the south was peaceful. The recent snowstorm had dusted everything in white, and you could hardly tell you were entering the poorer part of the city.

He hadn't come across another soul for a good half of his trip. Since the murder, nightfall acted like a curfew, and it was rare to see anybody out after dark, especially alone.

Nick wasn't sure what made him feel like he had immunity from Isaac. He just figured if Isaac was going to kill him, he would've done it already. He knew it wasn't confidence but stupidity that led him to think that.

The Sparrow was quiet, but it seemed even the threat of death wasn't enough for some patrons, so Nick played until the last one left. He'd taken to walking Celia home at the end of the night, and when he left her at her apartment, she told him the same thing she said every time they parted.

"Go straight home and be careful."

Nick nodded. "Of course."

But it wasn't a simple walk home tonight because as he neared the end of Celia's street, a shadow appeared before him. He was familiar with this shadow now: the kind that was darker than night. So it wasn't a surprise when Isaac revealed himself.

"Ives. Here to kill me?" Although his voice didn't betray it, he felt a flicker of fear as he looked at Isaac. Nick wondered how his brother had felt when faced with death. Although he had sometimes thought about it, Nick didn't want to die, least of all alone.

"No. Unlike your brother, you're not worth the trouble."

"Charming. Where have you been hiding?" Isaac looked thinner: not gaunt, but his cheekbones were sharper and his eyes were darker, as though he had absorbed death itself.

Isaac strode towards him. "Here and there."

"Bronte's not around if that's who you're waiting for."

Isaac waved off Nick's words. "I don't need to kill her yet. There will be time."

"What are you doing here?" Nick's eyes darted around for anything he could use to maim Isaac with. But the street was empty, and his powers were nothing against Isaac.

"I have another visit to make and just thought I'd stop by. But you're as boring as ever, so I'm not sure why I bothered." He disappeared into his shadows without another word.

Nick froze. Isaac was after another enchanter, that was the only thing that made sense. But if that person wasn't Bronte, it meant someone else in Namire was in danger. Nick began running to the nearest Arch. He had to get to the palace to alert the High Alchemist.

Bronte arrived at breakfast that morning and instantly sensed something was wrong. "What's happened?" she asked as she sat beside her father.

There were large bags under her father's eyes, and his face looked ashen. "There has been another murder."

Bronte paled. "You found someone?"

He nodded. "Your friend Nick came to the castle to alert the High Guard that Isaac had appeared to him, claiming he sought another enchanter. When I was notified, I'd hoped it was merely a hoax, but the Guard found a body by the Canal early this morning. A young man called Fai."

Bronte knew she'd heard that name, but she hoped she was wrong. "Fai, who works at Nina's apothecary?"

Her father nodded. "It appears he was doing a stock count and stayed late."

Bronte thought of Nina and how heartbroken she would be. She could imagine the way her face would fold when she heard the news.

"We can't let him run around murdering all the enchanters. We have to do something."

"We know he's searching for the other necklaces. Isaac likely won't come for you until he's found them all and can finally claim their power. We have time to build a plan."

"We can't wait for him to succeed. Let me go after the necklaces. If he gets a hold of them, he'll become even more dangerous. If I can beat him to it . . ."

"No, the deal was you go to school, and you come home. That's it. Have you forgotten you failed your training drill again yesterday? That means you're as good as dead if you get into a fight with Isaac. Until you can hold your own, I won't let you put yourself in that position."

"So, you'd rather innocents die?"

"Of course not, but I have my people searching for the necklaces, and they will also be the ones to find Isaac, not you."

"I'd rather feel I was doing something tangible to prevent it."

"You can stay here and train. That's still doing something."

"It's not enough."

Bronte could hear the frustration growing in her father's tone, but she couldn't stop pushing.

"Bronte, I don't want to hear anymore. You will stay here where you're safe. I have a meeting with Sloane to discuss our next moves. Finish your breakfast, and we can train later."

Her father walked out of the room before she could argue. Peirce was standing by the door. Usually, Bronte didn't mind having him around, but his presence annoyed her this morning. She sat in silence, toying with her food while pretending he wasn't there.

"I think you're right." Peirce's voice was low, as though he was afraid to speak.

Bronte turned. "What?"

"I think you're right. You should be looking for the necklaces. They are yours by right and by blood, and to allow anyone else to find them would be wrong."

Bronte sighed. "I don't even know where to start, and I doubt my father will give me a clue."

"Luckily, I do."

Bronte stilled. "How? What do you mean?"

"I've sat in on meetings with them. I know what they're thinking. One of the necklaces is in Isaac's possession, as you know. Another one hasn't been seen in over a decade, but the third they believe is hidden at the centre of the Whispering Wood."

"Believed by who?"

"It is thought that when your mother died, she gave the necklaces to Emelia to protect. As we know, she took one with her, but the other two were clearly taken someplace else. Years ago, the Grand Shaman found a large source of energy emanating from the Whispering Wood. Assuming that's true, and the necklace is indeed there, the High Alchemist has so far refused to collect it. I presume that's because it is said to be protected by a great beast which dwells at the very heart of the Whispering Wood. I don't know what beast they speak of, but if the High Alchemist thinks it's safer that the beast protects the necklace, then I can only imagine it's something pretty terrifying. So, instead of retrieving it, he's put all his resources into finding the third pendant. So far, though, they have no leads to go on."

"Why didn't Emelia just take all three with her?"

"It was a risk even taking one. As I said, great power can always be traced."

"So, are you proposing that we go into the Whispering Wood?"

"If you want to find the necklaces, that's where we need to go. I can prepare everything. You just need to meet me by the courtyard door at midnight."

Bronte's heart knocked rapidly against her ribcage as she considered Peirce's proposal. "Do you really think this is a good idea?"

"You said yourself, you'd rather feel like you were doing something. This is something you can do."

"How will we even know where the necklace is?"

"If it's really there, wouldn't you know? Wouldn't you feel it? I thought they were meant to call to their owners."

Bronte thought of the necklace she'd worn for so long. How she'd felt it like a second heartbeat. "I guess."

"We're doing this then?"

Bronte chewed her lip. It was crazy even to think about, and her dad would be furious with her. But then she thought of Fai and the other murdered enchanter, and her mind was made up. "I'll see you at midnight."

CHAPTER 35

All day Bronte had been brimming with barely contained adrenaline. It was the weekend, and now that her exams were over, she had a short reprieve from homework which meant she had little to do but lounge around the palace.

Luckily, her father had been preoccupied by meetings all day. Otherwise, she was sure, she would've revealed her plan to him. It was difficult enough keeping her mouth shut throughout training and dinner.

The final hours leading up to midnight were the hardest. At a quarter to twelve, she eased her door open. Peirce was nowhere to be found, and she crept through the castle, stopping when she reached the courtyard door.

It was only five to twelve, and she stood in the dark waiting for Peirce to arrive. By the time it was five past, and Peirce still hadn't come, Bronte was beginning to think something had gone wrong. Then, at last, she heard movement from the other side of the door, and she tensed, hoping it wasn't another guard.

Thankfully, she heard Peirce's whispered voice. "Bronte?"

"I'm here." She edged the door open and saw Peirce waiting.

"This way."

He led her through the snow to the stables. He opened the gate and disappeared inside. Bronte had never visited the stables. She didn't have an affinity for horses. She'd never ridden one before and didn't have an interest in doing so now. But today would have to be the first time. She had no other choice.

Peirce returned, holding the reigns of two horses. One had a black coat, and the other was a very dusty white. Blankets had been thrown over their backs, cinched at their bellies, and two packs had been secured atop them. The black horse snorted and shook its head, making Bronte flinch.

"Don't be timid. They won't bite."

"Right," she said sceptically.

"Come here. I'll give you a leg up."

She did as she was told, and Peirce launched her onto the horse. It was much higher than she expected, and Bronte kept her gaze forward to avoid seeing how far away the ground was. Peirce mounted his horse and in turn dug his heels into its flanks, causing it to trot forward.

"Do the same," he instructed.

Bronte hesitantly squeezed her legs into the side of her horse, and it began moving beneath her. She was shifted awkwardly from side to side with every step it took, and she gripped the reigns tightly.

"What about the guards," she hissed as they neared the gate.

"I slipped something into their cups at dinner."

Sure enough, when they passed the gatehouse, the two guards on duty were slumped on the ground inside.

"They'll wake soon and not think anything of it," Peirce assured her. "No one wants to admit they fell asleep on the job, and night shift is always the hardest."

Leaving the castle, they travelled on through deserted city streets under the light of the moon. It was only once they reached the city limits that they encountered a problem: a stone wall more than ten meters high that extended around the entire perimeter. In front of them was a locked gate. And it was guarded, of course.

"No one goes through any of the gates after dark unless they have permission." The first guard told them flatly.

"We have the authority of the High Alchemist himself," Peirce replied smoothly, pointing to the symbol of the palace household on his tunic.

The guard frowned. "I don't see a letter of authority."

"Are you going to question the High Alchemist's power? We are on extremely important business, and holding us up will not reflect well on you. Do you want me to report back and tell him we were delayed from our task because you questioned his emissaries? That would make life very hard for both of you."

Bronte had never heard Peirce sound so serious. His jaw was clenched and, though she'd never been intimidated by him before, if he looked at her like that, her knees may've quaked a little.

The guards glanced at each other. "I can't risk losing my job, Calvin."

"If he's lying, you may not have a job tomorrow either," the first guard whispered.

"If he's lying, he'll be the one answering to the High Alchemist. If he's telling the truth, we will."

The first guard sighed. His shoulders relaxed and he stepped to one side, nodding to his companion to open the gate. "Fine. Enjoy your journey."

Peirce bowed his head to them as they passed. "Thank you."

It wasn't until they were safely out of earshot that Bronte spoke. "I didn't realise you were such a sweet talker."

"You thought that was sweet?"

"Well, no, but it did the job."

Peirce grinned. "The path we're on takes us straight to the centre of the Whispering Wood. It's a day's journey. We need to make sure we stay on the path. The Whispering Wood is a strange place. Playful spirits like to lure travelers away, but more sinister creatures lurk in the shadows off the track and we don't want to come into contact with them. As long as we stay on the path, though, we should be safe. It's been warded against evil."

Once they entered the cover of the trees, there was no moonlight, and it was impossible to see. Bronte had to summon fire into her palm to lead the way. They rode on in silence, listening to the sounds of the trees in the breeze as flames crackled in her hand. Thankfully, the sky eventually began to lighten, and she could extinguish the flames.

Bronte knew her father must by now have been alerted that she was no longer in the palace. She'd left a note on the dining table, so he didn't think she'd been abducted by Isaac, but she hadn't told him where she was going.

By midday, Bronte could count the things she liked about horse riding on one hand, and that was to say she didn't like anything. She had no problem with horses but being on top of one was not something she found enjoyable. Her tailbone had gone numb, and her legs had stiffened with the lack of movement. Peirce was humming to himself behind her when her stomach gave a particularly loud grumble. She'd barely eaten dinner because she'd been too nervous about today, but now she regretted it.

"Hungry?" Peirce asked her sarcastically. "We'll take a break at this embankment."

They had been following the path alongside the river, and Peirce led his horse off the dirt trail onto a grassy patch by the water's edge. He jumped down from the horse and offered her a hand. Bronte managed to get her leg over and slid uncomfortably to the ground.

Peirce took hold of her horse's reigns, and tied both horses to the low-hanging branch of a tree. From the pack, he took out a blanket, wrapped sandwiches, apples, and a couple of muffins. He laid the blanket out for them and set the food in its centre.

"Dig in," he said, patting the space beside him.

Bronte groaned as she sat down, her muscles barking in protest. She devoured the food without speaking and took a gulp of water from the skein Peirce handed to her.

"What do you think my father will do when he realises I'm gone?"

"I can't imagine he's going to be very impressed. Not sure I'll even have a job when we get back."

Bronte liked that Peirce didn't use if, as though there was no question that they'd return. "I'll say I forced you to come."

"It's alright. I can take ownership of my decisions."

"You don't need to risk your livelihood for me."

"It's worth the risk. I just mean . . . it's worth stopping the deaths, stopping Isaac," he clarified hastily.

Bronte's cheeks grew warm. "Oh, of course." She hated that she felt disappointed he hadn't meant her. But she didn't want to think about what that feeling meant. "We should get going," she said quickly. "Don't want to be missing any longer than we have to."

Peirce cleared his throat. "Right." He packed the mat away and untied the horses. "Ready?"

Her legs ached, but she allowed him to lift her back onto the horse. His hand lingered for a moment on her waist. She looked down at him, meeting his grey eyes but they betrayed nothing of what he was feeling. He pulled his hand away, walking to his horse without a word.

They travelled in silence, the only sounds the crunching of leaves beneath their horses' hooves. Night was beginning to fall when the idle breeze which had been rustling the branches throughout the day begun to pick up. Whatever mysterious magic the Wood possessed made it sound like voices were whispering to each other above them and Bronte assumed this was what gave the Wood its name.

The wind continued to strengthen, eventually becoming so intense she worried she would be knocked off her horse. Bronte had to bend low, until she was almost lying flat atop the horse, to keep stable.

A loud crack sounded above them, and Bronte's head whipped around to see a thick branch fall between her and Peirce. As it fell, it grazed her horse's hind and suddenly she was lurching forward as her horse set off at a gallop.

She gripped the reigns, keeping her head low as they crashed through the trees. In its panic, her horse diverted from the path, plunging deeper into the Wood. She heard Peirce yelling after her, but there was nothing she could do.

The path had disappeared behind her, when suddenly the horse reared on its hind legs, and Bronte was thrown off the back, landing heavily on the ground. Her vision went black as pain shot through her body.

She heard the horse's hoofbeats receding as it continued on through the forest, and she struggled to call after it, but it was gone before she could sit up. Gasping for breath, lying tangled in the damp undergrowth, she tried to get her bearings.

Bronte realised, her heart sinking, that she could no longer hear Peirce. In fact, she couldn't hear anything. The wind had stopped as suddenly as it had begun, and along with it, the whispers had fallen silent. It was a lot darker off the path. No sunlight could find its way through the thick canopy of trees.

Bronte squinted as she stood unsteadily, brushing the dirt and leaves from her clothes. She thought about summoning a flame but Peirce's warning that dark creatures lurked in the woods echoed in her ears and she decided against it. Calling out to Peirce was out of the question too – it would only alert anything nearby to her presence. She was stuck, travelling through the woods in the dark hoping that she would somehow run into Peirce or find her way back to the path.

At first, Bronte searched for the hoof prints her horse must have left to trace her way back, but the ground around her appeared unmarked, as if smoothed over. There was no sign she had just fallen from her horse and no evidence that anything had disturbed the soil by running over it. By some strange magic everything around her now seemed untouched.

She heard something moving through the bushes nearby and hid behind the trunk of a tree waiting to see what emerged. Relief rushed through her when she saw Peirce's blonde hair.

"Peirce," she hissed when she emerged from behind the tree.

"Bronte! Are you alright?" He rushed to her side, scanning her body. "I followed straight after you. I've heard this Wood does mysterious things to erase any signs of life or movement. I knew if I lost you, we would be searching for each other all night."

"I'm fine, just a little sore. My horse ran off though."

"That doesn't matter, Bronte. What matters is that I found you. And now I can finally do something I've wanted to since the first moment I saw you."

He bent down, brushing his lips against hers. She became transfixed by him, falling into the kiss that a secret part of her had been growing increasingly curious.

"Bronte! Bronte!"

In a distant part of her brain, she was aware someone was calling to her, but she couldn't force herself to listen. Suddenly, her body was ripped away from Peirce and she blinked to find a second Peirce holding her by the arms. She looked back to the first Peirce but there was no one there.

"What . . . is happening?"

"Evil spirit, I can tell by the way your eyes were glazed when I found you. I'm guessing it's been enslaved by a crimson eater to entrap you. They usually do that by playing out a fantasy that's especially important to you. How they know your deepest thoughts is a mystery, but it's so realistic that you don't realise you're transfixed in place until it's too late. While you're standing still it goes back to its master to report your location. Then the eater can come and devour you, which means we need to move fast."

But they were too late. From the shadows a human-like creature emerged. Except it was anything but human. Its face was a mask of skin with no eyes and only vertical slits for a nose. There was a gaping hole where its mouth should've been, and it emitted a chilling moaning sound as it stood before them. Its hands were narrow, its fingers spindly points with sharp claws on the ends that reached down its thighs.

"It's blind, but it can scent human blood and it's freakishly fast. If it gets close enough to seize us it will latch onto our chest with its retractable razor-sharp teeth and gnaw until it reaches the heart which it will suck out of our bodies until we're nothing but a lifeless sack of flesh," Peirce whispered to her.

"Charming."

"The only thing it fears is fire. So you need to set it alight. And you need to do it now." His hand gripped her arm, but he spoke calmly, as though he was asking her to pour it a cup of tea.

"What?"

"You need to set it on fire. Right. Now."

The crimson eater had turned their way and its nostrils flared as it tilted its angular head to smell the air. Bronte focused her gaze on it, and just as it took a step towards them its body burst into flame. It emitted an unearthly shriek, its body contorting in agony, howling as the flames seared its skin.

"We need to go!" Peirce grabbed her hand tugging her away.

They sprinted through the woods. Stray branches grazed Bronte's arms as she followed Peirce, blindly trusting that he knew the way. Finally, they made it back to the path and Peirce threw Bronte onto his horse, leaping up behind her. He grabbed the reigns and suddenly they were galloping away. The crimson eater's agonised shrieks chased them relentlessly down the path as they made their escape.

CHAPTER 36

Night had fallen completely by the time they reached a wide lake. Moonlight shimmered on its inky surface illuminating the great falls in the distance which tumbled from an escarpment of jagged stone. They were too far away for the turbulence to reach the shore where Bronte and Peirce sat slumped on Peirce's exhausted horse. They hadn't spoken since they'd escaped the crimson eater and adrenaline still pumped through Bronte as she climbed awkwardly to the ground and stumbled to the shore. She could hear Peirce following behind her.

"What did you see?"

Bronte didn't have to ask to know what he meant. She kept her gaze forward as she lied. "Just my mum. Um, Emelia I mean." She was grateful the dark hid the red that crept across her cheeks. She thought about Pierce's lips on hers. She couldn't believe she had been fooled into thinking it was real.

"It must be hard, not knowing what to call her."

"She was my mum, in every way that mattered."

"Even so."

Bronte shifted uncomfortably. "How did you know to set the crimson eater on fire?"

"All the guards are trained to understand every possible threat to Namire, which includes a large number of creatures who live in the Whispering Wood. You may think the crimson eater looked terrifying, but compared to some of the beasts I've learnt about it's as timid as a furrow."

Bronte shivered, imagining what her fate could've been if Peirce hadn't found her.

"Do you sense the necklace?" he asked. "The lake marks the center of the Whispering Wood; it should be around here somewhere."

Bronte felt nothing but the soreness of her body. "No."

"Try again," he urged.

She sat down by the water and slowed her breathing. Eventually, Bronte could hear a pulse. It was like a second heart calling to her. But it was coming from far across the water, where the falls were.

"I think it's on the other side of the lake."

Peirce frowned. "We'll have to go around."

Bronte nodded, looking out over the dark water. Peirce offered his hand to help her up and they went back to the horse.

The track around the lake was uneven, and they struggled to make their way in the dark. When they eventually reached the falls, they found themselves on a flat platform of worn stone, ten or fifteen meters above the surface of the lake. It was bordered by stunted trees, their branches stripped of leaves. Torrents of water thundered down before them at a deafening level. Behind the falls, there was a space between the tumbling water and the black stone of the mountain. Filled with mist, and on a night without moonlight, it was difficult to make out what lay beyond.

"I think the pendant must be inside or behind the falls." Bronte hesitated. She could feel the call of the necklace, but it was muted as though blocked by something.

Peirce helped her off the horse then he tied the reigns to one of the low branches. They climbed down and over the rocks, getting as close as they dared to the water.

"Can you part the water as it's falling?" Peirce asked. "If you can, we might be able to slip through and see what's behind."

Bronte didn't answer, but she drew herself up and gritted her teeth. Channelling all her power, she separated the waterfall into two wavering streams. Once the water was cleared, they could make out a series of square stepping stones leading to a stone archway in the base of the cliff. Peirce took Bronte's hand, and they darted through. The water immediately closed again behind them, blocking them off from the outside world.

It was damp and cool in the tunnel, and their clothes were soaked by the fine mist of spray from the falls. With a wavering flame in her outstretched palm, Bronte motioned for Peirce to follow where the necklace was calling her. It was too loud to talk over the roar of the water so they walked in silence. As they went deeper, the tunnel led them into a system of caves and chambers that honeycombed the heart of the mountain.

They walked until the deafening sound of the falls receded to a distant rumble. As it faded into the background, it was replaced by a vicious, earsplitting snarl which echoed off the stone, coming from somewhere further ahead. They stopped in their tracks. Bronte glanced at Peirce; the trepidation on her face written also on his. The snarling was followed by a very human grunt.

She signalled for Peirce to come closer. "There's someone else here."

"You don't think it's . . ."

"Isaac?"

Peirce gripped her arm. "Are you sure you're ready for this?"

"I don't have a choice. We need the necklace. Seems like he's having enough trouble with the beast so hopefully he'll be distracted. Between the beast and me he should be occupied enough so you'll have time to find the necklace."

They crept to the end of the tunnel, until it opened into a vast cavern lit by a pale blue light that seemed to emanate from the stone vault above them. The far wall was lost in the gloom. Immediately in front of them, a narrow stone bridge spanned a chasm, its edges jagged and fissured. On the far side was an island of rubble, immense slabs of stone jumbled into an uneven pyramid in its centre. Between the bridge and the pyramid of stone a towering, formless creature, its upper limbs extended above its head, its torso matted with filthy fur, stood roaring at Isaac. Bronte recognised him immediately. He was crouched behind a large boulder, and there appeared to be a sizeable wound in his left leg. His trousers were soaked, and blood was pouring down his calf and pooling on the ground at his feet.

"It's a kringet." Peirce sighed.

"And what is that?" The beast was the size of a small tree and had fangs that curved outside its mouth reaching down towards its chin.

"They're extremely vicious and volatile creatures. They choose one object and protect it like a mother protects her child. Usually, you have to offer a kringet something better than it already has if you want to take the thing it's protecting. And if it doesn't like what you have to offer then your chances of leaving alive, or getting anywhere near the object, are slim."

"We don't have anything to offer."

"Seems like Isaac didn't either."

The kringet let out a shattering roar, hefting a boulder with one of its huge paws and hurling it toward where Isaac was kneeling. The boulder smashed into the ground only centimeters away from him, splitting into pieces and covering him in dust and fragments of stone.

Neither the kringet nor Isaac had noticed them yet. Staying low, they edged closer, until they were crouched at the base of the narrow bridge.

"We need a distraction. Something to give us enough time to run across the chasm," Peirce said.

Bronte peered over the edge of the path into the deep abyss. One wrong move and they would be plunging to their deaths. The creature had its powerful back turned to them as it tried to locate Isaac, who was scrambling along near the edge of the abyss, attempting to keep a mass of rock between himself and the kringet.

"Now!" she hissed to Peirce.

They darted out, sprinting across the chasm. By the time they were halfway across their pounding footsteps had alerted the kringet to their presence. It turned sharply, gathering the nearest boulder and throwing it towards them as they ran. Bronte's legs trembled as it crashed into the bridge just behind them, the sound of shattering rock echoing in its wake. Reaching the island they hurled themselves to the ground behind the nearest boulder, hoping it would give them at least some temporary protection.

Isaac was now beside them, resting his hands on his knees, his back pressed against the stone, panting loudly. It wasn't until he looked up that his eyes locked on hers.

"You," Isaac breathed. Blood and sweat dripped down his face. "You just can't leave things alone, can you."

"You're the one who's determined to kill me."

Isaac sniffed. "I realised that was foolish until I have all the necklaces. I've been searching for months, and now you think you're going to snatch it from me after all I've been through?" He laughed coldly. "And you even brought your watchdog along to help. How sweet."

Isaac's speech was interrupted as another boulder hurtled through the air towards them. Bronte flung up a barrier to shield her and Peirce, jolting as stray rocks struck its outer edges. There was a grunt beside her, and Isaac dropped to the ground. His injuries had obviously taken a toll on his power, and his shield had faltered. Bronte was instantly at his side, despite their history. Thankfully, he was still breathing, and his pulse was strong, although he lay motionless.

"I think he's just knocked out," she told Peirce.

She risked a look above the rock. Behind where the kringet stood panting was a pyramid of smaller rocks, like a nest, and at the top was a golden box.

"That has to be the necklace." Bronte nudged Peirce, indicating the box. Since they'd entered the cave the necklace's power had grown taunt within her, and Bronte knew it was close by. The kringet wasn't leaving its spot in front of the pyramid, though, and to get to the necklace they needed to get past it.

"I'll try and lure it away and you get the box. Isaac should be safe here behind this rock. We're no help to him if we get hit too."

Peirce nodded, taking her hand, and squeezing it once. Bronte pulled her hand away with a shaky smile.

"Just like training," Peirce told her. "Except this time, I won't be standing watch."

"Just like training," she repeated, more as a mantra to herself than as a response to Peirce.

Taking a deep breath in preparation she darted out from behind the rock and ran to the opposite side of the platform. The kringet's gaze followed her instantly. It picked up the closest boulder it could find, and in one motion hurled it in her direction. Bronte put up a barrier and the rock deflected from her shield, dropping with a thundering crash onto the ground before her. Not waiting a beat, she drew up a cache of stray rocks from around her feet and launched them in a torrent at the kringet. The creature howled in rage, flailing its arms, attempting to bat away the rocks as they rained down.

Bronte moved further away from the kringet, getting as close as she dared to the edge of the abyss, hoping to lure it away from the necklace. Hesitantly, the kringet took half a step toward her, torn between chasing its prey and protecting its possession. All the while, it continued to hurl rocks at her, and she continued to block them. At a tantalisingly slow pace, the kringet moved toward her, edging further and further away from its nest.

Bronte felt like she was back in the courtyard dodging casts from her dad, except this time her life was at stake. Sweat drenched her skin despite the coolness of the cave and her arms shook as she produced barrier after barrier.

Behind the kringet Peirce had made his way to the bottom of the uneven pyramid of rocks. As she watched, he began to scramble up the side, checking as he went that the kringet remained distracted. Bronte refused to look at him, worried that her gaze would alert the kringet to his movements. Instead, she relied on the hazy vision of him in the foreground to track his progress.

Finally, he reached the top of the pyramid. Steadying himself, he grabbed the box. Tucking it safely beneath his arm, he immediately began his descent. Bronte didn't let her concentration waver as Peirce made his way ever closer to the ground, knowing that one mis-formed barrier would see her toppling into the abyss. As Peirce was navigating the final rocks, one of them slipped from its place beneath him and he was sent tumbling to the ground.

The kringet whipped around and its roar of despair was loud enough to shake the cavern as it realised what had been taken. Since it was no longer forced to remain in front of its nest, Peirce's life was forfeit if Bronte didn't do something fast.

Gathering all her strength, she focused her gaze on the biggest boulder she could find. She screamed as she lifted it into the air and flung it at the kringet's back, projecting the full might of her power in a single cast. The boulder stuck the kringet just below its shoulders, hurling it forward and slamming its body into the ground mere centimeters from where Peirce lay twisted on the stone.

Bronte ran to his side. He was breathing heavily, but otherwise seemed unharmed. The box was clasped in his hand, but she didn't bother to open it yet.

"We need to get out of here." Bronte pulled him up.

His face was a mask of shock after what had just happened. The kringet was already stirring and she knew that, if they didn't move fast, they would never make it out of the cave alive.

Isaac's body lay a few meters away still concealed by the rock. "I can't leave him." She wished she could. She wished she was as cold hearted as him. But she would throw her own body into the abyss before she left Isaac here alone. Lifting him into the air, Bronte levitated him in front of her as they began the walk back through the cave system.

They travelled in silence. Her legs shook with every step as the adrenaline left her body, but she didn't stop. A bone chilling howl filled the tunnel as they neared the exit. Bronte quaked in relief at the sight of the thundering water ahead. As they emerged, she gently lowered Isaac to the ground, unable to hold him up any longer. Then she knelt beside him and took back her necklace. She had noticed the flash of the chain immediately, but she hadn't had a moment to take it until now. Bronte fastened it around her neck, and as it settled again on her sternum, she felt like she could finally breathe again.

"Do you want to open the box?" Peirce asked.

"Won't the kringet be after us? Should we wait until we're somewhere safe?"

"Once a kringet loses it's possession it goes into a period of mourning before it seeks something new. It won't be leaving its den anytime soon."

"You open it."

Peirce lifted the latch and opened the lid, his brow furrowing as he looked at whatever was inside. "There's only a note."

"What?" Bronte blurted. Instantly, she was on her feet. She took the box from Peirce and inside the small felt-lined case was a slip of paper.

"It appears someone beat us to the necklace."

Bronte unfolded the paper. "Up on the hill, but underground, the thing you seek will surely be found," she read. "But . . . but I felt it. It drew me to this place. I couldn't be mistaken, could I?"

"No, not mistaken. What you were feeling must have been the necklace Isaac was wearing," Peirce said in resignation.

The cold seeped into her. "No." Her bones ached, and her head had begun to throb from exhaustion. They had risked everything for nothing. For a silly riddle that they would now have to solve. "But didn't the Grand Shaman detect a great source of energy coming from this area. How could she have been wrong?"

Peirce shrugged. "This box has likely been spelled to deter anyone from realising the necklace has been taken. Whoever stole it would want to cover their tracks."

Bronte heard movement behind them, and she whipped around. Isaac was on his feet, blinking away his haziness. She snapped the lid shut.

Isaac's eyes narrowed on the box. "Give it to me."

"No." Bronte's voice was defiant.

"I won't ask twice." Isaac lashed out, and Peirce was flung against the nearby rocks.

"No!" Bronte yelled. She sent a stunning cast at Isaac, but he instantly blocked it.

"I see the games have begun," he drawled.

Not waiting a beat, Isaac drew all the debris from the ground at his feet and speared it at her in a cast of immense power. Bronte didn't even flinch as she threw up a barrier before it could reach her.

Bronte set the ground around Isaac on fire, trapping him in a ring of flames. In the flickering light, she could see him struggling to breathe, and she pushed harder, drawing all the available air away until the heat of the flames was only centimeters from his skin. He dropped to his knees, gasping for breath, but he managed to turn the fire away from him, and it dissipated in a wave of heat.

She couldn't get an edge on him. Bronte knew his tells, the way his mouth twitched when he was about to cast, but he knew her tells as well. Finally, one of her casts managed to slip through Isaac's barrier, slamming into his chest and he crumpled to the ground. She knew he wouldn't be knocked out for long. Her cast had been weak after all the energy she'd used already.

Bronte ran to Peirce's side. He was still breathing but there was a cut on his temple where his head had struck the rock. Parting the water, she quickly levitated him back through the falls to where their horse was tethered. She slung him over its back and using the rocks nearby climbed on behind him, quickly securing the box in the pack as she did so. Ignoring the dark and the danger of the trail, Bronte dug her heels into the horse's flank. It took off down the path, away from the falls and away from Isaac.

Bronte had just reached the opposite shore when a darkness she recognised only too well exploded in front of her. Isaac appeared as it parted before her, kneeling on the ground. He rose dripping wet, his hair hanging down in front of his eyes, which were gleaming at her with the promise of death.

"Did you really think you could get away so easily?"

He didn't let her reply as he lashed out, flinging cast after cast at her. Bronte jumped from the horse, dodging and weaving to avoid his attack. But with each new cast she was forced towards the lake's edge.

They parried back and forth, but Isaac was more ferocious than before, as though he were really going to kill her now. A dangerous gleam shone behind his eyes, but she did everything she could, fighting grimly to hold him at bay.

Her feet edged closer to the water as she blocked his casts, and with each new assault, she struggled to regain her balance. The sky had clouded over, and wind whipped through her hair, catching on the loose strands, blowing them across her face. Bronte had no time to brush them away. She didn't have a second to spare. Distant thunder rumbled around them, but neither she nor Isaac was powerful enough to control the weather, and they fought on as the rain began to fall.

Her breath came in short gasps, and Bronte felt dangerously close to another burnout, just like the one she'd experience on the Lost Night. Resembling the storm around them, the same storm was raging within. The initial adrenaline from their last fight had left her body, and her muscles were aching with exhaustion.

She could feel herself slowly collapsing. Rain fell from the skies, and Bronte could no longer make out Isaac's face through the downpour. The best she could do was block the fuzzy stream of white light coming toward her in intermittent waves. Her whole body was aflame despite the freezing rain, until she didn't think she could go on. Any second now, it would be over. Any second now, she could be put to rest.

At that moment, Bronte pictured Fai's kindly face, and she thought of the destruction Isaac had caused and forced herself to keep fighting. Her necklace pulsed against her skin, and she latched onto its beat. She felt the well of power within her begin to expand, and when she hurled her next cast at Isaac, it destroyed his barrier, forcing him back. She'd regained an edge, and she wasn't relenting.

Through the storm, Bronte heard the pounding of hoofbeats and from the trees she saw her father emerge at the head of a group of riders, Sloane among them. Isaac heard them too, and before any of them could react, he'd summoned the box out of her pack and disappeared into a cloud of darkness.

Bronte collapsed to the ground. The driving rain pummeled her skin, yet she barely noticed the cold. She felt her father at her side, lifting her up, but she couldn't open her eyes.

"Peirce," she mumbled. "Go to Peirce."

Bronte remembered almost nothing of the ride back to the palace. She slipped in and out of consciousness, and it wasn't until they were on home soil that she felt like she could walk again. But by that time, her father, who had remained silent the whole journey back, looked as though he couldn't contain his rage anymore. In the palace, he carried her into the dining room and sat her gently on a chair. Food was placed before her, and it was only after he'd watched her eat a full meal that he finally spoke.

"That you are still alive is a miracle, Bronte. What were you thinking! What you did was extremely irresponsible. It put both of your lives at risk and could easily have played into Isaac's hands."

Bronte remained defiant. After all, they had retrieved her original necklace and, despite failing to claim the second one, they at least had a clue to its location. Unfortunately, Isaac now had that clue too, but that was a loss Bronte was willing to deal with. "It was necessary."

"Maybe so, but you should've waited for my permission."

"You were never going to give me permission."

Her father frowned. "Bronte, all I want is for you to be safe . . ."

"Everyone's been trying to protect me my whole life, but it isn't going to work. I'm involved in this now, and the sooner you accept that - the sooner everyone accepts that - the better it will be."

Her father's shoulders sagged with resignation. "You're not going to stop, are you?"

"No, but I would appreciate all the help I know you can offer with my training. If you allow me to work with you, I think I could be useful. We retrieved a box tonight with a note in it about the current location of one of the other pendants. Once I figure out where it is, I'll be going after it."

"What about your school?"

"There are more important things than school. I can study at home, if necessary. But we both know Isaac isn't waiting until I've graduated to strike, which means we can't either."

He ran a hand over his face. "This isn't the life I wanted for you."

"We can't change things now. I've accepted that. I suggest you do too." Her father remained silent, taken aback by her directness, and she took that as a momentary win. "What happened to Peirce? Is he alright?"

"He has a cracked rib and a mild concussion, but he's been taken to the healer, and he should be fine. He'll be stationed outside for a week as a punishment, though. I have no doubt you talked him into this, but he won't get out of it scot-free."

"May I see him?" She was damp and desperately needed a shower, and sleep, but she needed to know he was alright before she did any of those things.

"You're going to do what you want no matter what I say." He smiled ruefully. "So yes, you may see Peirce before you sleep. But keep it brief."

Bronte found the healer's room and peeked inside. Peirce was resting on a cot. He was dry and in a fresh change of clothes, and there seemed to be no signs of damage to him, thankfully.

"So, this is the consequence of your unauthorised actions? Being pampered by the palace healer."

Peirce's eyes opened slowly, revealing their steely grey colour, and Bronte finally let herself breathe a sigh of relief.

"Would you rather I stayed in pain?" He sat up gingerly, even though his wounds were gone.

Bronte rolled her eyes as she came to his bedside and perched on the edge of the cot. "Always so dramatic." He gave her a soft smile, and her heart lurched. "Are you really, okay?"

"I'm fine. I'll be out in the cold, freezing my arse off, in no time." She nodded, but she couldn't shake her guilt. Peirce took her hand. "You're ice cold. Take my spare blanket."

He threw a bundle of soft wool at her. Bronte hadn't even realised her temperature. She'd been too focused on him, but now that he'd mentioned it, she couldn't ignore how cold she was. She'd come back from the edge of a burnout, and her body was left aching and weary. She drew the blanket around her shoulders and across her chest.

"You're still shivering. Come here." He patted the space beside him. "Body heat, we can't have you getting sick."

With the blanket wrapped around her, she slowly moved to his side and curled into him. She couldn't allow herself to relax, though. His body was hard and warm against her, and Nick's face flashed across her mind.

"Thanks for not leaving me." His grey eyes looked deep into hers, and she could feel her heart pounding in her chest. She blinked, turning away. Coming here had been a mistake. Bronte needed their easy banter back, not whatever unknown territory they'd entered into.

She cleared her throat. "What do you think the note meant?"

Peirce tilted his head, considering. "Sounded like something a Fae would write. My guess is that some little faerie has gotten its hands on the necklace and thought it would be a lark to leave a treasure hunt behind."

"So, we're going on a treasure hunt next?"

"We're not going anywhere. You'll be lucky to be let out of the palace ever again after the stunt you just pulled."

"I think I've convinced my father otherwise."

Peirce squeezed her arm. "You surprised me. I didn't think I would like facing death with you so much."

Her body hummed at his words. "You surprised me too."

Yet she didn't know if that was a good thing. Or what it meant for her and Nick if she was here with Peirce and she didn't want to pull away from him when he looked into her eyes. But she would think about that some other night.

They drifted into silence. It wasn't long before Peirce's head dropped against her shoulder as he dozed soundly. Resigned that she couldn't move now, she lay awake beside him.

A tiny statue of Hecate watched over her from the healer's shelves. Bronte recognised the three women conjoined on the statue, representing Hecate's three forms. Mother. Maiden. Crone. The necklaces took after those forms, reflecting the stages of the moon. She reached a hand to her necklace, and held the cool metal, vowing that she would never let Isaac get his hands on it again.

Bronte wasn't going to submit to anything anymore. Isaac thought she could be taken advantage of and manipulated. But now it was her turn to become the villain he'd made her out to be. She hadn't thought herself capable of bloodlust, but being timid wasn't going to serve her now. If Isaac wanted to kill her, she would make it so goddamn hard that he would fear even coming near her.

The statue's unseeing eyes watched over her from its perch, and Bronte found herself doing the one thing that she had never thought would serve her. She found herself praying. Praying to Hecate to give strength to her enemies. Because she was going to make herself like a god and, so help them, she would fight like one too.

ACKNOWLEDGMENTS

The three years it's taken for this book to go from inception to publication has been an extremely challenging and solitary time. However, that's not to say there isn't a long list of people I would like to thank, who have helped me on this journey.

Firstly, I'm eternally grateful to my editor, Craig Reynolds. He worked tirelessly to shape this novel into the book it is today.

To my wonderfully amazing best friends, Remy Tidy, Emily Su, and Keely Ralphs, you have been there for me through everything. Thank you for listening to me constantly rant about this book, and offering endless support when I spiralled. I am so lucky to have each of you in my life. I could write a novel about how much I appreciate you.

I owe a big thank you to my followers on TikTok, who were there to encourage me from the very beginning. Also, a special thank you to my beta-readers who read a very early draft of this novel (one I shudder to even think about now) and offered invaluable feedback.

To all the little interactions I've had over the years with people in my life, whether it be co-workers, acquaintances, or strangers, thank you for taking an interest in my work and making me feel as though it was worth something.

Thank you to my parents, Kathryn and Tony, for never telling me to give up on this dream. It is important to believe in yourself, but it is easier to do so when the people you love believe in you too.

Lastly, to you, reader, thank you for giving this book a chance.

ABOUT THE AUTHOR

J.B. Croft is an emerging author from Sydney, Australia. *When Blood Divides* is her first novel.

Stay in touch!
jbcroft.com
Instagram: @j.b.croft
TikTok: @jasminebeacroft

Printed in Great Britain
by Amazon